Dragonflies

Dragonflies

*Fiction by Chinese Women
in the Twentieth Century*

Edited by
Shu-ning Sciban
and Fred Edwards

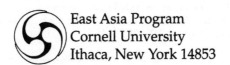
East Asia Program
Cornell University
Ithaca, New York 14853

The Cornell East Asia Series is published by the Cornell University East Asia Program (distinct from Cornell University Press). We publish affordably priced books on a variety of scholarly topics relating to East Asia as a service to the academic community and the general public. Standing orders, which provide for automatic billing and shipping of each title in the series upon publication, are accepted.

If after review by internal and external readers a manuscript is accepted for publication, it is published on the basis of camera-ready copy provided by the volume author. Each author is thus responsible for any necessary copy-editing and for manuscript formatting. Address submission inquiries to CEAS Editorial Board, East Asia Program, Cornell University, Ithaca, New York 14853-7601.

Cover design by Fred Edwards and Karen K. Smith, cover photograph by Donna Maloney, calligraphy and dragonfly artwork by Kuang-yean Huang, chapter header pages designed by Shu-chin Albert.

Number 115 in the Cornell East Asia Series
Copyright © 2003 by Shu-ning Sciban and Fred Edwards. All rights reserved
ISSN 1050-2955
ISBN 1-885445-15-6 pb
Library of Congress Control Number 2003107101
Printed in the United States of America
20 19 18 17 16 15 14 13 12 11 10 09 08 07 06 05 03   9 8 7 6 5 4 3 2 1

⊗ The paper in this book meets the requirements for permanence of ISO 9706:1994.

Contents

Acknowledgments

The publication of *Dragonflies: Fiction by Chinese Women in the Twentieth Century* engaged us in the profound experience of meeting many people who genuinely care about Chinese literature and willingly and unselfishly gave their support whenever and however they could.

First of all, we express our heartfelt gratitude to the translators. Their dedication to literary translation and the moral support they gave the editors were vital to the completion and publication of this anthology. Without them, *Dragonflies* never would have taken flight.

Second, we wish to thank those who generously provided or assisted us in one way or another to obtain permission to translate and publish these twelve works of short fiction. There is, in fact, a touching story behind each permission received. The editors want to thank Mrs. Hsiao-ying Chen Chinnery, Professor Chen Shu, Ms. Wu Qing, Mr. Ping Yun of Huangguan Publishing Company, Ms. Wei Junyi, Ms. Yang Tuan, Ms. Kang Yunwei, Ms. Ping Lu, Ms. Liao Huiying, Ms. Chi Li, Mr. Chen Yuhang of Maitian Publishing Company, Ms. Wang Anyi, Ms. Jiang Zidan and Ms. Xi Xi, for granting us translation permission. We also are grateful to Ms. Daisy Chang, Ms. Wu Liwan, Professor William Tay, Professor Pang-yuan Chi, Dr. Julie Chang, Dr. Shaobo Xie, Ms. Deng Tianmei, Ms. Lin Peini, Mr. Ye Burong of Hongfan Bookstore Publishing Company, Renmin Wenxue Press (Beijing) and Tiandi Publishing Company for their assistance and advice as we sought permission to translate and publish these stories.

We also want to thank the University of Calgary for providing a grant to cover data collection and travel expenses. Dr. Hermina Joldersma's encouragement and assistance in the grant application are much appreciated. Ms. Karen Smith, the Managing Editor of the Cornell East Asia Series, provided support and timely advice on issues ranging from editing and copyright to manuscript preparation. Our families also contributed to the final version of *Dragonflies*. Donna Maloney, Fred's wife and an editor herself, read the manuscript and made valuable suggestions for improvements. She also generously provided the cover photograph, shot in Beijing in 1990. The paintings of dragonflies and the calligraphy used in *Dragonflies* belong to Kuang-yean Huang, Shu-ning's father. We also want to thank Shu-chin Albert, Shu-ning's sister, for her beautifully designed author pages. Last but not least, we wish to thank our spouses (Donna and Lloyd) and children (Rowan and Rya) for their love and support throughout the years.

Introduction

In the past two decades, Chinese women have been a popular research subject in many disciplines. The portraits of women by women in twentieth-century Chinese literature are particularly interesting to researchers because they reveal firsthand information about women's lives. The purpose of this anthology is two-fold. On one hand, it provides English readers with a general introduction to Chinese literature and culture through excellent stories by twentieth-century women writers from mainland China, Taiwan and Hong Kong. On the other hand, considering that literary work reflects a specific social milieu, the anthology is designed to promote understanding about the development of Chinese women and Chinese women's literature in the twentieth century.

This anthology consists of twelve stories by eleven female writers. These stories were chosen based on two considerations. First, they display a high standard of artistic achievement. All eleven writers are prominent in their regions and all the stories are well-known works. Second, the images portrayed in these stories are those of "ordinary" women. What do we mean by "ordinary"? This refers to female personalities who, regardless of family or educational background, are neither revolutionary nor ambitious, may be somewhat traditional and domestic but, most important, who seek no more than a simple and happy life. Obviously, this is just one type of Chinese woman. However, such women are prevalent in Chinese society and a common image in Chinese literature. For this reason, the editors chose to focus on them in this anthology.

The twelve stories, dating from the 1920s to the 1990s, are arranged chronologically according to their publication dates. This provides a historical perspective on the development of Chinese women in the twentieth century. Readers are encouraged to compare heroines in an earlier story with a later one to appreciate the evolution of twentieth-century Chinese women.

Concerning this evolution, it would be beneficial to review briefly some important issues that had a bearing on women's living conditions and were subject to passionate discussion by intellectuals from the late nineteenth century to the beginning of the twentieth century. To those familiar with Chinese culture and history, it is common knowledge that footbinding, chastity, polygamy and limited educational opportunities were four of the major issues

1

concerning women in premodern times. The situation worsened in the Song (960-1279) and Ming (1368-1644) Dynasties; by the time of the Qing Dynasty (1644-1911), women's status had reached its lowest point in all of Chinese history.[1]

Some literati in imperial China recognized these problems and criticized many social norms regarding the treatment of women. For instance, Che Ruoshui of the Song Dynasty opposed footbinding;[2] Li Zhi (1527-1602) and Yu Zhengye (1775-1840) attacked the beliefs that widows should not be allowed to remarry and that women were less intelligent than men;[3] Wu Weiye (1609-1672), Mao Qiling (1623-1713) and Wang Shizhen (1634-1711) encouraged women's literature; Yuan Mei (1716-1798) even promoted women's education by teaching women himself.[4] So these problems were not unknown to society at the time, but real action did not take place until the second half of the nineteenth century.

In the last sixty years of the Qing Dynasty, the decline of the Qing court's power and the intrusion of Western imperialism caused a number of insurrections. In order to gain as much support as possible, reformers encouraged women to participate in military and political uprisings and social reforms. Concepts such as opposition to footbinding and the promotion of women's education were advocated. Two common slogans were: "to strengthen a nation, one must strengthen all the mothers in the nation" and "the establishment of women's schools creates good mothers."[5] During this period, the Taiping Rebellion (1851-1864), Western missionaries, members and associates of the Hundred Days' Reform (1898) and members of Sun Yat-sen's Revolutionist Party all made significant contributions to the improvement in women's lives. At the beginning of its reign, the Nanjing-based Taiping regime prohibited prostitution, footbinding, polygamy and mercenary marriage, and formally practised equality between men and women.[6] Though these ideals were not fully implemented, they provided an alternative view of women's status.[7]

---

1. Bao Jialin, "Xu," *Zhongguo funüshi lunji*, Vol. 1, ed. Bao Jialin (Taipei: Daoxiang chubanshe, 1979), 39.

2. Gu Mou, "Funüjie zhi juexing," in *Zhongguo funüshi lunwenji* Vol. 1, eds. Li Youning and Zhang Yufa (Taipei: Taiwan Shangwu yinshuguan, 1981), 294.

3. Liu Ningyuan, ed. *Zhongguo nüxingshi leibian*, (Beijing: Beijing shifan daxue chubanshe, 1999), 11-4,

4. Ibid.

5. Lin Weihong, "Qingjide funü buchanzu yundong," in *Zhongguo funüshi lunji* , Vol. 3, ed. Bao Jialin (Taipei: Daoxiang chubanshe, 1993), 187-94; Huang Yanli, "Zhongguo funü jiaoyu zhi jinxi," in *Zhongguo funüshi lunji*, Vol. 2, ed. Bao Jialin (Taipei: Daoxiang chubanshe, 1991), 270-1.

6. Jin Zhenhe, "Taiping Tianguo shiqide funü wenti," in *Collected Essays on the History of Chinese Women* Vol. 1, 104.

7. Chen Zhongyu, "Taiping Tianguo de funü zhengce," in *Essays on the History of Chinese Women* Vol. 1, 253-62.

While Western missionaries were not directly involved in political activities, their views on footbinding and women's education were influential. The first anti-footbinding organization was formed in 1875 by Rev. John MacGowan.[8] The first girls' school was established by Miss Aldersay, a British missionary, in 1844 at Ningbo.[9] Members of the Hundred Days' Reform and the Revolutionist Party actively promoted women's education and opposed footbinding. Kang Youwei (1858-1927), a leader of the Hundred Days' Reform, founded an anti-footbinding organization in Guangdong province.[10] There also were some female members among the Revolutionists, such as Gao Baishu and Qiu Jin (1875-1907), who said that from a woman's point of view, not binding one's feet marked only the beginning of emancipation. They encouraged women to seek education and ultimately equal rights.[11] Scholars today view the rise of the women's emancipation movement at the turn of the twentieth century as a development beyond the expectation of contemporary political and social reformers.[12] By the beginning of the twentieth century, many girls' schools had appeared, and in 1920 women finally were allowed to study in universities.[13]

In the history of the development of Chinese women, one should not overlook the contributions made by the male intellectuals of the May Fourth era (1917-1927), such as Hu Shi, Li Dazhao, Chen Duxiu, Wu Yu, Lu Xun, Huang Rikui, Tian Han, Shen Yanbing, Chen Wangdao and so on. They were frequent contributors to *Xin Qingnian* (New Youth), a leading journal in which major social issues were debated. According to Liu Ningyuan, the main women's issues addressed by the May Fourth intellectuals were female emancipation, chastity, marriage-related family conflicts, education, and economic independence.[14] In their writings, orthodox Confucian notions about gender were criticized.[15] Support from May Fourth male intellectuals provided impetus to the women's emancipation movement during its initial stage. Without this support, women's fight against feudal concepts would have been much more difficult. But while the support of May Fourth male intellectuals was indispensable to the women's emancipation movement in the 1910s and

---

8. Lin Weihong, 202.

9. Huang Yanli, 269-70.

10. Lin Weihong, 204.

11. Ibid., 201-2.

12. Amy D. Dooling and Kristina M. Torgeson, eds. *Writing Women in Modern China: An Anthology of Women's Literature from the Early Twentieth Century* (New York: Columbia University Press, 1998), 5.

13. Huang Yanli, 279; Liu Ningyuan, 250.

14. Liu Ningyuan, 29-30.

15. Many of the discussions are translated into English and published in Hua Lan and Vanessa Fong's *Women in Republican China: A Sourcebook* (New York: M.E. Sharpe, 1999).

1920s, women themselves continued the battle for true equality for the remainder of the twentieth century.

Women participated in both social and political movements. In pre-1949 China, these included Sun Yat-sen's revolution (from the end of the nineteenth century to 1911), the May Fourth Movement (1919), the Sino-Japanese War (1937-1945) and the conflicts between the Nationalists and Communists, roughly from the late 1920s to 1949. Through participation in political events, women discovered an opportunity to make a contribution to their country and also proved themselves as capable as men, deserving of equal treatment. However, in their pursuit of equal rights in politics and the law, modern Chinese women often experienced disappointment and frustration.[16] The women's suffrage movement provides an example. Immediately after the success of Sun Yat-sen's 1911 revolution, many women's suffrage organizations were established in China.[17] It was not until 1947, however, that the Constitution of the Nationalist Government finally recognized equality between women and men.[18]

Prior to 1949, women were encouraged by the Chinese Communist Party to participate in the revolution and, along with peasants, were regarded by the party as prime candidates for liberation. In responding to the call, women fought along with men in guerrilla warfare, laid mines, dug tunnels and acted as nurses, messengers and food collectors.[19] In Ding Ling's 1941 work "Wo zai Xiacun de shihou" (When I was in Xia Village), we even see women conducting intelligence operations and serving as spies. Following the overthrow of the Nationalist government in 1949, Communist China announced two key measures: the 1950 Marriage Law, which legalized freedom of marriage, equal rights for both sexes in the marital relationship and women's right to divorce; and Land Reform, also in 1950, which gave women the right to inherit and own land.[20] The All-China Women's Federation also was established in 1949 to protect women's rights. Nevertheless, women's political status rose and fell many times along with the tides of political and economic events in the second half of the twentieth century, such as the Great Leap Forward from 1958 to 1960, the Cultural Revolution in the decade from 1966 to 1976 and the economic reform of the 1980s and 1990s. During the first three decades of Communist rule, women were encouraged to join the labor force

---

16. Gu Mou, "Women's Awakening;" Liu Ningyuan, 110-113 and 174-82.

17. Wang Jiajian, "Minchu de nüzi canzheng yundong," *Zhongguo furushi lunwenji,* Vol. 2, eds. Li Youning and Zhang Yufa (Taipei: Taiwan Shangwu yinshuguan, 1988), 582.

18. Esther S. Lee Yao, *Chinese Women: Past and Present* (Mesquite: Ide House, 1983), 200.

19. Referred to by Yao, 156, from Delia Davin's *Women-work: Women and the Party in Revolutionary China* (Oxford: Clarendon Press, 1976).

20. Yao, 159. The English translation of "The Marriage Law of People's Republic of China" is included in Elisabeth Croll's *The Women's Movement in China: A Selection of Readings, 1949-1973* (London: Anglo-Chinese Education Institute, 1974), 107-12.

and some did achieve success in finding better positions in work or politics. Though both historians and sociologists confirm a certain degree of progress, traditional family concepts—such as preference for male over female children, inferior female social status, and the perception of housework and motherhood as binding female duties—are still prevalent.[21] This situation is more severe in the countryside than the cities.

In addition, the state-party's tight ideological control completely subordinated personal individuality from 1949 to the end of the Cultural Revolution. In a study of the contemporary literature of this period, Meng Yue states in her conclusion, "Years after the revolution, the most important effort in cultural production to achieve ideological control and eliminate distracting difference has achieved only one thing: the survival of a nation totally subordinating itself to the state, in economics, social life, ideology, culture and personal life."[22] In this period, women not only lived under male domination but also lost their femininity. This situation is described well by Li Xiaojiang: "'Women,' as an issue, have posed a challenge—a challenge to the rights, already won, that are threatening to revert to traditional ways; a challenge to the thousands of years of that tradition; and a challenge to the new tradition of 'sexual sameness,' which has dominated social relationships in China for the last forty years."[23] Many stories written in the late 1970s and the early 1980s by female writers reflect the awakening of the female identity and revisit themes, such as love and marriage, that were popular in women's literature in the 1920s. In her study of post-Mao fiction, Lai-fong Leung says, "Since 1979, with the relaxation of literary policies, they (young women writers) have written a body of material that manifests a considerable degree of uniform concern. They call for the return of feminine dignity, which has been distorted by puritanism and political dogmatism, for a re-emphasis on the individual, which had been eclipsed by collective ideals, and for the realization of the potential and talent of the female self, which had been overwhelmed by the male sex."[24] Zhang Xinxin's "Wo zai nar cuoguo le ni" (Where Did I Miss You?), published in 1981, is a good example of this outlook.

---

21. Many researchers have reached the same conclusion, for example: Margery Wolf, "Eating Bitterness," *Revolution Postponed: Women in Contemporary China* (Stanford, Stanford UP, 1985), 1-27; Emily Honig and Gail Hershatter, "Introduction," *Personal Voices: Chinese Women in the 1980s* (Stanford: Stanford UP, 1988), 1-12.

22. Meng Yue, "Female Images and National Myth," *Gender Politics in Modern China*, ed. Tani E. Barlow (Durham and London: Duke University Press, 1993), 136.

23. Li Xiaojiang, "Introduction," in Diana B Kingsbury's trans. *I Wish I Were a Wolf: The New Voice in Chinese Women's Literature* (Beijing: New World Press, 1994), 5.

24. Lai-fong Leung, "In Search of Love and Self: the Image of Young Female Intellectuals in Post-Mao Women's Fiction," in *Modern Chinese Women Writers*, ed. Michael Duke (New York: M.E. Sharpe, Inc, 1989), 136.

Since the latter half of the 1980s, women generally have been more fortunate than their predecessors. The political atmosphere has been much more relaxed, providing space for the development of personal life. According to reports, "some 82 percent of working-age women in the cities hold jobs;"[25] "on average, Chinese women earn between 80-90 percent of what men earn, much higher than the worldwide average of 60 to 70 percent;"[26] "China has the highest percentage of women in parliament, 21 percent, in Asia;"[27] and women accounted for 38.7 percent of university students in 1997, up from 23.4 percent in 1980 and 19.8 percent in 1949.[28] In literature, some successful career women have appeared as characters in fiction. For the first time in Chinese literature, these new women display self-confidence. Zhang Xin's "Ai you ruhe" (Love, So What, 1995) is a good example. These female characters are portrayed as capable of taking care of their own lives. However, they have stopped believing in love; they may love certain men during their lives, but do not expect relationships to last forever. The other new theme that appeared in women's fiction during this time was sexual liberation. Wang Anyi's (b.1954) famous "three loves"—*Xiaocheng zhi lian* (Love in a Small Town, 1986), *Huangshan zhi lian* (Love on a Barren Mountain, 1986), and *Jinxiugu zhi lian* (Love in a Brocade Valley, 1988)—are among the most widely read representatives of this kind of story. In these novels, the desires of women and men are treated equally as part of human nature. Although they all end tragically, the author's sympathy is obvious. While in the 1980s, according to Lai-fong Leung, sexually liberated women were, "without exception, morally condemned,"[29] in Wang's "Wo ai Bier" (I Love Bill, 1996) and Tie Ning's "Dui mian" (The Other Side of the Street, 1993), images of such women are no longer completely negative.

However, this picture of women's condition in China at the present time is not complete. What's missing is the effect of economic reform on women and women's lives in the countryside. Emily Honig and Gail Hershatter describe what economic reform has wrought:

---

25. Sheryl WuDunn and Nicholas Kristof, *China Wakes* (New York: Vintage Books, 1995), 213-4.

26. Vikram Nehru, ed. *China 2020: Development Challenges in the New Century* (Washington, D.C.: World Bank, 1997), 57.

27. "High-ranking positions elude Asian women," *Globe and Mail*, August 3, 1996, A18.

28. Ma Wanhua, Institute of Higher Education, Beijing University, September 4, 1999, lecture at the University of Calgary; Grace C. L. Mak, "Development and Women's Higher Education: A Comparative Study of China and Hong Kong," in Fanny M. Cheung and et al. eds. *Selected Papers of Conference on Gender Studies in Chinese Societies* (Hong Kong: Hong Kong Institute of Asia-Pacific Studies, the University of Hong Kong, 1991), 219.

29. Leung, 148.

"Beginning in 1978, economic reforms began to restructure the lives of women. In the countryside, agriculture was decollectivized and production was reorganized with households as the basic unit. Peasants were encouraged to engage in sideline production, private markets were permitted, and the government raised the prices it paid for farm produce. These new policies increased women's opportunities to earn income, but also placed their labor firmly under the control of the head of the household rather than the collective, reinforcing familial authority. In the cities, industrial enterprises were given expanded powers to hire and fire, and were made responsible for their own profits and losses. Since urban unemployment was a problem at the beginning of the 1980s, they had a large labor pool from which to draw. Many promptly decided that they would prefer to hire men rather than women, who were considered unreliable workers because of their responsibilities in the home."[30]

This observation matches what the 1999 United Nations' report on China's human development had to say. Under the subtitle "Women and the Transition: Some New Problems," the report pointed out that "with the ideological relaxation of recent years, old-fashioned sexist attitudes have re-emerged in public, shouldering aside the principle of ensuring equal rights and opportunities for women," and concluded: "There is much room, therefore, for continued efforts to promote gender equality in China. From the poor, rural hinterland, where girls are often kept from school, to the burgeoning cities, where women constitute more than their fair share of the unemployed, there is an agenda of issues that can be addressed by enlightened public policy."[31]

In the new era of economic reform, working women also found their lives much busier than before.[32] Since many people still believe that housework, child-care and elder-care are female responsibilities, women who work outside the home have to endure the burden of "two jobs." In the meantime, prostitution, which disappeared after 1949, has now returned. Chen Danyan's "Banü Linda" (The Bar Girl Called Linda, 1991) is a story about women in this profession.

As for women in the countryside, news reports about how they live are frequent. For instance, girls comprise 70 percent of all school dropouts;[33]

---

30. Honig and Hershatter, 5.

31. The United Nations Development Programme, China, *The China Human Development Report* (New York: Oxford UP, 1999), 52.

32. A three-city (Beijing, Shanghai and Guangzhou) survey shows that 72 percent of married women are not satisfied with their present life; the most important reason for their dissatisfaction is the housework burden. Xiao Wei, "Nanren lanzuo jiawu shi nüren guande?" *Zhongguo Funü*, August 1999, 50.

33. Wang Jun, "Nüxing jiaoyu: tiaozhan 'ling yizhong pinkun,'" *Women of China*, May 2000, 5.

country girls from poor families are sent to Beijing to sell flowers on the street;[34] women are battered or killed by husbands (sometimes with their in-laws' involvement);[35] the sex ratio for newborn infants was 112 boys for every 100 girls in the late 1980s, 118.5 to 100 in 1992,[36] and 116.3 to 100 in 1994,[37] much higher than the natural ratio of 105 or 106 male births for every 100 female births, suggesting either female infanticide or non-registration of female newborns. For these reasons, many feminist researchers regard female emancipation in China as still far from complete; some even claim it has failed.[38]

Due to the different political environment that has prevailed in Taiwan over most of the past one hundred years, Taiwanese women have taken a different route in their search for equality than their sisters in mainland China. Taiwan was ceded and became a Japanese colony in 1895, returning to the government of the Republic of China in 1945 after World War II. However, the Nationalist government retreated to Taiwan in 1949 and the island again became politically separate from mainland China. During the fifty-year Japanese occupation, Taiwanese culture was influenced greatly by Japan, and, Esther S. Lee Yao states, "The social status of Taiwanese women was as suppressed as their counterparts' in Japan. Both were expected to be totally subservient to their husbands."[39] The women's emancipation movement during the May Fourth era did not reach the island. Liao Huiying's "Youma caizi" (Rapeseed, 1982), contained in this anthology, allows us to gain some understanding of this influence. After 1949, the Constitution of the Nationalist Government (formally adopted in 1947) and the Civil Laws (1936) applied to people in Taiwan, granting women equality with men. The government, though, has been more interested in political and military issues and been passive in the area of improving women's status. Therefore, what the law says often is not the same as social practice. Property inheritance provides an example. According to local Taiwanese custom, a daughter is not entitled to a family's inherited property, i.e., property not acquired by her father but

---

34. Zhao Jin, "Ni daxue sheng tanmi huatong yu huatong zhixiang," *Women of China*, June 2000, 4-5.

35. According to Zhang Xihui, family violence in China often takes place in cases where the husband's family has a lower educational background, such as among laborers and peasants. See Guo Chi, "Funü yanjiu, mianxiang xin shijide sikao,"*Women of China*, March 2000, 5. A case of wife killing in Fengyang, Anhui Province, is reported by Liu Zhuying, "Yiqi lingren fazhideshaoqi an," *Women of China*, July 2000, 29-30.

36. WuDunn and Kristof, 228, 229.

37. The United Nations Development Programme, China, 48.

38. Tonglin Lu, "Introduction," in her ed. *Gender and Sexuality in Twentieth-Century Chinese Literature and Society* (Albany: State University of New York Press, 1993), 18.

39. Yao, 199.

inherited from his father or others.[40] Polygamy is another example. Although polygamy is against the law, it still occurs and is tolerated to a certain degree in modern Taiwanese society. For example, concubines' right to alimony in "divorce" cases has been legitimized.[41] At the same time, men do not suffer the same social stigma that women do for extramarital affairs.[42] Extramarital affairs are so common that they became one of the main themes in women's fiction in the 1980s.

In the first thirty years of the post-World War II period, Taiwanese society could justly be proud of its achievements in many aspects of development. In addition to the economy, education is an area that deserves our praise because of its impact on the improvement in women's well-being. According to the Ministry of Education's "Educational Statistics of the Republic of China in 1980," 99.67 percent of school-age girls entered elementary schools; 93.39 percent of elementary female graduates entered junior high schools; 61.44 percent of junior high female graduates entered senior high; and 85.80 percent of senior high female graduates entered universities, colleges and junior colleges.[43] Moreover, during the 1970s, the female literacy rate in Taiwan rose from 9.8 percent to 83.6 percent.[44] Given the opportunities provided by women's educational attainments in postwar Taiwan, one might expect that the conservatism towards women mentioned above would not be tolerated by the highly educated female population. The first wave of the Taiwanese women's movement finally emerged in 1972. Since then, there have been second and third waves in 1982 and 1993. The first wave was led by Lü Xiulian, today's vice-president of Taiwan. Aware of the social tolerance for patriarchy, Lü did not attack fundamental issues like the marriage system but instead promoted comparatively minor issues, such as women's equality before the law, mutual loyalty between husband and wife, and men sharing in the housework. The second-wave women's movement was led by Li Yuanzhen. Li established a publishing company named "Funü xinzhi" (Awakening) with a group of friends. Through a magazine of the same name, they aimed at raising women's consciousness and encouraging self-development. They translated feminist writings from the West, explored Chinese women's history and reviewed laws and politics from a feminist perspective. Among the

---

40. Lung-sheng Sung, "Property and Family Division," Emily Ahern and Hill Gates' eds. *The Anthropology of Taiwanese Society* (Stanford: Stanford UP, 1981), 367; Hill Gates, *Chinese Working-Class Lives: Getting by in Taiwan* (Ithaca: Cornell UP, 1987), 104. In addition, a couple of similar cases occurred to personal friends from Taiwan in the 1980s.

41.The law is vague but does exist. See the discussion on a concubine's right to alimony in Chen Meiling, "Lihun xiaoguo zhong shanyangfei jifu zhidu zhi yanjiu," Master's thesis at the Law School, National Taiwan University, June 1984, 90-1.

42. Yao, 203.

43. Ibid., 209-10.

44. Ibid., 208.

activities this organization initiated were opposition to trafficking in women and protection of child prostitutes. After the lifting of martial law in 1987, social movements gained political space and opportunities to spread. In the 1990s, many women's organizations appeared. Unlike the first and second waves of feminism in Taiwan, the third wave has displayed diversity, with each group having its own particular interest, including the rights of lesbians, establishing women's shelters and emergency telephone lines and revising laws that discriminate against women. Among the movement's many accomplishments, in 1996 Taiwan finally changed its discriminatory laws against women concerning child custody and ownership of a wife's property.[45] Given that more and more highly educated and professional women participate actively in the third-wave women's movement in Taiwan—most of the leaders of the women's movement were educated in the United States and have postgraduate degrees in various fields—the advancement of Taiwanese women's welfare should have a bright future, assuming socioeconomic development continues its steady progress.

In terms of economic and social development, Hong Kong is in many ways comparable to Taiwan. It emerged from a poor colonial state in the nineteenth century, experienced an economic boom in the 1970s, and developed into Asia's international financial center in the 1980s. Hong Kong island was ceded to Britain and became a British colony in 1842; the Kowloon (or Jiulong) Peninsula was ceded in 1860; the New Territories (or Xinjie) were leased for ninety-nine years beginning July 1, 1898. All three Hong Kong regions were returned to China in 1997. Given that Hong Kong was under British rule for about one hundred and fifty years and English was the colonial government's official language, Hong Kong people had an opportunity to make contact with Western thinking, including Western notions of women's rights. One idea that took root was women's education. Documents show that women had a fair opportunity to receive formal education. In 1870, there were 111 girls, 8.5 percent of the total, enrolled in schools; in 1900, the number rose to 3,092 or 41 percent.[46] In 1902, the Hong Kong government established a provision granting girls the same educational rights as boys.[47] From the 1910s to the 1930s, expatriates and Chinese Christians were actively involved in the movement to abolish the "meizai" (female bondservants) system. However,

---

45. Introductions to the Taiwan women's movement used here include Gu Yanling (Yenlin Ku), "Taiwan fuyun de kaizhan," W.M.Semi-Annual, No. 1 (February 1989), 264-70; Yenlin Ku, "The Uneasy Marriage between Women's Studies and Feminism in Taiwan," Gail Hershatter et al eds. *Guide to Women's Studies in China* (Berkeley: Institute of East Asian Studies, University of California, 1998), 115-34; Wang Yage, *Taiwan funü jiefang yundongshi,* (Taipei: Juliu tushu gongsi, 1999).

46. Mak, 220.

47. Ibid.

researchers today do not believe Western influence caused significant changes in the lives of Hong Kong women. Hon-ming Yip states, "While Hong Kong's women may appear 'Westernized' on the outside, they may not realize the extent to which they are traditional and Chinese inside."[48] According to the Hong Kong Women's Coalition for Beijing 1995, "Gender stereotyping is still prevalent in Hong Kong. In 1991, 83 percent of women between the ages of 20 and 24 were involved in the labor force. Between the ages of 30 and 34 and 35 and 39, the numbers dropped drastically to 60 percent and 50 percent respectively."[49] The reason for the high dropout rate is women's family responsibilities, which would seem to support Yip's argument.

Although Hong Kong was under British rule for one hundred and fifty years, in the areas of family structure and male-female relations, traditional Chinese patriarchy remained dominant. Its persistence is illustrated in two particular cases: the "meizai" system and women's land inheritance rights in the New Territories. A "meizai" is a female bondservant usually purchased at a very young age to serve the son or daughter of a rich man. When a woman from a rich family got married, she could bring her own "meizai" to her husband's home. The Anti-Muijai (meizai) Society was formed in 1921 by a group of expatriates and Chinese Christians to campaign for the abolition of the "meizai" system. However, they encountered extraordinary obstacles from the Chinese elite in Hong Kong society. The sale and transfer of women as adopted daughters, concubines and bondservants did not stop until the 1950s.[50] The "meizai" problem was more complicated than simply being an issue of child slavery; it also mingled with the problem of concubinage, as many of these "meizais" grew up to become their master's concubines. Concubines were not banned until 1971 in Hong Kong.[51] As for women's right of inheritance, several related laws were passed in the 1970s to grant daughters the right to an equal share in property inheritance but land in the New Territories has remained exempt to this day.[52]

Despite these problems, contemporary Hong Kong women generally do enjoy more opportunities for self-development as a result of Hong Kong's economic and social progress. In her study of women's higher education in China and Hong Kong, Grace Mak says that "the experiences of the women in

---

48. Hon-ming Yip, "Into the Postcolonial Era: Women's Studies in Hong Kong," *Guide to Women's Studies in China*, 78.

49. Hong Kong Women's Coalition for Beijing 1995, "Alternative Report on Women in Hong Kong," in Fanny M. Cheung's ed. *EnGendering Hong Kong Society: A Gender Perspective of Women's Status* (Hong Kong: The Chinese UP, 1997), 386.

50. Hon-ming Yip, "Women and Cultural Tradition in Hong Kong," in *EnGendering Hong Kong Society*, 312, 310.

51. Fanny M. Cheung and et al, "Gender Role Identity, Stereotypes, and Attitudes in Hong Kong," in *EnGendering Hong Kong Society*, 209.

52. Ibid.

this study suggest that in China women's opportunity in higher education has been shaped primarily by politics, whereas in Hong Kong it has generally been a result of economic development."[53] Statistics show that women accounted for nearly 40 percent of university enrollment in 1986.[54] Along with higher education, more and more local women's groups were established in the 1980s and 1990s to protect and improve Hong Kong women's living conditions,[55] a phenomenon similar to what occurred in Taiwan. Due to the existence of these groups oriented toward protecting women's interests and steady social progress, further advancement in the status of Hong Kong women could be expected, although some concern about interference from the Beijing government has been expressed since 1997.[56]

At the beginning of the 21st century, it is obvious that there has been a transformation in the development of women's living conditions in the past one hundred years. With the exception of remote areas of China, Chinese women in all three regions—mainland China, Taiwan and Hong Kong—now enjoy opportunities for a formal education, better jobs and higher income. Though true equality has not been achieved, women are aware of their rights and have established a number of women's groups to continue moving toward that goal, while at the same time reaching out to less fortunate women.

This anthology consists of stories about and by women from the 1920s to the 1990s. These stories provide one version of the history of the development of Chinese women in the twentieth century. Each of the twelve stories selected represents a type of woman common at that period of time. Three stories were written in pre-1949 China; nine in post-1949 Taiwan, Hong Kong and mainland China. It is apparent that more weight has been put on women's development after 1949. This is because changes in women and women's issues were greater in the second half of the twentieth century and the diversity among the three regions is worth noting.

As mentioned above, the first half of the twentieth century was a time when concepts about the role of women were challenged and gradually evolved from traditional to modern. Educated Chinese women actively participated in the cultural transition that began at the end of the nineteenth century. In the ten years of the May Fourth era, a group of female university students emerged as writers who used their pens to record their observations about women's lives, express their feelings about being women, and protest against the oppression women had endured. The fashionable literary trend of "turning inward" at that time gave these women writers a powerful tool to depict women and women's

53. Mak, 216.
54. Ibid., 222.
55. Choi, Po-king. "Identities and Diversities: Hong Kong Women's Movement in 1980s and 1990s," *Hong Kong Cultural Studies Bulletin Issue 4* (Winter 1995), 95.
56. Choi, 100-1.

experiences. Our first story, Ling Shuhua's (1904-1990) "Xiu zhen" (The Embroidered Cushions, 1925), is a good example of this kind of work. Writing during the May Fourth era, Ling described the reflections and recollections of a young lady from an old-fashioned family about an attempt to arrange a marriage two years earlier. The story illustrated the negative aspect of arranged marriages adopted in traditional patriarchal society, a not uncommon problem before 1949. Many unmarried young women (men, as well, in some cases) at the time were expected to obey their parents and accept the marriage arranged for them. Sometimes, as in "The Embroidered Cushions," they might not even have a chance to see what their husbands-to-be looked like. Although there must have been many loving parents who considered their daughter's happiness first in their selection of a husband for her, often it was the family's interests, not the woman's, which were paramount, as depicted in the story. The saddest thing about arranged marriages was that for many women in traditional society the only thing that mattered during their entire lives was marriage, yet it was a matter utterly beyond their control. While a woman might have to endure a lifetime of unhappiness if she married an unsuitable man, men had many other chances to avoid that fate by taking a second wife, a concubine or even visiting a brothel. The heroine's anonymity in "The Embroidered Cushions" suggests the universality of her condition at that time.

Like Ling Shuhua, many other female writers, as well as male writers, such as Feng Wanjun (1900-1974) and Ba Jin (b.1904), shared the same opinion about arranged marriages. Xiao Hong (1911-1942), a talented and famous female writer in the 1930s, was a victim of an arranged marriage herself. Therefore, it is no surprise that some modern women writers openly promoted the concept of marrying for love's sake.

While Ling Shuhua exposed Chinese women's lack of freedom of choice in a matter as basic as marriage, the second story speaks to the importance of women's economic independence. Eileen Chang's (Zhang Ailing, 1920-1995) "Qingcheng zhi lian" (Love in the Fallen City, 1943) is about a woman from Shanghai, one of the cities in China that first confronted Western influence and modernization. Here we see the two social norms, modern and traditional, battling each other. Young women in that environment might have been able to enjoy a semi-liberated lifestyle, such as going to movie theaters and dance halls, but they could not ignore tradition when it came to gender issues. This story takes on the issue of divorce to lament the dilemma a divorced woman faced. In traditional society, as depicted in this story and the following "My Neighbor" by Bing Xin, financial independence was extremely difficult for women to achieve, and a husband was regarded as a woman's be-all and end-all. In his frequently quoted article "Nala zou hou" (After Nora's Departure, 1926), referring to Ibsen's "A Doll's House," Lu Xun predicted: "(A Chinese) Nora's sole solution after her departure is either a return to her husband's house or prostitution."[57] In pre-1949 China, divorce could cost a woman her financial support and, worst of all, her dignity. Remarriage would have been a convenient solution to this problem, but that meant enduring slanders against one's reputation and the danger of falling again into the same situation. This is why Liusu, the heroine of "Love in the Fallen City," is shown as reluctant and extremely calculating in her courtship with Liuyuan. Although Chang gave "Love in the Fallen City" a happy ending, such endings were rare in her writing. Divorce initiated by women was possible in Chinese society before 1949 but could lead to hardship. As testified by Zhang Jie's (b. 1937) "Fangzhou" (The Ark, 1982), it still is not easy for women in contemporary China.

Our third story is about the appearance in modern China of "new women" who were lucky enough to have wealthy and open-minded parents and who received the same kind of higher education as men from a similar background. This sort of woman usually enjoyed many of the conveniences and opportunities of modern urban life. However, as soon as she married, being a good housewife and a good mother became her central roles, regardless of her talent and educational achievements earlier in life. In "Wode linju" (My Neighbor, 1943), Bing Xin (1900-1998) portrayed the married life of a university-educated woman. Echoing what Lu Yin (1898-1934), another prominent female writer of the 1920s, wrote in her "Shengli zhi hou" (After Victory, 1925), Bing Xin showed that although a modern educated woman might be free to marry and receive a higher education, she was not guaranteed harmony between marriage and career. The heroine, Mrs. M, despite talent in creative writing and qualifications as a teacher, is accused by her husband's family of being incapable of handling the housework. Because of her gender, she also experiences the frustration of not being able to find a job that would allow her to bring home an income and reduce her husband's financial burden in raising the family. Worst of all, her husband, an intellectual himself, fails to recognize his wife's value and provides no support either inside or outside the home. Bing Xin published "My Neighbor" under the pseudonym "Nanshi" (a man) and adopted a male persona in depicting Mrs. M. With its sympathetic tone, this story invites us to think about what education means for women, especially as we observe that contemporary women continue to experience similar problems.

Female writers in the first half of the twentieth century created a literary tradition of writing about women.[58] In their work, they cited many grievances against the unjustified oppression of women. Their writings were more than a

---

57. Lu Xun, *Lu Xun quanji*, Vol. 1 (Beijing: Renmin wenxue chubanshe, 1981), 159. The translation is by Tonglin Lu, 4.

58. Meng Yue and Dai Jinhua, *Fuchu lishi dibiao* (Taipei: Shibao wenhua, 1993), 133.

fictional representation of their views; instead their stories contained a large portion of autobiography and biographical material from friends and relatives. As Bing Xin said in the preface of the second edition of *Guanyu nüren* (About Women), which included "My Neighbor," the fourteen stories in that collection were the result of "inspiration" from her female friends.[59] This kind of writing also can be seen in stories by Lu Yin, Feng Wanjun, Su Xuelin (b.1899), Ding Ling (1904-1986), Xiao Hong, and Eileen Chang.

The first three stories in this anthology reveal certain difficulties women experienced in the first half of the twentieth century—arranged marriages, conflict between career and family obligation, divorce and economic independence. Bing Xin, who came from a loving family and usually viewed things positively, borrowed a male pseudonym to publish all the stories in *About Women* in the 1940s. In the postscript, still in the male persona, she wrote that "women indeed are to be pitied. Over the course of forty years I have observed and discovered a truth, which, in fact, was first said by our ancients. That is, 'Men live for career; women for love.' Though there may be one exception out of a million cases, it is indeed pitiable and dangerous to live one's life depending on love. . . . I cannot effectively prevent men from destroying women by means of marriage, but I can at least prohibit myself from doing so."[60] Radicalism never was Bing Xin's style. However, under the guise of a male persona, she employed a critical tone when writing about the Chinese marriage system and blamed men for the unfortunate women she observed around her. A strong aversion to chauvinism must have been felt among the female population at that time.

As mentioned above, the Chinese Communist Party advocated equal rights for men and women in the early stages of the revolution. In 1950, the new Marriage Law was passed to further guarantee women's equal status with legal protection. For the first time in history, this gave Chinese women the hope of being treated in their own homes with the respect and dignity men had enjoyed for centuries. However, after successfully overthrowing the Nationalist Party, traditional patriarchal concepts found ways to subvert the new policies. In offices, men occupied leading positions and told their female comrades that women were given less burdensome jobs for their own good. Women's main role was still at home. Wei Junyi's "Nüren" (Women, 1956), which portrays a woman with a patriotic heart who finds it hard to accept this change in the 1950s, was a clear protest against the return of patriarchy in Communist China.

---

59. Bing Xin, "Guanyu nüren zaiban zixu,"*Guanyu nüren*, 2nd edition (Chongqing: Kaiming shudian, 1945), page number unknown. This preface is reprinted in Bing Xin sanwen, (Hangzhou: Zhejiang wenyi chubanshe, 1999), 253-4. The quoted passage is on page 253.

60. Bing Xin, "Guanyu nüren houji," Guanyu nüren (Chongqing: Tiandi chubanshe, 1943), page number unknown. The postscript is reprinted in *Prose by Bing Xin*, 342-5. The quoted passages are on pages 342-4.

In 1980, Wei Junyi recalled the reason why she had written "Women":

> "At that time (1956), China had been liberated for more than seven years, and I was unconditionally supportive of the party's policy. However, I could sense that some party members were gradually moving away from the precious tradition established in the first liberated district—to strive hard. I was worried. . . . I saw them (some female comrades from liberated districts) become lazy. They did not consider that not working was shameful; instead they were proud of it. They began to accompany their husbands on holidays. . . . Of course, a woman should be like a man, be independent, interested in career, have lofty ideas. All these ideas were in my mind when I wrote the story, but they are not the main points. The main point is not the differences between men and women, but different philosophies and attitudes."[61]

The heroine of "Women" personifies the ideology the Communist Party promoted among women, that "women hold up half the sky." Indeed, there were changes in the law that benefitted women and had a positive influence on subsequent generations, particularly in the cities. Nevertheless, some Sinologists suspect the true reason for the reforms was to mobilize support for Communist rule rather than an honest effort to promote full-scale equality between men and women. In addition, because of the Sino-Japanese War, Chinese fiction from the late 1930s to 1949, both by men and women, had a patriotic character. Mao Zedong's "Yan'an wenyi zuotanhui jianghua" (Talks at the Yan'an Forum on Literature and Art) in 1942 entrenched the idea that literature should serve politics. This situation continued in mainland China until the end of the Cultural Revolution in the late 1970s. For this reason, many critics do not perceive any true "women's fiction" during this period. However, some women writers were enthusiastic participants in the social reforms in the 1950s and 1960s, and Wei's "Women" is a good example of this attitude.

Due to political separation from the mainland and differences in ideology, literature in Taiwan after 1949 developed a tradition of its own. Defeated by the Communist Party in 1949, the Nationalist government retreated to Taiwan, where the antagonistic relationship with the People's Republic helped to create a tense political atmosphere. Cultural conservatism was also encouraged, and concepts such as loyalty, filial piety and family values were stressed. Women writers in postwar Taiwan joined male writers in producing anti-communist fiction (*fangong xiaoshuo*) and nostalgic literature (*huaixiang wenxue*) in the 1950s and 1960s. In addition, considerable energy was employed in writing melodramatic love stories in the first thirty years of postwar Taiwan. For this reason, some women writers born after World War II, such as Li Ang (b.1952),

---

61. Wei Junyi, "Guanyu 'Nüren,' " in *Zhongguo nü zuojia xiaoshuo xuan,shangce.* eds. Yu Min and Qu Yuxiu (Yangzhou: Jiangsu renmin chubanshe, 1981), 362.

prefer not to be considered as "women writers" but simply as "writers," and some, such as Ping Lu (b.1953), even wrote with a male persona in some of their early works. The situation changed in the 1980s when, all of a sudden, there emerged a group of writers who put women's issues in the forefront of their work. This change could be a result of Taiwan's successful education system, which provides equal access for boys and girls to formal education. It also could be a response to the first and second waves of the Taiwan feminist movement in the 1970s and 1980s. Though sharing some common themes with popular romance writers—love, extra-marital affairs, love triangles, marital problems—these new women writers had sophisticated literary skills and projected feminist insights onto the problems they portrayed. After 1987, when martial law was lifted after forty years, the thematic diversity of Taiwanese women's literature became apparent. While there is still interest in personal independence and seeking harmony in the male-female relationship, we also observe a growing enthusiasm for pursuing the development of feminine identity, personal expression, especially through writing about women's sensual experiences, and politics. This marks a rebirth and continuation of the spirit of May Fourth women writers in contemporary Taiwanese literature.

There are three stories in this anthology by three prominent writers from postwar Taiwan. Told in the first person, Kang Yunwei's (b.1936) "Zheyang hao de xingqitian" (Such a Beautiful Sunday, 1966) was written not long before the first wave of feminism hit Taiwan in 1972.[62] Though living a comfortable life, the heroine feels a sense of dissatisfaction. The story represents a generation of women who fell into the pattern of receiving a good education, falling in love in their early twenties, marrying the men they loved and then becoming housewives for the rest of their lives. Well-educated but given no chance to develop or utilize their talents, such women remained limited in outlook and ignorant about the outside world. Writing in a conservative atmosphere, Kang offered neither harsh criticism nor bitter satire against traditional male-dominated Chinese culture. However, this story provides a vivid depiction of house-bound women's frustrating daily life in modern times.

Kang Yunwei was one of the few women writers in the 1960s who wrote about the problems women faced in their daily life. However, in the literature of Taiwan, the notorious first challenge to patriarchal society came in the next story, "Youma caizi" (Rapeseed, 1982) by Liao Huiying (b. 1948).

Liao Huiying is a writer of many talents. Most of her published work, fiction and non-fiction, focuses on social problems facing women. Liao says

---

62. There is a brief history of Taiwan's feminist movement by Ku Yen-lin. "The first wave of feminism" refers to the series of protests against unfair treatment led by Lü Xiulian in the 1970s. Ku Yen-lin, "The Feminist Movement in Taiwan, 1972-87," *Bulletin of Concerned Asian Scholars*, 20.1 (January-March 1989):12-22.

"Rapeseed" describes the slow progress of Chinese women in contemporary society.[63] The life of traditional Chinese women is vividly portrayed through the heroine Ah-hui's observation of her mother. A woman is said to be like a rapeseed; her fate is decided by whom she marries, just as a rapeseed's survival depends on where it lands. Regardless of how unlucky she is, she has to accept her fate. Liao made a valuable contribution to women's literature by recording the ironic fact that women in traditional society, despite being victims of the patriarchal social system themselves, perpetuate it by being partial to sons over daughters. Ah-hui, growing up in this traditional family yet receiving a modern education at school, is able to question the validity of the patriarchal tradition. She is a symbolic figure for contemporary women. Through the juxtaposition of the mother's and daughter's perspectives, the change in the condition of Chinese women in contemporary society becomes crystal clear.

In "Ai yu" (Jade, 1985), Ping Lu (b. 1953) displays her keen observation of various old problems women continue to face in both Hong Kong and Taiwan. These include women's lack of financial and emotional independence, men's extra-marital affairs, and destructive relationships among women themselves. The jade bracelet is a symbol; like marriage, it traps the heroine. Women's incompetence in seeking financial independence forces them to accept humiliation from their husbands. That includes the revival of polygamy in the form of extra-marital relationships, a common social problem in Taiwan, Hong Kong and even urban society in mainland China. "Sisterhood" with her female friends in the story does not seem to exist when the heroine loses her dignity by embracing a dead marriage for the financial security it provides. Through the symbol of jade, Ping Lu criticizes every character in the story.

In this anthology there are only two stories from Hong Kong, each by the same author. Though a culturally unique city, Hong Kong nurtured few native writers before the 1980s. The most important reason for this situation involved language. Hong Kong is a Cantonese-speaking region. The language used in daily life is Cantonese (or Guangdonghua), while the written language is Mandarin, as in mainland China and Taiwan. As a result, many Hong Kong people have not felt confident about writing. Those who have enjoyed some kind of literary reputation tended to be those who migrated from China after 1949 for economic or political reasons, the so-called "nanlai" (coming to the south) writers. They often wrote nostalgically about the homes they had left behind and their work lacked local Hong Kong flavor. However, in the 1980s, some writers appeared who, although they might have been born in China, grew up in Hong Kong and began to put Hong Kong into their work. While Hong Kong has a number of successful female romance writers, there are only

---

63. Liao Huiying, "Bashi niandai nüxing chuangzuo yu shehui wenhua zhi guanxi," *Wenxue zazhi*, No. 127 (May 1996): 44.

a few female writers of serious fiction. Xi Xi (b.1938) is one of the most celebrated contemporary women writers in Hong Kong. Though she made her reputation first in Taiwan, Xi Xi has a genuine affection for Hong Kong. This is manifested by her descriptions of the people and the city in her writing.

Xi Xi's "Wan" (Bowls) and "Jianguo" (Frying Pan) were written in 1980. Both stories employ a unique technique of interior monologue. "Bowls" is about two women who were good friends in middle school and who run into each other ten years after graduation. This short story consists of four paragraphs—four interior monologues by these two women—reflecting on their unexpected meeting. These two female characters embody two modern types. Yu, although she enjoys a high level of comfort in her rather westernized lifestyle, does not exhibit much of her modern educational background. Instead, she measures people's value by the amount of money they make and has traditional stereotypical attitudes regarding gender: girls should play piano and learn ballet but not play soccer. Hence, her life focuses on vain affairs like parties and gossip, and she pays great attention to stocks, diamonds and real estate. Ye, on the other hand, is genuinely liberated from all stereotypes about what a person should be. She may not be "successful" in her career, but she is self-sufficient. Reading and staying close to the natural world bring her a sense of happiness. The "Bowls" of the title are the thematic symbol of the story. These two women bump into each other while they are on their way to buy bowls. Yu, in fact, already has a luxurious dinner set but she needs to buy a new set for a party she is going to give because one soup bowl is broken and its replacement is not of the same famous brand. Ye is also looking for a bowl but any bowl will do for her. The kinds of bowls the two women want to buy and their reasons for buying a bowl illustrate the sharp contrast between the two characters.

Hong Kong, an international city, provides its citizens with opportunities to absorb influences from both oriental and occidental culture. The two women in "Bowls" help us to see some possible combinations of the two cultural influences on women. Given the apparent similarities between the character Ye and the author Xi Xi, it seems that Xi Xi wants to show the reader what her ideal modern woman is like, and also her opposite. While "Bowls" is "personal," as Xi Xi once referred to it,[64] "Frying Pan" is a story that targets educational and economic problems in Hong Kong. "Frying Pan," like "Bowls," consists of four interior monologues, but each of the four involves the thoughts of the four members of one family, namely the mother, father, daughter and younger brother. Though this story is not a discussion of women's issues, it reflects the difference between middle-aged women and the

---

64. He Furen, "Tonghua xiaoshuo—yu Xi Xi tan tade zuopin he qita," in Xiang wo zheyangde yige nüzi, by Xi Xi (Taipei: Hongfan shudian, 1984), 219.

younger generation in contemporary Hong Kong. Through the way it depicts the parents' lifestyle, the story shows how a married woman of the older generation stayed at home taking care of her husband and children, while the financial responsibility fell entirely on the shoulders of the husband. The wife is not able to do anything to assist the husband, except worry, if he runs into trouble at work.

This is not the case for young women. As we see in the daughter of the story, young women are now better educated and have plans for themselves. Aware of the necessity of improving themselves, they take action to pursue a better future. They are lucky to have the freedom to choose what they want, and they are independent—they will get what they want by themselves, not through the actions of others. "Frying Pan" constructs a positive and self-assertive image of modern women in contemporary Hong Kong.

The last three stories in this anthology are by three prominent contemporary Chinese women writers. As mentioned earlier, there was little development in women's literature in the thirty years from the 1950s through the 1970s in mainland China due to Beijing's tight control over the arts and literature. At the end of the 1970s, however, what has come to be called "New Period Literature" arrived and continued to flourish in the 1980s and 1990s with the loosening of the political atmosphere. Like male writers of this period, female writers enjoyed more creative freedom. The suppression of women's femininity in the previous three decades now ironically provided endless themes for female writers to explore. The achievements of women's literature in the last two decades surpass any previous period in Chinese history. Major themes include women's demand of the right to love; the awakening of gender consciousness; the search for a modern female identity; ever deeper examination of the relationship with men; the conflict between career and family duty, and sexuality. In brief, women writers have exposed the problems encountered and tolerated by ordinary Chinese women for centuries. At the same time, they have triggered a re-examination of women's issues from a variety of perspectives. Women have gone from confusion, anger and frustration to rational analysis and, finally, self-assertion.[65]

Three stories were chosen from this period. "Dengdai huanghun" (Waiting for Dusk, 1990) by Jiang Zidan (b. 1951) looks at women's lives from the point of view of a sophisticated intellectual. "Leng ye hao, re ye hao, huozhe

---

65. Three articles that are particularly clear in delineating the development of women's literature in the 1980s and 1990s are the following: Zhao Mei, "Zhishi nüxing de kunhuo yu xunqiu," in Wang Shichang and Wang Jingtao, eds. *Miandui shidai de xuanze—tansuo zhong de xin shiqi wenxue* (Shenyang: Liaoning jiaoyu chubanshe, 1988), 101-116. Yu Qing, "Liangxing shijie de duili yu hezuo," *Xiaoshuo pinglun,* June 1988, 19-22 & 47. Ren Yimin, "Jiushi niandai: nüxing wenxue dui nüxing mingyun de guanzhu yu tansuo—jian yu bashi niandai nüxing wenxue bijiao," *Xiaoshuo pinglun,* January 1996, 40-45.

jiu hao" (Hot or Cold, Life's Okay, 1991) by Chi Li (b. 1957) portrays the life of a modern urban worker. "Jiemeimen" (Sisters, 1996) by Wang Anyi (b. 1954) depicts women in the countryside in contemporary China. While the last story shows little change in women's lot from the past, the first two stories document the progress made by urban Chinese women.

"Waiting for Dusk" is an ambitious work. Jiang uses the modernist technique of fragmenting time and space and reassembling the fragments in a non-linear narrative. While this makes the job of answering "what" and "when" questions rather challenging; the fragmentation functions as a method of poeticizing the narrative prose, combining the use of symbols and poetic images in the novella. Every character and object can be interpreted on both realistic and symbolic levels, creating a dense semantic fabric—Jiang is a writer who demands her readers' full attention. In this story, she asks us to consider the meaning of a woman's life. Should we draw an equal sign between womanhood and motherhood for the entire female population of the world? Is motherhood women's binding duty? This question reminds us of the goals of those who promoted women's education at the end of the nineteenth century in China: that by giving women formal education, China would make women better mothers and better mothers would raise better children. In this story, the frequently recurring image of a red dragonfly represents a woman at the peak of life, young and beautiful. What will happen after reaching that peak? After giving birth, a woman has fulfilled her obligations and the remainder of her life becomes one long anti-climax. The murder by Sumi, a friend of the narrator, of her own children is a symbolic protest against the obligation nature and society force upon women. Sumi, therefore, is a notion, an ideal who challenges all women—embodied in the narrator—to reconsider the meaning of their personal life and womanhood in the context of traditional Chinese culture. The narrator represents contemporary women who are living in a world where old and new ideas about women co-exist. Yet, women nowadays have many choices; the meaning of one's life is decided by the individual.

While "Waiting for Dusk" is a story that demands a re-examination of fundamental questions about the existential meaning of being a woman, Chi Li's "Hot or Cold, Life's Okay" gives a positive description of everyday life. "Hot of Cold, Life's Okay" is set in the city of Wuhan. Its characters are all working people with average jobs. They have no great dreams but they enjoy their lives. In this modern urban world, the boundary between men and women is blurred. For instance, Yanhua, the main female character, is a bus driver, usually regarded as a man's job. Another female character, Xiao Mie, talks as rudely as any man, if not ruder. At night, these young women dress up and have fun together strolling through the city. Neither the young unmarried women nor the married women in the story display resentment toward men or society. To some degree, they seem to receive more respect from men than men do from women. Men and women may behave differently but they live together in harmony. Such a relaxed atmosphere between men and women was never portrayed in the literature of the first half of the twentieth century. This testifies to the improvement in women's status in contemporary urban society. Yanhua, as Chi Li puts it, is "a woman hero" of our time.[66]

For the conclusion of this anthology, we have chosen Wang Anyi's "Sisters." While Chi Li tells a happy story about women in the cities, Wang Anyi reminds us of the unchanging character of the suffocating life women live in the countryside. Wang Anyi is an internationally celebrated Shanghai writer. She likes to fill her work with facts and details, sometimes too many, but her appeal is probably best described by Helmut Martin, who says she is a "versatile writer with a special humane sensitivity, an idealist in quest of a friendlier, more civilized, and egalitarian society—among the classes and among the sexes, who must coexist in China's modern megalopolises."[67] "Sisters" is a story that documents the life of women in the countryside as Wang observed it during the Cultural Revolution. This piece of writing, though written in a very different style, reminds us of some of Xiao Hong's stories in the 1930s. In "Sisters," Wang adapts the rhetorical technique Sima Qian (c. 145 - c. 85 B.C.) used in the biographies contained in his *Shi Ji* (Records of the Grand Historian). Instead of describing one character in one biography, Sima Qian wrote about groups of personages. By comparing and contrasting a number of historical figures, Sima Qian revealed his own opinions. In "Sisters," Wang displays deep compassion toward women in the villages. By depicting the change in a girl's personality before and after marriage, and the reoccurrence of the change in almost every female in the village, the author effectively conveys her unspoken criticism of chauvinism.

The term "sister" is preserved for unmarried girls in the village. They are full of life, each of them possessing distinctive characteristics and self-esteem. Together, they are like flowers, adding color to the plain life of the village. Not only their parents, but the entire village treasures them. After marriage, however, they wilt. Married women are the lowest class in agricultural society, with no right to anything. They become bitter, vulgar, sloppy and nar-row-minded. The image presented of these women draws our attention to the countryside and the question of why progress there is so slow.

Chinese women in the twentieth century went through many stages of development. In the early part of the century, the individual woman's fate generally was decided by social and familial conditions. Gradually, personal talent and self-consciousness came to play a role. Today, a woman's individual

---

66. Chi Li, "Wo tanshuai shu," *Chi Li's Collected Prose*, Vol. 4, 224.
67. Helmut Martin and Jeffrey Kinkley, eds. *Modern Chinese Writers: Self-Portrayals* (New York: M.E. Sharpe, Inc., 1992), 123.

ability still may not be the most important factor in her life, but has become a crucial one. Although conditions in the countryside and the cities are oceans apart, women in urban society, especially those with advanced education, have overcome many of the difficulties their mothers and grandmothers experienced. This anthology, with only twelve stories, cannot include all the images of women portrayed in women's writing of the previous century, but it does reflect the changes that have occurred in many lives.

Due to reasons of length as well as thematic considerations, this anthology has not included countless masterpieces about Chinese women by many talented writers.[68] To gain a deeper understanding of the development of Chinese women, the reader should consult other excellent anthologies with different themes, particularly those about ground-breaking or revolutionary women whom this volume purposely avoids. In the end, I wish to pay tribute to those who, by whatever means, made an effort to improve the life of Chinese women in the twentieth century, and I look forward to further progress in the future.

Shu-ning Sciban
University of Calgary
2001

---

68. In addition to stories by Ding Ling and Xiao Hong, stories written in the 1980s and 1990s by brilliant writers such as Zhang Jie, Zhang Xinxin, Zhang Kangkang and Tie Ning in China, Zhong Xiaoyang in Hong Kong, and Li Ang, Su Weizhen and Zhu Tianxin in Taiwan, all deserve our applause.

凌叔華

Ling Shuhua (1904-1990) was born and raised in
Beijing, where she received formal training in
traditional painting and literature from the age of six.
She made a name for herself as a writer with the
publication of "After Drinking" (Jiu hou) in 1924 in
Modern Criticism (Xiandai pinglun), which was
edited by Chen Yuan (also known as Chen Xiying),
whom she later married. Ling's work tended to focus
on powerless women trapped by traditional social
conventions. She published four volumes of fiction:
The Flower Temple (Hua zhi si, 1928), *Women*
(Nüren, 1930), *Children* (Xiaohai, 1930), and *Little
Brothers* (Xiaogeer lia, 1935).

The Embroidered Cushions
❖
1925

Eldest Young Mistress sat with her head lowered, embroidering a cushion. The weather was hot and stuffy. A small lap dog lay beneath the table with its tongue hanging out, panting. In the heat, a fly spun around the glass at the window, lazy and confused. Zhangma stood behind her young mistress, fanning her. Streams of perspiration ran down Zhangma's face. She wiped it constantly with a towel but it would not stay dry. Just a moment ago, the tip of her nose had been dry, but now there were beads of sweat appearing at the corner of her mouth. Zhangma looked down to see how her mistress was faring. Though she was not perspiring nearly so much, her face was flushed, and the back of her fine white linen dress was damp with perspiration. Zhangma couldn't resist speaking:

"Miss, rest for a while. Cool down a bit. Although your father said this cushion must be delivered tomorrow, it hasn't been decided whether it will be in the morning or the evening."

"He said it is better to do it before twelve o'clock tomorrow. I can't afford not to rush. Come stand over here and fan me." When Eldest Young Mistress finished answering Zhangma, she lowered her head again and continued her work.

Zhangma moved to the left side of her mistress to fan her. The older woman looked at the embroidery on the cushion and could not help clicking her tongue in praise:

"I've heard people tell stories about pretty girls who were both intelligent and clever with their hands. I always thought these people were just weaving stories with their tongues. How could I know there was truth in it? Right here there is such a young lady, who looks as delicate as a porcelain vase and possesses such talent. People surely will love this embroidered bird more than anything else!" At the corner of the young woman's mouth, a dimple appeared for an instant but then it was gone. Zhangma's unending chatter continued:

"Humph, you can present this cushion at Official Bai's place. Everyone will see it. There will be countless people coming here to act as a matchmaker. . . . The door will be worn down from the crowds trying to push their way in. . . . I heard that Official Bai's second son is in his twenties and still has no

26

suitable match. Now, I know your father's intent. The fortune-teller told your mother that this was an auspicious year for you to marry . . ."

"Zhangma, such nonsense." Eldest Young Mistress stopped stitching and spoke no further. Her face had turned slightly red.

The room became quiet again. Only the sound of embroidering could be heard, the needle piercing the satin, in and out, and the slight rustle of the wind. Suddenly, from outside the bamboo curtain, a teenage girl called out:

"Ma, I'm coming."

"Xiaoniu? What are you doing here on such a hot day?" Zhangma wasted no time in asking. The young girl wore a dark blue cotton pantsuit. Her head was beaded with sweat and her face was purple from the heat. Quickly she pushed the curtain aside and entered the room. As if in a trance, she gazed at the young woman and with a deep breath said:

"Ma, yesterday Saozi told me that this young lady has spent ages embroidering a pair of cushions with great skill, and that she has used thirty or forty different types of thread for one bird alone. I didn't believe that anyone could use so many colors, so Saozi said if I didn't believe her I should go and see for myself. She also said that in two days these cushions would be presented to someone else. So today, I came to town right after I ate. Ma, can I take a look?"

After Zhangma had taken in the girl's words, she promptly asked with a smile:

"Miss, my daughter would like to see your handiwork, is that all right?"

Eldest Young Mistress raised her head to look at Xiaoniu. Her clothes were very dirty and the greyish towel she held was only smearing the sweat across her face. A wide grin came over the girl's face, revealing her yellowed front teeth. Her eyes were wide open as she looked into the room. The mistress frowned at the girl and replied:

"Tell her to go outside and wait for a while."

Zhangma knew that Eldest Young Mistress did not want Xiaoniu to look at her work because her daughter was dirty. Zhangma immediately scolded the girl, saying: "Look at the sweat on your nose. Quit wiping your face. There is some water for washing up in my room. On a hot day like this you'll poison the mistress with your smell."

Disappointment crept over the young girl's face. Even after her mother had spoken, she did not want to go. Zhangma saw that her daughter was not moving. She had to look at Xiaoniu directly and say: "Go to my room and wash your face. Go on. I'll come in a moment."

Pouting, Xiaoniu lifted the curtain and left. The mistress, while changing thread, raised her head and looked out the window. She only saw the girl wiping the sweat from her forehead with the front of her shirt, which was soaked through. In the courtyard stood a pomegranate tree on fire with blood-red blossoms. The sun was shining straight down, making the day seem even hotter. She looked down at her own clothes, and under each arm was a large, wet patch of perspiration.

Two years passed. Eldest Young Mistress again was sitting in her room doing needlework. Xiaoniu had grown as tall as her mother and had learned to wear clean clothes. Now, if her mother asked for leave to return home, she would be capable of taking over for her.

One summer evening, the girl had just sat down beside a lamp to stitch a pillow, when suddenly she heard the mistress call out to her. She laid her needlework down and ran into the main room.

Xiaoniu massaged her mistress's leg, gently pounding it with two fists. On and off, they spoke casually:

"Miss, the day before yesterday my godmother gave me a pair of beautiful pillows. On one there is only a kingfisher and on the other there is a phoenix."

"How could a person embroider such mismatched birds?"

It seemed as if Eldest Young Mistress was making fun of the girl's words.

"To explain about these pillows takes a long time. You know, because of them, my godmother's daughter and I were angry with each other for some time. Originally, Wang gave them to my godmother. She said these birds were cut from two large, dirty cushions. They were extremely beautiful when they were new. One embroidered cushion had a lotus flower and a kingfisher on it. The other had a phoenix standing on top of a rock. The first day the two cushions were given to Wang's master, he put them on a chair in the parlor. That evening, a drunken guest threw up all over one of them. Another person playing mahjongg threw the other one on the floor, which made everyone think it was a floor mat. The beautiful satin cushion was covered with muddy footprints. The young master of the house saw them and told Wang to throw them away. Later, my godmother asked if Wang would give them to her and she, in turn, gave them to me. I looked at them a long time that evening when I first got them. I loved them beyond anything else. The tail of the phoenix alone was made with more than forty different colors of thread. The eyes of the kingfisher, gazing at a tiny fish in the pond, looked so real. The eyes were shining. I wondered what kind of thread had been used to embroider them."

As Eldest Young Mistress listened to Xiaoniu's words, her heart became heavy with sadness. The girl continued:

"It's a real shame that these beautiful things were ruined. My godmother came to see me the day before yesterday and taught me how to trim away the dirty areas, and how to stitch the good parts on a pair of pillows. Who knew that godmother's older daughter would be so petty. She said I only asked her mother for all the beautiful things I saw they had."

Eldest Young Mistress stopped paying attention to the girl's words. She could only think back to that hot summer day the year before last when she meticulously embroidered a pair of cushions—they also had a kingfisher and a phoenix on them. The days were too hot to work with a needle, so she often embroidered in the evenings. When she was finished, her eyes ached for more than ten days. She was curious to compare this girl's birds with her own. She instructed Xiaoniu to bring the pillows at once.

Holding the pillows Xiaoniu said:

"Miss, see how the base of this dark blue satin is all dirty. I heard that before these birds were protruding right out of the pillow. Now, they are sunken in. Look! This bird's crest and red mouth, the colors are still bright. Wang said that this bird's eyes used to be inlaid with real pearls. This lotus is no good though. It's turned grey. And this lotus leaf is too big. There is no use for it on my pillow. . . . There are still some small flowers beside this rock. ..."

Eldest Young Mistress just sat there, hypnotized by the two pieces of embroidery. Whatever Xiaoniu was saying, she did not hear any of it. She was remembering when she had to undo the embroidery on the crest of the bird. Three times she had redone it. The first time, sweat had stained the delicate yellow threads. It had not become apparent until she had finished embroidering. The second time she mixed the wrong green pigments for the threads. In the evening, she had picked the wrong color. She could not quite remember what happened the last time. The pink threads for the lotus petals were so fair that even after she had finished washing her hands she was afraid to touch them. So she had covered her hands with talcum powder to continue embroidering. The lotus leaf was too big. The embroidery was more difficult. If she had used the same shade of green for the whole leaf, it would have been too dull, so she used twelve different greens. After she finished the cushions, she presented them to the Bai family. Many relatives and friends offered words of flattery to her parents. Her friends also teased her. Usually, when they did this she would smile slightly and blush. In the evenings, she would dream of being charming and delicate, or of being proud and wearing clothes she had never worn before. Many young girls would chase after her with admiration, and many of her companions would be green with envy. But that was all a dream world. Not long after that she had come to understand the whole situation, and hoped never to be reminded of it. But today, by chance, it had come up again and she remembered.

Xiaoniu watched her sitting silently, not saying a word, eyes gazing straight ahead just looking at the pillows. She said:

"Does Miss also like it? People surely will love this needlework more than anything else. Tomorrow, you can use this as a model for your embroidery. Is that okay?"

Eldest Young Mistress did not hear what the young girl said. She only shook her head in reply.

Translated by Heather Schmidt

張愛玲

Eileen Chang (Zhang Ailing, 1920-1995) came from
an illustrious family. Her grandfather, Zhang Peilun,
was an official in the Manchu court and was married
to the daughter of Li Hongzhang, the most powerful
Chinese political figure in the latter half of the
nineteenth century. Zhang was a literary prodigy who
began to write at age seven. Between 1943 and 1945,
while living in Japanese-occupied Shanghai, she
enjoyed a burst of productivity, publishing eighteen
short stories and novelettes, plus a collection of thirty
articles. "Love in the Fallen City" (Qingcheng zhi
lian, 1943) dates from this period.

Love in the Fallen City

❖

1943

To save daylight, the people of Shanghai turned their clocks one hour ahead. But the Bai family said, "We use the old time." Therefore, what was ten o'clock to them was eleven to others. It was as if the family sang out of tune with the melody of life.

A *huqin* squeaked on a night full of twinkling lights. The melody ran up and down the scale, telling such an endless and sorrowful tale that it would be better not to ask about it! The stories told by a *huqin* should be performed by a gorgeously dressed actress whose delicate nose narrows between two long, rouged cheeks. She sings, she smiles and she covers her mouth with a sleeve . . . but, actually there was only Fourth Master Bai[1] sitting alone on the gloomy, dilapidated balcony playing the *huqin*.

While he played, the doorbell rang. It was uncommon that this should happen in the Bai household. Following an old custom, the Bai family never went out to visit friends in the evening. If they had visitors at night, or by chance received a telegram, it meant there must be a dire emergency. In most cases, it meant that someone had just died.

The Fourth Master listened without moving, and, as expected, he heard Third Master, Third Madam and Fourth Madam making a fuss as they climbed the stairs, but they spoke so fast that he could not understand what they were talking about. In the main room facing the balcony, sat Sixth, Seventh and Eighth Misses and the children of Third and Fourth Masters. All of them were anxious. Seated in the darkness on the balcony, Fourth Master could clearly see everything that was happening in the lighted room. All of a sudden, he saw the

---

1. In traditional Chinese society, family members tended not to call one another by their first name as Westerners do. Instead, they addressed one another according to their relationship with that person or the seniority of a son or daughter in the family. In this story, for example, there are "Fourth Brother," "Sixth Sister," "Seventh Sister" and "Fourth Sister-in-law." However, male outsiders are always called "Master," women "Miss" and men's wives "Madam." So we see "Third Master," "Third Madam" and "Seventh Miss" as terms of address. In the story, "Third Master" is "Third Brother"; "Fourth Madam" is "Fourth Sister-in-law" and also "Fourth Master's Wife." Bai Liusu is known as "Sixth Sister," "Sixth Miss" or "Sixth Aunt," depending on who is addressing her.

door open, and Third Master entered wearing an undershirt and a pair of shorts. He stood in the doorway with his legs spread. As he put his hands behind him to slap the mosquitos buzzing around his thighs, he called, "Fourth Eldest, guess what? Sixth Sister's ex-husband has died of pneumonia!"

Fourth Master put down the *huqin* and walked into the room. "Who brought over the message?" he asked.

"Mrs. Xu." Saying this, Third Master turned his head, waved his fan to shoo away Third Madam and said to her, "Don't bother us now. Mrs. Xu is still downstairs. She is overweight and afraid of climbing the stairs. You'd better hurry up and assist her!"

After Third Madam had gone, Fourth Master seemed lost in thought and said, "Isn't the dead man a relative of Mrs. Xu?"

Third Master answered, "He is. It looks to me as if they specially sent Mrs. Xu to give us this news, which must mean something."

Fourth Master asked, "Can it be that they want Sixth Sister to attend the funeral as a member of their family?"

Third Master scratched his head with the handle of his fan and said, "As a rule, it is only right that . . ."

Simultaneously, both of them glanced at Sixth Miss Bai Liusu while she sat in the corner of the room, calmly embroidering a pair of slippers. While Third Master and Fourth Master had been talking, there had been no opportunity for her to speak. Only now she nonchalantly said, "I've already divorced him; if I were to return to his home as his widow, people would laugh their heads off." She continued working on her slippers as if nothing had happened, but cold sweat broke out on her hands. The needle became hard to handle, and she could not remove it from her work.

Third Master said, "Sixth Sister, it's not what you think. We all know that he let you down. Now he's dead. Can you still be letting it weigh on you? Naturally, the two concubines he left behind won't be able to bear living out the rest of their lives as widows. If you return all dignified and impressive, decked out in mourning, who would dare laugh at you? Though you don't have any children, he has many nephews. You can choose one of them to adopt.[2] His estate may not be much, but his family is a prosperous one. Even if they sent you to look after the clan hall, you and the child would never starve."

Bai Liusu responded with a cold smile, "You are very thoughtful on my account; unfortunately it's a bit too late. I've been divorced for seven years. According to the way you talk, the legal procedure we went through was a joke! We can't fool with the law!"

---

2. In traditional society, boys were more important than girls because they carried the family name and continued the family line. Moreover, even after marriage boys lived in their parents' home, taking care of the family business and supporting their aging parents. That's why Liusu is encouraged to adopt a boy from among her ex-husband's nephews as security for old age.

Third Master answered, "Don't use the law to scare me. Laws are changed every day while the natural feelings and human relationships that I'm talking about are unchangeable. Alive, you are a member of their family; dead, you are their ghost. No matter how towering a tree is, the leaves always return to the roots when they fall."

Liusu stood up and asked, "Why didn't you say so seven years ago?"

Third Master replied, "I was afraid you might be suspicious that we didn't want you."

"Ah, you are not afraid that I'm suspicious now? You spent all of my money. Don't you worry that I'm suspicious?"

Leaning closer to her face, Third Master exclaimed, "I spent your money! How much money did I spend? You live in our house, eat our food, and drink our water. It was okay to support one more person before. It meant nothing to add one more pair of chopsticks. But now, you should go out and ask what the price of rice is. I didn't mention money, so how could you?"

Fourth Madam stood behind Third Master, laughed and added, "Normally, one's own flesh and blood should never mention money; if one does, then it leads to more trouble. I told your Fourth Brother long ago, 'Fourth Eldest, you should persuade Third Master that they shouldn't use Sixth Sister's money to buy gold and stocks; otherwise bad luck will surely strike!' Don't you see: as soon as she married, her husband became a spendthrift; and then, since she has returned home, the family has been bled dry. That one's a born jinx!"

Third Master continued, "Fourth Madam is right. If we had not let her join in our business at the beginning, we wouldn't have had to suffer such a crushing defeat."

Liusu was so angry that her whole body trembled uncontrollably. She put the half-embroidered slippers against her quivering chin.

Third Master spoke again, "I recall the time you came back crying and raised hell to get a divorce. I have to blame my strong sense of justice: When I saw you had been beaten so seriously, I had no heart to refuse you. So I struck my chest and said, 'All right! Although I am poor, there will always be a bowl of rice in my house for my sister!' I thought every young couple needed to let off a little steam, and I guessed that you would change your minds. If I had known that you were serious about making a clean break, do you think I would have helped you get divorced? Splitting up a marriage breaks a family line. I have sons, and I still hope they will support me in my old age."

As angry as she was, Liusu nevertheless laughed loudly and said, "Yes, yes, it's my fault. You became poor because I sucked you dry; your business failed because I tied you down; if one of your sons should die, this would also be a result of my damaging your unrewarded virtues!"

Fourth Madam immediately grabbed her son's collar and pushed him into Liusu, bumping his head. She exclaimed, "You put a curse on these boys without any reason. After what you've said, if my son dies, I will hold you responsible!"

Dodging out of the way, Liusu ran to Fourth Master. She held him and cried, "Fourth Brother, look—Give us your honest opinion!"

Fourth Master said, "Don't get excited. If you have something to say, say it calmly. Let's plan for the long term. Actually what Third Brother says is all for your own good . . ."

In a rage, Liusu let go of him and walked into the inner bedroom.

There was no light in that room. She peered through the gauze bed-curtains and could dimly make out her mother lying in the big redwood bed, waving a white round fan. Liusu stepped to the front of the bed and then, suddenly feeling weak in the knees, knelt down. She bent over the edge of the bed and cried, "Ma!"

Old Mrs. Bai's ears were not bad. She had heard the entire argument in the outer room. She coughed and held out her hand for the spittoon beside the pillow. She spat into it and said, "Your Fourth Sister-in-law is too talkative; you shouldn't pay any attention to her. As you know, everybody has their own problems. Your Fourth Sister-in-law was born with a strong personality. She used to run the house, but your Fourth Brother disappointed her, constantly whoring and gambling. What he did not only damaged his own health—what's worse is that he also embezzled the family's funds, which shamed your Fourth Sister-in-law terribly. Therefore, she had to let your Third Sister-in-law manage the household. That's hard for her to take, so she always feels unhappy. In addition, your Third Sister-in-law is not very healthy. To sustain this family is not easy for her. In any case, you should try to show them a little consideration."

Liusu saw that her mother had taken the easy way out, so she said nothing.

Old Mrs. Bai turned over to face the wall and tried to sleep. Then she added, "During the past two years, we scraped things together and sold some land which gave us just enough to live on for two years. Now, things are different. I am getting old, and will die anytime. I can't take care of you any longer. Besides, there's not a banquet in the world that doesn't have an ending. Staying with me is not a permanent solution. You'd better go back, adopt a child, suffer for ten more years. Then you'll be able to lift your head again some day."

Just then, the door-curtain moved. Old Mrs. Bai asked, "Who is it?"

Fourth Madam stuck in her head, "Mother, Mrs. Xu is still downstairs, waiting to discuss Seventh Sister's marriage matter with you."

Old Mrs. Bai answered, "I'm coming. You turn on the light." The room brightened. Fourth Madam propped the old lady up and waited on her as she put on her clothes. Then she helped her get out of bed. Old Mrs. Bai asked, "Has Mrs. Xu found anyone suitable?"

Fourth Madam replied, "According to her, the one she found seems not too bad, but he is a few years older."

Old Mrs. Bai coughed and said, "Baoluo will be twenty-four this year, which really is a thorn in my heart. All my worrying about her has been for nothing. People all said that since she is not really my child, I have delayed her marriage on purpose." Old Mrs. Bai walked out of the room, supported by Fourth Madam. Old Mrs. Bai said to her, "Go get my new tea leaves to make a bowl of tea for Mrs. Xu. The stuff in the green tin box is Longjing tea given to me by Eldest Aunt last year; the other in the long box is Biluochun. Don't mix them up."

Fourth Madam nodded in agreement and at the same time shouted, "Hey! Somebody turn on the light!" There was a sound of footsteps, and then some rough looking young servants came in to help the maid support the old lady down the stairs.

Fourth Madam remained in the outer room by herself, going through all the drawers in search of the old lady's private stock of tea leaves. All of a sudden, she began to laugh, "Hey! Seventh Sister, where have you been hiding? You scared me! I was just wondering where you had disappeared to!"

Baoluo answered in a soft voice, "I was on the balcony catching the breeze."

Fourth Madam tittered, "Bashful are you? Let me tell you, Seventh Sister. In the future, when you have a husband, you should be more careful. Don't give in to your temper. Do you think divorce is a simple matter? Some people just split up whenever they feel like it; it's so commonplace! Indeed, is it really that easy? Your Fourth Brother wasn't successful, but did I divorce him? I still have my own home. I'm not the one who has no place to go. But even during those bad times, I had to take all that into consideration. I am conscientious and I have enough self-control not to impose on others. I still possess a certain sense of shame!"

Kneeling desolately in front of her mother's bed, Bai Liusu listened to Fourth Madam's words. She clasped the embroidered slippers against her chest. A needle in the slippers pricked her fingers, but she was oblivious to the pain. She murmured, "This house is impossible to live in . . . impossible." Her voice was discouraged and light at the same time, as stringy as a broken cobweb. It was as if she were in a dream, and her head and face were veiled with dust-covered strands of webbing. In a fog, she threw herself forward to embrace her mother's knees like cushions and began to sob, "Ma, you must stand up for me!"

In her imagination, her mother began to smile silently, but without any emotion. She held her mother's legs and shook them vigorously. She cried, "Ma! Ma!" It seemed like many years before. She was only about ten years old. After coming out of the theater in a downpour, she had been jostled and separated from her family. She stood alone on the sidewalk, staring at people who were staring at her through rain-splattered car windows—layer upon layer of transparent glass—countless strangers they were. Everyone was isolated in small individual worlds. Even if she smashed her head against the barrier she could never break into their lives. It was as if she were paralyzed. Suddenly, she heard footsteps behind her and guessed that it was her mother coming. She tried hard to pull herself together, not saying a word. However, the mother she prayed to and her real mother were two completely different individuals.

Someone walked to the edge of the bed and sat down. But when she spoke, it was in Mrs. Xu's voice.

Mrs. Xu tried to calm her down. "Sixth Miss, don't be sad. Get up; get up; it's so hot . . ."

Liusu propped herself on the bed and stood up with difficulty, saying, "Auntie, I . . . I can't bear it here any longer. I've known for some time that they disliked me, but they'd never quite come out and said it. But today they've banged the battle gongs and war drums and declared war. I have no face to go on living here."

Mrs. Xu pulled her down to sit on the edge of the bed with her, and whispered, "You are too honest—no wonder the others have taken advantage of you. Your brothers transferred your money from here to there, and finally spent it all! So it's quite fitting if they have to support you for the rest of your life."

Liusu rarely heard fair words like these. Without asking if Mrs. Xu really meant what she said, she felt a warmth emanating from her heart, and tears fell like rain. She said, "How could I have been so stupid! It's just this little bit of money that's forcing me to stay even if I want to leave!"

Mrs. Xu said, "Young people like you have their lives in front of them."

Liusu replied, "If I had a life in front of me, I would have left earlier! I don't have much education, and I'm not strong enough to do anything physical. What kind of job can I get?"

"Finding a job is just a joke," Mrs. Xu said. "Finding a man is something true."

"I'm afraid it won't work," Liusu answered. "My life was finished a long time ago."

Mrs. Xu disagreed. "Only rich people who don't have to worry about food and clothes have the right to say such things. A penniless person can't end his life even if he wants to! Even if you shave your head and become a nun, or you beg for alms, you'll still be part of this earthly world—you can't escape from men!"

Liusu lowered her head and kept quiet. Mrs. Xu continued, "If you had asked me to take on this matter two years earlier, it would have been much easier."

With a slight smile, Liusu said, "That's for sure! I'm already twenty-eight."

Mrs. Xu soothed her, "A talented person like you needn't worry about being twenty-eight. I'll keep my eyes open for you. While we're on the subject, I have to find fault with one thing. You've been divorced for almost eight years. If you had made your decision to flee earlier, you would have saved yourself a lot of embarrassment!"

Liusu explained, "Auntie, you must know, how can a family like ours allow its members to go out and make friends? How could I depend on them to find me a match? They wouldn't approve, but even if they did, I still have two younger sisters who aren't yet married. Then there are the daughters of my Third and Fourth Brothers who are also growing up. There's not even enough time to arrange their marriages. How can they take care of mine?"

Mrs. Xu smiled and said, "Speaking of your younger sisters, I'm still waiting for their answers."

Liusu asked, "Is there any hope for Seventh Sister's marriage?"

Mrs. Xu said, "It is beginning to take shape. Just now, I left mother and daughter alone on purpose to discuss it. I told them I would come up to see you for a while. Now I must leave. Would you please accompany me downstairs?"

Liusu had no choice but to help her down. The stairs were old, and Mrs. Xu was quite plump, so each step was accompanied by a loud creak. When they came to the main room, Liusu wanted to turn on the light but Mrs. Xu said, "Please don't, I can see. They are in the east room. Come with me and we'll all have a nice chat and the matter will pass. Otherwise, tomorrow when you sit down to eat and can't avoid seeing each other, it will be awkward and unpleasant."

Liusu couldn't bear to hear the word "eat"; pain stabbed her heart. Choked with misery but forcing a smile, she said, "Thank you very much, Auntie. But I don't feel well now, and I'm really not up to seeing the others. I'm afraid I'm so despondent that I may say something to cause a catastrophe, and let you down after all your concern for me."

Seeing Liusu's determination not to go, Mrs. Xu gave up. She pushed open the door herself and entered.

The door closed again, and the main hall remained in darkness. Through the lattice glass on the top of the door, two squares of yellow light shone down on the green tile floor. Dimly, one could see a row of bookcases piled along the wall. The cases, made of red sandalwood, were carved with a few characters painted green. In the center of the wall, above the stool and in a glass cover, sat an enamel chiming clock. Its mechanism had worn out years ago. Hanging on either side were two red paper scrolls embossed with glittering "Longevity" characters. They contained a set of couplets written in bold, black strokes. In the faint light, each word seemed to float in space, far from the paper's surface. Liusu felt as unreal as one of those characters, drifting and unconnected. The Bai house was a little like a fairy's cave. When one idled away a day here, a thousand years passed on Earth. But a thousand years here was also the same as one day because every day was the same: dull and boring. Liusu crossed her arms and held her neck. Seven years had passed in the twinkling of an eye. Was she still young? It didn't matter; in another two years she'd be old. Here, youth was not cherished. There was plenty of youth here—babies were being born one after another, new shining eyes, new tender rosy mouths, new wisdom. Then, as the years passed, the eyes got weaker, the body got weaker, and then another generation was born. Each generation was absorbed into the glorious gold-sprinkled vermilion background, and little by little the sparkling gold became the frightened eyes of men gone by.

Liusu suddenly cried out. She covered her own eyes, staggered up the stairs, up the stairs . . . to the second floor. When she entered her own room, she turned on the light and leaned toward the dressing mirror, examining herself carefully. It was all right; she still was not too old. Liusu's tiny figure was the kind that didn't show age. She would always have a splendid waistline and child-like budding breasts. Her face, normally as white as porcelain, had changed to a jade color—a half transparent, light green jade. Her chin had been round, but in recent years it had gradually become pointed, which made her small face even more lovely. Her face was fairly narrow, but the distance between her eyebrows was quite wide. In addition, she had a pair of delicate, charming, liquid eyes. On the balcony, Fourth Master began to play the *huqin* again. Hearing the melodious sound, Liusu could not help turning her head. She cast a fleeting glance and made a gesture. Because of her performance in the mirror, the *huqin* did not sound like a *huqin* anymore, but rather the profound temple dance music played with pan pipes, flute and zither. She took a few steps to the left, and then a few to the right. Each step seemed to be in time with the beat of some lost, ancient music. All of a sudden, she smiled—an ominous malicious smile—and the music stopped. Outside, the *huqin* continued, but the distant moral tales the *huqin* was playing no longer had anything to do with her.

Fourth Master stayed away from everybody and played the *huqin* on the balcony alone because he knew he would have no opportunity to speak at the family meeting downstairs. After Mrs. Xu left, the Bai family continued deliberating and analyzing her suggestions. Mrs. Xu planned to match Baoluo to a man named Fan, who had quite close ties with Mr. Xu in the mining business. Mrs. Xu was familiar with his family background, and she thought he was absolutely dependable. Fan Liuyuan's father was a famous overseas Chinese who had a lot of property scattered in Ceylon, Malaysia and other places. Fan Liuyuan was thirty-two this year and his parents had both passed away. When the Bai family questioned Mrs. Xu as to why such a perfect marriage partner was still unattached, Mrs. Xu told them that when Fan Liuyuan came back from England, many women shamelessly had tried to force their daughters upon him. They made a huge fuss, plotting and scrapping, each trying to display her own talents.

This kind of flattery had spoiled him. Since then, he had regarded women as so much mud under his feet. Owing to his rather unusual childhood environment, his temperament was a bit odd from the start. His parents' marriage had not been legal. His father, already married, had gone abroad on an inspection tour. While he was in London, he met an overseas Chinese woman, a real social butterfly, and they married secretly. His original wife eventually caught wind of this and, fearing her revenge, the second wife had never dared return to China. The result of all this was that Fan Liuyuan had been brought up in England. After his father's death, Fan Liuyuan had his fingers burned many times trying to define his legal status in spite of the fact that the first wife only had two daughters. He had wandered destitute in England and suffered a good deal. Finally, he won his right of inheritance. Even now, Fan's family was still hostile to him. Therefore, he stayed in Shanghai most of the time, avoiding the family home in Guangzhou unless it was absolutely necessary. Because he had suffered such emotional hardship when he was young, he grew up to be a playboy. He patronized brothels and gambling dens and everything else. The pleasures of marital bliss didn't interest him.

"A person like him must be very fussy," Fourth Madam said. "Seventh Sister is not the child of the first wife. I am afraid that he won't even give her a second glance. What a pity if we let such a good match pass by."

Third Master said, "He himself is illegitimate."

"But look, what a smart fellow he is!" Fourth Madam answered. "How can you hope to catch him with naive Seventh Miss? On the contrary, my eldest girl is quite clever. Don't look down on her. Although she is small, she has a big heart. She's really very intelligent!"

"But their ages are too far apart," Third Madam said.

Fourth Madam disagreed, "Hey! You don't know. That kind of man likes young girls. If my eldest one isn't right, I still have my second daughter."

Third Madam laughed and said, "Your second one is twenty years younger than Mr. Fan."

Fourth Madam tugged her sister-in-law's arm. With a serious look on her face she said, "Third Sister-in-Law, don't be so foolish! You protect Seventh Miss, but what is she to the Bai family? She came from the belly of another woman. What's she to us? If she marries him, nobody can expect to get any benefit from it! I'm just thinking about our welfare."

But old Mrs. Bai was anxious to avoid the relatives saying she mistreated Seventh Miss. So she decided to go along with the original plan: let Mrs. Xu select a date to arrange a meeting and introduce Baoluo to Fan Liuyuan.

In the second prong of her strategy, Mrs. Xu also found Liusu a man named Jiang, who worked in the customs house. He recently had become widowed and was left with five children, so he was eager to remarry. Mrs. Xu thought it better to finish with Baoluo first, then try this match for Liusu, because Fan Liuyuan would be leaving soon for Singapore.

As for Liusu getting married again, the Bai family basically regarded it as a joke. They wanted her out of the house but couldn't be bothered to deal with her situation. They preferred to let Mrs. Xu grapple with it. In contrast, in regards to Baoluo's marriage matter, everyone was cackling and flying about. Both of them were daughters, but for one they were burning up the place, while for the other they were as cold as could be! It was hard for Liusu to bear.

Old Mrs. Bai got everybody in the family to dig out all their jewelry. Whatever she could put on Baoluo, she did. Old Mrs. Bai also forced Third Madam to take out the piece of silk that her daughter had received from her godmother on her birthday, and had it made into a *qipao* for Baoluo. The old lady's private collection from many years ago included many furs. Since Baoluo could not wear fur in the summer, old Mrs. Bai pawned a mink coat and used the money to reset some of the jewelry into a more fashionable style. The value of these things, like the pearl earrings, jade bracelet and emerald ring, need not be mentioned. The idea was that they had to dress up Baoluo as opulently as possible.

When the appointed day came, the old lady, Third Master, Third Madam, Fourth Master and Fourth Madam all felt they had to go along. Baoluo had heard indirectly about Fourth Madam's plot and was furious. She was determined not to go out with Fourth Madam's two daughters but was too embarrassed to say so. Instead, she insisted that Liusu accompany her. That meant seven people had to cram into the taxi, leaving no room for anyone else, which eliminated Fourth Madam's forlorn daughters Jinzhi and Jinchan from the party.

They left at five o'clock in the afternoon, and didn't come home until eleven. With all the excitement, how could Jinzhi and Jinchan relax and go to sleep? They watched as everybody came back, but not one of them said a word. With a long face, Baoluo walked into the old lady's room. Like a gust of wind, she quickly took off all the jewelry, gave it back to old Mrs. Bai and silently returned to her bedroom. Jinzhi and Jinchan dragged Fourth Madam to the balcony and bombarded her with questions about the party.

Angrily, Fourth Madam said, "I've never seen girls like you! It wasn't you who had a marriage interview. What are you both so hot about?"

Third Madam followed them out onto the balcony, and said to them in a soft voice, "Don't let your talk arouse other people's suspicions."

At that, Fourth Madam turned her face toward Liusu's room and yelled, "I was just pointing to the pot and calling the kettle black. So I cursed her. So what? It's not that she hasn't seen a man for centuries, but why did she become befuddled as soon as she saw a strange man? Has she gone crazy?"

Jinzhi and Jinchan were confused by their mother's anger.

Third Madam tried her best to calm down Fourth Madam, then she told the two girls, "At the beginning we went to see a movie."

Jinzhi cried in surprise, "A movie?"

Third Madam continued, "Isn't that strange? The purpose of this interview was to let them see each other, but sitting in that kind of darkness, you can't see a thing. Mrs. Xu told me later that it had all been Mr. Fan's idea; he was playing a dirty trick. He wanted her to wait for two or three hours, until the oil had come out of her face and the makeup had faded. Then he'd be able to see what she was really like. But this is only what Mrs. Xu speculated. In my opinion, that Mr. Fan wasn't sincere from the beginning. He took us to the movies because he was too lazy to entertain us. After the theater, didn't he try to sneak away?"

Fourth Madam couldn't help interrupting, "Who says? Today's interview started off well. If our own people hadn't been causing such a ruckus in there, then we probably would have had a seventy or eighty percent chance!"

Jinzhi and Jinchan asked simultaneously, "What happened then, Third Auntie?"

Third Madam replied, "Then, Mrs. Xu grabbed him and suggested we all go for a meal. He said he would treat us."

Fourth Madam clapped her hands and said, "Having a meal is having a meal, but he knew perfectly well that our Seventh Miss couldn't dance. So why did he take us to the dance hall? The fact is, Third Brother is to blame. He's always out running around. When he heard Fan telling the driver to head to the dance hall, why didn't he stop him?"

Third Madam quickly answered, "There are so many big hotels in Shanghai, how could he know which ones have dance halls and which ones don't. He is not like Fourth Master, who has plenty of time on his hands. He doesn't have time to check out things like that!"

Jinzhi and Jinchan would have liked to know what happened afterwards, but Fourth Madam kept butting in, and Third Madam lost interest in giving them any more details. She just said, "Then we went for a supper. After the supper, we came home."

Jinchan asked again, "What kind of person is that Fan Liuyuan?"

Third Madam answered, "How would I know? Altogether, I didn't hear him say more than three sentences." After thinking for a while, she added, "I suppose he dances fairly well!"

"What?" Jinzhi asked in surprise, "Who did he dance with?"

Fourth Madam hurried to answer, "Who else? It could only be your Sixth Aunt! We're a literary family, and none of us was allowed to learn dancing. It's only after getting married that she learned that trick from her good-for-nothing husband. Shameless! If someone asks you, you just have to tell him that you can't, and that's that! Not knowing how to dance is nothing to be ashamed of. Like your Third Auntie and like me, we're all from wealthy families. Having already lived half of our lives, what haven't we seen? We just can't dance!"

Third Madam sighed and said, "Once, perhaps, out of politeness. But she had to dance twice, and even a third time!"

Hearing this, Jinzhi and Jinchan were aghast and tongue-tied.

Turning her face toward Liusu's room again, Fourth Madam cursed, "Heartless idiot! If you think that by destroying your sister's affair, you would have a chance, then I'm telling you now that you'd better forget it! There have been countless young girls that he wouldn't even look at. Do you think he'd want a withered flower like you?"

Liusu and Baoluo were sharing a bedroom. By this time Baoluo had already gone to sleep. Liusu was squatting on the floor groping in the dark trying to light a mosquito coil. She heard the talk on the balcony clearly, but this time she was very calm. She lit a match, and watched it burn. The little pennant-like flame flickered in its own air currents. It moved closer and closer to her fingers. She gave a puff and blew out the flame. Now only the glowing red stick was left. Gradually, the matchstick shriveled down into a ghostly curled ashen-colored figure. She threw the scorched match into the ashtray. What had happened today, she had not done on purpose. Nevertheless, she'd taught them a lesson. They thought her life had finished? It was still early yet! She smiled. In her heart, Baoluo had to be cursing her, probably even much more unpleasantly than Fourth Madam had. But she knew that although Baoluo hated her, Baoluo would look at her now with new eyes, regarding her with deep respect. It does not matter how good a woman is, if she cannot obtain a man's love, she cannot win respect from the members of her own sex. Women are really low that way.

Was Liuyuan really fond of her? Not likely. She did not believe a word he had said. She could tell that he was the kind of man who was used to telling lies to women. She could not be careless—she had no relatives to rely upon. She only had herself. Her thin, moonlight-white *qipao* hung on the bed frame. Bending over, she sat on the floor, held onto the hem of the *qipao* and quietly snuggled it to her cheeks. The green smoke of the mosquito coil drifted up one curl after another, seeping its way into her brain. In her eyes, tears were glistening.

A few days later, Mrs. Xu came to the Bai house again. Fourth Madam already had made a prediction: "Since our Sixth Miss has messed up everything, it's obvious that it's all over for Seventh Miss as well. How could Mrs. Xu not be angry? If Mrs. Xu blamed Sixth Miss, would she still be willing to find a match for her? This would be the same as going for wool and coming back fleeced."

As expected, Mrs. Xu was not as eager to help as before. She beat around the bush, explaining why she had not come in the past two days. Her husband was leaving for Hong Kong on business. If everything went smoothly, they would consider renting a house and living there for six months or a year. Therefore, she had been busy packing for the last two days preparing to go with him. As for Baoluo's matter, because Mr. Fan had already left Shanghai, she had to put it aside for the time being. And regarding Liusu's possible match with Mr. Jiang, Mrs. Xu had found out that he already had someone else. To separate them would be difficult. It would be best to forget about it. When Third and Fourth Madam heard what Mrs. Xu had said, they gave each other knowing looks and suppressed their smiles.

Mrs. Xu frowned and continued, "My husband has quite a few friends in Hong Kong, but too bad they're all so far away . . . However, if Sixth Miss can make the trip, she may have many opportunities. In the past two years, a wealth of talented people from Shanghai have flocked to Hong Kong. Shanghainese are naturally attracted to Shanghainese, so hometown girls are very welcome there. If Sixth Miss went, would she have to worry about not being able to find someone suitable? In fact, she could pick a bunch and then choose one!"

Everybody felt that Mrs. Xu had a way with words. Just two days earlier she had been matchmaking vigorously, but now that all her plans had vanished like smoke she couldn't back down with good grace, so she nattered on, making these perfunctory excuses.

Old Mrs. Bai sighed and said, "Making a trip to Hong Kong is easy to talk about, but actually . . . "

Mrs. Xu abruptly cut her off. "If Sixth Miss is willing to go, it'll be on me. I agreed to help her and help her I must."

Everyone looked at each other in surprise—even Liusu was shocked. Originally, she'd thought that Mrs. Xu had volunteered to find her a match out of sympathy for her situation and a sense of justice. That Mrs. Xu would do some legwork in trying to find a beau, and even arrange a banquet with Mr. Jiang—well, their friendship was strong enough for that. But to pay for the travel expenses and take her along to Hong Kong would cost Mrs. Xu a fortune! Why would Mrs. Xu want to spend this money on her without a reason? Although there are many good people in the world, there are not many fools willing to part with money for the sake of friendship. Mrs. Xu obviously had something in the back of her mind. Could it be Fan Liuyuan's trick? Mrs. Xu had once mentioned that her husband kept quite close contact with Fan Liuyuan on business. Both the husband and wife were probably eager to ingratiate themselves with Fan Liuyuan. It also was possible that they wanted to fawn on him by sacrificing an unimportant and helpless relative.

While Liusu was still lost in her thoughts, old Mrs. Bai started to talk, "How could we do that? We could never let you . . ."

Roaring with laughter, Mrs. Xu said, "Never mind. This is but a small treat—I can afford it! Besides, I'm actually hoping Sixth Miss can help me. I'm taking along two children. I have high blood pressure, and I can't afford to get very tired. If she is on the journey, then everything will be taken care of. I'm not taking her as an outsider; I may be giving her a lot of trouble!"

Old Mrs. Bai quickly said a few polite words for Liusu.

Mrs. Xu then turned to Liusu, and asked directly, "Well, Sixth Miss, how about coming along with us? Even if it's just sightseeing, it's still worth it."

Liusu lowered her head and answered with a smile, "You treat me too well." At the same time, she made a quick calculation of the situation. The Mr. Jiang matter was hopeless. Later on, if anyone made another match for her, he probably would be more or less the same type as Mr. Jiang, or perhaps even worse. Liusu's father had been a famous gambler who lost the family fortune. He had led them along the road to poverty. Liusu's hands had never touched dominoes or dice but she also liked gambling. Now she decided to wager her future. If she lost, her reputation would be ruined, and she wouldn't even be able to be the stepmother of the five children. If she won, she might obtain what everybody coveted most: Fan Liuyuan. This would give her some measure of revenge.

She accepted Mrs. Xu's invitation. Mrs. Xu wanted to leave within the week, so Liusu got busy packing. Even though she did not have many valuable possessions, and there really wasn't anything to pack, this occupied her for several days. She sold some odds and ends to buy a few dresses. Despite all the preparations, Mrs. Xu still found time to give her some advice. Seeing that Mrs. Xu still favored Liusu so, the Bai family gradually developed a renewed interest in her. They still were suspicious of her, but also more cautious. They whispered about her behind her back, but to her face, they were not quite as accusatory as before. Once in a while, they would even call her "Sixth Aunt," or "Sixth Miss" because they were afraid that she really would marry a rich Hong Kong man and return home in glory one day. They had to protect some face against that eventuality; offending her was not worth the risk.

Together with the children, Mr. and Mrs. Xu picked her up and drove her to the harbor. They had a first class cabin on a Dutch boat. The boat was small and rocked violently. As soon as Mr. and Mrs. Xu boarded, both of them just lay down and were terribly seasick. The two children cried all the way. Liusu waited on them for the entire trip. It was not until the boat docked that she finally had the opportunity to go on deck to see the ocean. It was a baking-hot afternoon. From what she could see, the most conspicuous things surrounding the dock area were those huge advertising billboards. Red ones, orange ones and pink ones were reflected in the dazzling slick green sea. These brilliant colors contrasted sharply with each other, like so many swords bobbing and fighting violently in the water. In this city of contrasts, even just stumbling probably would be much more painful than it was in other places, Liusu thought. She couldn't help being nervous. Suddenly she felt someone run over and hug her legs, almost knocking her over. She was startled, but when she bent down to look, it was only Mrs. Xu's child. She pulled herself together and went back to help Mrs. Xu. It was impossible to assemble the ten pieces of luggage and the two children in the same place. When the luggage was together, in a flash they would be short one child. Liusu got so tired of running here and there that she did not bother going back again to look at the view.

After disembarking, they took two cabs to the Repulse Bay Hotel. When the cars left the downtown area they climbed between yellow and red hillsides, gaps in the hills revealing dense green trees on the turquoise sea. As they approached Repulse Bay, the hillsides and trees seemed to grow brighter and brighter. Many tourists were coming back from the mountains, each car jammed with flowers. Fragments of laughter could be heard on the breeze.

When the car stopped in front of the hotel gate, they still could not see where the hotel was. They got out and walked up broad stone stairs. It was not until they reached a terrace filled with a beautiful display of plants and flowers that they saw two yellow buildings above them. Mr. Xu had reserved rooms long before. The waiters led them along a gravel path, through a dim dining room and musky hall, then up to the second floor. When they turned, they saw a door leading to a small balcony with a vine-covered trellis; the sun was shining on half the wall. There were two people talking on the balcony, but they could only see the back of a girl with long, jet-black hair hanging straight down to her ankles, on which she wore gold-plaited bracelets. Her legs were bare, but it was hard to see if she was wearing any sandals. A little above her ankles the bottom of a pair of narrow Indian-style trousers could be seen.

Concealed behind the girl was a man, who called out all of a sudden, "Hey! Mrs. Xu!" He walked over, saying hello to Mr. and Mrs. Xu. He bowed slightly to Liusu with a gentle smile on his face.

Then Liusu saw that it was Fan Liuyuan. Earlier, she'd had a feeling she might meet him, but now that he was there in person she could not stop her heart from pounding. The girl on the balcony vanished. Liuyuan accompanied them upstairs. On the way, everyone acted as if they had just run into an old friend in a distant land, continually expressing their surprise and delight. Although Fan Liuyuan could not be considered handsome, he had a certain rugged masculinity.

While Mr. and Mrs. Xu were directing waiters to move their luggage, Liuyuan and Liusu walked on ahead. Smiling, Liusu asked Liuyuan, "Mr. Fan, didn't you go to Singapore?"

Liuyuan replied in a soft voice, "I have been here, waiting for you."

Liusu had not expected him to be so frank and dared not pursue the matter further, fearing that if he said it was actually he and not Mrs. Xu who had invited her to Hong Kong, she would be unable to get out of the predicament in which she found herself. She decided to dismiss his remark as a joke and just smiled at him.

When Liuyuan asked, Liusu told him that her room number was 130. He stopped in front of a room, saying, "Here we are."

The bellboy brought the key and opened the door for them. Liusu entered and couldn't help walking directly to the window. The whole room was just like a dark yellow picture frame, and the window was the picture. The surging waves outside seemed to splash on the curtains, coloring their edges blue.

Liuyuan told the bellboy, "Put the bags in front of the closet." His voice, so close to her ear, startled her. She turned and found that the porter was already gone but had left the door open. Liuyuan leaned against the windowsill with one arm on the frame, blocking her vision. He gazed at her with a smile on his lips. Liusu lowered her head.

Liuyuan laughed, "You know what? The way you drop your head is one of your strong points."

Liusu raised her head, laughed and said, "What? I don't understand."

Liuyuan said, "Some people are good at talking or laughing, and some at housekeeping, but you are good at bending your head."

Liusu replied, "I know I can't do anything; I am just terribly useless."

Liuyuan laughed, "A useless woman is the cleverest woman."

Liusu walked away laughing, "Let's not continue this. How about going next door and looking around."

"Next door?" Liuyuan asked. "My room or Mrs. Xu's?"

Liusu was shocked again. She asked, "Do you live next door?"

Liuyuan had already opened the door for her and said, "My room is very messy, I can't let you see it."

He knocked on the door of No. 131. Mrs. Xu opened the door to let them in. "Have a cup of tea with us; we have a living room." Then she rang a bell to order some pastries as well.

Mr. Xu, coming out of the bedroom, said, "I just phoned Lao Zhu. He insisted on giving a banquet in honor of our visit. He invited everybody to the Hong Kong Hotel. Today!" Turning toward Liuyuan, he continued, "Including you!"

Mrs. Xu said, "You're certainly in a good mood. Having been seasick for a few days, don't you want to get to bed early? Let's just forget about tonight."

Liuyuan laughed, "The Hong Kong Hotel's ballroom is so passé. The building, the lights, the decoration and the band are all old English style. It was fashionable forty or fifty years ago, but it's not interesting anymore. There's not too much to see there, except for those queer looking foreigners who model themselves after Northerners and wear trousers gathered tight at the ankles even in this hot weather."

"Why?" Liusu asked.

"To get into the 'Chinese mood'!" he replied.

Mr. Xu laughed, "Since we are here, we've got to look at everything! I hope you'll put up with the torture and accompany us!"

Liuyuan smiled, "I can't say for sure yet. Don't wait for me."

Liusu saw that he did not want to go. Mr. Xu, on the other hand—not the kind of person who frequented dance halls—seldom seemed so happy. It appeared that he really was serious about introducing his friends to her. She was more puzzled than ever.

All those who went to the Hong Kong Hotel that night for the welcoming party were either older couples or bachelors in their early twenties. While Liusu was dancing, Fan Liuyuan suddenly appeared and cut in on another man. Under the lichee-colored lights, she couldn't see his dark face clearly, and only felt that he was abnormally quiet. Liusu smiled, asking, "Why aren't you talking?"

Liuyuan answered with a smile of his own, "I've already said everything that I can say in front of others."

Liusu tittered, "What do you have to say behind others' backs, sneaking around like this?"

Liuyuan answered, "Just some foolish thoughts. Not only can't I say them in front of others, but I don't even want to hear them myself. They embarrass even me. Words like 'I love you', 'I'll love you forever'."

Liusu turned her face aside and said softly, "That's nonsense!"

Liuyuan said, "First you blame me for not talking and now you're criticizing me for talking too much!"

Liusu laughed, "Let me ask you, why didn't you want us to come to the dance hall?"

Liuyuan explained, "Most men like to corrupt good women, and to reform bad women. I'm not like them, looking to make work for myself. I think good women should remain good."

Liusu cast a sidelong glance at him and said, "You think you are different from other men? But I think you're just as selfish as the rest of them."

Liuyuan laughed, "What selfishness?"

In her heart, Liusu thought, "Your lofty ideal of a woman is someone who is incorruptible as well as tantalizing. Incorruptible to others, and tantalizing to yourself! If I were a thoroughly good woman, you probably never would have noticed me!" She tilted her head towards him and asked, "You want me to be a good woman in front of others, but to be a bad woman with you."

Liuyuan thought for a while and replied, "I don't get you."

Liusu explained again, "You want me to be bad to others, but be good to you."

Liuyuan laughed and said, "What? Now you've reversed them again? You're making me more and more confused!" He was silent for a while before adding, "You're wrong."

"Oh," Liusu laughed, "now you understand."

Liuyuan said, "I don't care whether you're good or bad, I don't want you to change. It's hard to meet a genuine Chinese woman like you."

Uttering a sigh, Liusu answered, "I'm old-fashioned."

Liuyuan said, "A genuine Chinese woman is the most beautiful, and will never be old-fashioned."

Liusu smiled, "A modern person like you . . ."

Liuyuan interrupted, "Modern—you mean westernized, I guess. I certainly don't count as a typical Chinese. It's only in the past few years that I've become more Chinese. But you know, a foreigner who becomes Chinese is even more reactionary than an old Chinese scholar."

Liusu laughed, saying, "You're reactionary; I am too. And as you said, the dance hall at the Hong Kong Hotel is the most old-fashioned . . ."

They both burst into laughter just as the music stopped. Liuyuan held her arm as they returned to their seats. He smiled to all the people at the table, "Miss Bai has a headache, so I think I'll take her home now."

Liusu couldn't have predicted that he'd do this, and she didn't know how to respond. Then again she didn't want to offend him. Their relationship was not close enough yet to have an argument. All she could do was let him drape her coat over her shoulders and make her apologies to everyone as they left the hall together.

Walking toward them was a group of foreign gentlemen. Like stars surrounding the moon, they were crowded around a woman Liusu had noticed earlier. She had long jet-black hair, now braided into two plaits coiled high on the top of her head. It was that Indian woman. Though she wore a Western-style outfit, she still had the pronounced color of the East. Under her fine, black cloak, she was wearing a long, tight, goldfish-colored dress that covered even her arms and hands except for her glittering fingernails. The collar of her dress was v-shaped, and opened right down to her waist. This was the most fashionable style in Paris now; it had been dubbed "Ligne du Ciel." Her face was rich and tawny, like a gold-plated Goddess of Mercy, but her deep, black eyes seemed to have the devil in them. She had a straight, classical nose, but it was a bit too sharp and thin. Her thick, pink, pouty lips seemed a little swollen. Liuyuan stopped and bowed slightly to her. As Liusu stood there looking at her, the woman gazed back in a dignified fashion. That pair of proud-looking eyes seemed a thousand miles away, staring at people from a distance.

Liuyuan introduced them, "This is Miss Bai. This is Princess Saheiyini."

Despite herself, Liusu felt a sense of respect.

Princess Saheiyini stretched out one arm, touching Liusu's hand with one fingertip and asked Liuyuan in English, "Is this Miss Bai also from Shanghai?"

Liuyuan nodded.

The princess smiled, and said, "She doesn't look like a Shanghainese."

Liuyuan smiled and asked her, "Then, what does she look like?"

After pressing her index finger to her cheek, the princess opened her hands wide as though she were going to describe her, but couldn't find the right words. She shrugged her shoulders with a smile and walked inside.

Holding Liusu's arm, Liuyuan walked out of the hotel with her. Although Liusu did not understand much English, from their facial expressions, she realized what they had talked about. She then said with a smile, "It's clear I'm a country bumpkin!"

Liuyuan said, "I just told you; you are a typical Chinese. Naturally you're a bit different from what she called Shanghainese."

After they got into a car, Liuyuan spoke again, "Don't think the airs that she is putting on are justified. Outside, she tells people that she is Prince Krishna Kramupa's legitimate daughter. Because her mother fell out of the prince's favor and was ordered to die, Saheiyini was then sent into exile, destined to roam in foreign countries without being able to return home. Actually, it is true about her not being able to return home, but as for the rest, nobody can prove it."

Liusu asked, "Has she been to Shanghai?"

Liuyuan replied, "She was quite well known in Shanghai. But later on she came to Hong Kong with an old Englishman. Did you notice the old man behind her? That's who supports her now."

Liusu smiled, "You men are just like this. To her face, you always flatter her, but behind her back, you say she's worthless. I wonder what you would say about me—the daughter of an old official's family whose fortunes have been going downhill and with a social status even lower than hers!"

Liuyuan laughed, "Who would dare to put your names together in one breath?"

Twitching her lips, Liusu said, "Maybe it is because her name is so long you can't say it in one breath!"

Liuyuan replied, "Don't worry. I'll take you for whatever kind of person you are. Make no mistake about that."

Liusu seemed to relax and leaned against the car window. She asked in a low voice, "Really?"

Liuyuan had not sounded sarcastic. Gradually she was discovering that when they were alone together, he was respectful, like a gentleman. She did not understand why he was so dignified in private and so uninhibited in front of others. She couldn't figure out if it was just his odd personality, or if there was some other reason.

When they arrived at the Repulse Bay Hotel, he helped her out of the car and pointed at the thick woods beside the road, saying "Look at those trees. They only grow in the South. The English call it 'flame of the forest.' "

Liusu asked, "Are they red?"

"Yes!" Liuyuan exclaimed.

In the darkness, she couldn't see the red, but instinctively she knew it was as red as could be—an uncontrollable red. Clusters and clusters of small flowers, hiding in the towering trees, were just like fire crackling and burning all along the path, even tinting the purple sky red. She lifted her face to look at them.

Liuyuan continued, "The Cantonese call it the 'shadow tree.' Look at the leaves." The leaves were just like ferns. When the wind blew, the delicate black shadows shivered. One could almost hear a melody, not yet a song, just like the tinkling made by wind chimes hanging on the eaves of a house.

Liuyuan said to her, "Let's take a walk over there." Liusu did not answer him, but when he began to move, she followed. The hour was still early, so there were still many people strolling on the path—it didn't matter. Some distance from the Repulse Bay Hotel a bridge arched through the air. On the far side was a hill, and on this side there was a grey brick retaining wall. Liuyuan leaned against the wall as did Liusu. She looked up. The wall was very high; she could not see its upper edge. It was also cold and rough, the color of death. Against it her face looked different. She was real flesh and blood with red lips, liquid eyes, and an intelligent face.

Liuyuan looked at her and said, "I don't know why, but this wall reminds me of ageless testaments of love. . . . One day when our civilization is completely ruined and everything is destroyed—burned, bombed or collapsing, perhaps the only thing remaining will be this wall. Liusu, if we should meet then at the foot of this wall . . . Liusu, maybe then you will be sincere to me, and maybe I would be sincere to you."

Liusu was annoyed and said, "You admit yourself to pretending. You don't have to drag me in! When did you catch me lying?"

Liuyuan burst into laughter. "Right, you are the most innocent person in the world," he said.

Liusu replied, "Hold on, don't tease me!"

After being quiet for a while, Liuyuan sighed. Liusu asked, "Is something bothering you?"

"Lots," Liuyuan replied.

Liusu sighed, "If a person as carefree as you can complain about his fate, then somebody like me should have hanged herself a long time ago."

"I know you are not happy," Liuyuan said. "I know you've seen enough bad things and bad people around you, but if this is the first time you have seen them, it's even harder on you. I was just like that. When I first came to China, I was already twenty-four. I had dreamed of home many times. You can imagine how disappointed I was. I couldn't stand the shock. I had no control and just became more and more corrupt. If . . . if you had known me then, you would probably forgive the way I am now."

Liusu tried to recall the first time she had seen her Fourth Sister-in-law. Then she exclaimed: "Even so, that's still better. The first time you see something, no matter how bad or how dirty it is, those things and people aren't a part of you. But if you mix with them for a long time, how can you distinguish what they are made of from what you are made of?"

Liuyuan fell into silence. He did not say anything for a few moments. Then he said, "Maybe you are right. Maybe what I've said was nothing but an excuse, and I'm deceiving myself." Suddenly, he began laughing and said, "Actually, I don't need any excuse! I love playing around—I've got the money and the time. Do I need to look for a good reason?" He thought for a while, again becoming perplexed, and said to her, "I don't even understand myself—but I want you to understand me! I want you to understand me!" Although these were his words, in his heart he had already despaired. Still he stubbornly begged, "I want you to understand me!"

Liusu was willing to try. In fact, within certain limits, she was willing to try anything. She turned her face toward him, and whispered: "I understand, I understand." She consoled him, but she couldn't help thinking of her own face in the moonlight . . . her delicate profile, eyes and eyebrows, the beauty was incredible and yet intangible. She slowly dropped her head.

Liuyuan started to chuckle. Changing the tone of his voice, he said with a smile, "Right, let's not forget, your specialty is the way you bow your head. However, some people say it is only teen-aged girls who are good at bowing. Those who are good at it are forever doing it. You know, if you do it too often, it may make your neck get wrinkled!"

Liusu's expression changed. She couldn't help but lift her hand and feel her neck.

Liuyuan laughed, "Don't worry, you definitely don't have any. In a while, when you return to your room and nobody's around, you can open the button of your collar to have a good look."

Liusu didn't say anything; she just turned and left.

Liuyuan caught up to her and laughed. "I'll tell you why you are able to keep your beauty. Once Saheiyini said she dared not get married because once Indian women become idle, just staying in the house and sitting around all day, they get fat. But I said, "What about Chinese women? Even when they are just sitting around, they don't want to get fat because getting fat still requires the use of a little bit of energy. Being lazy has its own advantages!"

Liusu ignored him. All the way back, Liuyuan was on his best behavior, talking and joking to cool her down. Her expression did not warm up until she got into the hotel, and they each returned to their individual rooms. Liusu concluded that Fan Liuyuan was interested in spiritual love. She had to agree, because the result of spiritual love is marriage, while sexual love usually levels off at a certain stage with little hope of marriage. Spiritual love has just one flaw: in the course of love, women never understand what men are saying. But that is not of any great importance. After all, it always ends in marriage, finding a house, buying furniture, hiring servants, and so forth. In this regard, women are more capable than men. When she thought of this, she put today's little misunderstanding out of her mind.

The next morning she did not hear a sound from Mr. and Mrs. Xu's room and knew they would be getting up very late. Mrs. Xu had mentioned if you ordered breakfast in your room in the hotel, you had to pay extra as well as give a tip. Therefore, Liusu decided to save them a little bit of money and go to the dining room. Just after she finished washing and dressing and was leaving her room, a bellboy waiting outside saw her and went to knock on Fan Liuyuan's door.

Liuyuan came out immediately, smiled to her and said, "Let's eat together." Then as they walked, he asked, "Have Mr. and Mrs. Xu got up yet?"

Liusu smiled: "They must have had a good time yesterday! I didn't hear them return; it must have been close to dawn."

They chose a table on the terrace outside the dining room and sat down. Outside the stone fence was a tall palm tree, its shiny leaves spread in every direction shivering slightly in the sunlight like a glorious, spurting fountain. There was a real fountain beneath the tree, but it wasn't all that splendid.

Liuyuan asked, "What do Mr. and Mrs. Xu plan to do today?"

Liusu answered, "I heard they are going to look for a place."

Liuyuan said, "Let them look for one. We'll enjoy ourselves. Would you rather go to the beach or downtown and look around?"

The afternoon before, Liusu had used binoculars to look at the nearby beach. It had been crowded—things really were jumping, but she found the people's behavior a bit too free. Her natural caution prompted her to propose they go into town. They caught a special hotel bus and went into the heart of the city.

Liuyuan took her to the Great China Restaurant to eat. As soon as Liusu noticed that the waiters spoke Shanghainese, and that the sounds coming from every table in the room were also in her native dialect, she asked in surprise, "Is this a Shanghainese restaurant?"

Liuyuan smiled, "Aren't you homesick?"

Liusu laughed, "But . . . to come all the way to Hong Kong to eat Shanghai food seems foolish!"

Liuyuan said, "When I'm with you, I like to do foolish things . . . even riding nowhere on a trolley, or watching a movie I've already seen twice . . ."

Liusu said, "That's because you've been affected by my foolishness, right?"

Liuyuan laughed and said, "You can explain it any way you like."

After eating, Liuyuan picked up his glass and drank his tea in one gulp. He lifted the glass up high and looked intently inside.

Liusu asked, "If there is something to see let me see it too."

Liuyuan said, "Face the light and look. The scene inside reminds me of the jungle in Malaya." The leaves left inside stuck to the glass, forming a special pattern. Viewed against the light and from below, they looked like real banana trees. The tea leaves piled up at the bottom were all jumbled, just like rootless creepers or rushes.

Liusu lifted the glass to look, Liuyuan then bent over to point. Through the dark green of the glass, Liusu suddenly felt his gaze; his eyes seemed to be smiling but actually were not as he stared at her. Smiling, she put down the glass.

Liuyuan said, "I'll accompany you to Malaya."

"To do what?" Liusu asked.

Liuyuan answered, "To return to nature." Then, his train of thought changed, and he added, "There is only one thing, I can't imagine you wearing a *qipao* running in the jungle . . . On the other hand, I can't imagine you not wearing a *qipao* either."

Liusu turned serious and said, "Don't talk nonsense!"

Liuyuan replied, "I am serious. The first time I saw you, I just felt you shouldn't wear those fashionable long vests that show your upper arms; at the same time you shouldn't wear western clothes either. Perhaps the Manchurian *qipao* would be a little bit more suitable, but its lines are too harsh."

Liusu said, "In short, I'm ugly! No matter how I dress, it doesn't look good!"

Liuyuan laughed, "Don't get me wrong again! I mean you don't seem like someone from this world. You have small gestures that have a romantic air to them, almost like you were singing Peking opera!"

Liusu raised her eyebrows, and laughed sarcastically. "Singing opera? Not by myself! Whenever I put on an act . . . I am forced to do so. If people play a small trick on me, and I don't do the same back, they would take me for a fool and pick on me!"

Liuyuan was dejected by these words. He lifted the empty glass, tried to get a mouthful, and put it down again. He sighed, "Right, blame everything on me. I'm used to pretending because everybody pretends with me. Only you did I say a few words of truth, but you didn't recognize it."

Liusu said, "How do I know what's going on inside you?"

Liuyuan replied, "Right, blame it all on me. But I've given you a great deal of thought. The first time I met you in Shanghai, I thought if you got away from your family, you might become a little bit more natural. Waiting to see you in Hong Kong was hard on me . . . and now I want to take you to Malaya, to the primitive jungle . . ." He laughed at himself, his voice hoarse and dry, and called the waiter to bring the check. By the time they had paid and left, he'd returned to his original self and regained his high-class airs—and very refined they were!

After that, he took her everywhere and had fun doing everything: movies, Cantonese opera, casinos, the Gloucester Restaurant, Szeho Inn, the Green Bird Coffee Shop, an Indian silk store, a Sichuan Food Restaurant in Kowloon . . . In the evening, they often went out for walks till the very late hours. She could not believe that until now he had hardly even touched her hand. She was always alert in case he would drop his mask suddenly and grab her. However, the days passed one after another, and he still maintained his gentlemanly conduct. She felt as if she were facing a formidable enemy, but there was no movement at all. At first, she felt uneasy, like going downstairs and missing a step. Although she always was anxious, she gradually got used to it.

There was just that one time at the beach. By then Liusu was more familiar with Liuyuan, and she felt that it would not do any harm to go, so they went and spent one morning there. They were sitting side by side, but one facing east and one facing west when Liusu cried out that there were mosquitos.

Liuyuan said, "They're not mosquitos, but a kind of insect called sandflies. When they bite, they leave a small red mark just like a red mole."

Liusu went on, "I can't stand the sun."

Liuyuan comforted her: "Let's get a little more sun, then we'll move under a sun shelter. I've rented one over there."

The thirsty sun lapped up the sea, gurgling and churning, making loud sounds. It also sucked the moisture from people's bodies. Everyone was like a dried golden leaf floating in the air. Liusu felt a strange dizziness and happiness but she could not help crying out, "A mosquito is biting me!" She twisted her head and slapped her naked back.

Liuyuan laughed, "That's difficult. I'll slap them for you and you slap them for me."

Indeed, Liusu watched and aimed carefully and then slapped his back. She cried out, "Darn! I missed it!"

Liuyuan was also watching. They slapped back and forth at each other and laughed heartily together. All of sudden, Liusu had had enough. She stood up and started walking toward the hotel. This time, Liuyuan did not follow her. Liusu walked under the shade of a tree. On the stone path between two reed sun shelters she stopped to shake the sand off her skirt. Turning, she noticed Liuyuan still in the same place, lying on his back with his hands cushioned beneath his neck. Apparently he was daydreaming under the sun there, still turning into a golden leaf. After Liusu returned to her room, she took out the binoculars and looked out her window. Now there was a woman lying beside him with braids coiled on her head. Even if Saheiyini was burnt to ashes, Liusu could recognize her.

From that day on, Liuyuan flirted with Saheiyini every day. He probably had decided some time ago to give Liusu the cold shoulder for a while. Liusu was used to going out every day, but now she suddenly had a lot of time on her hands, which she could not explain to Mr. and Mrs. Xu. So she told them she'd caught a cold and stayed in her room for two days. Fortunately, the gods understood and made it drizzle. This proved a further excuse, so she did not need to go out.

One afternoon, holding an umbrella, she went for a walk in the hotel's garden. When she returned, the sky was getting dark. She thought Mrs. Xu and her family would be returning from their house-hunting very soon, so she sat under the eaves of the hall waiting for them. She opened the colorful oil-paper umbrella, and hung it on the railing to cover her face. The umbrella had a pink background with a pattern of dark green lotus leaves. Rain drops rolled one after another down its ribs. It began to rain more heavily. There was the splashing sound of cars driving in the rain. A group of laughing men and women came upstairs pushing and holding onto one another. At their head was Fan Liuyuan. On his arm, was a disheveled-looking Saheiyini. Her bare legs were splattered with mud. She took off her big straw hat and shook the water on to the ground. Liuyuan glanced at Liusu's umbrella. He said a few words to Saheiyini by the banister at the foot of the stairs. Saheiyini went upstairs by herself. Liuyuan came over, pulled out his handkerchief and wiped off his drenched clothes and face. Liusu could not avoid exchanging a few words with him.

Liuyuan sat down and said, "Did I hear that you weren't very well a couple of days ago?"

Liusu answered, "It was just a summer cold."

"This weather is terribly muggy," he said. "Just a while ago I went to the Englishman's yacht for a picnic. We sailed over to Tsing-yi Island."

Following his lead, Liusu asked about the scenery on Tsing-yi Island. While they were talking, Saheiyini came downstairs again. She had changed into Indian clothes and wore a floor-length gosling-yellow shawl. On the shawl, there was a floral design embroidered with silver thread, each of the flowers was at least two inches wide. Holding on to the railing, she picked out a table on the far side of the veranda. She sat down with one arm leisurely draped across the back of a chair; her fingernails were covered with silver polish.

With a smile, Liusu said to Liuyuan, "Aren't you going over?"

Liuyuan replied, "She already has her man!"

Liusu said, "That old Englishman? How can he manage her?"

Liuyuan smiled and said, "He can't control her, but you can control me!"

Liusu compressed her lips into a smile. "Oh! Even if I were the Governor of Hong Kong or the city god and governed all the people here, I still couldn't control you!"

Shaking his head, Liuyuan said, "Any woman who isn't jealous is a bit abnormal!"

Liusu burst into laughter. After a while, she asked, "What are you looking at me for?"

Liuyuan also laughed, "I'm looking to see if you are prepared to treat me better from now on."

Liusu answered, "Have you ever cared whether I treated you well or badly?"

Liuyuan clapped his hands, saying, "Now you are saying something! Your tone seems a little bitter."

Liusu could not help laughing aloud and said, "I've never seen anyone as shameless as you trying to make others jealous!"

At that point, the two of them decided to make up and have supper together. On the surface, Liusu was warmer toward him but her heart remained cautious. By trying to make her jealous, he was just trying to goad her into throwing herself into his arms. She had held him off so far. But if she made up with him now she would be sacrificing herself for nothing. He'd just think she'd fallen into his trap. Even in her wildest dreams she could forget about him marrying her . . . It was clear that he wanted her but wasn't willing to marry her. Although her family was poor, they still were respectable, and everyone involved was a member of the same social set. He could not afford to be accused of seducing her, so he'd adopted this open and above-board attitude. Now she knew it had been pretense. He shirked all responsibilities. If one day she was abandoned, she would not have anyone to blame.

Thinking about this, Liusu unconsciously ground her teeth and grunted bitterly. Outwardly, she went through the motions with him as usual. Mrs. Xu had rented a house in Happy Valley and was going to move very soon. Liusu wanted to move with them, but she was aware that she had imposed on them for more than a month. If she stayed any longer, it would be very embarrassing. Remaining in a deadlock like this was not right, but she could not decide to advance or retreat. One night, long after she had gone to bed and while she lay there tossing and turning unable to sleep, the telephone at the head of the bed began to ring.

As soon as she picked it up she recognized Liuyuan's voice saying, "I love you." Then he hung up.

Liusu's heart went pit-a-pat. She held on to the receiver, stunned for a moment; then, she gently placed it back on its cradle. Who could have guessed that as soon as she put it down, it would ring again.

She picked it up again. Liuyuan was on the other end saying, "I forgot to ask you something, do you love me?"

Liusu coughed and then opened her mouth, but her voice was still hoarse. She spoke in a low voice, "You should have known long ago. Why do you think I came to Hong Kong?"

Liuyuan sighed, "I've known for a long time, but, even though it's obvious, I simply wouldn't believe it. Liusu, you don't love me!"

Liusu asked, "How do you know I don't?"

Liuyuan did not say anything. Then, after a long time, he said, "There is a poem in *The Book of Songs* . . ."

Liusu quickly interrupted him: "I don't understand!"

Liuyuan was impatient, "I know you don't. If you did, there would be no need for me to tell you! I'll read it for you:

'Till death do us part.

To you I pledge my word.

I hold your hands,

Wanting to grow old together.'

"My Chinese is quite bad. I don't know whether I can explain it correctly or not. I see it as the saddest of all poems. Life, death and departure, they're all major issues beyond our control. Compared to the strength of the outside world, we human beings are so small, so small! However, we are determined to say, 'I'll be with you forever. For our entire lives, we will never leave each other'—as if we were able to be our own masters!"

Liusu considered this for a moment, and then became uncontrollably angry: "Why don't you say frankly that you don't want to marry, and that's all there is to it? Why do you have to beat around the bush saying how you can't be the master of your fate? Even a conservative like me still says 'a first marriage is decided by one's parents; second marriages are decided by one's own self!' You are a person without any ties. If you can't be your own master, who will be?"

Liuyuan answered coldly, "If you don't love me, what can you do? Can you be your own master?"

Liusu said, "If you really loved me, would you care about these things?"

Liuyuan replied, "I'm not that stupid. It's not worthwhile for me to spend my money marrying someone with no feelings for me, someone who is going to restrict me. That's too unfair. It's not fair to you either. Hey, maybe you don't care. Basically you think marriage is just long-term prostitution . . ."

Liusu did not wait for him to finish, but slammed the receiver down with a bang. Her face was flushed with anger. How dare he insult her like this, how dare he! She sat on the bed. The darkness of the scorching night enveloped her like a purple blanket. Her whole body was wet and itchy with perspiration. The ends of her hair on her neck and back were so prickly that it was almost unbearable. She pressed her hands to her cheeks and found her palms were cold.

The phone rang again. She didn't answer it and just let it ring. "Ring... .ring . . ." The sound waves were especially piercing to her ears in the tranquility of her room, the tranquility of the hotel and the tranquility of Repulse Bay. Liusu suddenly came to her senses and realized that she could not let the phone wake up the entire Repulse Bay Hotel. First, Mrs. Xu was in the next room. Cautiously she picked up the receiver and placed it on the bed sheet.

The air around her was too quiet, however, and although it was far away from her, she could still hear Liuyuan's voice calmly saying, "Liusu, can you see the moon through the window?"

Liusu did not know why, but all of a sudden she was choked with sobs. Through her tears, the moon appeared big and vague, silver with little green rays.

Liuyuan continued, "Over here, there is a flowering plant hanging in the window, blocking half of it. Maybe it's a rose; maybe it's not." He didn't say anymore, but he did not hang up the phone either.

After a long, long time, Liusu wondered if he had dozed off. Eventually though, there was a clicking sound as he lightly hung up. With trembling hand, Liusu picked up the receiver from the bed sheet and put it back. She was afraid that he might phone her back a fourth time, but he did not. It had all been a dream—the more she thought about it, the more it seemed like a dream.

The next morning she did not dare to ask him about it because he would certainly mock her, saying, "Dreams are what your heart is thinking!" Was it true that she missed him so much that even in her dreams he would call to say, "I love you!"

His attitude was no different than usual. They went out for the day as always. Liusu suddenly noticed how many people regarded them as man and wife. There were lots and lots of them—waiters, as well as some old wives and old ladies in the hotel who stopped and chatted with her. She could not blame them for being mistaken. Liuyuan was living next door to her, and they always went out and came in side by side. Late at night they still went down to the beach to walk, not concerned about what other people might think. A nanny pushing a baby stroller walked by and nodded to Liusu, calling her, "Mrs. Fan." Liusu's face stiffened; she did not know whether to smile or frown. She could only knit her eyebrows, glance at Liuyuan and whisper, "They don't know what to think!"

Liuyuan laughed, "Don't worry about those who call you Mrs. Fan. It's those who call you Miss Bai that you should worry about!"

Liusu frowned.

Liuyuan rubbed his hand over his chin and smiled, "You'd better not do injustice to this undeserved reputation!"

Liusu was astounded and looked at him. She suddenly realized how wicked this man really was. He purposely had acted familiar and intimate with her in front of other people, leaving her no way to prove that they did not have a physical relationship. Now she was in an awkward position with no line of retreat. She could not go home, could not see her parents; she had no recourse than to become his mistress. But if she compromised herself with him, not only would all her precious efforts be wasted, but she never would be able to recover in the future. She was determined not to! Besides, even if she had this false reputation, he had managed to take advantage of her in name only. The truth was that he still had not possessed her. And since he had not possessed her, maybe one day he would return to her with a somewhat more acceptable proposal.

She made up her mind and told Liuyuan that she planned to return to Shanghai. Liuyuan did not insist on keeping her. On the contrary, he volunteered to accompany her back. Liusu said, "There's no need of it. Don't you want to go to Singapore?"

Liuyuan answered, "Since I have already delayed that trip, there is no harm in delaying it a little more. Besides, I've got something to take care of in Shanghai as well."

Liusu knew that he was playing the same game; he was afraid of people not talking about them. The more people had to talk about, the less able Liusu was to defend herself. Naturally she wouldn't be able to settle down in Shanghai. But Liusu calculated that even if she did not let him take her back, she couldn't hide anything from her family. She had forged ahead with no thought of the consequences, so she might as well let him accompany her on this journey.

Mrs. Xu had seen that they had been hot as fire for each other, and now all of a sudden they wanted to split up. She was amazed and questioned Liusu and Liuyuan. Although both of them tried to whitewash the matter in the same way, Mrs. Xu didn't believe anything they said.

On the boat, there were many opportunities for them to get closer, but if Liuyuan could resist the moonlight of Repulse Bay, he could withstand the moonlight on the deck. From the beginning to the end, he did not say anything solid. He seemed indifferent but Liusu sensed that it was the indifference of a complacent man who was sure she could not elude his grasp.

When they arrived in Shanghai, he took her home but did not get out of the car himself. The Bai family already had heard the gossip and were convinced the Sixth Miss and Fan Liuyuan had lived together in Hong Kong. Now, after fooling around with him for over a month, she came back as though nothing had happened. Clearly she intended to hurt the Bai family's honor.

Liusu had seduced Fan Liuyuan for nothing but his money. But if she really had got his money, she wouldn't have returned home so quietly. Obviously, she hadn't obtained anything from him. Ordinarily when a woman falls into a man's trap, she should die for her sins, but if a woman entraps a man, that makes her even more of a whore. If a woman wants to entrap a man but fails and, on the contrary, falls into the man's trap, then she is doubly a whore. Killing her would defile the knife.

In the Bai household, it was normal for the whole family to explode over even the tiniest indiscretion. But when there was a really sensational scandal, all of them were stunned speechless. They reached a decision: "The family's shame must not be publicized." Then they all went off on their own to tell relatives and friends, swearing them to secrecy. Later, they quietly asked these relatives and friends one by one if they knew about the affair or how much they had heard about it. Finally, when they felt they couldn't conceal the matter any longer, they decided to open it up for discussion. They sat around, dejectedly slapping their thighs, and talked about the affair. This kept them busy for the entire autumn, which gave them no time to take action against Liusu.

Liusu knew full well that after returning this time, her life would be worse than before. Her ties of affection and loyalty to the family already were severed. She thought about looking for a job to support herself in a simple lifestyle. Although it wouldn't be easy, it was better than staying at home and taking their abuse. But if she took a low-class job, she would forfeit her status as a lady. That status was intangible, but giving it up would be a pity, especially at the present time, as she still had not given up all hope concerning Fan Liuyuan. She could not degrade herself. That would just give him another excuse for refusing to marry her. So, no matter what, she had to tolerate the situation for a while longer.

She managed until the end of November, when Fan Liuyuan, as she had expected, sent a telegram from Hong Kong. Not until everyone in the Bai household had passed the telegram around did old Mrs. Bai send for Liusu and give it to her. There were only a few words: "PLEASE COME TO HK. BOAT TICKET ALREADY ARRANGED BY THOMAS COOK."

Mrs. Bai sighed and said, "Since he wants you to go, you might as well go!"

Was she so cheap? Tears rolled from her eyes. She lost her self-control; she could not stand it any longer. In one autumn, she had aged two years—she could not afford to get old! So she left her family to go to Hong Kong again, but this time without her previous cheerful eagerness for adventure. She felt she had been destroyed. Of course, everyone likes to feel subjugated once in a while, but within certain limits. If she had been overpowered by Fan Liuyuan's looks and manner, it would have been another story, but the most painful part was the pressure her family put on her.

Fan Liuyuan met her on the dock in the misty rain. He told her that her green transparent raincoat was like a bottle, and then added: "A medicine bottle!"

She thought he was sneering at her weakness, but then he whispered in her ear, "And you are my medicine." She blushed and gave him a cold look.

He had reserved her old room for her. That night when she returned to her room, it was already two o'clock. After putting on her night cream, she turned off the light and walked out of the bathroom. Then she recalled that the bedroom light switch was at the head of the bed. Groping her way in the dark, she suddenly stepped on a leather shoe and nearly fell on the floor. As she was blaming herself for not putting her shoes in the proper place, she suddenly heard someone in the bed laugh out loud, "Don't be scared! They are my shoes!"

Liusu hesitated for a moment and asked, "What are you doing here?"

Liuyuan replied, "I've always wanted to look at the moon from here."

. . . The telephone call that night had been him for sure—it had not been a dream! He did love her. This poisonous man, he did love her, but he did not treat her any better than this! She could not help feeling bitterly disappointed and turned to the front of the dressing table. The slender late November moon was a white hook, like frost on the window. Enough moonlight shone on the sea to reflect through the window and glow in the mirror. Liusu slowly took off her hairnet, messing up her hair. The hairpins fell tinkling to the floor. She put the hairnet back on, angrily pushing the end of the net into her mouth to hold it. Frowning, she squatted down to pick up the pins one by one.

Liuyuan walked up behind her barefoot. He put one hand on her head, turned her around and kissed her mouth. The hairnet slipped to the floor. This was the first time he had kissed her, but both of them suspected it was not really the first time because it had happened many times in their fantasies. They'd had several opportunities in the past—proper place and proper atmosphere. He had thought about it, and she also had considered the possibility. Both of them had been very keen, but they had been taking things too carefully, and neither of them was willing to be reckless. Now that it was happening, both became confused. Liusu felt like she was walking round and round, finally bumping into the mirror, her back tightly pressed against the mirror. They seemed to fall into the mirror, into a dark world that was hot and cold at the same time, a world with wild sparks that consumed their bodies.

The next day he told her that he was going to England in a week. She asked him to take her with him, but he answered that it was impossible. He suggested that he rent a house in Hong Kong for her, and after a year or so he would return. If she wanted to stay at home in Shanghai, he would agree to that as well. Of course, she didn't want to return to Shanghai. Her family—the farther away the better. As for staying in Hong Kong by herself, if it was going to be lonely, it would be lonely.

The real problem would be when he came back. Whether the situation changed or not depended completely on him. Could one week's love win his heart? On the other hand, Liuyuan was a restless man. This kind of quick fling would not give him a chance to get rid of her, which was to her advantage. One week could be more memorable than a year. If he, full of passionate memories, really came back to look for her, she might have changed herself! A woman near thirty can be inexplicably lovely but that loveliness can fade in the twinkling of an eye. In short, trying to hang on to a man for a long period without the guarantee of marriage was difficult and painful, just about impossible. Well, who cared! She admitted Liuyuan was lovable and she found him wonderfully stimulating. Her purpose in staying with him, however, was economic security. On this point she knew she did not have to worry.

They found a house on Babbington Street located on the side of a hill. After the house was painted, they hired a Cantonese maid named Ah Li. They purchased only a few essential pieces of furniture, and then it was time for Liuyuan's departure. Everything else was left for Liusu to manage in her own good time. Since the kitchen was not ready yet, on that winter's night when Liusu saw Liuyuan off on the boat, she picked at some sandwiches in the ship's restaurant. Because she was so dejected, Liusu drank a few more glasses of wine than usual. On the way home, with the sea breeze blowing in her face, she felt a bit tipsy. When she entered the house, Ah Li was in the kitchen heating water to wash the feet of the child she had brought with her. Liusu looked around everywhere. Wherever she went, she would turn on the light. The green paint on the living room door and windows was not yet dry. She tested it with her index finger and then stuck her sticky finger on the walls, each touch leaving a green print. Why not? This was not illegal! This was her home! She laughed, and felt she might as well put on a clear palm print on the dandelion-colored plaster walls.

With faltering steps she walked into the next room. Empty rooms, one after another—it was an empty world. She felt she could fly to the ceiling. Stepping on the empty floor was like moving on the dustless ceiling. The room was empty, so empty she could not help filling it with light. Even so, she told herself to remember to change the bulbs for a few stronger ones tomorrow.

She went upstairs. It was good that it was empty. She was in desperate need of absolute quiet. She felt extremely tired; pleasing Liuyuan was too tiring. His mood was always changing, and ever since he'd fallen in love with her, he'd become even stranger with her, never happy. He had gone, which wasn't too bad. It would give her a chance to catch her breath. Now she wanted nobody—detestable people, lovable people, she wanted none of them. Ever since childhood, her world had been too crowded. Pushing, squeezing, trampling, holding, carrying, old and young, there were people everywhere. There had been twenty or more in the family, all living together. Even if you cut your fingernails, someone would be watching through holes in the window. It hadn't been easy to flee far away to this place where there was no one. If she had legally become Mrs. Fan, then she would have had all sorts of responsibilities and never would be able to get away from people. Now she was nothing more than Fan Liuyuan's mistress, and did not want to appear in public. She should avoid people and people should avoid her.

The problem with solitude was that she wasn't interested in anything other than people. The only thing she'd been trained for was to be a dutiful wife and a considerate mother. But here she was a soldier without a battlefield, a homemaker with no "home" to run. As for children, Liuyuan did not want any. And there was no need to be thrifty because she didn't need to worry about money. How then would she pass the time in the future? Would she look for Mrs. Xu to play mahjongg or go to the opera? And later would she gradually have affairs with actors, smoke opium, and go the way of concubines? She stood up abruptly, straightening herself with her two hands clasped behind her back. No, she would not be like that! She was not low class like that. She would control herself. But . . . could she prevent herself from going mad? The three rooms upstairs and three rooms downstairs, all arranged in a triangle, were brightly lit. The waxed floor glistened like snow. There was not a soul! One room after another, the screaming emptiness . . . Liusu lay on the bed. She thought about going down to shut off the lights but she could not move. Later on she heard Ah Li, wearing her wooden slippers, coming upstairs, clicking off the lights as she went. Finally her strained nerves relaxed.

That was December 7th. On December 8, 1941, the cannons roared. Amid the cannon shots, the white winter fog of early morning slowly dispersed. On the mountain tops and in the valleys, everywhere on the island, people were looking out at the sea saying, "The war's begun! The war's begun!" Nobody believed it, but in the end the war had started. Liusu was living on Babbington Street by herself, so how could she know anything? Not until Ah Li picked up the news from the neighborhood and woke her up in panic did she learn that the battle was already raging. Not too far away from Babbington was a scientific experimental station with an anti-aircraft gun on the roof. The shells constantly flew over screaming, "Rrrrr . . ." and then, "Boom!" as they hit the ground. The shells screamed one after another, "Rrrrr . . ." as they cut through the air and frayed nerves. The light blue curtain of the sky was torn into strips that fluttered in the cold wind. Also floating in the wind were countless shattered nerve endings.

Liusu's house was empty; her mind was empty; and because there was no rice in the kitchen, her stomach was empty as well. The feeling of emptiness fed her sense of fear. She tried to phone Mr. and Mrs. Xu in Happy Valley, but it took ages to get a line because everyone who had a phone was using it, trying to find out which areas were safe so they could plan an escape route. Liusu didn't get through until the afternoon, but although the phone rang and rang, nobody answered it. She thought Mr. and Mrs. Xu must have left in a hurry, moving some place where it was a little quieter. As Liusu was running out of ideas, the shelling became even more ferocious. The anti-aircraft gun in the neighborhood had become the target of those airplanes buzzing around the sky. "Bzzzzz . . . " they circled around and around, "Bzzzz . . ." as painful as a dentist's drill, the sound stabbed the depths of their souls. Ah Li, holding her crying child, sat by the living room door. She seemed dazed, rocking side to side, softly singing in a dreamy voice and patting the child in order to calm him. Outside there was another "Rrrr . . ." and "Boom!" A corner of the eave was blasted away, scattering bits of rock in every direction. Ah Li made a horrible cry, jumped up, and ran outside carrying her child. Liusu caught up with her at the front gate, grabbed her with one hand and asked, "Where are you going?"

"I can't stay here! I . . . I'm taking her to hide in the sewer!" Ah Li cried.

Liusu yelled, "Are you crazy? You'll die!"

Ah Li continued, "Let me go! My child . . . my only child . . . can't die . . . got to hide in the sewer . . ."

Liusu held on to her with all her might, but Ah Li pushed Liusu down and rushed out the gate.

Just at that moment the sky split open with a violent roar that made the ground tremble. The whole world turned black, as if a huge trunk had slammed shut, trapping uncountable agonies and hatreds within.

Liusu was sure she had died; who would have guessed she would live! Opening her eyes, she could see that the ground was covered with broken glass and sunlight. She struggled up and went to look for Ah Li. Ah Li was still clutching her child, her forehead drooped against the cement wall of the entrance way. She had been shocked silly. As soon as Liusu pulled her in, she heard the blast of another bomb that fell next door and blew a big crater in the garden. Although the trunk was shut tight, there still was no place to hide from the overwhelming noise. The "bang, bang, bang" continued on and on. It seemed like someone was hammering nails into the lid of the trunk with a hammer, and the hammering never let up from dawn to dark and from dark to dawn.

Liusu thought of Liuyuan and wondered if his boat had made it out of the harbor or whether it had been sunk. Nevertheless, as she thought of him, she felt he was far, far away, just as if he were in another world. These events were cut off from her past, which now seemed like a half-sung song on the radio interrupted by the crackles of static caused by a terrible storm. After the crackling had passed, the song would continue on as before. But she was afraid the song might have finished by then, and there would be nothing left to hear.

The next day, after Liusu, Ah Li and her child had divided up and finished the last few cookies in the can, their spirits began to decline. The whizzing fragments of bullets made a noise like someone slapping her face. A military truck chugged down the street stopping, to everyone's surprise, in front of the door. When the doorbell rang, Liusu opened the door herself. Seeing Liuyuan, she grasped his hand and clutched his arm just like Ah Li held on to her child. She fell forwards and banged her head on the concrete wall of the doorway.

Liuyuan used his other hand to lift her head and hurriedly said, "Were you frightened? Don't worry. Go get some essentials then; we'll go to Repulse Bay. Hurry!"

Liusu staggered inside asking, "Is Repulse Bay okay?"

Liuyuan answered, "Everybody says they won't come ashore over there. Besides, there will be food at the hotel; they usually stock a great supply."

Liusu asked, "Your boat . . ."

"The boat didn't sail. They sent the passengers from the first class cabin to the Repulse Bay Hotel. Actually, I was going to come to pick you up yesterday, but I couldn't find a car, and the buses were too crowded to get on. I had a hard time finding this truck today."

Liusu couldn't calm down enough to pack the luggage, so instead tied up a small bundle. Liuyuan gave Ah Li two months' wages, telling her to take care of the house. After the two of them got on the truck, they lay face down, side by side on the floor in the cargo area, covered with a khaki oilcloth. The truck bumped along the way, and their elbows and knees were rubbed raw.

"This bombing has blasted away the ends of many stories," Liuyuan sighed.

Dejected, Liusu didn't respond to him for a while. Then she said, "If you were blown up, my story would be finished as well. If I were blown up, your story would still go on!"

Liuyuan laughed, "Did you intend to be a widow on my account?" Overcome with an odd giddiness, they laughed heartily. Once they had started, they couldn't stop. Finally, when they did stop, their bodies trembled all over.

Through the screaming of the steady stream of bombs, the truck eventually arrived at the Repulse Bay Hotel. The main floor of the hotel was occupied by the army. Liuyuan and Liusu stayed in their old room. After they had settled down, they discovered that although the hotel had stored many provisions, it was all for the soldiers. Besides cans of milk, beef, mutton and fruit, there were also loaves of white and whole wheat bread. But all they had for the guests at each meal were two soda crackers and two cubes of sugar. Everybody was so hungry they were almost starving.

For the first two days, Repulse Bay remained quiet. Then conditions changed, gradually becoming more intense. There was no shelter upstairs, so everyone moved downstairs to stay in the dining hall. The glass door was wide open. Sandbags were piled up in front. The English soldiers set up a cannon there and were blasting away. The warships in the bay located the cannon and returned fire one by one. Across the palm trees and the fountain, the bullets zinged back and forth. Liusu and Liuyuan did as everybody else did, pressing their backs against the wall of the hall. The murky scene was like an old Persian carpet—all kinds of people were woven into it: lords, princesses, brilliant men and beautiful women. The carpet was hanging on a bamboo rod facing the wind so that the dust could be beaten out of it. Wham! Wham! It was beaten with such force that the characters on it had no place to escape. When the bullets were fired here, the people ran over there. When the bullets were shot there, they ran over here. In no time, the spacious hall had been blasted with thousands of holes. One of the walls had collapsed. They had no place to run now and could only sit on the ground and submit themselves to the will of Heaven.

Once Liusu got to this stage, she regretted having Liuyuan beside her. She was like one person with two bodies, and it doubled the danger as well. A bullet that missed her might get him. If he died or became disabled, her fate would be unthinkable. Because she was so afraid of burdening him if she were wounded, she could only harden her heart, looking for death. Even if she died, it wouldn't be as simple and easy as dying alone. She suspected Liuyuan felt the same way. All she knew was that at this moment she only had him, and he only had her.

The fighting stopped. The men and women trapped in the Repulse Bay Hotel slowly made their way back toward the city center. They passed yellow hillsides and red hillsides, and then more red hillsides and yellow hillsides. They almost suspected they were on the wrong road and were circling back again, but they weren't. The previous stretch did not have holes blasted in it that had been filled with rubble. Liuyuan and Liusu said little. Before, when they took a short car ride, they'd have a long talk. Now, even riding for a few dozen miles as they were, they had nothing to say. Occasionally one of them would begin speaking, but before being half finished, the other one would know exactly what was going to be said, and so there was no need to continue.

Liuyuan said, "Look! On the beach!"

"I see it," Liusu answered. Barbed wire entanglements were scattered here and there all along the beach. On the other side of the barbed wire, the white sea lapped up on to the pale yellow sand. The clear winter sky was a gentle blue. The season when the flame of the forest flowered was over.

"That wall . . . ," Liusu said.

"I didn't go to see it," Liuyuan replied.

She sighed and said, "Never mind."

Liuyuan was hot from walking. He took off his coat and hung it over his arm, which also began to sweat.

Liusu said to him, "You don't like the heat, let me carry it for you." If it had been a few days earlier, he certainly wouldn't have let her, but he wasn't so gentlemanly any longer, so he handed it over. A little further along, the hills were higher. They wondered if it was the wind blowing the trees or the movement of the clouds, but the yellowish green foot of the hill seemed to darken. When they looked closer, however, they saw it wasn't the wind or clouds, but rather that the sun had slowly crossed the mountaintop, throwing half the slope into a huge blue shadow. Up on the mountain, a few houses were burning. The smoke appeared white, but against the sunny part it was black. In any case, the sun was just leisurely moving over the crest of the mountain.

When they reached their home and pushed open the door, which was already ajar, a flock of pigeons flew out. Dust and pigeon droppings covered the hallways. Liusu walked to the foot of the stairs, and cried out, "Oh God!"

On the second floor, her new trunk was wide open, lying askew. Two other trunks had fallen down the stairs. The foot of the stairs was buried in a flood of clothes. Liusu bent down to pick up a light, honey-brown velvet *qipao*. It wasn't hers. It was full of sweat stains, cigarette burns and the smell of cheap perfume. She also discovered some female stranger's belongings, old magazines, and an opened can of lichees—its syrup had spilled on her clothes. Had soldiers lived here before? English soldiers with their women? They seemed to have left in a great hurry. The local poor folk who looted door by door probably had not come yet, otherwise none of these things would have been left here. Liuyuan helped her call Ah Li. The last grey-backed pigeon abruptly flew out through the door and into the golden sunlight.

Ah Li had disappeared to who knew where. Nevertheless, the two of them had to go on without her. Before cleaning the house, they went out to get something to eat. After a long time, they finally paid a stiff price for a bag of rice. Fortunately, the gas supply had not been cut off, but there was no water. Liuyuan took a lead bucket to get some spring water from the mountain in order to start cooking. From that moment they spent all their time busily cooking and cleaning the house. Liuyuan was able to manage every job, sweeping and wiping the floor as well as helping Liusu hang the heavy bed sheets to dry. Although Liusu was cooking for the first time, her food had a surprising hometown Shanghai flavor. Since Liuyuan missed Malayan food, she also learned to deep fry satay and to make curried fish. Although they became more interested in food than ever before, they still tried their best to be frugal. Liuyuan was not carrying many Hong Kong dollars with him, so as soon as there was a boat, they had to try to find a way to go back to Shanghai.

After the attack, living in Hong Kong was not a long-range plan. They struggled through the days at a hectic pace, but as soon as it was dark in this dead city with no lights and no human sounds, only the cold, fierce wind blew its three different notes: "Woo . . . Hoo . . . Ooo . . . ," it cried endlessly. When one gust stopped, another would start. They were like three grey dragons flying line abreast, their bodies so long that their tails never came into sight. "Woo . . . Hoo . . . Ooo . . . ," it cried until even the dragons had vanished leaving a stream of empty air, an empty bridge that led into darkness, into the void of voids. Everything was in ruins; there was only debris. The civilized people who had lost their memories staggered and fumbled in the dusk as though they were looking for something, but everything was destroyed.

Clutching a quilt, Liusu sat down and listened to the mournful wind. She was certain that the grey brick wall near the Repulse Bay Hotel was still standing. The wind had slackened, and it seemed as though those three grey dragons were resting on the top of the wall with their scales glittering in the moonlight. Trance-like, she walked to the foot of the wall. Liuyuan was approaching. Finally, she met Liuyuan! . . . In this turbulent world, money, property and everything else that would last as long as heaven and earth, all these were unreliable. The only thing that was reliable was the breath of life in her body and in the man sleeping beside her. Suddenly she climbed over to Liuyuan, and embraced him through his quilt. He took his hand out from under the quilt and held her hand. Now they finally understood each other completely. It was only an instant of understanding, but that instant would be enough for them to live harmoniously together for eight or ten years.

He was just a selfish man, and she just a selfish woman. In this age of military turmoil, there was no place for individualism, but there was always a place for an ordinary couple.

One day when they were out buying groceries, they ran into Princess Saheiyini. Saheiyini's face was a sickly yellow. She had carelessly made a bun with her loose braids. She wore a green cotton robe borrowed from heaven knows where. On her feet, however, she still wore the embroidered leather Indian sandals. She shook hands with them warmly, asked them where they lived now and was eager to see their new house. She noticed there were some small shucked oysters in Liusu's basket, and she said that she wanted Liusu to teach her how to make oyster soup. Without thinking, Liuyuan invited her over for supper, and she happily accompanied them. When she called Liusu "Miss Bai," Liuyuan smiled and said, "This is my wife. You should congratulate me!"

"Really?" asked the princess, "When did you get married?"

Shrugging his shoulders, Liuyuan replied, "We only put an announcement in the Chinese newspapers. You know, marriages in wartime are always arranged in a haphazard fashion . . ."

Liusu didn't understand what they were saying. Saheiyini kissed him and then kissed her. The meal was arranged quite simply, and Liuyuan made a point of saying they seldom had oyster soup. Saheiyini never visited again.

As they saw the princess off, Liusu stood in the doorway, with Liuyuan just behind her. His hands covered hers, and he said, "I say, when shall we get married?"

Liusu heard but did not say a word. She bowed her head and some tears rolled down her face. Liuyuan held her hands tightly and said, "Come, come. Let's go to the newspapers today and put in an announcement. But perhaps you would like to wait for a while, maybe until we return to Shanghai so that we can put on an elaborate wedding with all the trimmings and invite all of the relatives!"

"Pooh," Liusu uttered. "They don't deserve it!" Saying this, she broke into laughter and fell back, leaning against his body.

Liuyuan lifted his hand and stroked her cheek with his index finger, making fun of her, and said, "You're crying and laughing at the same time!"

The two of them went downtown together. When they approached a bend in the road, it suddenly sank away. There was nothing in front of them but a void—except for the moist, deep grey sky. Nearby there was a small iron gate with a ceramic sign that said, "Dr. Zhao Xiangqing, Dentist." The metal hanger of the sign squeaked in the wind; behind the sign, only the empty sky.

Liuyuan stopped and looked for a moment. He felt the terror in that commonplace scene, and suddenly a shiver ran down his back. He said to Liusu, "Now you should believe: 'Till death do us part.' How can we be the masters of our own fate? When they are bombing, if one had unfortunately . . ."

Liusu interrupted in annoyance, "Even now, you're still talking about being unable to be your own master!"

Liuyuan smiled and said, "I'm not beating a retreat! My meaning is . . ." He looked at her expression, laughed and said, "I won't say any more, no more!"

They continued walking, and then he spoke again, "It must be the doings of gods or ghosts that made us really fall in love!"

Liusu said, "You told me you loved me a long time ago."

Liuyuan laughed, "That didn't count. At that time, we were too busy talking about love. How could we have the time to actually be in love?"

The wedding announcement came out in the newspaper. Mr. and Mrs. Xu came over to congratulate them. Liusu was not very happy though, because during the siege of the city the old couple had taken refuge in a safe area without caring a bit if she lived or died. Nevertheless, she had to greet them with a smile. Liuyuan arranged a banquet as a delayed wedding celebration for their friends' sake. Not long after, communications between Hong Kong and Shanghai were restored, so they were able to return to Shanghai.

Liusu went back to the Bai home only once because she was afraid that there were too many people who might gossip and make trouble. However, trouble was hard to avoid. Fourth Madam decided to begin divorce proceedings against Fourth Master. Behind her back, everyone blamed Liusu for it. Liusu was divorced and remarried. It had been a shocking achievement! It was no wonder that others would want to follow her example.

Liusu squatted down in the light and lit the mosquito coil. Thinking of Fourth Madam, she smiled.

From then on, Liuyuan never joked around with her, he saved his wisecracks for other women. That was a good sign. It indicated that he had accepted her as a full member of his own family—a bona fide wife. Nevertheless, Liusu still was a little disappointed.

The fall of Hong Kong had helped her achieve her aim. But in this absurd world, who knew which was the cause and which the result? Who knew? Maybe just because the big city had wanted to help her accomplish her goal, it had been destroyed. Thousands of people had died, thousands of people had suffered, and what followed was an earth-shaking change . . . Liusu felt that she didn't amount to a pinhole in history. She just smiled and stood up, kicking the mosquito coil underneath the table.

The legendary women who caused countries and cities to fall had been like her. Although there are legends everywhere, they do not necessarily end happily like this.

A *huqin* squeaked on a night full of twinkling lights. The melody ran up and down the scale telling such an endless and sorrowful tale that it would be better not to ask about it!

Translated by Shu-ning Sciban

Bing Xin (1900-1999), one of the best-known and most prolific writers in twentieth-century China, was born into a wealthy family from Fuzhou but grew up in the port city of Yantai. Not surprisingly, maritime imagery became a feature of her prose. Common themes she explored include motherhood and childhood, as well as pressing social problems. In the 1940s, adopting a male persona and writing under the pen name "Gentleman" (Nanshi), she published a series of prose works about women. "My Neighbor" (Wode linju) is one of them.

My Neighbor
❖
1945

Mrs. M was my colleague's daughter. She also was my student and now is my neighbor.

The first time I saw her was at her father's house—it was the year I assumed my university teaching post and I was paying courtesy visits to senior members of the department. Her father proudly introduced her, saying, "Mr. X, this is my oldest daughter. This year she is fifteen. She's very bright and studies hard. She especially likes foreign literature. Perhaps you would be kind enough to give her some advice."

At that time, Mrs. M was still just a girl, thin and small with a pale complexion and two short, thick braids hanging behind her head. She was extremely shy when she spoke but really quite sweet when she smiled. She frequently used a finger to poke her glasses back into place.

I chatted with her briefly and was amazed at what she already had read in English literature: for example, most of Hardy's novels, and she could recite from memory several major English nineteenth-century narrative poems. Her father happily fetched a small notebook and gave it to me to read. On the front was a title, *Dew Drops*. Inside were more than two hundred poems in the style of Bing Xin's *Starry Sky*. I briefly flipped through them. I remember one or two poems that I felt were particularly bright and fresh, just like little pearls of dew on a spring morning.

After I had praised them, her father said with a smile, "She's even written a novel—go get your novel and show it to Mr. X!"

"Papa's always the same! I haven't finished it yet!" she said blushing before lifting the curtain and dashing off. She didn't come back. "You see, she is spoiled, not well-behaved in the least!" her father said smiling at me. "She's the smartest of my children. Unfortunately, her health isn't good."

A year later, she had become my student. Because the first-year university class was so large, I had few opportunities to deal with her directly, but from her compositions I could see she had a brilliant future in creative writing. Her well-conceived ideas and exquisite descriptions were beyond the capabilities of any of her classmates.

Later, however, because I was the faculty adviser for student publications, and she was an important member of the staff, we often had opportunities to talk. For the next few years her progress was swift, her articles often appearing in literary journals off campus. Her skill and her ideas matured and the literary world gradually became aware of her brilliance.

After graduating, she married Mr. M, also a writer. They moved to Nanjing and for seven or eight years I had no news of her.

A year before the end of the war against Japan, I went to Kunming. Friends found a place for me to live. They said there was a certain Professor M who could rent a room on the second floor of his house. The location was good, too, very close to the university. When we went to take a look, I discovered that Mrs. M was none other than my former colleague's daughter! I was delighted to see her, although the room was small and the light poor. It came from one tall window with a view of the verdant western mountains. The M family also consisted of Mr. M's elderly mother and four children, their ages close together with the youngest not yet two. Mrs. M was paler than ever; her frail body appeared to have aged—she looked well past thirty.

Having decided to take the room, I moved a few simple bags and a box of books upstairs. That evening, I went to see Mr. M. He, too, was thinner, also rather more irascible. Nothing seemed to please him. He was with the three oldest children, eating supper beneath the gloomy light of a coal-oil lamp. Granny was in the kitchen busy with something or other. Mrs. M was holding the youngest child, going back and forth between the two rooms to help with the meal. No one said anything. Reluctantly, I sat at the table for a while before going back upstairs.

Less than half a month passed before I decided to move: This household was far from peaceful and the somber atmosphere was actually frightening. Those children! I don't know if they weren't getting enough food or there were other reasons, but they cried constantly. Granny chattered away, often complaining to me that Mrs. M was incapable of doing anything. Only when Mr. M came home in the evening was the crying and whining momentarily brought under control; but it wasn't long before the first floor was throbbing again with his angry, worried and complaining voice scolding the children, cursing his wife and detesting the whole world. Their bedroom was right under mine. The floor boards were broken and nothing could block out the sounds from below. I was alone and have always been a very quiet person, but the voices downstairs continued all night, accusing, weeping. Sometimes I would hear Mr. M suddenly break something and shout angrily. Then the children would begin crying and I'd be awake half the night.

Early on the morning I was thinking of moving, I went downstairs and discovered complete quiet—there was no one about. I called and saw Mrs. M reach out from the kitchen. She brushed a stray hair from her face and asked, "What do you want Mr. X? They've all gone out." I knew "they" referred to

Granny and Mr. M, so I asked, "Children, too?" She said, "They also went out. The breakfast wasn't made properly and we're out of pickles again. They said they'd go out and get something." Her lips twitched briefly into a pitiful smile and she said, "I really am a useless person. Even when I was small I never studied these things. My mother always said, 'A few *mao* for making a suit of clothes, one or two *kuai* for a pair of shoes, girls really don't need to go to school to do this kind of work. But education is important and can help to earn money. When I was that age I wanted to study but never had a chance to go to school.'

"My father let me do as I pleased. I simply didn't go into the kitchen—as you've seen, when I light the fire to make dinner, I just end up with a kitchen full of smoke." As she spoke, she used the back of her blackened hand to rub her eyes. In the entire time I'd been there, she hadn't spoken so much. I saw her eyes were red and swollen, and her voice was husky. I knew she had been crying again, so I said, "Since the others have gone out, you don't have to light the fire. Wash you hands. I have some snacks upstairs and a can of milk powder, we can make some milk with water from the thermos bottle. You wait here while I fetch it." I didn't wait for her answer before going upstairs. Holding back her tears, she stood beside the stairs and watched me dully as I went.

Mrs. M stirred her milk and ate the snacks silently with her head lowered. After an eternity, I said, "Kunming certainly is nice; the sky is as blue as the ocean. You remember Mrs. Browning's poem . . ." I had barely got the words out when we heard the long miserable bleating of a horn. Then it sounded as if there were horns all around us and we heard people running outside. Mrs. M immediately stood up and said in a trembling voice, "That's the air raid alarm! Where are the children?" I also jumped up and said, "Don't be afraid, they must be nearby. Wait while I go and find them." Just as we reached the door to look out, Granny arrived leading the four children, crawling and stumbling. Mr. M had said there was a manuscript at his office at the university. He'd gone to rescue it but had sent his children, young and old, back home!

While I helped Mrs. M carry the two youngest, she frantically said, "Mr. X, we should hide, shouldn't we?" "Good idea," I said. "The children will be less frightened." Quickly, we packed some things, gathered up the children and went outside. Granny suddenly emerged carrying a large bundle wrapped in blue cloth. Flustered and stumbling, she said, "Don't go! Wait for me!" At that moment, the deafening roar of aircraft rumbled over us. I lifted my head to look. White light glimmered in the azure sky. Nine silver airplanes deployed in neat rows flew over relentlessly. A machine-gun fired, then heaven and earth seemed to erupt with noise, rattling doors and windows. The little children burst out crying. Granny stood paralyzed by the door. We all squeezed into the doorway. Mrs. M was deathly pale, clutching her children. In a low voice she said, "Don't be afraid, don't be afraid, Mr. X is here." I turned to the old lady and said, "Don't be nervous, the planes are gone already." Just then there was the sound of voices as people poured out of every house, their words anxious and confused. Mrs. M stood up, smoothed her clothes and pushed the children through the door. We stood listening for a moment; there wasn't a sound in the sky. I said, "Let's go inside and rest, the enemy planes have gone." Mrs. M nodded and I helped her hustle the children inside before I went upstairs. As soon as I sat down, I heard Mr. M return. Once inside he shouted, "This is just great! Now no place is safe—they've chased us all the way to Kunming! I was just picking up my briefcase to leave my office and there was an explosion, damn thing!"

From that day on, there was an alarm almost every day. Mr. M always went out before the alarm and wouldn't return until after the all-clear had sounded, complaining that dinner hadn't been prepared. Mrs. M wouldn't say anything—her eyes would swell, she'd lower her head and leave the room. Some mornings, when she was in the kitchen and I was coming downstairs to wash, she would ask softly with a bitter smile, "Mr. X, you won't go out today?" I usually said, "I won't go out when I don't have classes. Feel free to call on me."

Granny wouldn't go out into the countryside because she was afraid it wasn't safe. She always hid in an air raid shelter beside the city wall. Mrs. M and I then would take the children out of the city. We selected a trench-like place beneath some large trees that was protected on three sides by earthen walls. The children, used to the air raid warnings, now began building a little house of mud bricks and sticks. They continued their work every day, although the smallest often fell asleep in his mother's arms. Sometimes I brought along a book to read. At noon, if the alert had not been lifted, we would stay outdoors and eat some dried snacks to ease our hunger.

We chatted to fend off boredom. From bits and pieces of Mrs. M's conversation, I could guess at her many grievances. She never complained about anyone, even her less than likable children. She rarely raised family matters but I could tell from her clothes and diet that the family was destitute. Watching her wither day by day, I wanted to help her a little. I asked if she wanted to do some teaching or write some articles to earn a bit of money. Granny could take care of the house and they also could hire a maid; everything would be fine. She'd never liked housework, so why not do what she was good at?

Sitting cross-legged, Mrs. M held her children, swaying gently as she listened. A long time passed before she answered. "Mr. X, thank you for your concern. I've already thought about these things. When we first moved here, I taught for a while. The school was happier with my teaching than with my husband's." She laughed softly; it was the first time I had seen her laugh. She paused for a moment before continuing. "Later, I don't know why, he opposed my going out to teach, and his mother said the children were too much for her.

So I returned to the household. Then several friends and colleagues came and asked me to write some articles. Mr. X, you know that ever since I was a girl I've enjoyed writing. As soon as I picked up the pen, my heart . . . my heart was on fire. Everything before my eyes would go blurry. When I was writing, I could escape from reality." She lowered her head to the children playing with the buttons on the front of her dress and sighed faintly. "But reality still is reality. The children cried, guests arrived, old Mrs. M rambled on and the maid asked about this and that—all that broke my train of thought. I haven't been able to pick up my pen for ages. Besides, writing requires a certain inner peace, if not actual happiness. But look at me now. It's so, so difficult to talk about peace of mind, not to mention happiness.

"I wrote a couple of articles. Then my husband discovered it wasn't worth the effort. It seemed like wages were increasing 100 times faster than whatever I could earn from writing. And the price of clothes and shoes was increasing even faster. To depend on my writing to pay for the children's clothes was just a dream—a 5,000-character story couldn't even buy a small pair of shoes. There was no encouragement, no hope. Writing just broke my heart. When family members started pointing their fingers at me, I had to dismiss our servant. Actually, she'd wanted to leave earlier. Our family doesn't have much money but has a lot of children and ill-tempered adults. Nothing could make her stay, not like me. For me, there's no escape.

"Making a fire, cleaning rice, washing vegetables, sewing shoes, darning socks—my heart is like a withered tree, empty, numb. During the war against Japan, who has had an easy life? Those who've had easy lives aren't real people! I don't seek comfort. Just because I never learned how to keep house, doesn't mean I can't do it—I'm not afraid to do it. There is happiness in physical work. I just want to have a little inner comfort, warmth . . .

"I never said anything to anyone. I am bitter enough. In these difficult years, why tell my story to other people and make their lives even more miserable? I especially avoided telling my parents. Letters came from my father in the north. They always said, 'The rich beauty of the southern landscape must have widened the subject matter for your poetry. Why not send some short poems so Papa can have a look?' Recently, someone, I don't know who, told my parents about the real situation here. My mother wrote a very worried letter. It said, 'I didn't know you were living that way down there. Should Mother come and help you a bit? If I could have foreseen this, I never would have let you read and write; it just ruins your health and you can't do your housework.' She blames herself. When I read that, it was like a knife in the heart. My personal suffering isn't important, but I've also disappointed my father and broken my mother's heart. Mr. X, this really is like Cai Zhonglang in *The Lute,* when he says, 'Education disappoints me and I disappoint my parents.' "

She couldn't bear to continue—she pushed her children to one side, covered her face with the front of her blouse and cried uncontrollably. The children probably were used to seeing their mother cry. They stood and watched blankly for a moment but gradually resumed playing. As for me, I didn't know how to encourage her. I thought of her hiding in her dreary household all day. Here in the open country I let her display her grief, show her feelings. Slowly, I stepped away.

I really didn't want to live with the M family any longer. School was out for the summer. One day the air raid shelter was flattened, crushing many people. Fortunately, old Mrs. M wasn't hurt but I urged them to move to the countryside. I also moved far away to live in a temple in another town—and there I met another woman!

Translated by Fred Edwards

韋君宜

Beijing-born Wei Junyi (b. 1917) participated in
student political movements at university and
worked underground for the Communist party in the
early years of the Sino-Japanese War. Her political
commitment was carried over into her fiction. Her
heroines tend to personify the ideology the party
promoted among women, that "women hold up half
of the sky." Wei Junyi was an editor for a variety of
publishing houses and magazines, including *Renmin
wenxue* (People's Literature). Her fiction has been
collected in several anthologies, including *Women*
(Nüren ji, 1980) and *Mothers and Sons* (Mu yu zi,
1986).

Women

❖

1956

Lin Yun and her husband, Song Cheng, were attending a cocktail party in a large hall. She wanted to leave, and nudged him with her finger to indicate as much, but he, as usual, muttered under his breath: "Just wait a while."

At this moment, the music rose to a crescendo near the end of a song, sounding like a flock of nightingales singing at dawn. The two of them were still whispering beside the door when a person suddenly approached and greeted them. It was Chief Wang, an acquaintance of Song Cheng's. From behind, Wang patted Song Cheng's shoulder, then shook hands with Lin Yun, even bowing slightly. He wanted to invite Lin Yun to dance. He had overheard their dispute and said: "Lin Yun wants to go? No problem! I'll accompany her! You don't have to go yet, Song Cheng. I'll take her myself in my car!" Lin Yun politely declined and eventually Wang stopped persisting. Then he turned to look for a table, pulled out a chair and invited her to sit down. Turning his head, he called for someone to get him a drink. Lin Yun could do nothing but sit there. She looked at Chief Wang while he poured her a soda. She was thinking that ordinarily when she saw him—in the office—he was quite difficult. But here, this evening, he treated her so respectfully. She knew this honor was the result of her relationship with Song Cheng, not because of her own hard work. At first, she had been sensitive to these things and, recalling them to mind here, felt unhappy. She did not say a word. Chief Wang and Song Cheng spoke for a while. Then, with a smile on his face, Wang turned towards her and said in loud voice:

"First I'll tell you some good news. The office has already decided that soon you and Comrade Ma Su are to be transferred. Both of you finally will return to your ancestral home just like leaves return to their roots. You will go to work with Song Cheng. This will set your mind at rest."

The last sentence was spoken with laughter while he looked at Song Cheng. When he was finished speaking, he stood up to leave and greet other people. Lin Yun was shocked and pursued him saying: "I still need to talk with you! You don't have to . . . leaders don't need to show such consideration for me." Wang just waved his hand and said: "This has already been decided by the party." He left quickly to join the crowd. The only thing she could do now

80

was sit down and discuss the matter with Song Cheng. She stamped her foot and asked reproachfully, "Was it you who asked for my transfer? Didn't I say earlier I didn't want this? Why are you being so persistent?"

But Song Cheng only smiled. He deeply inhaled a mouthful of smoke from his cigarette and exhaled slowly. Then he looked at her and said: "Is this good for you? I'm afraid your job will put a strain on you. Look, Ma Su asked for a transfer as soon as possible. Why don't you try to transfer together?" Ma Su was the wife of Song Cheng's assistant, Li Wenguang, and also a personal acquaintance.

Lin Yun shook her head repeatedly and said: "No, I don't want it! I didn't even know in advance. Why did you . . ."

Song Cheng noticed two people sitting at a nearby table turning their heads to watch. He immediately made a downward gesture with his hands to tell her not to speak. In a low voice, he said: "How could you not know? Wasn't it discussed earlier? Obviously you're tired. You can't endure that job much longer. You practically have no time to come home on Saturdays. But still those youths in your unit criticize you for this . . ."

She cut him off and shot back: "That doesn't matter. It doesn't matter. I can't . . ."

He shook one hand and covered his mouth with the other to stop her from speaking further. Softly he said: "Others are listening. Why do you still quarrel? Look!" He pointed across the room at Ma Su, about whom they had been talking earlier. Ma Su's clothes flowed gracefully down her body. Her steps were delicate and airy. She seemed to move as effortlessly as a cloud. Ma Su saw the two of them and waved immediately. As if floating, she moved across the room to shake hands. Lin Yun was barely able to ask her: "Are you going to be transferred?" Ma Su tilted her chin upwards, and with a smile said only one sentence: "I must obey orders!" Then she turned and floated back into the middle of the hall.

Song Cheng watched Lin Yun with a smile, but she did not say anything. All the way home she had nothing to say.

When they arrived at home, Song Cheng turned on the desk lamp. He took out a folder and spread its contents across the table. Lin Yun also sat down in front of her own small desk, and began writing on an unfinished document. Song Cheng glanced in her direction, but saw only her lowered head. He turned toward the papers on his own desk. After writing comments on just two or three of them, he couldn't help looking up at her again.

The weather that day was not hot, but just now in the hall she had been sweating. Her hair, which she had combed so carelessly earlier, was wet with perspiration; each strand was glued to her forehead. It made her appear soft and delicate. Looking at her closely, one could see she was not unattractive. The contours of her face were classic. The well-proportioned lines of her lips and face looked as if they had been crafted with fine workmanship. There were no apparent shortcomings. She was not very old, but all day she appeared to be. In this, she and Ma Su differed, and Song Cheng felt embarrassed. It was his wife who had shared all the joys and hardships for so many years, not anyone else! Why shouldn't he show her some consideration and give her some happiness?

They had been married for fourteen years. When they married, Lin Yun was nineteen and Song Cheng twenty-seven. They had both attended training classes to become cadres. She was a student and Song Cheng was her group's political instructor. The Lin Yun of that time was held in high esteem by her female classmates. Though her education level was not that high, she was clever. She was also gentle and serene, a good wife. They were married less than a year when she gave birth to their first child. That first child had not yet learned to walk when she gave birth to the second. In all, Lin Yun had four children, one after the other. At that time, living conditions in the valley were not good. In between each birth, she worked off and on. When she could find a nursery for the children to attend she would go to work; when another child was born, she would stay at home for a while. After the children had grown a little, a government-sponsored worker came to help out with household chores. This allowed Lin Yun to work longer hours. During this period, she also had to take care of Song Cheng. She mended his shoes and clothes, and made the children go outside if they were too loud when Song Cheng worked at home. This lifestyle continued for ten years. In those days, such hard conditions were quite common among married women. Some of the female comrades complained, but complaining was futile: women could never do much. Still, they would continue working as long as there was work to do. Every time Song Cheng saw the lines at the corner of Lin Yun's eyes, thinking of how she had let her youth slip away in this manner, he felt he owed her some kind of debt and that he should repay her. Now, he had the means to care for her by transferring her to a better job. This would help to alleviate her weariness. He thought she should understand this.

But Lin Yun didn't think this way. She sat there, her unit's welfare documents spread out before her. She could not continue to look at them. Her mind was filled with thoughts about her transfer. With it, she would become Song Cheng's secretary! She thought of all the young people in her office, like Xiaotao and Xiaoqu. If they knew, what would they say? They wouldn't understand that she could be transferred without her consent. And Director Liu, although he wouldn't say anything, what would he think? The more she thought about it, the more misunderstood she felt. She looked at Song Cheng, who was writing on some documents. She knew now that she would not be able to discuss it with him. If she did, he would just shake his hand and say: "Let's not talk about it! Don't quarrel!" Her only course of action was to meet with Chief Wang and express her opinion to him directly. She herself was a cadre under Wang, not just his friend's wife.

By the next morning, however, she had changed her mind. When she entered the office doorway, she decided not to meet with Chief Wang. After thinking it over, she knew it would be useless. Instead, she preferred to go to the head of her own unit, Director Liu. Perhaps he would listen to her. Director Liu, an urban cadre, had just turned thirty. He went through his formative years during the period of the student movements. Now, he was an experienced and energetic young leader. He handled his affairs with unfaltering strictness. He treated her the same as other cadres even though he knew she was the wife of a higher leader. If she didn't do her work well, he wouldn't let her off easy but instead criticized favored treatment and would add one sentence: "Old Comrade, you should put in more effort!" Frankly, she was a little afraid of Director Liu. But in spite of this, she still intended to see him. In the past, if she failed in an assigned task, Liu would neither take it away nor pass it to another comrade. Instead, he always asked her to do it again and do it better. On the basis of this experience, she assumed he would not let her leave easily. Besides, he was also the leader of her party group.

She went to the office and knocked on the door. Inside, she heard three or four voices saying simultaneously: "Come in!" She knew then that she had come at the wrong time. As expected, when she opened the door she saw four people sitting around Director Liu's desk discussing something. Among them was Xiaoqu. Lin Yun was panic-stricken. Xiaoqu immediately got up to greet her, calling out: "Hi, Deputy-Director Lin!" Director Liu raised his head to look at Lin Yun. His eyes remained on her face for a moment. He nodded his head. Using a red pencil, Liu pointed away from his desk toward a chair by the window and said: "I didn't need to see you. This business is urgent; it will take a few more days to complete. You really don't have to concern yourself with this any more. Are you . . . here to talk about your transfer? Just wait a moment. We'll be done soon."

Lin Yun had no alternative but to sit down in the chair indicated by Director Liu. Between her fingers, she held a corner of the curtain that lay on the back of the chair. Her eyes settled on the trunk of a small birch tree outside the window, but she heard every word they said. They were discussing work assignments. They were to go to basic-level work units and collect information about the workers' complaints about the many meetings after work, and problems with living quarters and medical treatment. The five of them spoke so loudly that they sounded like a group of twenty or thirty people arguing over who would go here, and who would go there. After they were finished talking, Director Liu stood up and dismissed them all. He turned his head to look at Lin Yun sitting by the window and waved at her to come sit near his desk.

Lin Yun felt a little uncomfortable. She was barely able to open her mouth, but Director Liu began first. Speaking slowly, he said: "We didn't show you enough consideration in the past. For this I am responsible. A cadre's family life ought to be attended to . . ." It seemed as if he were making a self-criticism, as if he were doing his political duty. His soft voice was gentle, not the slightest bit angry. Unexpectedly, she began to withdraw from him. None of the words she had prepared would come out. Lin Yun only lowered her head, looking at the top of the desk. She spoke only one sentence clearly: "I don't want the transfer." Director Liu did not seem as patient as usual, neither was he very attentive to her words, but continuing in a gentle manner he said: "It has already been decided by higher authorities. That's the way it is." It seemed as if the matter had been settled long ago.

She could not accept this. Biting her lip, she continued: "This can't happen! Director Liu, I have an objection and you should listen to my opinion." Lin Yun lifted her head and looked directly at him, speaking in a loud voice. Liu noticed this and saw that she was making a great effort to remain calm. He was beginning to understand a little. Nodding his head he said: "You have a great deal to say, eh? But honestly, today I'm too busy. Look . . ." He wanted to explain, but suddenly she stood up, saying quickly: "Since work is so busy, why are you so inclined to have me transferred out of here? Am I really that useless? Even . . ." She couldn't continue. Her voice had begun to tremble. Liu waved his hands at Lin Yun and, looking at her, replied in a gentle, sighing tone: "I understand your objection. Wait and I will discuss it with the leaders. I'll let you know." With this, Lin Yun had no choice but to leave.

Lin Yun didn't know that three days earlier Director Liu had argued with Chief Wang about her transfer. Wang said they wanted Lin Yun transferred out and, noting that the decision was not subject to change, said the matter was settled. In the end, Director Liu had sighed and shaken his head, saying: "Please don't send any more of those cadres' wives to my office again." Chief Wang seemed sympathetic, and expressed his own opinion at great length: "Yes, it's hard to have this kind of female comrade as a cadre. You can't demand too much from them. You have to admit it! Forget it! If you don't permit her transfer now, then later, when her husband needs her company for a holiday or when she is needed at home, you'll have the same trouble . . . There is no loss in giving up such a female comrade . . ."

About these disputes, these words, Lin Yun knew nothing.

Lin Yun left the Director's office and stood in the corridor. Her heart was heavy. What was happening? Even Director Liu behaved so unexpectedly; he apologized for not showing enough consideration for a cadre's family! Was there ever any leader who apologized for not being considerate about his subordinates' professional performance and development? Who am I? Am I not a party member? A cadre? I have received so much consideration and respect, but now I will have no more work to do! The grief and indignation she felt were difficult to suppress. Moreover, it was impossible to explain to others and make them understand because they thought she had requested the transfer and the leaders were just granting it out of consideration! She thought she should go to the party committee. But in the end, she held back and controlled her anger even though Liu was wrong. She decided to try and persuade Song Cheng first.

She stayed in the corridor for a while, then entered the office of her own unit. The four young people on her staff were talking loudly but they went silent as soon as they saw her enter the room. She tried her best to smile and sat down with them. She asked gently: "Are you talking about your new tasks? Will you leave today?" Only one of the youths answered: "Tomorrow." Xiaotao, a girl with two long braids, moved closer and took a look at her, then softly asked: "Are you going to be transferred?"

Lin Yun noticed the girl was gazing at her with a pair of sparkling eyes. She couldn't prevent herself from turning her head aside to avoid meeting that gaze. At that moment, a clear thought came into her mind—Go! Go to work! I have not been transferred yet! Why not go to work with them? She didn't answer Xiaotao's question. Instead, she pretended that nothing had happened. She said in her usual manner: "I'll go with you on your new task!"

"Are you going with us? Of course you are!" The four young people cheered and clapped their hands. Xiaotao smiled. Holding Lin Yun's hands, she said: "Let them carry your bags this time." The other three raised their voices again. Lin Yun observed the situation and understood quite well that they must have been talking about her before she entered the room.

When Lin Yun walked out of the office, Xiaotao followed and caught up with her in the corridor. First, she looked around to make sure there was no one else nearby, then moved closer to Lin Yun's shoulder from behind. Xiaotao addressed her in a low voice: "Comrade Lin Yun," instead of "Deputy-Director Lin" as usual, "Please don't leave! Why do you want to leave? Is it because of the unjust criticism from the other three? I thought you wouldn't . . ." She spoke very quickly and, as soon as she saw someone approaching, she quickly moved away. Hearing Xiaotao's words, Lin Yun had a sudden impulse to tell her the whole story, regardless of their relationship as superior and subordinate. However, she didn't say anything at all. Shaking her head, Lin Yun lowered her voice to say: "Truly, I'm not willing to leave." Then, with a profound feeling of sadness, she added: ". . . It's hard for you to understand." Quickly, Xiaotao grasped Lin Yun's shoulders to stop her from leaving. In a low but firm voice, Xiaotao said: "I do understand! There are many young women in our Youth Union who often cry after they get married. Comrade Lin . . ." She held Lin Yun's hands. "Don't leave! We all want you to stay. Decide on this and leave all the other problems for later!" Lin Yun nodded to her.

When Lin Yun arrived home that evening, her children ran and gathered around her but she sent all of them away. Song Cheng wasn't home yet. She was in a big room by herself with only the small desk lamp for light. She couldn't sit down in front of the desk to read. She realized that only those who had caused the problem could solve it. She must have a talk with Song Cheng, a serious talk, just like a discussion between two cadres. She would tell him that she definitely was not interested in a transfer, that she wasn't tired from working, and that she was willing to work just like anybody else . . .

She thought carefully and prepared her words in more detail than she had for Director Liu. Song Cheng suddenly opened the door and turned on the two lights that hung down from the ceiling. The abrupt brightness shocked her out of her concentration. Song Cheng put his briefcase on the table and walked over to her. He held Lin Yun's arms then said: "Don't be in such a daze. Come here and have a rest!" She didn't move. He pressed her shoulders again and said with a smile: "Are you still not satisfied? Come, please put up with me this time and do as I say." After this, he lowered his head and moved his face to hers, as if he were going to give her a kiss, but she turned her face aside. He then stroked her hair and she had no choice but to sit still. She didn't know how to start talking about what she had prepared. She looked at his shaved face, which was filled with satisfaction. "I still don't want to transfer!" she said simply.

He took her hands and held her up to move her over to the sofa. A titter came from his mouth, as if she had surprised him with a joke. Song Cheng stretched and yawned in the middle of the room and said: "Are you really still thinking of this matter? You are obsessed by this, you know. I'm very tired. I have to attend another meeting soon. I just came back to rest for a while. Let's enjoy ourselves. Can we change the topic?" He raised his left hand and waved, as if he wanted to wave away all nonsense. But Lin Yun sat up straight and said: "No! I don't agree!"

Song Cheng did not argue with her. Suddenly he opened the screen door facing the opposite yard and called out: "Ma Su! Ma Su!" Then he turned his head toward Lin Yun and said: "I've called Ma Su over here to divert you. Is that okay? Don't torment yourself any more!"

Ma Su came over as soon as she heard his voice. Song Cheng pointed to Lin Yun and said to Ma Su: "Look at her! She is unhappy again!"

"Why are you unhappy again? Is somebody bothering you? Is it Old Song?" Ma Su didn't wait for an invitation to sit down. She took Lin Yun by the hand, pushed her over and sat down beside her. Lin Yun looked at her and felt she had nothing to say in return. She only smiled and said: "Don't believe him! Nobody is unhappy!"

Song Cheng refused to accept this. He insisted on exposing the matter to Ma Su. "How could she say she's not angry? She's behaving like a child. She just wants to save face, so now she's acting rashly. She still insists that she doesn't want to transfer."

"She doesn't want to transfer? That's strange! And you still say that it's not your fault? You must have provoked her in some way so now she won't cooperate with you. Say sorry to Lin Yun quickly!" Ma Su ended with a shrill laugh. She stood up on one foot and turned herself around on tiptoe as if she were about to conduct a dance recital. The sound of her laughter spun in the air at the same time. Her laugh embarrassed Lin Yun, who stood up and took some apples from the cabinet. She peeled one and gave a piece to Ma Su. "Taste it!" said Lin Yun. Ma Su, still on tiptoe, tasted the apple and, as if something suddenly came to mind, asked Lin Yun in a serious manner: "Did you taste the honey melons that just arrived two days ago?"

Lin Yun just answered with one word: "No." Immediately, Ma Su laughed heartily, as if she had just heard a clown telling a silly joke. After a moment, she managed to control her laughter and, pointing to Lin Yun with her finger, said: "You are really . . ." Ma Su didn't continue. It seemed she didn't know how to describe Lin Yun. After that, her attitude became more serious and she stopped tapping her feet. She pulled Lin Yun over to the sofa to sit down. Then, speaking very slowly and sincerely, she said, "Lin Yun, I'm not complaining about you, but why are you spending so much time being upset about something so irrelevant? Why don't you pay more attention to your life with Old Song? Okay?"

Lin Yun couldn't bear any more. She put down the fruit-knife and the expression on her face turned more serious. Just as she was about to protest, Ma Su intervened: "I understand your reason! But don't you also have a responsibility for Old Song? What does he eat everyday? Food delivered from a public kitchen! I have never seen any kind of seasonable fruit in your home! What kind of life is this?" Ma Su seemed to be moved by her own words and her voice began to tremble: "And he is a leader in charge of important work. If his physical condition is poor, shouldn't you take responsibility for that? Look at yourself . . ." The more she spoke, the louder her voice became. Her tone verged on the reproachful. Song Cheng had been listening with a smile but he could see from Lin Yun's face that her mood was changing. In order to prevent Lin Yun from misunderstanding, Song Cheng cut off Ma Su: "Not just for me! The main purpose is for herself!"

But Ma Su couldn't stop talking once she began. She took over from Song Cheng: "I just said it's for herself. Look at yourself!" She turned to face Lin Yun and continued: "Why should it be like this? Do you really want those women, who are capitalists, business women, and urban petty bourgeoisie, to laugh at us as bumpkins? I can't accept this! Are they really more experienced? Why should we consider ourselves lower than them? I would like to let them know who the real pioneers are!"

Ma Su paused and stood up. Raising her head a little, she pursed her lips and cast a sidelong glance at both of them, as if she really was vying for position with such opponents. Song Cheng and Lin Yun couldn't help staring at Ma Su. The fact was that nobody could know her true social standing if she herself didn't say anything. This woman was the same age as Lin Yun and had shared almost the same experiences. But looking at them together now their lives seemed to have nothing in common. Ma Su's age was not obvious. Only a careful examination might reveal some small lines around her eyes. Her lips were like a pomegranate flower in bloom. The curls of her hair were shining, quite different from those who were just learning to be fashionable by perming their hair! She looked as if she were ready for a banquet at all times. Ma Su had been Li Wenguang's secretary for six years before being transferred to the Industry Bureau. But in less than one month she was transferred back again to be Li Wenguang's secretary and, as usual, was on a recuperative holiday. What her exact illness was, only a very few could know. There was something wrong with her head. Her stomach was not quite right, either. There were some troubles with her eyes as well. When she met with someone she hadn't seen for a long time, and he inquired about her health, her answer was never the same. Sometimes it was her eyes, sometimes her stomach, sometimes other parts of her body. As for acquaintances such as Song Cheng and Lin Yun, they never even asked the question. They had forgotten about it a long time ago. Now, Song Cheng listened to her words, which were full of conceit, and observed her fervent manner. He couldn't prevent himself from bursting into laughter. He took a puff of his cigarette and said: "Of course, you are the pioneer of this trend."

Lin Yun made no comment. Ma Su heard this satirical praise and rolled her eyes. She raised her head slightly and smiled faintly at Lin Yun. She felt so full of energy tonight that she decided to have a long and detailed conversation with Lin Yun. Ma Su then began speaking loudly: "I heard that even in the Soviet Union there are still many women who are just housewives. People who don't know this don't even know what socialism is!" She talked not only about facts but also theory. Her voice was shrill and high-pitched, her speech fast and continuous. Lin Yun had no chance to cut in. By this time, Song had finished several cigarettes and it was time for his meeting, so he left.

Ma Su stopped talking as soon as Song Cheng left. Sitting closer to Lin Yun, she held Lin Yun's hands gently and lowered her voice: "What have you thought about me all these years?"

Lin Yun didn't quite follow her: "What have I thought?"

Unexpectedly, Ma Su sighed deeply and shook her head. The bright expression on her face became more somber. Speaking slowly, word-by-word, she said: "Women! Women are women after all." She paused for a moment, reflecting, and then continued: "Lin Yun, you tell me. Didn't I carry a rucksack during the marches? Didn't I work night duty? Don't talk about the childish ideas we held when we were young. Now I am older and realize; physically, emotionally and mentally, there is no comparison! None at all! ... After all, we are only women."

"You are a woman, so you give up?" Lin Yun shot back.

"What can you do except give up?" Ma Su laid back and spread out her slender white hands along the back of the sofa. "Don't be silly! We are inferior to men! Don't think that can be changed. If you really possessed some special abilities, then maybe it could. But in fact, you don't! You work so hard, and for what?"

At this moment, she sat up straight and faced Lin Yun again. "I know that you don't agree with my opinion. Maybe, in your mind, you look down upon me. Think about your own situation. You are subordinate to that young leader, who was just an elementary student when we were fighting for Liberation. Does he really respect you? You work so hard and still it is uncertain whether you can get even one word of praise. What's it for? Whoever wants to say that I am backsliding, then so be it. I tolerate the criticisms, and life still keeps going—I've freed my own thoughts. Lin Yun, we are still attending the revolution, even if you don't continue in your present job! We are not common people. Who has the right to say that we are not in the revolution?"

Lin Yun's heart trembled when Ma Su mentioned that young leader. She didn't think it was unfair to be his subordinate. She was certain that he was superior to her. In fact, even though she worked conscientiously under his leadership, she could make no claims of outstanding performance. Maybe he paid more regard to the young Xiaotao and Xiaoqu. Evaluating herself, she thought: "I have no high level of theory to analyze situations. As for running errands, my physical condition is not as good as the younger people's. And though they consider me a veteran, in terms of personal experience, I really have not done much independently. Now, I will be transferred out!" Ma Su had touched a tender spot. Lin Yun consoled herself silently and couldn't think of anything to say in return. It was not easy to judge Ma Su with one sentence, to decide that she was not active in the revolution. Besides, it was difficult to refute her words. Ma Su noted her silence and put her hand on Lin Yun's shoulder. As though speaking a secret, Ma Su lowered her voice and softly said: "You should take more care of Old Song. Maybe you can stew some tonic soup or food for him. You should also pay more attention to your own appearance—we have grown a little older. Old Song has behaved well till now but, with one wrong step, who knows what would happen . . ." At this moment, she was so close to Lin Yun that she almost touched her ear. There was a strange scent of perfume and tobacco in the air. Lin Yun could barely hear anything Ma Su said. Her ears were filled with a continuous humming. Once more her heart seemed filled with heaviness. She gazed at the ground and saw only Ma Su's thin green shoes decorated with golden flowers. She kept silent. There was just one simple thought in her mind: leave me alone.

After Ma Su left, Lin Yun turned off the two lights on the ceiling and sat on the sofa alone. Ma Su's comments were ridiculous and her actions were shameful. Lin Yun knew that clearly. However, Ma Su's question, "Who has the right to say that we are not in the revolution?" was a paradox to her. It would be unimaginable for a male comrade, such as Song Cheng, to act as Ma Su did. But because it was Ma Su, it was another story. Nobody felt strange about it. Was there really such a double standard? Progressive labor was part of the revolution, and doing nothing was part of the revolution too?! A woman could endure all hardship and try her best to work diligently, but compared to those women who do nothing, there was no difference in the eyes of others.

Thinking of this, she suddenly felt cold. Half closing her eyes, she supported her head with her left hand and used her fingers to cover her eyelids slightly. The window above the sofa was half open and a gust of night wind blew in, causing the curtains to flutter. Lin Yun felt the wind rush up her sleeves, chilling her arms, so she moved her hands away from her face. Her eyes were heavy with weariness and she felt like there was mist in the room from the weak light. It seemed like her eyes were covered by Ma Su's slender white hands. She rubbed her eyes. Something more came to her mind concerning Ma Su . . .

When she first met Ma Su, they were both young girls. That year, they were in a propaganda team with more than twenty male cadres. In one day, they would carry their rucksacks for at least seventeen miles. In the daytime, male cadres always joked: "You can't walk anymore! Give us your rucksacks! We can carry them for you!" Neither of them gave in. Instead they retorted: "If anyone of you can't walk any more, we can carry both you and your rucksack!" They walked in front of the male cadres every day. One night, in the camp, they lowered their voices and said: "It's so tiring!" They sat on the warm *kang*[1] rubbing each others' legs and looking at the blisters on the bottom of their feet. From outside the window, some mischievous boys overheard them talking and rushed into the room laughing and clapping, disturbing them for the rest of the night. At that time, Ma Su wore her hair in two long braids and had such round eyes. She looked so much like today's Xiaotao! . . . When she recalled this memory, she was no longer disgusted with Ma Su. She felt so sad that she almost started crying. She really didn't know where this sadness came from, or who it was for. It was so difficult to understand someone else's state of mind. In just over ten years, Ma Su had come to believe: "I am inferior!"

"I'm no use any more! I'm old." Lin Yun suddenly remembered there was another woman who had often said these words: her dead mother. Her mother had graduated from a female teachers' training college in 1912, the first year of the Republic of China. In Lin Yun's memory, her mother always wore wide-legged, satin pants and a pair of silk slippers. From morning till night, she would sit on a bamboo chair under the eaves of the veranda holding an old issue of a women's magazine published by the Shangwu Press seven or eight years previously. Whenever somebody asked her to fill a teaching position, she always said the same two familiar sentences. The clearest image in Lin Yun's memory was of the afternoon she went to join the People's Liberation Army.

---

1. A heatable, brick sleeping platform.

Her mother remained sitting on that bamboo chair after trying to persuade her to stay. Then she called Lin Yun over to her and said with a low voice: "I am old. I don't know how many more years I have to live . . . Maybe I won't see you again . . ." Her mother cried as she spoke. Lin Yun was eighteen. Part of her felt sad but she had grown tired of those familiar words. She swore to herself: "If you want to be old, then be old! I'll never follow in your footsteps, even till the day I die!" How old had her mother been then? Just thirty-eight.

At the thought of this, Lin Yun felt as if she had been stabbed by a needle. In the twinkling of an eye, she had become thirty-something. She nearly jumped up. It was impossible! She felt as though she were in the shadow of her mother's ghost, which was part of a mountain made from a thousand years' worth of generations. In among all of this was Ma Su's slender shadow. The apparitions were chasing her and trying to consume her. She wanted to raise her arms and shout: "No!"

She was thinking about so many things when the door creaked. Song Cheng had come back. It was already eleven o'clock. He saw that she was still up alone. He walked over to her, patted her on the back and said in a tender voice: "Forget it. Go to bed."

She raised her head and looked at him. She tried her best to control her discontent, then said calmly: "Cheng! I ask you. Please withdraw that transfer tomorrow. I won't go to your office. I would like to work like everybody else."

Song Cheng didn't notice the trembling in her voice. He said casually: "Don't be silly. Other people are other people. Don't be afraid of others laughing at you. It was an official transfer. Who would dare to say anything? What can you do if you listen to other people's childish talking?" As he spoke, he grasped her and tried to pull her up.

She sat there, not wanting to get up. Instead, she prevented him from standing up, indicating that she wanted to continue talking. She tried softly to say all she had prepared in advance. She was willing to work, and she felt guilty for leaving when her office was so busy. Having such leisure would not bring happiness, but bitterness. Clearly, he didn't need her to work in his office. She would do anything if he would let her stay in her own unit.

But still, he shook his head and said thoughtlessly: "Stop arguing. Leave it alone. It has already been decided."

She looked at him, her eyes full of disappointment, surprise and doubt, as if she were looking at a stranger. He stood up and bent down to find his slippers under the table. He was sleepy and needed to go to bed.

She rubbed her hands together forcefully while still looking at him. He was concentrating on finding his shoes. Lin Yun realized that she had said too much. There was nothing more to say—although she hadn't yet spoken of the troubles plaguing her, he had been so different before. Since the time they attended training classes together, Song Cheng had always been her closest friend, even before they fell in love. At that time, she discussed all her troubles with him, from becoming a party member to the emotional difficulties caused by some suitors. That was why they married. But now it seemed that he was more satisfied with being a responsible husband than a cadre. She could only talk with him about children and entertainment. With regards to politics, she could only be a good listener, hearing him chatter on about attending some congress and his own opinions on what had occurred. If she tried to say anything, he was not willing to listen. Moreover, the more serious she became, the more careless he behaved. Often, after she spoke, he would ask her: "What did you say?" She couldn't stand his attitude any more. Finally, she spoke the words that had been building up inside her: "When you act like this, I can't stand to be with you any more!"

He stood up straight and slid his feet into the slippers. After he heard Lin Yun's words, he burst out laughing: "Then, you will be the fleeing—Nora."[2]

Her temper flared at this and she stood up suddenly. Walking over to him, she spoke loudly face to face: "I am certainly not Nora, but you are really like Helmore!"

Song Cheng was shocked. He gazed at her. Her face turned red and her lips were pressed together. Only now did he realize that something was unusual, but still he didn't entirely grasp her meaning. He even shook his head and said: "Don't be so sensitive and feminist. Nowadays there is no Helmore!"

"Did you say there is no Helmore?" She flung her head upward and continued without stopping to take a breath: "Aren't you a Helmore? Please think about it by yourself and answer me honestly! The way you treat me now, was it the same during the Liberation era? Before I was your classmate and comrade. Now you treat me even worse than a child! You . . ."

"What are you saying?" His mood changed: "Why do you talk like this over such a trivial thing? I transferred you for your own sake, and you surprise me by reacting like this. Are you crazy?"

"I'm not crazy," she answered seriously.

"Not crazy?!" he moved closer to the sofa she was sitting on. This argument had come out of the blue. How could there be some ulterior motive in his having her transferred? It was ridiculous. Some husbands messed around behind their wives' backs and considered divorce a normal thing. But had he done something wrong to her? She had misunderstood him completely and should apologize. He was so angry that he lost control:

"If you're not crazy, then you must have something else in mind. You don't want to stay with me? Why else would you say such words to destroy our relationship? Are you being unfaithful?"

---

2. This is a reference to the heroine of Ibsen's play *A Doll's House*.

Her heart was full of so many emotions that she couldn't even think about what Song Cheng had just said. She responded at once: "If the sentiment has faded then it is hard to be faithful!"

He was so angry that he balled his hands into fists. He almost jumped up, but was afraid Li Wenguang and Ma Su would overhear. He watched Lin Yun's face, which had lost its youth and tenderness in this anger. Finally, he stopped the shouting. He ran to open the bedroom door and turned back to her saying: "I never thought that my good intentions would turn against me. I know that you are not really concerned about this job transfer. If you really intend to leave, then just leave. Don't torment me like this!" The door slammed as he went into the bedroom. He did not bother to look back. Lin Yun watched the door with a sense of emptiness. Then she bent over the sofa and cried.

It was so unexpected, things turning out this way. Originally, she had just wanted to discuss the transfer. How had the conversation digressed into an argument about love and marriage? Was it true that she didn't want to transfer to his office because she didn't love him any more? Thinking back, why had she said those words about unfaithfulness just now? She felt some remorse. She really didn't want to be separated from Song Cheng. She almost wanted to go into the bedroom and explain to him. But thinking further, she didn't have enough courage to take one step toward him. She raised her face with tears in her eyes. Through the tears, she saw Song Cheng's documents lying on the desk in disarray. Lin Yun walked over to the desk and tidied them up. Gradually, she calmed down. Her words really had been biting. Song Cheng wasn't a Helmore. He was the lover who had walked the revolutionary path together with her. Their hearts were connected by the same progressive ideal. But this common ideal had faded little by little during daily life. Love still existed, but they understood each other less. Could love that lacked understanding continue? This situation had to be changed! It had to be changed no matter what new problem arose tomorrow.

She opened the drawer and took out a clean handkerchief to wipe away her tears. The hot, confusing thoughts in her mind were clearer now. She slowly walked over to her own desk and took out a piece of paper. She picked up a pen to write a letter to Director Liu. She thought carefully for a while and then wrote:

"Director Liu:

"I really appreciate that higher authorities have showed so much consideration for my family life and working conditions . . ."

She couldn't continue. She shouldn't have to write this way. Why was she still writing in this manner? She looked at the letter again and then tore it up. She got another piece of paper and tried to start again:

"Comrade Liu Kewen and Party Committee:

"I hope that the leaders will no longer treat me only as a cadre's wife. Please consider me as a comrade . . ."

When these two lines were written down in black ink, she felt released from all the troubles she'd had for so long. She felt carefree.

Translated by Heather Schmidt and Yu-kun Yang

康芸薇

Kang Yunwei (b. 1936) was born in
Nanjing and began to write in the 1950s.
She has published five volumes of fiction.
"Twelve Golden Hairpins" (Shi'er jinchai,
1987) is her best known story. "Such a
Beautiful Sunday" (Zheyang hao de
xingqitian), written before the first wave of
feminism hit Taiwan, portrays a generation
who received a good education and were
free to marry the men they loved, but who
were fated to live as housewives.

Such a Beautiful Sunday

❖

1966

I followed him out of the room. I wanted to flee the cold interior to the outside where the sunshine was so wonderful! The sky was as blue as the sea but the sun wasn't shining into the room. There were no sunbeams, and the room was so dark it seemed as if mold would start to grow.

"I still have to wash my own clothes," he said, shaking his head and stopping beside the sink beneath the eaves.

"I can do it. I didn't say that I wouldn't wash them for you," I yelled at his back. I thought that just a moment ago I had been in the cold room, angry at that cold man. Trying to keep a calm voice, I called out, "It was me who washed the clothes you have on now."

"Twice, at most," he said indifferently, glancing my way. His expression matched his tone and made me feel as if I had received an insult from which there was no defense. I hollered angrily, "Six times already!"

"Alright, six times." He finished talking and started to wash his clothes.

Alright, six times. Why did he say it so insipidly like that? When the sweat flowed from my forehead doing his clothes, I hoped that I could do everything for him, but that flat "Alright, six times" terminated that desire. Full of indignation, I stood behind him, unable to think of any words he would find unbearable. I didn't have any experience in deliberately hurting other people. That was something best left to the genuinely callous. I despised myself. Like a lion with an ant crawling around his ear, I had to accept being treated like a fool.

He graciously continued to wash his clothes, and soon the sink was filled with white, soapy bubbles. The anger still swelled in my chest, like the bubbles that were about to overflow the sink. Why are some people so indifferent to other people's embarrassment, why? I just can't understand it. A trace of pity, some compassion between oneself and others, shatters anger; it shatters willpower and strength.

I looked at him with a blank expression. His arms were covered with the white soap bubbles. There was a spot on the cement underneath the sink where the water had overflowed. The spot had long since become discolored from a history of being soaked with wash water. I suddenly felt that those white bubbles would be fun to play with and wanted to stretch my hand into the sink and wash clothes just like him. I couldn't say why I wanted to burst into tears; it was just that I wanted that kind of simple, carefree happiness. I wearily raised my eyelids and watched him turn on the tap and wash off the white soapy foam.

I walked unhurriedly to the lawn inside the courtyard and sat down. As I gazed up at the blue sky, I kept thinking of those funny bubbles that had been washed away. When I was still a girl, I used to enjoy sitting by the small river near the church and look at the blue sky's reflection in the water, or put on my glasses to gaze at the faraway green hills and the red-brick buildings. The white clouds, the blue sky, the faraway hills, and the red-brick buildings inside the church compound seemed like they were from a fairy tale. After I put on my glasses, they turned so bright and pretty.

I lowered my head and saw the "sweet 'n' sour" plants I'd long-since forgotten about. I picked one, put it in my mouth and chewed it. I don't know its real name, but it's a kind of creeper that lies on the ground and has round leaves and a sour-tasting stem. When I was a carefree young girl, I used to call them "sweet 'n' sours."

"We have to be careful about Shanshan," I said chewing the sour-tasting little grass stems. Suddenly I remembered something: "The Yang child had a series of illnesses and ruined his health."

"That's the ninth time you've told me."

He hadn't turned his head, but from the sound of his voice I could see the mocking line of his mouth and couldn't help smiling. Maybe I had said it eight times already. He had just shown that he was going to ignore my chatter by running out to wash his clothes. Am I so talkative that I make it unbearable for other people? Where is that peaceful young girl, sitting by the stream beside the church, looking at the reflection of the blue sky falling into the river?

Biting my lip and smiling, I watched him quietly. Absorbed in the washing of his clothes seemed a kind of pleasure to him. There wasn't anything that could bother him. Even my pain during childbirth didn't trouble him. He once wrote a letter to his friend: "We arrived at the hospital at two o'clock in the morning. I brought a pile of newspapers and magazines to read. When I heard her shrill cries coming from the delivery room, I knew it would be soon. The other men like me who were waiting outside the delivery room acted like there was some kind of impending doom, pacing back and forth in the hallway. I really wanted to tell them to take it easy, sit down and read the paper. The ripe fruit will fall by itself—why get so nervous?"

Nothing can make him nervous. He doesn't know that man is a living, feeling animal. Even if I live to be a hundred, I will never forget that cold night. As I lay in the delivery room in agony, thinking that I was going to die, he suddenly appeared beside my bed like a ray of light. I looked at him. My heart waited for him to grasp my hand, to give me strength. But instead, he stood there strangely, watching me suffer like he didn't recognize me.

"I want some water. I feel like I'm going to die!" I cried. "I don't want to have a baby!" I yelled out inconsolably. I was so disappointed. In my pain, I grasped the iron railing at the top of the bed. My fingernails dug into the cold iron so hard that they made a terrible scratching noise. I often recall that terrifying scratching sound.

When I was in pain like that, he didn't extend his hand to me, although he said several times that it simply didn't occur to him to do so at that moment.

"It's a very natural action," I said, extremely unsatisfied. "Anyone in that situation would do it."

He emphasized that holding my hand wouldn't have made him bear any of the pain for me.

"At least it would have given me some comfort." Finally, I could not help saying: "You simply don't care about other people's suffering. You are a frightening, cold-hearted man."

"If that's the case, why did I sneak into the delivery room in the first place?" he asked. Unhappily he said, "Did you know that it's a restricted area people aren't allowed to enter?"

He went into the delivery room in order to care for me? But he looked at me with such strange eyes, like I was a stranger.

"And if I'd had a difficult delivery?"

"You didn't."

"I said 'if.' "

"Then I would have gone to save you, at any cost."

"Is it really like that?"

"What do you want?" he exclaimed. "Look, I don't want to talk about these things again. You're being deliberately provocative. Every day, so many women have babies. If it were as dangerous as you say, then we wouldn't have to worry about overpopulation!"

He could always reduce me to silence with just a few words. I looked up at the blue sky, feeling at a loss. Emotionally speaking, is my always wishing to be a little closer being "deliberately provocative"?

When Shanshan isn't feeling well, I tell myself that if she's sick, she should see a doctor. This is the Scientific Age. When doctors heal the sick, we shouldn't get emotional and complicate matters. But I can't be aloof like him, not caring about anything.

The wide open sky and the sweet 'n' sours weren't helping me any more. He finished washing the clothes and went back into the house. A kind of anger that came from being ignored made me feel dazed and confused once again. I stood up and followed him into the house. I would rather have stayed in the small courtyard, looking for some enjoyment from the wide-open sky and the sweet 'n' sour grass, but that anger from being ignored drowned out everything, making me scorn myself for no reason. Pitifully and humbly, I went back into the cold house, chasing my own self-worth in the face of that cold man.

He was sitting in great comfort on the couch with his legs stretched out to the coffee table. A record of folk songs by Hoffman was playing.

He held a cup of freshly brewed tea in his hands and said, "For a stupid person, even if there is gold everywhere, he still doesn't know where to look." He slowly sipped his tea. He drank very little, but his mouth let out a loud sound as if the tea were very sweet. "If you have nothing to do, you can listen to some records. I think it was you who bought them!" Then seriously, he said, "You're a very strange person, but you probably didn't know that, right?" He looked at me. Suddenly, as if bestowing a favor upon me, he said, "You look terrible. Go see a movie. Every life needs some excitement."

I looked terrible? Unconsciously, I lifted my hand and stroked my haggard face. Every life needs some excitement but I had made mine strange and pathetic. Perhaps I should wade into the crowds of Ximending for some excitement. I had hidden myself away in the dark for too long.

I washed my face and sat down at the dressing table. The mirror reflected my pale face. I picked up the comb and combed my hair back indifferently. I don't know when, but a slight, wicked smile appeared on my face. I put on some lipstick and penciled my eyebrows. Gradually I couldn't recognize myself in the mirror. Who was it that I looked like? I knitted my brow, and the wicked little smile on my lips grew deeper. I suddenly remembered a girl who looked like this in a movie I once saw. She was suffering from a serious case of schizophrenia and had many different personalities. I quickly moved the mirror away.

As she was dreaming, Shanshan let out a laugh. I quietly went to the front of her bed. The little green blanket set off her rosy face beautifully. As was my habit, I reached out my hand and stroked her forehead. Her temperature was normal now, but I still didn't know why she'd suddenly got a fever two nights before. I stared at her little face. I wanted to hug her close to my chest. Did she know that she was my precious jewel?

If someone could talk with me about Shanshan now, about her rosy face, the smile she just had, then I wouldn't have to go to Ximending. She was a four-month-old infant who was as delicate as a lemon blossom.

"Are you going out or not?" he asked impatiently. "If you don't want to go out, then I'm going to go out. It's such a beautiful Sunday."

The sun still had not shone into the room. I had been in the cold for too long. I had to get out quickly and roam about the jammed crowds of Ximending. I'm an ignorant person, unable to open the road to his heart.

I went to the sink and washed off my lipstick and penciled eyebrows. I scrubbed with a washcloth until my skin hurt.

"Take two hundred *kuai*," he said, looking surprised at my aching skin. "Buy something that you like to eat. Enjoy yourself. See a couple of movies."

I took the money. I knew he was sincere this time, but why couldn't we talk together about Shanshan? Or about some other things? Before we were married, we said endless sweet nothings to each other.

"Shanshan," I said. "When she wakes, she'll want some milk."

"I know. She eats every four hours, right?"

"Three spoons of milk powder, and a hundred and eighty milliliters of water."

"I know."

"Make sure to clean the bottle."

"Relax. Play to your heart's content; I'm responsible for Shanshan."

Why isn't he this good about everything? Why do I always want to talk with him about Shanshan?

"Change her diapers frequently. Don't let her keep crying."

"I know, I know."

He was obviously getting impatient. I still felt that there was something I hadn't said, but what did I want to say? Just like a talkative woman, I didn't know what I had already said and what I still needed to say. It was just that I felt I hadn't said something, that's all.

I pushed open the door and walked out feeling weak. Such a beautiful Sunday. Where should I go? I don't like going to movies alone. I stood hesitating in the courtyard when I heard Shanshan crying. I thought I should make some milk for her, then go.

"What are you doing back?" he asked. He was squatting on the bed changing Shanshan's diapers with his head turned to look at me.

"I'll make Shanshan's milk, then go," I said.

I watched him shake his head. I didn't say anything as I opened the water bottle to make some milk for Shanshan. I was used to this kind of disdain.

After I had made the milk, I handed the bottle to him.

With bright eyes, he looked at me, smiling. "After Lincoln freed the slaves, do you know what they did?" he said. "They refused to leave their masters' houses because they didn't know how they could make a living if they left."

I couldn't help laughing. I suddenly discovered that I had such a witty husband.

Shanshan's eyes stared at her bottle. I didn't look at her again. I put the arts section of the newspaper in my purse. Maybe I would watch three movies.

I hadn't taken the bus for a long time. In the crowded bus, I felt like I was going to vomit the whole time. This was impossible, because I thought that only country folk who rarely went out threw up on the bus. Of course, I didn't throw up. I didn't even throw up when I was pregnant with Shanshan, but still, the whole time I felt nauseous, like when you're sick.

The bus finally arrived at Ximending. The loud, untrained voices of the Beatles blared from the record store. I couldn't understand them. I also wasn't familiar with Ling Bo, the female star of the movie. The things I knew were already long gone. Now I had to be careful: several times I was almost hit by cars on the street.

Not until I had bought the movie ticket did I discover that my glasses weren't in my purse. Being as nearsighted as I am, without my glasses I simply couldn't watch the movie. I looked up at the advertisements for the coming attractions in the glass display case. A young girl trotted up to me and asked me to buy some of her melon seeds. I had long since lost the patience to eat seeds, but she wouldn't leave me alone and I didn't know how to get rid of her. I gave her the movie ticket, which I now had no use for. Her eyes opened wide and stared at it: she'd certainly never had something like this happen to her before.

From the movie theater I left the throng of people, not knowing where I wanted to go. I didn't dare cross the street by myself. I was afraid of that flowing river of cars. As I followed behind a crowd of people, a poem by Lamartine came to mind: "Perhaps among the crowd there is an unknown soul who knows my deepest heart, who can give me answers." Keeping this poem in mind, I followed the crowd and strolled from one side of the street to the other. I didn't know if I wanted to spend a whole day like this. I wasn't interested in looking around the shopping center. I didn't like the ladies behind the counter asking: "Can I help you? Can I help you?"

But I wouldn't return home. I wasn't willing to be like those slaves. Lincoln wasn't going to come and liberate me. After all, it was such a beautiful Sunday!

Translated by Martin Sulev

西 西

Xi Xi (b. 1938) was born in Shanghai but moved to Hong Kong in 1950. She graduated from the Grantham College of Education and worked as a teacher until the mid-1980s, when she decided to become a full-time writer. A student magazine published her first story, "Maria" (Maliya), in 1965. "A Girl Like Me" (Xiang wo zheyangde yige nüzi) won Taiwan's *Lianhe Bao* (United Daily) prize for fiction in 1982. Xi Xi acknowledges the influence of South American writers such as Mario Vargas Llosa and Gabriel Garcia Marquez on her work. Besides short fiction, Xi Xi has produced three novels about Hong Kong: *My City* (Wo cheng, 1979), *The Beautiful Building* (Meili dasha, 1990) and *Migratory Birds* (Hou niao, 1991).

Bowls

❖

1980

I ran into Ye Qinqin. She was wearing a pair of the blue jeans everyone is wearing nowadays, and a cotton blouse of red and green plaid. Her disheveled hair was like a pile of hay. The last time I'd seen her, she'd looked the same, a pair of blue jeans and a plaid blouse with the same limited colors. The only difference was that it was summertime; it was very hot and her blouse was short-sleeved. Her arms were tanned dark. The last time I met Ye Qinqin was many years ago, I think. I wasn't married and had just found a job. She said she was a school teacher. Now, my daughter Françoise is already several years old. I calculate that Ye Qinqin and I have not seen each other for more than ten years. In the past, when we were in school, we saw each other every day. We would even get together on Sunday to play soccer with a group of people. I don't know who started this. Someone asked why girls shouldn't play soccer, then we began to kick the ball. Really! If Françoise told me tonight that she played soccer at school during the day, I'd have to find a way to stop it. But Françoise certainly wouldn't play soccer. She'd obediently continue to study ballet. In a moment, I have to pick her up from her ballet teacher's place and take her to Miss Yang's to learn piano. I'd better take this opportunity to go to the store. I need to see if they still have that set of green-glazed dinnerware with the soft-colored butterfly pattern. We are going to entertain next week. I can't use the old set, the orchid-blue glazed porcelain. It's really elegant but one of the soup bowls is broken. After a careful search, I could find only a second-class product. The bottom of the bowl didn't have the authentic "Jingde County" trademark[1] but rather that of "Ruanyu." God knows what it means. A set of dark green dinnerware with a soft-colored butterfly pattern should be suitable for the spring season. It will go well with a pink water-lily embroidered tablecloth and the new ivory chopsticks. It would be even more splendid if all the purple, white and red African violets on the balcony bloomed at the same time that day.

---

1. Jingde is well known in China for its porcelain industry.

104

On the way back from the zoological-botanical gardens, it occurred to me that I could buy a bowl. I walked around to look for one. Any grocery should have bowls, and any plain bowl would do. There was a rice bowl I'd used for many years, a thick and heavy one. Although it looked cumbersome, it survived several bangs. Walking by a stall on the street one day, I had suddenly, and without knowing why, decided to buy a goldfish. Holding the elastic that sealed the top of the plastic bag, I went home. I couldn't find anything like a glass fish tank at the time, so I put the goldfish in the rice bowl. I didn't know how to raise goldfish. I gave it many worms to eat, and it didn't take long before it turned upside down. The goldfish's white belly floated on the surface while those worms that hadn't been eaten darted in all directions. I threw away the fish and dared not use that bowl again because I knew I'd think of the belly-up goldfish whenever I ate. I didn't even plant a cactus or anything else in it. In fact, I threw that bowl away. That's why I wanted to buy a new one. It was when I was on my way to buy a bowl that I ran into my classmate from middle school, Yu Meili.

More than half of my middle-school classmates' whereabouts are unknown to me. I only know that Mimi is a clerk in the United Nations. She's not bad; she can speak five languages. The Du sisters emigrated to Canada with their family. Fairy Han got married and moved to Hawaii. Lu Min, who used to be afraid of hearing people with headaches cry, is now a head nurse. As for Ye Qinqin, I only knew that she had been teaching. She and another seven classmates had passed the normal school entrance examination immediately after graduation. The day when everyone returned to the school to receive their graduation diplomas, Lin Zhenhua even wore her normal school uniform onto the stage. Her chin was raised very high—but it was nothing but a normal school. At the Christmas Eve party, David's colleague, Bradley Feng and his wife, Margaret, were there. Margaret Feng was the principal of Ye Qinqin's school. She said Ye Qinqin is no longer teaching. As far as she knew, she did not take another job. This brought a few new topics into our conversation, in addition to flower arranging, diamonds, real estate, stocks. We spent half an hour chatting about women's emancipation, social responsibility, the economic situation and so on. I think that if you don't work, you become a social parasite. Modern women should establish their economic independence, and no one can feel secure without a salary of more than five thousand Hong Kong dollars per month. Anyone who has received professional teacher training and doesn't use it to contribute to society is failing to live up to society's expectations and wasting taxpayers' money. In a society where inflation is severe, anyone who gives up a good job is mentally ill. Those who do not like to work are lazy, irresponsible, antisocial, antihuman, uncooperative, unsociable and selfish.

Today I went to the zoological-botanical gardens to look at some animals and plants. I have been there many times, and always thought it was too small. Today, however, I felt different. I stayed for a long time. Slowly and carefully, I looked at the grass, the flowers, the colorful feathers of a bird. I went to the garden very early in the morning. It was a sunny day. The sun shone warmly on my back, the hot needles of its light acupunctured my bones, woke them from hibernation. I walked slowly in the garden to appreciate the blooming flowers surrounding the pond this spring day. In the rose section, there was a series of odd names: colored box, peace, Chicago. In the ape cage, there were several parrots. One of them hung upside down from the water pipe to drink the water dripping down from the tap. I'd seen a similar photo in a geographic magazine. After all, every parrot has the same capabilities. The jaguar, which I took for a leopard, has spots all over its body. Both of the zoo's two jaguars have square faces. This was the first time I'd seen a cat with that shape of face. The sun continued shining on the grass, making morning and afternoon inseparable. I sat on a bench in the garden, eating a dry, hard piece of bread and reading a book at the same time. I've read many books this year, many more than I've read in many years. I think I am happy. The trees nearby all had their own names. A leaf fell on my head. By following the information provided by its appearance, I found its mother: a Seven-star Maple. It made me raise my head to see the high, far away top. When I looked up at the tree, the sky, I saw clouds flying without any wings.

Translated by Shu-ning Sciban

Frying Pan
❖
1980

The woman said:

He finally went to work, with both eyes red and swollen. Last night, he did not close his eyes at all. Why did the manager of the company all of a sudden summon him, alone, to the office? Why didn't he send for Stationmasters Huang and Li? Aren't they usually together? It must be because of his age. The company knew a long time ago that he'd passed fifty-five. Because he's older than fifty-five, he should be retired. If it weren't for the old manager's understanding, why would a big company like this one have kept on an old worker who is close to sixty? The old manager passed away several years ago; naturally, the present manager has different policies. How will we live in the future? This family has no savings; the burden will fall on our daughter's shoulders. She is a nurse in the small medical clinic. She handles registrations and takes temperatures. Her salary is lower than she'd make in any other profession, even a female textile worker. Inflation is worse and worse every day. Cabbage suddenly is eight dollars per *jin*,[1] and the electricity bill received yesterday contained a two-dollar rate increase. Alas, life is getting harder and harder. Our son is still in school; he has two more years until graduation and we should let him finish. If he doesn't continue, he won't get a good education and it will be hard to find a decent job. What would we do then? Yes, with one less income, we'd have serious problems.

The old man said:

I feel as though a load has been taken off my mind! In the beginning, I was terribly worried; my palms sweated constantly. But the reason the manager asked me to see him today was that the company has a new development. They have installed a radio system to be used for the deployment of all the buses. Considering the years I have served the company and my familiarity with the bus lines and all the company's departments, the manager decided to appoint

---

1. One *jin*, a traditional Chinese measurement for weight, is about a pound, or half a kilogram. A Hong Kong dollar is worth about 12 cents U.S.

me Director of the Radio Office. This really was a surprise. Stationmasters Huang and Li, who are the same rank as I am, both congratulated me. They even said that they wanted to take me out right away to eat and drink to celebrate. Naturally, I was extremely happy. In the afternoon, I went to the office. It is located on the third floor of the company's new building. In more than one thousand square meters of floor space, there is just this new machine and a big chair right in the middle, to be controlled by me alone. The room is quite cool. The building has a central air conditioning system but the third floor has its own that won't be affected by power failures. Because of the machine, a different temperature is maintained in this room than the others. I've tried the machine. There are small red and green lights that go on when certain buttons are pushed. It's not hard to operate. When any special circumstance arises, a button lights up. I pushed one button and heard someone on the line say: "Patrol Car Number One reporting. Number 7396 Bus on Line Six is broken down, currently parked near the end of Milton Avenue. Off." I didn't know what "off" meant. My trainer told me "off" meant one had finished speaking. I then told the patrol car: "Inform Guantang Yard immediately to send for another bus. It will be able to pick up the passengers within fifteen minutes. As well, contact the service department. Tell them to send a tow truck over to tow the broken bus back to Lichee Corner Yard to fix. Off."

The daughter said:

When I took the secondary school entrance exam, I chose to go to a Chinese school. At the time, I thought that because I was Chinese, I should enter a school where Chinese was the dominant language. Could it be my choice was wrong? If not, why has the road been so rugged and rough for me since graduation? I can't even help my father solve his problem today. Since becoming Director of the Radio Office, Father doesn't have to work as hard as before. He doesn't need to be on his feet waving his arms under the burning sun when he deploys the buses, nor does he need to push his way through a packed bus to check tickets when the temperature is 40 degrees Celsius. But there's another problem. He often has to write reports. All reports need to be written in English. This baffles him. One day, he sat in a chair staring blankly for a long time after coming home from the office. I could do nothing to help him. If I had gone to an English school, I'd be able to help him write those reports. I've considered this problem for several nights and I understand something. I think it is not that my English isn't good enough, neither is it that I attended a Chinese school. The main thing may be that I haven't committed myself to studying hard. I remember there were a number of classmates whose English was very good. In the certificate examination, they all achieved high grades in English. Why is it only me whose English is so poor? Why is it that a graduate of a Chinese school is no comparison to a graduate of an English school in English?

Little brother said:

I found a grade one English textbook for the old man. There are four pictures in Lesson One. The first is a man, and the second is a frying pan. The other two are that of a man and a frying pan, and that of a frying pan and a man. I began to teach my old man English. He is serious and studies hard. His pronunciation isn't bad either. He said he wants to learn one lesson a day. He said he must work hard until he can write those reports by himself without asking me to do it. He asked me: "Is it possible?" I replied: "Yes." We sit at the table. When he's reading, I listen to him to check his accuracy. At the same time, I look at the pictures in the book. Sometimes the frying pan is big, bigger than the man, as if it could fry the man. In another picture, the frying pan is small and the man becomes huge, as if the man were going to pick up the pan to fry an egg. Lesson Two in this textbook is about eggs: a hen, an egg; an egg and a hen; a hen and an egg. I think that when I teach my old man Lesson Two, I'll consider the confusing problem of whether the chicken or egg came first. It's very quiet in the house. No one is watching TV. My sister is attending an evening class. She registered herself in a cultural association to study English. Mother has been in the kitchen for a long time. Hmm, it smells delicious! It must be the lotus and red bean soup.

Translated by Shu-ning Sciban

廖輝英

Liao Huiying (b. 1948) graduated from National Taiwan University with a major in Chinese literature but worked in the business world until 1982. In that year she won first prize in the *Zhongguo Shibao* (China Times) short story competition with her autobiographical "Rapeseed" (Youma caizi). Since then, she has been writing full-time. A number of her works published in the 1980s, such as *Road with No Return* (Bugui lu, 1983) and *Blind Spot* (Mangdian, 1986), are regarded in Taiwan as modern classics of women's fiction.

Rapeseed

❖

1982

Father was only twenty-three when Older Brother was born. Mother was young, too, just twenty-one, but had studied at a finishing school in Japan. She had brought a rich dowry to the marriage, twelve gold bars and twelve large boxes of silk cloth and woolens and some first-class furniture. They needed the black sedan and a truck to move it all.

My mother, the youngest of my grandfather's daughters, was known as "Black Kitten." He was the town doctor, and the combination of her beauty and family background brought out the matchmakers in droves; many a young doctor was left crestfallen on the doorstep. So eyebrows were raised when the man she married turned out not to have a medical background nor even to be of the same social class. He was just the son of a teacher in a neighboring town, a graduate of a technical college. It was said the doctor took a fancy to this young man because of his straightforward manner. His simply cut, prematurely gray hair made him seem more honest and reliable than my mother's other suitors, young doctors with their Western clothes and fancy French haircuts.

Then, just one year after the wedding, she gave birth to a son. This pleased my grandfather so much that he couldn't stop grinning. He had taken six concubines in his life but had never been able to produce a son of his own. Older Brother's birth also disappointed envious neighbors who had hoped the beautiful Black Kitten's marriage would fail.

I don't know how long those happy days continued. My earliest memories are of hiding in corners with Older Brother, watching Father furiously fling objects about while Mother, her hair streaming, called down laments from heaven. After particularly big fights, Mother often left home. Older Brother and I, who by this time did not cry easily and had learned to watch the adults closely, would be packed off to Auntie Fu's. A few days later, white-haired old Grandfather would bring Mother back, her face still filled with anger and resentment. Father, always sparing with words, would stand speechless before silent Grandfather. The two men would sit face-to-face by the door, wordless as the sun went down. Grandfather, a rich and influential man who'd once been able to make water freeze with a single glance, looked old and tired as the

112

sunlight illuminated his overlapping wrinkles. His silence was taken by his son-in-law not as a reproach but as a plea to treat his spoiled daughter better. But the tight-lipped young man no longer was the nervous youth who once had embarrassed himself by sitting on the commode while being sized up before the marriage.

I remember once pulling at my mother's skirt as we walked slowly with Grandfather back to his black car, parked at the entrance to the village. He turned to his daughter and said, "Kitten, a woman's fate is like a rapeseed. A father can only try to make the best selection but after all that searching we ended up with one like him. My love has been harmful to you but this is your destiny. Your old father is over seventy and can look out for you only for a few more years. You must endure everything. Your husband is not like your father; he will not spoil you as your father did."

When we returned to the house, Papa already had left. Mama held me in her arms and, between sobs, told Older Brother, "Silly boy, you think Mama has no place to go? Mama has one foot inside the door and one foot outside but because of you children she can't take a step."

This type of scene, Mama and the children crying together, was repeated many times when we were young. When we saw Mama cry, we were filled with panic and fear and joined in her wailing. How could we children understand this woman, standing in a corridor at dusk, holding her two children and sobbing?

Two years after Younger Brother was born, our ailing old grandfather finally died. Mama practically crawled back to her father's house all the way from the bus station. On the day of the funeral, Father took us three children but mingled distractedly among the relatives watching Mother cry like there was no tomorrow. I was used to her crying by then, but this wasn't the same as when she and Papa fought. This broken-hearted wailing arose from the loss of the only person under heaven she could rely on; even grandfather's widows had to comfort her.

Papa wore the mourning attire of a son-in-law but, compared to Mother, who was sprawled on the floor, he was unmoved. And he was impatient with us. When Younger Brother wouldn't stop crying, Father went so far as to curse him with some choice three-character phrases. That whole day I timidly followed him around; when he walked fast, I didn't dare reach out to grab his pant leg to slow him down. Later, it seemed to me that in those days Father didn't really belong to us. He only belonged to himself. He was trying to live the good life of a bachelor, which he missed. Now he was the father of three children, something he seemed to forget.

Still, he did pay attention to us sometimes. During that time when he was rushing about and rarely at home, one day he unexpectedly brought me a big doll with fluttering eyes. When he pulled out that golden-haired doll and called me to come to him, I stood at a distance, watching this unfamiliar man in a state of half-wonder, half-fear. His face must have been gentle, though. Otherwise, after so many years, how could I still remember how he patiently coaxed his frightened young daughter to accept his generous present in that old tile-roofed house in the country?

When I was six, I attended a free kindergarten attached to the factory where Father worked. Younger Brother went along with me but I attended the upper class and he the lower. At home, I helped Mama wash rice, wipe the tatami mats and play with nasty Younger Brother. Sometimes Mother would look up and say, "Ah-hui is a good girl. Girls from hard-up families are more sensible. Only you help your unlucky mother. Your Older Brother is a boy; all he knows how to do is play all day. He's not aware of his mother's suffering."

To tell the truth, I envied Older Brother. I think he certainly had a happier childhood. At least he was able to play outside all day with his friends—all types of games. He had no patience with crybaby Younger Brother; when Younger Brother cried, Older Brother just gave him a swat, so Mama never asked him to look after Younger Brother. Even luckier for him, he usually wasn't around when Mama and Papa went at it. He would be out playing or sleeping so soundly that nothing could wake him. I was the timid one. I simply couldn't abandon Mama and Younger Brother and go play in the orchard and paddy fields like the other kids as if I hadn't a care in the world.

Older Brother seemed to have no fear of Papa. Really, it was as if they lived in their own private country. When Papa came home, he often gave Older Brother magazines like *Oriental Youth* and *School Chums*. Because he could lend these out, the other children in the village sucked up to him and he became king of the village kids. One time when Mama hit him, he cried and said, "Okay, so you hit me. I'm going to tell Papa and he'll slug you!"

This only made Mother even angrier. She hit him harder, cursing him between breaths. "You disrespectful boy! You'll die young! I carried you for 10 months and gave birth to you but you say you'll get your shameless father to come and hit me! I'll beat you to death first!" She hit him and hit him, heaving great sobs between blows.

When I was seven, I went barefoot to the only elementary school in the village. I wasn't the only barefoot child in the class so I didn't feel singled out. But after one term I was elected class president and felt embarrassed to stand in the first rank with my two shiny feet sticking out. Besides, all the other barefoot children in the class came from farming families. I told Mother, "Teacher says Papa is a mechanical engineer and that our family isn't poor. She says he should buy me a pair of shoes. She also says that crossing the irrigation ditches barefoot is dangerous because there are water snakes and wild plants that can hurt a person."

Mother said nothing but that evening after supper, as soon as she had put my one-year-old sister to bed, she picked up a pencil and told me to put my foot on a piece of cardboard so she could trace it. Later she picked up a very small package wrapped in purple cloth and told me, "Ah-hui, Mama is going to Taizhong. You sleep now; when Mama returns, she will give you a pair of cotton shoes."

Pointing to the purple cloth, I asked, "What's that?"

"Something your Grandfather gave Mama. Mama is going to sell it to buy you shoes."

That evening, struggling to keep my eyes open, I lay on my pillow listening attentively for the bus, half believing, half doubting she would return with the shoes. Finally, despite my eagerness, I fell into a fitful sleep.

When I woke the next day, a pair of crimson cotton shoes was beside my pillow. I put them on proudly and walked back and forth on the tatami mats. Even better, breakfast that morning wasn't the usual rice porridge but a piece of red-bean-paste bread from Yifu Tang's. I ate it piece by small piece, peeling off the outer layers until only the small piece of red bean paste at the center was left, which I ate almost reluctantly.

After that, Mother often opened her trunk to take something out, and went to Taizhong in the evening. The next day we would eat a piece of red-bean bread, and the days after that a succession of tasty dishes would appear on the table. At these times, Mother always took the opportunity to lecture me: "Ah-hui, you are a girl. In the future, you will manage a household. Mama will give you some advice: Go to the market at midday, when the merchants want to close up, and you can get things cheap. In the future, if fate is good to you, so be it. But if fate is unkind, then you'll have to take care of yourself."

Gradually, Papa began coming home more often but he still went regularly to Taizhong after tidying up. And he still yelled crudely at Mama at the top of his voice in our small two-room apartment. They had no patience with each other, as though it were some unimaginable luxury to speak quietly and softly together. They had been raising the roof for so long by this time that it became hard to tell whether they really were quarreling or not. Over and over again, the same scene was repeated in front of our eyes: Father's angry face and Mother's sharp curses, and later him throwing her to the floor and punching and kicking her.

This was how the days dragged by. One day after Mama had looked in Papa's pay envelope, she threw it on the tatami, cursing in a loud voice, "You shameless four-legged beast! Besides keeping that disgusting woman, what else do you do? If these four children had to rely on you, they would have starved to death long ago. Out of a salary of more than a thousand *kuai*, there's just two hundred left. How am I supposed to raise these four children?! When you are with your stinking cheap woman, don't you think of your own children, who are about to die of starvation? What a disgrace. Providing for another man's wife! Are her little bastards yours? Don't tell me that these four aren't yours!"

They cursed each other. I crouched in a corner with Younger Brother and Younger Sister. Suddenly Papa took a meat cleaver and threw it at Mama; the blade nicked her ankle. For a moment, time stood still. The fresh red blood oozed out like poisonous red snakes crawling down Mama's white foot. Only then did I cry out in fear, followed by my brother and sister, who began to wail. Papa looked at the three of us crying children before angrily shuffling out of the room in his wooden clogs. Mama didn't cry but just gathered up some cigarette butts, broke them open and used the tobacco to stop the bleeding.

That night, I felt very cold, dreaming continuously of Mama's body covered with blood. I cried out that I would avenge her.

When I was promoted to the second grade, I was still the top student in the class and designated a "model pupil." But my classmate Ah-chuan, who lived in my village, told our classmates, "Li Renhui's father is a bad man. He's the lover of a woman in our village. How can she be a model student?"

I took off the round badge of a model student and hid it in my school bag. I didn't wear it again that term and never again spoke with Ah-chuan. Every day I still wore my crimson cotton shoes, now with gaping holes at the toes, and crossed the paddy swinging a rice stalk on the way to school. But, oh, how I wished I could leave, leave this place with its corrupt women and a schoolmate who talked behind my back. Surely there was a place where no one knew about Papa's affairs. That was where I wanted to take Mama.

One night I was roused from sleep by strange sounds. I opened my eyes and heard the frightening noise of a violent storm battering the roof tiles and the trees outside the bamboo fence. Beside me, my two brothers and sister slept peacefully. In the darkness, I heard Mama calling me softly. I crawled over my brothers and sister and lay beside her. With a strained voice she said, "Ah-hui, the baby in Mama's belly is dead. I can't stop bleeding. Go get Auntie Chen and Auntie Fu to come and help. Do you think you can do it? I wanted to tell your Older Brother but he's fast asleep and I can't wake him."

Mama's face was like ice. She asked me to get a packet of toilet paper. I slipped out of the bed but suddenly, fearing Mama was going to die, I said in a loud voice, "Mama, you must not die! I'll get them! You must wait for me!"

I pulled on a raincoat and went out barefoot. The eucalyptus trees around the village were swaying, bending forward and backward like cackling witches. When I came to the grain-drying yard, I ignored Ah-chuan's stories that it was haunted and raced across it. But when I tripped and fell, I felt there were ghosts chasing me, so I scrambled to my feet and ran. The rain hit my eyes; it hurt so much I couldn't keep them open. I staggered all the way to the Fu family's house and pounded on the door for all I was worth. Auntie Fu told me to go to the Chens and ask Auntie Chen to go back with me while she herself went to get a doctor.

So I ran through the other half of the village. At the Chens', I ran right into their bamboo fence, setting off their big guard dog in its cage. When Auntie

Chen had heard me out, she picked up a flashlight, wrapped herself in her raincoat and followed me back into the rain.

"You poor child. Your dad's not at home?"

I shook my head. She looked at me and shook her head, too. Walking beside her, I suddenly felt the strength drain out of my body and almost couldn't make it home.

After the doctor had left and Mama had at last fallen into a deep sleep, Auntie Chen said, "Poor soul, what misfortune to be married to such a husband. If it hadn't been for this eight-year-old girl, her life would have ended today. I wonder what shenanigans that shameless husband is up to now."

I knelt beside Mama and stroked her face, wanting to make sure she was only sleeping. Auntie Fu pulled my hand away. "Ah-hui, your mother is all right. You go to sleep. Auntie is here to look over her. You can relax."

Mama's face looked so white that I refused to go to the inner room and sleep, but stubbornly lay down beside her, watching her intently. It wasn't long before I, too, was sleeping.

That year on New Year's Eve, the dough for the New Year's cake was already made—Mama was annoyed that it hadn't risen enough, indicating another year of bad luck—and now she was sharpening a cleaver to kill the big rooster we had raised for more than a year just for this occasion. Right then, four or five big guys came to the door and Papa looked queasy when they summoned him. They didn't come inside but sat by the door. Nor did they drink the tea Mama brewed for them, or pay attention to her small talk. They just peppered Papa with questions: "You are an educated man, how can you do such a vile thing?" "Another man's wife, how do you dare to sleep with her? Have you no moral principles?" "For this kind of behavior, you should be crippled, have your Achilles' tendon cut."

Papa bowed his head beneath their verbal barrage while Mother, red-eyed and muttering, sank into a chair. This racket went on all morning. I sat bored in the backyard, watching the big rooster. He was standing proudly on his two strong legs and shook his neck as he pecked at a smaller chicken. *Ai!* Today he probably wouldn't be killed after all, and Mama wouldn't be able to give me a fat wing to eat. With regret, I turned my attention to a group of young turkeys that probably wouldn't be ready for butchering until mid-summer. *Ai!* It was New Year's Eve but it looked like we wouldn't be getting new clothes and shoes, not even eating chicken and fried rice noodles. When were those rude men going to leave?

I could hear beastly Younger Brother begin to sob but I was too hungry to bother with him. Besides, I felt like crying myself so I stayed put in the backyard. He really began to wail, so Older Brother clapped a hand over his mouth. This only made him scream all the louder, so Older Brother hauled off and whacked him. Now Younger Brother lost control of himself completely and filled the air with his sobs. This set off Younger Sister, who had been lying quietly up to then.

Mama came out, smacked Older Brother and snarled, "Ah-hui, are you dead?"

I had no choice but to climb up on the tatami and pick up Younger Sister. At the same time, I snapped at Younger Brother, "Are you dead Ah-xin?"

Ai! You call this a New Year's celebration?

During this commotion, the men stood up and their leader said, "This is a shameful affair. Nothing less than two thousand *kuai* will get the bad taste out of our mouths. If your children didn't need to celebrate New Year's we wouldn't be so easy on you. This shameful affair must be resolved with a certain delicacy. Tonight at seven o'clock we'll be waiting for you at my place. If you're late, it will be ugly."

Kneeling by the front door, Father and Mother watched them swagger off. Mama then turned and went into the house and walked directly to the kitchen, where she took the fresh dough for the New Year's cake and cut it slice by slice. Papa stood by the door for a while before shuffling after her into the kitchen.

"The money for tonight, we have to think of a way to get it," he said.

When Mama heard this, the words poured out: "Have to get it?!" she yelled. "This dirty business was your doing. End it yourself! You slept with the woman; you think of a way to come up with the hush money. This is only because of your shameless lust. Is the fact that your children are starving to death of no importance? Are you really a man at all? You!"

Once Mama got started cursing him, nothing could stop her. She was cursing and crying at the same time. She took a long time to slice the cake but I hadn't seen her put it in the pan. The oven's air hole was still stuffed with cloth; if the cloth wasn't removed quickly, the fire wouldn't be hot enough to cook the cake. But she was so angry I didn't dare say a word to remind her.

At last, however, the cake was cooked. Mama then went to her leather trunk and spent a long time sorting through it. Red-eyed, she wrapped up a large bundle of things with a piece of cloth. Papa then brought around his new 20-inch Philips bicycle and stood by the door waiting for Mama. To Older Brother and me, Mama said, "Ah-jiang, Ah-hui, Mama is going out to sell some things and pawn the bicycle to pay those people. You older two look after the little ones. If you're hungry, have some cake. When Mama comes back, she'll cook something to eat. Behave yourselves, now. Do you hear?"

As I watched them go, I wanted to ask Mama whether we were still going to kill the rooster but I didn't dare open my mouth. Instead, I asked Older Brother, "Pawn, what does that mean?"

"Stupid! It means to sell something for money. Don't you understand anything?"

Mama and Papa didn't come back until late in the evening. Naturally, the rooster hadn't been killed. And because we didn't have the usual ceremony, there were no good things to eat. We just had some salted gruel that Mama made. Of course, the rooster could not escape his fate forever; sooner or later he would be slaughtered. With this shred of hope to console my disappointment over missing out on any New Year's money, I fell asleep.

After school started, Mama arranged a transfer for Older Brother and me. We were leaving this place! I was so happy that I ignored my earlier vow and ran up to Ah-chuan and announced to his face, "We're moving to Taibei!"

When I saw his startled, idiotic look, I triumphantly ran away. What a wonderful thing! And he was just a smelly boy who liked to badmouth others.

In Taibei, we rented a house from Aunt Cuihang. Mama kept the turkeys and the chickens near the water pump. She also bought some American broilers. It was said these grew fast and would be ready to lay eggs in just four months. Soon, it seemed, we would be eating these luxurious American eggs without having to pay!

Papa bought a second-hand bike that he rode to and from work every day. He came home early now. An easel was set up in the parlor. When he had the time, he would stand there in his shorts, painting. When our neighbors saw these paintings, they often came to ask for them, which made him paint all the more. Although Mama didn't tell him not to paint, she often would sneer and say, "What use is that? It brings in no food or money." When she was feeling particularly hard done by, she'd say, "Other people's husbands think of extra ways to feed their families and make their wives and children happy. But your old Dad, hah! He just brings home his regular pay. It's never enough."

Despite this sniping, I was happy to see Papa at home more often. Besides, he and Mama weren't fighting like they used to. He still rarely spoke to me but I think this was because he really didn't know how. Ever since I was little, I seemed to see him from a distance. But when he took Younger Brother by the hand and, carrying Younger Sister, went to buy blood pudding, he never forgot to bring a piece for Older Brother and me.

Older Brother and I both joined the elementary school across the bridge. It was already the middle of term. He was in grade five; I was in grade three. In those days, cramming began as early as grade three. The five or six students who weren't planning to attend high school helped the teacher with odd jobs. But because the rest of us would be taking the city-wide examinations, we had no choice but to participate in the cram sessions, especially since that was the only time certain important lessons were taught.

After transferring, I discovered that teachers in Taibei based their assignments on supplementary reference books. In the country, we'd never heard of them. One reference book cost more than 10 *kuai* and we couldn't afford to buy all those we needed. Because Older Brother was in a higher grade and closer to taking the city-wide exams, he needed several each term. So

Mama decided to concentrate on buying the ones he needed. The result was that for the next three or four weeks the teacher lashed my palms with a thick rattan strap every day because I hadn't done my homework. He probably thought this rural kid was a hopeless case.

At the end of the month, the teacher announced, "Cramming fees are due tomorrow." The next day, I saw more than 60 of my classmates line up one by one to pay. The cramming fees were 30 *kuai* a month, although the rich kids paid one or two hundred. Blushing with shame, I sat in my seat watching the grand procession go forward. Later, I braced myself for the teacher's loud announcement of the names of the students who hadn't paid. Almost every day for the next two weeks the teachers called out the names until mine was the only one left. When I couldn't take it any more, I told Mama, "I don't want any more tutoring."

"But aren't many lessons taught only in the cram sessions?"

I nodded and said, "I'm not certain I want to take the junior high exams."

"Do you want the kind of life your Mama has?" Her face darkened as she scolded me. "A woman without skills will always have to depend on a man to put food on the table. If she finds a reliable husband, that's all to the good. But if she marries an irresponsible layabout, what's she going to eat? Sand? Ah! Your Mama isn't without schooling, you know. I even studied in Japan for a few years. I'd even say my youth was happy. But then I weighed myself down with a husband and children. I can't go out and work. This half of my life can't be compared with other people's."

"But," I said haltingly, fingering my shirt, "I haven't paid the cramming fees. The teacher calls my name every day. Everyone turns and looks at me like I'm a freak."

"In a couple of days Mama will be able to give you 20 *kuai* to pay."

"Everyone else pays at least 30 *kuai*!"

"Be happy we can pay anything. Ten *kuai* less is neither here nor there. We're poor, eh?"

Every month we scraped together the cramming fees in this long drawn-out manner. Often, I had just completed the last month's payment when my classmates began paying the next month's. The sense of shame I felt over the teacher constantly announcing my name and the sniggering glances of my classmates was eased by being among the best in each monthly examination.

A year later, Older Brother fell 1.5 marks short and had to accept his second choice of schools. Although this was a little disappointing, Mama still was quite happy. He was her first born, a child from the country who, despite having no contact with supplementary reference books or cramming until the second term of his fifth year, had squeezed through the narrow gates of a provincial high school. Even our emotionally detached Father seemed happy. But because Mama had to get together more than 200 *kuai* for school fees plus tens more for uniforms, she was really squeezed. Like an ostrich, Papa hid from the matter. Even when Mama cursed him for the thousandth time, calling him "useless" as she raged about the house, he just stayed in his corner, painting his pictures.

Every morning during these years, Mama would go out in the misty light of dawn to start a fire. She would roll up two or three sheets from our old exercise books and pile on some wood shavings and briquettes. When we got up, there would be two bowls of rice waiting for us. In Older Brother's bowl, there would be two eggs; in mine, just one.

Mama's explanation for this difference was that because Older Brother was a growing boy, he needed to eat more rice and the extra egg.

One day I had eaten all the mixed-up egg and rice but there were two mouthfuls of plain rice left over that I refused to eat. Mama scolded me, "What a waste! Ah-hui, do you know how much a *jin*[1] of rice costs?"

"Why can't I have two eggs?" I muttered. "It's me who cleans out the chicken droppings every night. Dear brother never has to do it."

Mama was taken aback. After a goodly pause she said, "What are you fussing about? A woman's fate is like a rapeseed. It grows where it falls. The good fortune of an unmarried woman hardly matters. Mama is fair to you. We are poor but let you go to school. In another family, you'd have been sent out as a factory worker long ago. Your brother has to continue the Li family line. So what are you fussing about? You don't even know what name you'll end up with!"

Mama gradually lowered her voice, collected the dishes and went back inside. After that, I learned to eat my rice mixed with one egg quietly and never again complained about the many chores I had to do after my cramming sessions, even though Older Brother could spend all day goofing off, swimming, playing basketball—and he never had to do the dishes.

In the two years before the city-wide exams, there was a lot of homework. I dutifully did my work at school but at home only completed compulsory assignments and no longer tore into the books. When I thought of how the whole household had fallen into crisis over Older Brother's school registration fee, and how Mama had struggled to make up the difference out of the housekeeping expenses, I decided that if I didn't pass I wouldn't continue with school.

In grade six, I entered the school-wide fine arts competition and won first prize, a box of twenty-four watercolors and two brushes. I returned home triumphantly to show off my prize but Mama, who was doing the dishes, just rolled her eyes and said harshly, "You think that's really something, eh? You want to be like your useless Papa; paint, paint, paint. Will your painting

---

1. A *jin* is half a kilogram.

produce any money? You'd better put away those useless things before it's too late."

I don't think Mama had ever been so scornful of me. So although my prize was something we never could have afforded, I lost interest in it. And later when I entered composition or poster competitions, I never mentioned them at home. When I brought home my report cards, Mama read them and affixed her seal without asking why I had slipped back to second in the class or praising me for being first. What did it matter whether I studied hard or not? Nobody cared anyway. So I didn't bother with the cramming sessions any more, although I remained among the top three in the class.

The day the results of the city-wide exams for junior high school were announced, Mother shook me out of my afternoon nap. "Have you died in your sleep? The radio has been announcing the results all afternoon. If you didn't make the grade, I doubt you'd still be able to sleep as soundly as a pig!"

I got up and stood on the next door neighbor's porch to listen to the broadcast. They still were reading the boys' names and I stood there so long I thought my legs would break. I didn't dare go home but wondered how long I'd have to wait. While I was hesitating, I could see Papa coming home on his bicycle. Even before he reached the house he called out happily, "You passed! You passed!"

Mama came out and said sharply, "We had no doubt she passed. The question is, which school?"

"Her first choice! I knew it would be her first choice!" Papa parked his bike. His face glowing, he gestured for me to come to him. "The newspaper was pasted up. You didn't need to keep listening."

I was in my glory. Father, who never seemed to have taken much interest in my affairs, repeatedly told other people, "She was well above the admission mark, got 25 for composition, really high!"

I couldn't tell whether Mama was happy. She never said anything to anyone and kept to her usual busy routine. When the time for my household chores rolled around, I wasn't able to escape them just because of my high marks.

It was around this time that Papa got some work doing mechanical drawings. He didn't bother to negotiate a fair price, and Mama berated him for not knowing how to haggle. He replied earnestly, "It won't happen, won't happen. They won't cheat us." But when he received payment for his long nights of work, Papa could only stare at the meager sum. After that, he wasn't eager to take any more such work.

When it came time to register for school, Papa took a day off so he could take me on his bicycle. We spent all morning in long queues in the auditorium, going from one desk to another. I don't know what came over Papa but he seemed unable to stand quietly. Instead, he chatted eagerly with the other parents, asking them about their children's marks and where they'd attended elementary school. Whenever he found out that someone had lower marks than me, he seemed especially pleased and said to me, "You see, several points lower than you, nearly had to take their second choice!" When I was being measured for a school uniform, he couldn't keep his mouth shut, repeatedly saying, "In all Taibei, only your school has this type of uniform."

At lunch that day, Papa took me for a bowl of beef noodles and then gave me five *kuai*. He urged me not to tell Mother about it. "We'll just say it was part of the registration fees."

Although I felt guilty about cheating thrifty Mama, I knew Father had always been too hard up to show any concern for me. So I felt I had to keep silent.

After school started, Papa was more enthusiastic about my homework than I was. Every time he saw me opening my English textbook, he would say with great zest, "Come on, Papa will help you." He would take the book and, forgetting about me altogether, read on and on in a Japanese accent until Mama began cursing him, "Crazy! How can the girl study with you making that racket. Don't you know she has an exam tomorrow morning?"

During these junior high school years, Papa enthusiastically helped me with my homework. He often said, "Ah-hui is like me" or "Ah-hui has beautiful calligraphy just like me." It seemed that anything good about me came from him. Mama always mercilessly poured cold water on him, "Like you? Then there's no hope for her!"

But Papa must have been very content in those years. He often slipped me small change and then told me not to tell anyone. Many times I saw him hide money clumsily in a shoe. I could tell Mama would find it and she did. After that he began hiding money all over the house in places he thought were safe. But perhaps because he had little time and was nervous or flustered when he hid the money, or had too many hiding places, whenever he wanted to retrieve it he'd look all over the place unsuccessfully. He would end up covered in sweat and, risking Mama's caustic scorn, have to ask her. The result was either a nasty quarrel or we'd all end up looking for the money. In the end, his private savings would be expropriated. Although I knew he kept money on hand to buy a pack of cigarettes or give us kids some change, I couldn't bear to tell Mama. Perhaps because he was so much like a careless child, and so transparent, I felt it was pointless to plot against him.

Although he usually had some petty cash, school registration time usually found him in straitened circumstances. Mama, though, would direct us to him whenever we wanted money. He'd usually say, "Ask your Mother."

"Mama told us to ask you."

"Where will I get it? I give my entire salary to her. I don't know how to make gold!"

If we hammered away at him he would flare with some of the old anger, "No money? Quit school!"

This happened over and over again. I felt that Father was like a caged beast who couldn't find a way out. He was an unconventional person, suited only to lead a carefree life by himself. He was incapable of assuming the burdens of the head of the household. Their problems were the same: He had married too young, and Mama had seen her dreams die too early. They each had retreated into their own private world and neither knew how to deal with the crude realities of married life.

The days passed by. I half accepted my fate, and half raged against it. Mama got pregnant again at 37 with my youngest brother. Every day I saw the silhouette of her protruding belly waddling around the house as she bitterly went about her chores, squatting by the faucet doing laundry or taking care of this or that. Before the baby was born, I took my piggy bank, which contained more than two years' savings, from its hiding spot under my bed and silently gave it to Mama. She took a rusty hatchet and handed it to me, saying, "It's your money. You break it."

Even before she finished speaking, she started to cry. With one stroke I smashed open the bank and the coins cascaded over the floor. My dream of going on the cross-island hike was smashed with it. Later, mother and daughter sat facing each other in a dark corner of the kitchen, silently piling up the coins, one *jiao*, two *jiao* . . .

Why was life like that?

After I graduated from junior high, I passed the entrance exams for both senior high and the normal school for girls. Mama pressed me to attend the girls' normal school: "It's free, and besides, why do girls need such highfalutin talents. You don't want to be an old maid. A reliable job is all you need."

I don't know whether it was because this was the first time I resisted Mama's will, or because that year Father went to work at a high-paying job in the Philippines, but Mother unexpectedly gave her consent for me to continue in senior high.

Those years, unlike the difficult past, seemed to slip by smoothly and quickly. Working in a distant country, Father was able to set aside enough of his salary to live contentedly again as a single man. With my parents separated by oceans and mountains, the sharp conflicts of the past were becalmed. Each week he sent back surprising letters full of sentiment and solicitude, making careful references to each family member. Sometimes, he would entrust someone from that distant country to bring each of us not entirely practical gifts. Or, using the same hands that had beaten us and held us, he would carefully wrap parcels of clothes he had bought in the sizes he recalled us as being, and shipped them by air.

Mama still nattered sometimes about his past transgressions but looked forward to his letters and packages, half-complaining but unable to resist a smile. Who could say this wasn't a good life? At last we had money to buy a few frills and Mama no longer had to wrack her brains over basic items.

But when I passed the college entrance exam, for which Mama had prayed and lit incense morning and night, she looked at my results with a curled lip and muttered, "Fat grows on the dog rather than the pig."

That certainly deflated me. But then she seemed to forget her own words and busily laid out fresh flowers and fruit on the family altar and told me to kneel before the Buddha and kowtow twelve times. In the smoke from the incense, Mama's kindly, peaceful face looked down on me just like Guanyin, the Goddess of Mercy, in the family shrine.

I continued to muddle through life, neither struggling to achieve nor to avoid anything. Like other college students, I tutored children and started to write articles to make a few *kuai*. In those four not very exciting years in college, I also had to take on the almost maternal responsibilities of an older sister and care for a procession of younger siblings. Mother—I'm not sure when—began going to temple regularly, became a vegetarian and semi-retired as a housewife. So all the children's mundane affairs became my responsibility.

Father's glorious years came to an end. After he returned home, he was too old to get a regular job. Although he was able to get some work because of his experience and technical skill, I think he found it unsatisfying. He became moody and unpredictable. Sometimes when he changed buses on the way home after work, he would go to the Buddhist temple and buy vegetarian noodles for Mama and then, with a great show of concern, press her to eat them while they were still hot. But at other times, he would fly into a rage because Mama had gone to the temple herself to eat. He got so angry that he'd threaten to smash all the idols in the family shrine. Sometimes, he would patiently explain each sentence so Mama could follow foreign or Mandarin language programs on the TV. But at other times, he would ridicule her for not knowing how to get around on the bus or how to speak even simple Mandarin. As for Mama, after so many bitter years her tongue was like an axe splitting firewood, each blow cutting all the way through. Again and again, she dredged up Father's past misdeeds. Father resented the fact that Mama was unable to get work outside the home and share his financial burden. Here they were: one a bent-over old man with gray hair and loose teeth; the other an old woman with white hair and failing eyesight who'd run a household on a shoestring for thirty years. Their arguments were still as heated and as frequent as when they were a young couple. After thirty years of living together and tormenting each other, they still hadn't learned about peaceful co-existence. Hadn't we all paid some price for this? All those hurts; what possibly could compensate for them?

In those years, Older Brother was unwilling to follow Father's example of looking for a salaried job. Instead, he tried to set up his own business from scratch, an endeavor that sucked him dry and left him no time for the family. So the responsibility automatically fell on to my shoulders. You could say I was lucky, as well as having been driven by a stubborn desire to help the family, but I made quite a lot of money through my hard work and moonlighting, and our home suddenly looked a lot different.

But my character also changed; I was more anxious. Sometimes I felt overwhelmed by the business world. My old life, drifting along with fate, seemed so far away.

Mother also had changed. Perhaps she was just reverting to her pre-marriage character, or maybe she wanted something in return for thirty sour years, but she abruptly became demanding and difficult to please. She even changed the way she dressed. In the past, when caring for her children, she had been unkempt and disheveled, going years without buying a new outfit. Once she even was mistaken for a scullery maid. Now when I went shopping with her, she selected only imported Swiss or Japanese material. Whatever clothes I bought for my own work were too ordinary for her. After a few of these shopping sprees, I suddenly found myself on the list of favored customers. Every time new material arrived, my office phone would ring. I did what I could, always thinking that I had lots of energy and would never be short of money. Besides, I really felt Mama had put up with a lot over the years. I couldn't give back those thirty years to her, so how could I be stingy? Season after season I took along big wads of cash and paid for her purchases.

Mama wasn't able to do the family shopping, so besides buying her items, I also had to estimate Father's size and purchase his shirts, pants, sweaters and undershirts. Mama now considered herself beyond such mundane concerns, although she never was able to rise above such earthly emotions as love and hate. She had long ago relinquished her control over many minor but practical matters. Whenever I bought an outfit for myself, I bought one for Younger Sister, too. I became a real little housewife, not only looking after food, clothes, transportation and living expenses, but also had my younger brothers and sisters rushing off here and there for various lessons after school. I was afraid they would turn out like me, dull, cautious and good only at school work. I thought they should develop many different skills in order to secure a worry-free future. Now that I think of it, my fears were just like Mama's. It's no surprise I devoted myself to making as much money as possible.

As for Mama, I don't know whether poverty had instilled in her a fear of destitute old age, but she constantly complained about how hard up she was. She even took to citing other families we knew as examples, embellishing her descriptions of how able and filial their children were. Clearly, I didn't measure up.

A few years ago, I had a serious operation and was bedridden for forty days. Friends took care of the medical expenses but I realized then how frightening it was not to have any savings. So, without telling Mother, I joined a private loan association organized by some colleagues at the company. She suspected something, however, and interrogated me in a thousand and one little ways. She wasn't at all happy about my secret stash but her own secret savings couldn't have been anything less than several hundred thousand *kuai*. She didn't keep it in a bank but locked up in the depths of her wardrobe. Money came first with her. If anyone other than her beloved oldest son asked for some, she'd let fly with a stream of curses. In the end, she usually opened her miserly hand but always gave less than what was asked. She'd even throw the money to a far corner of the room where the borrower, teeth gritted, had to pick it up.

Her temper worsened even as our family's fortunes improved. Every day, one of us, old or young, would be cast into the outer darkness. She would go from room to room hurling abuse in her shrill voice—really, it was quite unreasonable behavior. The young ones would argue back after just a few words, provoking Mother into loud lamentations about her bitter fate while tears rolled down her face and her nose ran. If just one of us defied her, she would rhyme off everything each family member had done to her over the years. She went through us one by one—it could go on for days. I came to dread these endless diatribes so I tried to stop anyone from crossing her and learned not to rise to her bait. My brothers and sisters accused me of indulging her and mocked my "stupid filial piety." They said I was making them look bad by comparison. But after all that had happened in the past, how could we not obey her now? We owed her that much.

During those ten years, she disapproved of all my boyfriends. Sometimes she would be rude to them on the phone; sometimes she would keep them waiting outside in the rain. On the rare occasions when I came home late, she wouldn't let anyone open the door for me, forcing me to stand in the pitch-black alley listening to her unbearable curses rain down from her fourth-floor apartment—and I was an adult in my twenties!

Surely she still loved me? When the others disobeyed her, she'd suddenly remember that it was only this daughter who understood her silent pain. Although I didn't eat at home much any more, whenever she went to the market she would never forget to buy kidneys for me. Many evenings when I was worn out from work and ready to drop off, she would come into my room and chatter about this and that. Before my drowsy eyes, I sometimes saw that same loving face like the Goddess of Mercy, the one who looked down on me as I lit the incense and kowtowed after passing my college entrance examinations.

I had no plans for marriage. This wasn't because I was respecting her wishes; there wasn't anyone I was that interested in. And I was too tired. I just wanted to hide somewhere where there was no quarreling or hatred, and where I didn't have to sweat blood to get ahead. Mother continually cited the many examples of failed marriages among our friends and relatives as a warning to me, especially her and Father, who had been like fire and water. "Remaining single isn't necessarily a misfortune. A girl's fate is like a rapeseed. Fall into a bad marriage and you can't escape. This has been your mother's fate. Look at you now. You dress nicely every day to go off to the office and you don't have to wait on anyone in the evening. Isn't this a good life? Why would you want to marry?"

For more than thirty years, Mama's spirit had been chained in a dark and fearful place. Now that her life had entered dusk, she'd become a devout Buddhist in the hope that life would treat her better. But she remained dissatisfied. My brothers' and sisters' careers, their friends, their marriages; all these seemed a betrayal of Mother's wishes. What was most unbearable to her was that not one of her three sons could stand the atmosphere at home and moved out. Who would continue the family line? Who would burn incense for the ancestors? As far as she was concerned, a daughter couldn't do these things; only a son could keep the Li family incense burning. Marriage became something she abhorred.

Unfortunately, this was precisely the time I decided to get married. Whether Mama simply was weary or saw that I was unyielding, she did not object strenuously. In fact, when she feebly gave her consent, I could hardly stand it. After the final decision was made, she told me over and over, "For better or worse, it's your life. You chose it yourself."

The wedding ceremony was arranged quickly and with few complications. But when Mama found out from her horoscope that our wedding day was inauspicious for her, she decided she could not see me off personally. She was genuinely regretful: "The Goddess of Brides is great. I must stay away. I raised this girl but I can't even see her in her wedding gown. Other people will have that good fortune; someone else will see her out of the house. It's really not fair."

The fact that Mother could not see me off in my white veil saddened me even more than her. During those difficult, bitter years, she had sheltered me and made me what I was. No matter what, she should be seeing me off personally. In my opinion, the Goddess of Brides couldn't overshadow a mother. Mother, however, preferred her own beliefs.

The night before my wedding, I put on my dress just for her. She knelt down on the floor of the apartment we had lived in for the last ten years, one hand on the trailing white veil as she looked up at this rapeseed who was about to fall into an unknown field. I stroked her white hair with my white gloves. Her image in the mirror seemed so old and helpless; she seemed unable to see where this rapeseed would fall. I knelt down and for the first time in my life held her in my arms and pressed her face against my white wedding dress. I wanted to tell her not to worry, that I would be happy. But when I looked at her face, that old face shadowed by past hardships, I could only cry out, "Mama, Mama!"

Translated by Fred Edwards

平 路

Ping Lu (b. 1953) is a graduate of National
Taiwan University and received a Masters
degree in statistics in the United States. She
began writing in 1983 and twice won the
Lianhe Newspaper Literary Award with her
"Death in the Corn Field" (Yumitian zhi si,
1983) and "The Taiwan Miracle" (Taiwan
qiji, 1989). She moved back to Taipei from
America in 1994 to become a writer and
editor at *Zhongguo shibao* (China Times).
In 1998 alone, she published five books:
two collections of non-fiction about
women, a volume of autobiographical
articles, and two short-story anthologies.

Jade

❖

1985

Imagine, originally she never even liked jade!

That was when she had just married into the unfamiliar lifestyle of Hong Kong. Her husband's older brother, a cop, clearly knowing that she wasn't used to the sophisticated ways of the city, insisted on showing off by taking his younger brother and new sister-in-law on a tour of his beat, including a stop at the jade market.

"Buy a little something: Big Brother's here, so everything's at a discount!" her husband said gently while looking at his wife's dainty hands.

They had walked up a wide avenue where the sky was filled with hanging shop signs and clothes suspended on bamboo poles drying in the sun. They ended up in the hubbub in front of a vendor's stall. Her heart skipped a beat in surprise as, in an instant, the jade dealer quickly, almost rudely, forced a jade bracelet on to her exquisite wrist.

After the bracelet was on, she felt a hot stabbing pain that would flare up as soon as she touched the bracelet. She wanted to take it off immediately: it seemed as if the chafing of the bracelet would break the skin on her wrist before long. It hurt so much that she wanted to cry. Her face turned a deep red, but the more she tried to take it off, the tighter the bracelet became. Around her, she could hear some joking laughter emanating from the crowd of curious onlookers who had gathered to view the show. For a flustered moment, she did not know what to do.

Standing at her side, her husband tenderly took her red, chafed hand in both of his and rubbed it gently for her. He turned to his brother and said that now he might as well buy it, instead of making her suffer the pain of taking it off again.

Only when she was listening to the two men haggling with the jade dealer about the price of the bracelet did she understand that it actually was a piece of jewelry originally made for a child. It was only because her hands were so small, with joints so small as to seem boneless, that it had been barely possible to squeeze on the bracelet in the first place.

In the end, it was easy to strike a bargain with the vendor for the piece of dense white jade mixed with swirling bands of deep green: after all, it was only a child's plaything.

From that time on, the jade stayed on her wrist day and night. But from the day she got it, she never really liked it. When she did housework, the jade was a nuisance as it banged repeatedly against the dishes and china she was washing. With her apron hanging down, she stood by the sink and looked out the window at the dry, arid weather that all too often seemed to engulf Kowloon Bay. As she stared at the faucet in front of her, from which not a single drop of water had come for half a day, it dawned on her that she had grown to detest the kind of life she was living. But it frustrated her that she could not put her finger on exactly what it was that she had grown sick and tired of!

Every time she wrote a letter home, the pen she was holding would not have written even a few words before the clicking noises made by the jade clattering on the table would deepen her already depressed mood. At times like that, she could not help missing her family back on her own beautiful island. The locked iron bars in front of the window made her feel ill at ease: in the cramped, rented room, she felt tormented and was overcome by powerful feelings of homesickness.

During the times when she thought she could not endure it any more, she tried to take off the jade. But her hands, her once dainty hands, had been changed into rough, crude things by years of housework. The swelling caused by years of soapy water made it impossible to get the bracelet off no matter how hard she tried.

She was sick and tired of the jade, just as she was sick and tired of her never-changing married life and the unending stream of housework she forever seemed to be doing. What she did not realize was that even though the housework was boring in a thousand ways, in her heart she did not really harbor any resentment toward it.

Later in her life, she hated the jade with all her being. These feelings began when she read in a book somewhere that jade was often buried with the dead. As she contemplated that deep, dark netherworld beyond, she would raise her own wrist and stare deeply into the jade for a long time. She could not help wondering whether there had been a girl who had died young and worn her jade to the grave.

The odd thing was, not long after this queer line of thought entered her mind, something strange happened: she tripped and fell, causing her to lose the child that had been growing in her womb.

Holding his head sorrowfully in his hands, the man who so desired to be a father told her as she lay on the bed, "It was a girl!" From that moment on she started to loathe that piece of jade.

Sometimes, when she was gazing into the jade, she actually could perceive a deep blood-red streak inside it.

She tried determinedly to get the jade off in spite of the fact that the scraping on the back of her hand had already caused more than a trace of blood to appear. She was desperate, but no matter how hard she tried, she could not get it off. Full of hate, she continued to glare at the evil stream of blood on her wrist. Then in her heart, she realized something for the first time. It was this: as a woman, it was so easy—too easy—to be trapped into her kind of cursed existence.

Afterwards, her husband, who had gradually found his own fame and fortune in his career, spent more and more nights away from home. Later she realized that his finding a new sweetheart had been inevitable: after all, businessmen, for the sake of keeping face, could not tolerate not having a son somewhere!

She, his first wife, in addition to being heartbroken, could not bear this. Thinking about both the good times and bad times over the years, she was filled with anger. She made up her mind to smash the jade. Smash it once and for all!

But the strong and mysterious jade had become faithful and would not leave her. When she dashed it against the wall, the only result was a depression left in the wall. The jade stubbornly remained on her wrist.

She thought of finding a hammer to smash the jade, but after pausing to look at her thin, frail arm, she thought better of it. She imagined what a pitiful sight her torn, gaping flesh would present should she miss the jade and hit her arm instead. She could not suppress the fear in her heart. She just could not do it.

She plopped down on the bed and sighed. In her mind she knew she should think of her own safety first. After all, she would rather live for complete tiles rather than die for broken jade![1]

Over the years, the abandoned housewife managed to pass her days, and over the years she changed into a fat, middle-aged woman.

In time, her husband took a new wife (or should we say concubine!) named Ah-man into the household. Imagine, at the wedding banquet her appetite was not the least bit affected!

In the piled, fatty rolls of her arm, the jade was like a band deeply embedded in her fleshy limb. At least she didn't have to worry any more about the nuisance of the jade swinging back and forth on her wrist.

In fact, most of her time these days was spent at the mahjongg table. When she shuffled the tiles, the jade rang sweetly to her.

---

1. A play on an old saying, "Ning wei yu sui, bu wei wa quan," literally "Rather a broken piece of jade than a whole tile." The meaning is "better to die in glory than live in dishonor."

But now that she had become a fat old woman, even that sound was rarely heard, or perhaps she had just gradually forgotten about it, even forgotten that she had wanted to take it off!

It was only on the day when her mahjongg friends stared enviously at the band on her arm that she was shocked to realize the jade, after all these years, had changed color to a penetrating, translucent green, and it glittered splendidly.

She lowered her head to gaze upon the soft and beautiful complexion of the stone and the sleek veins that ran through it. Buried in the no longer resilient flesh of her arm, the jade seemed to be the only living, breathing thing there! At that moment she thought of the long road down which she had come and said to herself, "Jade, it must have been you who absorbed my lifeblood!"

As she continued to stare at the green jade, her mind sadly sailed back to the jade market all those years ago, and all those years wasted living in her birdcage of an apartment (what they used to call their "love-nest"). She thought of what her arm was like back then—so round and full, so fine, so soft and smooth with such a delicate pale complexion. As she continued to stare at the jade, the green glittered and shone. Slowly it seemed to start shimmering before her eyes, like jade ripples. Oh, that girl was so fresh and young, so beautiful and innocent. She had once been so full of her own hopes and dreams, but those dreams had just sunk away into the ripples of the jade.

That green jade! Its veins had been nourished at the cost of her life's vitality, and its texture had been drawn from the pool of her youth. No wonder it had that unreal green aura. Wrapped around her now aged wrist, the jade still bloomed and thrived vigorously, and was content to be brilliantly beautiful. After she strained to catch hold of that bright aura as it danced and leapt, she finally shut her tired, baggy eyes. When she opened her eyes again, her friends at the card table were chattering quietly among themselves as they admired the jade on her wrist.

"It's priceless!" the old ladies all chimed together. "You must love it dearly: it's flawless!" they said as they continued their appraisal. They all bent their heads down close to the jade to get a better look, scrutinizing it with intensity as if they would not cease until they found some tiny flaw in the jade.

"How on earth did you ever get it on? It's so small! You must have been a slender-waisted beauty back then!" one of her friends said as she gave up her search. Spoken with a glance toward her and laced with sarcasm, this comment immediately provoked a burst of uproarious laughter from the ladies, as if they had heard an absurd joke. Their laughter caused the card table to shake.

"Well, however you got it on, you might as well forget about taking it off! For sure, you and your jade are together now 'until death do you part'!" chimed another as the ladies continued their fun at her expense while shuffling the mahjongg tiles.

At almost the same instant, the corners of her slack mouth turned upwards into a gloomy smile. The smile grew wider and deeper. After a moment, a cold, almost miserable sound spilled from her mouth. The others went silent, fixed on the coarse voice that came from her throat.

"Ah-man just had a baby girl. The old bastard forces me to be its 'Godmother.' If Ah-man really does have a son some day, the old man will go crazy with joy and make everybody congratulate him. There's no guarantee—there's no guarantee that he won't suddenly remember this jade which has shackled my life—you can't be sure! He might want to cut this jade bracelet off so that he can use it to bind his treasured son!"

At this point, she paused briefly and then, tightly clamping her jaw shut, she spoke though clenched teeth word by word.

"Look! I – I – I'd rather die than give it to him! I will never let anyone cut it off! Cut – it – off! Take – it – away – to – help – someone – else!"

Having finished this venomous tirade, her face relaxed a little. Unhurriedly, she raised her left hand. Her plump, round fingers caressed the jade tenderly with an almost infinite reluctance. A moment passed, and then she pressed her cheek against it. Perhaps it was only because of the contrast of the jade, but her face slowly began to radiate a red light, like that of twilight, or a moonbeam, or even like the final radiance of a dying life. And in that glow, she seemed to be searching for something to treasure in her life. As her cheek stroked the jade, she seemed comforted and joyful; a satisfied smile emerged on her face.

From the eighteenth floor of the towering Meigui Apartments halfway up Taiping mountain, the sound of clicking mahjongg tiles spread across the sky.

Translated by Martin Sulev

蔣 子 丹

Jiang Zidan (b. 1951) was born in Beijing but grew up in Hunan province. She became a member of the Chinese Writers' Association in 1986. "Black" (Hei yanse, 1985) and "The List of Performers Who Will Travel Abroad" (Chuguo yanchu dui mingdan) are two of her prize-winning works. She moved to Hainan Island in 1988 and currently lives in Hainan City as a full-time writer.

Waiting for Dusk

❖

1990

I got sick. It was almost at the moment when I heard the terrifying news about Sumi that I clearly felt I was getting sick. The sickness landed on me, went right through me, like that red dragonfly.

I was thirteen when I saw that red dragonfly for the first time.

What happened to Sumi: it's barely credible, really. In any event, I couldn't imagine that slim and delicate woman doing that. How could she use her pale white fingers to squeeze her own two children's windpipes, and then slowly dismember them. That incomparably lovely woman.

It was mother who brought me the news. Her mind cracked. She spoke in somber tones, but I couldn't discern any trace of grief. She seemed beyond the reach of all compassion. Once again I felt loathing for her hateful profession. I had seen her with my own eyes tell a patient, all shrunk to skin and bones: You have cancer, an advanced stage. Go home and eat a bit of whatever you like. She spoke in that same somber voice. If it had been me, her daughter, lying there, all skin and bones, on the narrow examination table, waiting for her verdict, would she have spoken like that?

Surely not. It can't be true. She's surely not mad! I sprang up from the sofa, shouting hysterically. I saw the peacock feather in the flower vase rustle and tremble with fear. What do you mean, she can't be? Of course she is. Mother was insisting even more emphatically. When she diagnosed a patient, she would always very self-confidently get right up close in that insistent way. I hated this kind of self-confidence. This life-oppressing self-confidence. No, it just couldn't be. I felt crazed, hopeless. What do you understand? If she definitely was mad, at least she will be allowed to live. Suddenly, mother turned anxious. If she had got this anxious in the presence of patients wracked by incurable illness, then maybe I could have loved her. But now she didn't move me. It's not true! I screamed, and cried emotionlessly.

Rather than Sumi continuing to live with her madness, it would be better to end her beautiful life in a volley of rifle fire. Such was my brutal hope.

The first time I saw a red dragonfly, I was just a girl of thirteen.

A thirteen-year-old girl, walking the streets after a rain storm, brooding over torments she had no one to share with. The low oleander hedge was red with countless flowers, their petals dripping gently from the recent rain.

For several months already, she had felt constant anguish over the dark red blood that flowed from her body at regular intervals. She held back her light footsteps from jumping or running and constricted her belly so as to stop the blood from spilling out. Every time she felt a drop flowing it would arouse her panic. Everywhere she went she was obsessively cautious, for fear that anyone standing nearby could see right through her. Every boy and every girl suddenly became unapproachable, and the boys' attitude became especially equivocal. When a football hit her in the belly on the way back from the sports field, it felt no different than if a bullet had shot her in the chest. She knew what kind of boys were involved, and their apology proved to her that they had ulterior motives. She didn't dare ask the teacher to be excused from physical education class, as she decided that this young man, just out of physical education school, might well, from no good motives, ask her why. She had seen early on that this handsome physical education teacher had some kind of secret understanding with Wang Xiaoyan, the class's prettiest girl student. This made her hate Wang Xiaoyan, to the point of refusing to talk to her. Without a qualm, she took the eraser that she had lent to Wang Xiaoyan and threw it into the garbage. She abhorred the color red, and conceived the original idea of painting over in blue ink every red dot on the tablecloth. She refused to wear that three cornered red scarf, and many a time the busybody who was on daily duty at the door of the school had written her name up on the Criticism Board. Not that she cared. She comforted herself with the thought that in any case she would soon reach the age when she could leave the Young Pioneers.

A thirteen-year-old girl. Walking along on the street drenched in water from a rain shower, aching with the irrepressible desire to tell someone. She wanted to find someone to talk to, never mind about what. She had nothing particular to say, just to express herself. There had been times when she had thought of telling her mother the secret of her body, but she would change her mind right away. She worried that her mother would just serve up a lecture of common-places about Hygiene For The Young in her imperturbable tone. Her common-places would be sure to be very scientific and precise, since her mother was a pretty good gynecologist-obstetrician. If indeed her mother were to do that, no intimate word could possibly pass between mother and daughter again. She dreaded the thought that they would act out that scene; she sincerely hoped that her love of her mother would win out over her love of herself, and for her own sake she wanted to keep this hope alive.

I'm suddenly sick. The sickness took me by surprise as much as the awful news about Sumi. I'm absolutely convinced that it was all unavoidable.

I'm a sensitive woman. I'm sure that people talk about me behind my back, and say I'm a typical neurotic. Including my mother and my husband. I dare say they take no more exception to my sensitivity than strangers do: they just pretend to understand me, that's all. Nothing wrong with that. My fault, if it has to be counted a fault, is just that I've always been very concerned with my body and my life. Actually it's been a blazing passion. It started that year when I was thirteen, and for the next twenty years I concentrated my greatest energy on taking extremely good care of myself. Every little thing that wasn't quite right put me in a flurry and made me lose my head. The slightest cough, an occasional diarrhea or headache, even waking up at night in a sweat, or finding a red pimple or black mole on my skin, anything was enough to set me off on a long chain of imaginary terrors. My mother's huge handbook of clinical medicine was crammed with my slips of paper marking crucial pages. The book was a treasury of grotesque and bizarre pictures and descriptions of symptoms of every kind imaginable; these had become my favorite topics of conversation. I would relish giving vivid descriptions of my symptoms to everyone in sight, regardless of whether they had any inclination to listen, and nothing could stop me from getting to the end of what I had to say. I often devoted my utmost efforts to imagine what exactly one could do when one was faced with cancer. What to eat, what would be the best position to sleep in, how to deal with the men and women who came to visit, each in their own different moods. I turned these schemes over and over in my mind, without ever giving them definite shape. Only one thing stayed constant: when you got cancer, you should read nothing but the Old and New Testaments. I had my own copy of the Holy Book, in black hardcover, which I kept hidden in the most secret corner of the bookcase. I was afraid to leaf through the already brittle paper: I had to keep it safe for when it would really come in useful. The morgue held a mysterious fascination for me. Every day I passed in front of the hospital where my mother worked, and when I saw those black doors with their peeling paint, I was seized with an irresistible longing for them to open wide and reveal to me the mystery of death which they concealed. I heard that the deaf and dumb keeper of the morgue was about to marry, and without the slightest reason I presented him with a large gift, on which I spent far more than I would have if it had been my best friend who was getting married, to the complete bewilderment of the unfortunate bridegroom and his bride, fresh from her poverty-stricken mountain hamlet. Mother knew nothing of this. Had she known, God knows what she would have said. She snorted with contempt at all my eccentricities, while I took the view that my mother's excessive matter-of-factness was precisely her greatest fault. Had she been capable of a little more fantasy, perhaps she would have been a better mother. I could have been close to her then, closer than any mother and daughter on Earth. My father, when he was still alive, always said that my mother's profession had a bad influence on me, caused me to have a kind of oversensitivity to sickness.

But my mother never shared that opinion: so many doctors, she would say, and not one of them has a child like mine. That made me think my father loved me more than my mother did.

Thirteen years old that year. What really happened to me? Often I pondered this question long and hard. Apparently nothing really happened, I just vaguely remember seeing a red dragonfly. The first time I saw a red dragonfly.

That day, walking the streets after a rain storm, that thirteen-year-old girl walked along a hedge of oleanders. She could hear the pearls of water left on their leaves and petals anxiously dripping down, as if racing for the ground. A secret, intimate voice seemed to call out to her and checked her step. Sumi was the one, the only perfect woman: the thought suddenly came to her as she stopped by the oleanders, and an inexpressible regret welled up inside her—I would have liked that woman to be my mother, the mother who bore and raised me. She secretly harbored guilty feelings because of her blasphemous thoughts about her mother. But she thought Sumi was more like a real mother. Though she knew that Sumi wasn't quite twenty-five, and wasn't married, that didn't deter her from thinking that she was a better mother.

Sumi was a nurse in the obstetrics ward at the hospital. Her work was far from being as extraordinary as her looks. Maybe people always envy what they don't have: in particular, Sumi looked up to my mother. My mother was the director of the obstetrics ward, and with her own two hands she was reputed to have saved the lives of countless would-be mothers. Because of that, Sumi often gave her a friendly smile, and her head, usually held arrogantly high, bowed respectfully to my mother. It was thanks to my mother that I was on friendly terms with Sumi. If it hadn't been for that, it is hard to believe that someone as aloof and reserved as Sumi could have become friendly, even inseparable, with such a silly chit of a girl. She never doubted that Sumi treated her as if she were her most intimate friend, to the point where she didn't mind changing her underwear in front of her. With Sumi's resplendent body revealed to her eyes, she quietly shuddered in the depth of her heart. This innocent, still unopened flower of a child trembled with awe before the glamor of full-grown womanhood. In that evening dusk, as the autumn sun glowed behind the light blue curtain, Sumi's body engraved itself on her memory like that of a goddess. The curved line of her neck, her full breasts, her smooth thighs; nothing left her unmoved. From that time, she often couldn't stop herself thinking about Sumi, thinking about how she should be closer to her mother because of Sumi. When she stood before a mirror, full of gloom as she combed through her dry, brownish braids, she wondered what would happen if she herself had Sumi's thick black hair: would the weight of it drag her down so that she couldn't stand up straight? Only Sumi was worthy of such a head of hair. That was the ultimate conclusion. She despised herself for this, but also took pride in it. It made no sense at all.

When she was anxious to find someone to confide in, the only possible person was Sumi. She decided to tell her dark red secret to Sumi; she also wanted to know whether it was like that for Sumi, too. She paced up and down in front of the door of the admissions department for a long time, waiting for Sumi to come out after she finished work. When it was time to utter the first sentence, she could barely unclench her teeth, but then the terror in her heart poured out, magnified beyond all proportion. Sumi laughed carelessly, said it was just natural, every woman was like that. That made her feel somewhat dejected; she thought Sumi too casual, too off-hand; she didn't seem to pay any attention to her and even seemed contemptuous of her secret. She came close to deciding to distance herself from her friend. For a girl to find her secret belittled by her friend, even by her closest friend, was not to be endured. You should be glad, it means that you've become a real woman. There's nothing to be afraid of about that! But when the red flow stops, that's when old age is near: now that's the really scary thing. Sumi went on in this vein, but none of it calmed the girl's distress, because she was quite incapable of believing that she could possibly become a woman like Sumi, a real woman.

When she paused by the hedge of oleanders, she saw the little dragonfly pausing on a branch. Its rain-drenched wings beat heavily. When the red flow stops, then old age is drawing near. She rehearsed Sumi's words. At that moment, the red dragonfly's wings became a concrete symbol of life: she felt clearly the frailty of existence. She held her breath, and for a long time didn't dare move her feet, as if the slightest careless move might easily cause the voiceless and shapeless life inside her to disperse and fly away. The red dragonfly was the most beautiful red she had ever seen.

That year, she was thirteen.

It was long, long ago—it seemed like a hundred years. One afternoon after a rainfall, just the kind of time to awaken boundless nostalgia. I was with my son, and passed by a low hedge of oleanders. There were no blossoms on the oleanders, and their leaves were dripping pearls of rain. This boy walking by my side. I called him my son. They said he was my son. They swore up and down he was my son. Yet there were times when suddenly the meaning of that word *son* escaped me, when suddenly I didn't quite know where that boy came from. I just couldn't bring to mind who he was or where he came from.

Mummy, look. My son turned his head. Whenever he addressed me in his clever, articulate way, I got the feeling he was dropping a hint. A boy of five or six had somehow learned to drop some utterly untraceable hint—really, what could be more hateful? I'd rather he addressed me by my name, or better that he didn't address me at all. But no. He had to call me Mummy, he insisted on advertising the fact that he was my flesh and blood.

I saw that he was clutching something in his hand. It was a red dragonfly. It was the very one I had once seen, the one whose color was the most beautiful red ever seen by human eyes. I had decided that it was a manifestation of life that could never be repeated. The first time I saw it, I had just turned thirteen. But now it was being pinched tight in the hand of my son. I knew that the dragonfly's drenched wings were broken, so my voice was as ferocious as the fingers that held it. My son shuddered, and made me think of the trembling peacock feather rustling in the flower vase, that day I heard the terrifying news about Sumi. The dragonfly fell to the ground.

I never really saw what was different between that son of mine, who scampered off so fast, and any other boys on the street. His round cranium was covered with shiny black hair like that of a black colt. There were times when I conceived a desire to stroke that round head, even a really strong desire. Because that shiny black head of hair reminded me of a black cat we used to have at home.

Stepping wide over the dragonfly, I continued to walk. I didn't want to know whether or not it was still alive. Once the red blood no longer flows, old age is near. Sumi's voice seemed to resonate from far, far away. But when Sumi's own red blood stopped flowing forever, she was still in the graceful flower of her middle years.

I got really sick. I considered that to be sick at this time was really lucky. Had I not been sick, I don't know what I might have done about Sumi. I had a presentiment that Sumi's beautiful body would soon vanish altogether from the earth. It had never occurred to me before that being sick could actually make someone happy. Sumi would forgive me. I couldn't go and visit her, no one could see her before the end of her sentence. I could only lie in my warm bed, imagining her plight. If she was in no mood to wind her hair into that tasteful chignon, her thick black hair must be scattered like a wild forest all around her head, and this was bound to add even more heart-breaking pallor to her face. Surely, she must have turned pale indeed. Was she or was she not actually suffering from schizophrenia? This debate had already been raging for a long time, and not only between my mother and me. The entire courtroom, the entire prosecutor's office, the entire city debated the motives of the woman who had killed her children. The verdict hadn't come yet. I both longed for and feared the verdict. I was confident that her mind was entirely sound. She was the Creator's most perfect and most beautiful specimen: she never had and never could have any defect. Such perfection was precisely what showed that she was destined for destruction.

The rays of the autumn sun dimmed into dusk behind the light blue window curtains. The graceful, goddess-like body had disappeared in a twinkling like an imaginary mist. The full smooth curve seen once, under the gentle rays of the setting sun, would never exist again. Perhaps, when she was a thirteen-year-old girl, a child that trembled because of an allegory envisioned in the dusk, she already felt that all of it was just a fantasy about to vanish, all of it was but unreal beauty. She had been aware of it. Twenty years and more later, when she began to feel new life growing inside her, it was only then that she fully realized how profound it had been, that allegory in the dusk. Until then, for a life to be born or be snuffed out in death had seemed easily done, as in a carefree game.

This was harder to make sense of than anything I'd encountered. I was informed that I wasn't sick, my body was in fine health: it was just that I was pregnant. I stared wide-eyed at the white gauze mask in front of me, out of which spurted intermittent streams of hot air, unable to figure out what exactly was happening. The white gauze mask kept spurting hot air: Congratulations, you are soon to be a mother.

But I had no wish to be a mother. I had never had the desire to create a stranger's life. When I seethed with unexpressed anger at my mother, I often wondered how I could have been a part of her, how I could have come out of her body. If she enthusiastically brought me into the world, was it really for nothing other than to give her more opportunities for feeling wounded and unhappy, and to provide an object for the wanton expression of her emotions? She gave me life: because of that, she had the right to belittle me, to ridicule me, she had the right to interfere with any part of my life. I didn't think I was fit material to replicate the role of mother, it had never occurred to me to want to enjoy rights over another life and shoulder the responsibilities involved. What was worthy of rejoicing was that it wasn't my mother who told me the news. If she had, I probably would have had hysterics again. I would have been convinced that this was something she was forcing upon me, just as she had forced my own life on me.

I started vomiting as if my guts were spilling out. I couldn't get down a drop of water or a grain of rice. I had to be fed intravenously. I marveled at how my usually robust stomach could pour forth endless quantities of yellow-green liquid. Driven by a self-tormenting curiosity, with every explosion of vomit, as the bitter liquid spurted from my throat, I strained to complete the process even more thoroughly. The more violent the vomiting, the more I felt a kind of nameless joy, till it seemed that my whole body twitched in fits, shrinking and drying up till nothing remained but a bag of translucent skin. Only with the vomiting did the joy gradually subside. After that, very quickly I was able to think of Sumi, to think about how she could have used her pale white fingers to kill her two sons. Every time I vomited, it was a link to Sumi's tragedy, it seemed that vomiting was the only way I could express my longing for her.

My vomit diffused a foul smell, but I strenuously refused to let my husband remove the spittoon right away. I always thought there would be something unexpected inside it, such as a hair, a fingernail, or some other broken-off organ fragment of the fetus. Every time, before emptying out the spittoon, I had to inspect it minutely, which made my husband look at me suspiciously. What are you looking at? What's the point of looking at filth? he loudly reproached me more than once. I'd never experienced him scolding me in such a loud voice. I was already exhausted by the vomiting, and I hadn't the strength to tell him what I was thinking. He would have ridiculed me, and he and my mother would have seriously discussed sending me to be examined in the psychiatric ward. I really don't know whether I truly expected to find anything in my vomit. But what is certain is that every time my husband replaced the carefully washed spittoon next to my bed, I felt a kind of inexpressible disappointment. And the effect of my disappointment was another bout of even more violent vomiting.

I quickly lost weight. I knew that day by day the fetus that occupied my belly was horribly sucking my blood and consuming my flesh. I was helpless against it. Every day it got stronger, and every day I got weaker. Only the fact that my belly had not yet swollen may have given me a little comfort. Sometimes, I clearly heard the fetus pausing in his plundering growth, and quietly going to sleep. I longed for the muscles of my belly to tighten more and more strongly so that they could truss up that fetus in its sleep and stifle it. It wouldn't feel anything, it wouldn't suffer. That wouldn't be a crime. That couldn't be reckoned a crime. When I thought about that, my heart constricted, my blood ceased flowing in my veins.

It died, you see, it actually stopped growing, I said to my husband with trepidation. Don't abandon yourself to wild thoughts. It's still small, it hasn't grown yet, my husband said to me, and he had that kind smile again. Ever since the time he found out I was pregnant, he insisted on sporting a smile just like that. He was all too willing to do everything for me, including things he'd never agreed to do before. Whenever I was moved by his kindness, I felt a jealous hatred of that fetus inside my belly. His work, his solicitude, his smile—they were all for that life just forming, not for me. I vomited again. That was the life inside me denouncing me, it was still alive, it wanted to continue growing. You're tired, you have to rest. My husband earnestly beat my pillows to make them fluffy, propped me up and lay me down. Sleep for a while, have a nice dream. He smiled, kissed my forehead. I finally realized what's really meant by the saying that husbands and wives should treat each other like honored guests. That did move me.

She tried earnestly to have a nice dream. In the past, too many bad dreams had dominated her sleep; she no longer knew what kind of shapes a beautiful dream could bring. When you look at that tapestry, look at the leaves, you could think you are taking a walk in autumn woods. When you hear this fragment of music, it's the autumn wind blowing through a birch wood, with the leaves making a whistling sound, whistling the spiraling-down-to-the-ground tune. You're walking into the wood, ever forward, treading on the fallen leaves. The wood has no boundary, the fallen leaves spread out ever more thickly. When you can't go on any more, you lie down and rest, and the leaves keep falling, they cover up your body. You have gone to sleep, covered by the blanket of leaves. Her husband was by her side, like an earnest tour guide conscientiously describing everything to her, or like a magician, casting a spell to put her to sleep. She'd never known that this man, who was with her from morning till night, had such a gift for speech. She thought his silence was habitual. That a voiceless fetus had the power to conjure up the transformation of a silent man into one of such overflowing enthusiasm, that was hard to credit. Indeed, the tribute of her own flower of youth had not had the power to rouse him from his silence. She became afraid of this voiceless, soundless thing in her belly, and no longer dared to take it lightly; all she could do now was gingerly serve it. Already it had become the ruler of the household, and there was no way for her to contend with its power.

The white birch woods and the falling leaves stood out vividly; she felt that what the falling leaves signified was death, that picture was a picture of death.

She wanted to have a good dream. In her dream, there wouldn't be birches with their falling leaves, there would only be the evergreen hedge of oleanders. The oleanders might or might not be flowering, but the leaves would all be drenched with rain.

It's been a long time since I last heard news of Sumi. From the time I was definitely known to be pregnant, my mother and my husband sealed up all news of this kind in deep secrecy. The evening newspaper that got delivered to the house often went missing without reason. I suspected papers that disappeared in this way had contained a report about the trial of Nurse Sumi for killing her own children. They stopped me from watching television, claiming that the fluctuating images would make me dizzy. At first, I didn't understand their exaggerated solicitude. Every day, when she got home from work, my mother came to my bedside, and every time I inquired about Sumi. I don't know. There's no news. She bamboozled me. I thought the case hadn't come to public trial. Then, one day, the head nurse of the obstetrics ward came to our house to borrow some soy sauce. She was a loud-voiced woman, strong enough to lift a bull and dash it to the ground. I suspected that babies born into her large hands would get squeezed black and blue without her even noticing. The head nurse was gossiping with my mother in the kitchen, and her voice penetrated through the crack in the door to my bedroom. Suddenly, I heard her utter Sumi's name. It seemed Sumi was beyond saving: several hospitals had certified that she wasn't schizophrenic. What's more, it would be unthinkable to let someone like that live! She spoke in her loud cruel voice. I jumped out of bed, and was too befuddled to put on my slippers. I opened the door a crack, and glued my eyes to it. The woman's voice stopped abruptly, for all the world as if someone had just stopped up her mouth. I saw the glass door of the kitchen being closed, and the shadows of my mother and the head nurse whispering in each other's ears danced chaotically on the glass pane. That's when I realized that my mother had bamboozled me every day. She wouldn't apologize to me, she would just justify her deception with the usual highfalutin talk about how it was her duty as my mother to take care of me. But I'd rather have been one of the patients on her examining table, all skin and bones, hearing her inform me of my plight in her cold wooden voice. Between the real absence of love and the absence of real love, I would have chosen the former. Still, I couldn't complain, she did all a mother was supposed to do. It was that fetus inside me that had put me in this position where I had to suffer being duped: it was the fount of all lies. I felt sick again, and leaning against the door post I summoned up all my courage to vomit once more, and the filthy liquid was all over my body and my legs. Mother and the head nurse ran in as one, and found me standing bare-footed on the cold cement floor. They started wailing and shouting. The head nurse picked me up bodily and put me back on my bed. The power of those arms would have been a match for a hundred men's. I compared her to Sumi: for this person to be living out her life on Earth as a woman must have been the result of a mix-up.

Once again, I had no news of Sumi. The loud-voiced head nurse couldn't be expected to keep forgetting to buy soy sauce. Out of occasional clues and hints I constructed an edifice of guesswork. When the case first came to light, I chanced to hear someone say that she had used a scalpel to dismember the two children's bodies, and then had carefully placed arms, legs, hearts, and organs into separate piles, so that later, when the bodies were cremated, there was no way to tell them apart for sure. From what people said, every cut was done by the book, in the most fastidious way, more expertly than any of the residents in the surgical ward could have done. It was as if she had done it all with calm unhurried deliberation.

Once, Sumi had told me the story of Black Blade and Black Wolf. These were two dogs that her family had kept to guard the house when she was small. A once-in-a-century plague of locusts resulted in there not being a single grain harvested in the village of her birth. To save their lives, her father had hanged Black Blade and Black Wolf with a rope, put them both in a pot and cooked them into a thick meat stew. Their hunger dulled the children's sensibilities, and when they had finished eating the meat, they didn't feel any sorrow before the empty dog-house, but just thought about how good the dog meat tasted and tried to figure out which one, Black Blade or Black Wolf, was the more tasty. Sumi's brother and sister quarreled and came to blows. Her brother seized a chance to pull out a great handful of her sister's hair, and her sister scratched her brother's cheeks and drew blood. In the end, Sumi's verdict was that Black Wolf tasted better, because he had been more beautiful than Black Blade. How silly could we be! Tell me that! When she said that, she laughed, showing a perfect row of white teeth. Those teeth, really they were the teeth of a conqueror who carries all before her. Could it be that, when she carved up her children, she thought about Black Blade and Black Wolf?

When Sumi told me that story, we were on the pleasure boat in the public park. She was still single, and on Sundays she often took me for a stroll. I didn't understand why she would be so keen to keep her distance from her co-workers, and consent to idle time away with such a silly little chit of a girl. The lake surface was enshrouded with purple mist; there was a great stillness all around. On the shore, willow catkins were dancing in the air, some floating on the wind, others sinking down into the water. All around the boat, fish were jumping up with a swishing sound and sinking down again. They're spawning, Sumi said. I didn't really understand what that was, *spawning*. It's when fish make little fish, just like women giving birth to babies, she explained. At those words, *giving birth*, my heart gave a loud thump. Would you be able to give birth? Of course I could, but not just me, you can too, in time. Every woman can. We're just like those fish: we spawn and then we grow old, and then we die; our children will live on and replace us, and so life goes on. As Sumi talked, I watched the fish in the water, busily rushing up and down. So it seemed they came to the Earth just to spawn, just to die, and just so that others could continue to live in their place. Now, Sumi herself had severed the two lives that were meant to take her place. That woman, once so beautiful, once so good. Perhaps she didn't want to live on. Before she could reach old age, she had lost the desire to go on living, and she had no need for another life to be lived in her stead.

The wind began to blow. A little boat was gently bobbing up and down in the middle of the lake. On the boat, two girls, one older, the other a child. In the purple mist that enshrouded the water, the fish were busy spawning, aging, dying.

One afternoon after a rainfall, I watched my son squeeze a dragonfly between his fingers. It was tired of flying, could no longer flap its rain-drenched wings, dripping onto the oleander hedge. As I watched my son casually crush it, I suddenly knew how Sumi could have casually crushed her children, and how she could so casually have given up on herself. In truth, every life just born was indomitable, every life ended in haste. But when I was that thirteen-year-old girl, I knew already that life was as frail and flimsy as that red dragonfly's wings.

Oh bitter dragonfly on the low hedge of oleanders, how can it be that we met again? On yet another rainy afternoon, after what seems a hundred years. We walk in the vast confusion of time and of space, powerless to foresee our future or determine the direction of our path. One goal alone is common to all: old age and death.

In the end I accepted it, the savage invader of my body, the flesh and blood that usurped the warmth of my body, my nourishment, my life force, and which every day grew stronger. I couldn't control it in any way, so I let it twist my body into a distorted shape too horrible to look at. There was no defense against the force of its will.

The vomiting ceased. Now that my stomach was washed completely empty, it signaled me to eat this and that, to fill the limitless void, forcing my body to get more cumbersome every day. I was afraid to talk to any other woman, even those who were no longer young, and out of the ordinary; somehow they all made me feel ashamed of myself. And I was afraid to let my husband see how my body had become clumsy and fat, for I could easily see in his eyes the expression of weary disgust, and that in turn deepened my own resentment against him. I was no longer moved by his zeal. I knew it was the voiceless life in my belly that was cutting us off from one another, cutting me off from every other human being. It was a tyrant, who had invaded and possessed me. I asked for a long leave from work, shut my door and never came out. Once again I rehearsed the feeling of distance from my own kind, the feeling I had experienced long ago, when I was still an unformed girl.

I love myself too much. I'm a sensitive woman.

Suddenly, I started feeling close to my mother. She was once invaded and possessed by me, I had made her weak, made her cumbersome, made her awkward and embarrassed. But she'd forgiven me. She had a thousand reasons to mistreat me, to make me lie down, all skin and bones, on her examining table, and coldly to contemplate my living or dying. She was my benefactor. It was she who gave me my flesh and blood, my muscles and bones, my soul; any time she wanted them, she could take back these things which belonged to her. Were you happy in those days? I asked her. Of course I was happy. That was the happiest time of my life. As she answered me, a few white hairs floated down as if in time with the sound of her voice. I didn't believe her. I suspected that she said that only to win over even more of my feelings. You really should be happy, you know. To be a mother is a woman's heaven-given lot: only those women who have been mothers are fully women; without that, a woman is incomplete. She went on in a voice as aged as her white hair. I found nothing to answer, and my warm feelings silently left me. The same blood flowed in my mother's veins and mine, but we were wholly different women. Did it make her happy to sacrifice herself for me? I held her in high esteem. She had never contemplated what she might have lost: on the contrary, she thought my existence made her complete. She rejoiced in her happiness, and just hoped that by dint of giving birth she would perfect herself. So, there was no cause for me to feel guilty towards her; indeed, I might well envy the joy that I had once brought her.

From that time, the secretiveness began. She seemed to lose all her innocence and her joy. On the eve of summer, there were torrential rains, and afterwards, as usual, the intersection in front of the school door was knee-deep in water. The boys and girls coming out of class came out of the door in single file, and all bared their feet and jumped across with a plopping sound. Murky mud and water splashed high into the air in a great hullabaloo. Columns of cars and flocks of bicycles got in one another's way on the road in a great confusion of ringing bells and sounding horns. The grown-ups looked at the water, filthy with silt, made as if to step out but immediately paused; they frowned and complained about the building department's neglect of its duties. This just encouraged the children's frenzy. Even the girls who normally most liked neatness thought nothing of letting their short white nylon skirts get all stained with dirty water; now they jumped about in the water, screaming in high-pitched voices with total abandon. She alone stood stupidly on the stairs, unable to figure out why they should be driven wild with joy by a puddle of dirty water. She forgot that just a few weeks back, there had also been a big rainstorm; she had sat in a classroom, and tried to guess how much water would gather at the school gate and how many cars, bicycles and pedestrians would get bogged down, and tried to think how, when school was let out, she and her friends might splash merrily through the mud under the eyes of the staring crowds. But now, as she gazed blankly at her fellow pupils, it seemed to her they looked as distasteful a sight as a troop of monkeys injected with stimulants. Some people, in the grip of their wild fantasy, were calling her name, thinking to lure her to their crazy gang. They were astonished for a while when they saw her just standing there motionless, and they all stared at her, as with a single pair of eyes. Their stare was like the stare of people who have called out to stop a thief—all eyes are on the pickpocket who failed to get away with it. Luckily this didn't last, since no one was willing to delay the great moment of wading into the water. But just in that short blink of an eye, she felt the world to which she had once belonged was stripped away from her. Wading into the water was something that earned her mother's reproach. This aroused her deep resentment; but her father had egged her on to wade in, and that had aroused such strong gratitude in her that she felt on the point of tears—an attitude that now seemed endearing, laughable, and incomprehensible. In that short moment, her childhood had left her.

At that time, I didn't know we were parting forever.

It's as if we had parted a few centuries ago: how could I not bring to mind where it was that I saw Sumi for the last time, how could I not remember the circumstances of our last parting. Perhaps we just said, "See you soon," just like we always used to. In reality, however, we would never see one another again. I spent whole days in my bedroom, and she was escorted to death row. We spent our days alike: whiling away the time in front of a white wall. But she was waiting for death, and I was waiting for the rest of my life. Two different vigils indeed.

I swore to myself that I would remember our last parting, in every minute detail. But perhaps it was because our meetings and our partings were too numerous; or perhaps it was because we assumed we would see each other again that we took no special notice of our parting. However it may be, I just couldn't remember what it had been like. Could it be that Sumi was no longer so important to me? This discovery amazed me. From when, behind those light blue window drapes, in the dimly glowing rays of the autumn evening sun, Sumi had stripped her body for me, as lovely as a goddess, and at that moment started me trembling all over with adoration, she had become for me all at once an idol and an imaginary emblem of my whole life. At that time, I truly believed that without Sumi this world would turn dark and colorless, and that my life would lose all its savor.

Many years later, one afternoon after a rainstorm that had revived so many memories, I walked with my son along a low hedge of oleanders. Once again I saw that red dragonfly. I started thinking that, because of Sumi, that red dragonfly had actually become a sacred figure in my mind. It still seemed so fragile, it still retained its lustrous red color. But now Sumi was nothing but a handful of bones and dust, and everything about her had vanished, all sound and color lost, sunk without trace in the deepest wells of memory. The truth is that every human being walks on their lonely way along the path of time, but no two lives are ever really linked. Thus I will never know where this child by my side, whom others say is my son, really comes from, nor will I ever be able to predict where he is destined to end up. Sumi is dead, and I'm still perfectly all right. You couldn't really say that she matters to me. Just so, when I die, and my son is still perfectly all right, I won't be of any importance to him then either.

When Sumi told me the news of her intended marriage, I had just used a ladle to pour water on her hair for her. Her neck stretched out elegantly, and a column of water flowed evenly from the roots of her hair to the tips, like a jet-black waterfall. She picked that moment to tell me, as casually as possible, of her momentous decision. To this day I have no way of judging whether she did this unthinkingly, or whether it was carefully planned. My hand gave a start, and half the contents of a ladle spilled under the collar of her shirt. She stopped speaking for a while, and I thought she would ask me to hand her a dry towel. But she said nothing, and didn't change her position. She went on holding her hair out with her hand, waiting for me to sprinkle it with water. Without waiting for her to pat her hair dry, I took my leave. I was afraid that she would see that there was something strange about me. I thought my cheeks must have surely turned pale, I must have been biting my lips. Maybe it was from that moment on that Sumi was no longer important to me. That year, I was twenty.

Seeing that thirteen-year old standing stupidly on the steps of the school gate, staring at her schoolmates jumping joyfully into the puddle left by the rain, I understood at last that on that day, at that moment, I had become a woman.

She thought she had not so much seen him as felt him. She was inclined to say that if instead it had happened to be the other way around, she would never have come to know him. That morning, she had got stuck in the door of the streetcar, which was so crowded that you couldn't get in. In this situation, in which she could move neither forward nor backward, she felt a powerful shoulder pushing up against her backbone. Suddenly feeling secure, she was sure that the person behind her was a big strong man. The might of that shoulder awakened in her virginal heart an obscure longing. This man behind her, whose face she had never seen, he might be old or young, he might be handsome or ugly; but in one mad moment he had become someone to whom she might be close. It was only many years later, when she brought that scene to mind, that she was clearly conscious of the fact that this was the first time she had fallen in love with a man. The man had got out at the same station, and had walked straight in front of her into the school gate. That whole time, she never got to see his face clearly; but viewed from the back, he seemed as strongly built as his shoulders, and it made her long to be close to him.

To be sure, he must have been very young. At the moment that his back vanished in the thick of the grove, she suddenly felt a pang of joy.

Many days later, when she really did see that face clearly, all her feelings could be summed up in one sentence: that she would rather always be looking at his back. Even when she was getting ready to give herself to him, there still was no way she could deny that his face had proved a disappointment. What was strange was that this didn't cause her to withdraw from him; instead she still hoped to get closer to him. It seemed that from the instant when his shoulder had leaned against her back, that man had already drawn her into his magnetic field. Who knows when exactly it began, but they began to acknowledge one another with a nod or a vague greeting. Then there were conversations, short, and long. She knew that he came from a border town in the South, and that he was studying for an MA in philosophy at the university she attended. In order to escape the noise of the dormitory, he had temporary lodgings with his aunt, who lived only two stops away from her home. So they often found themselves squeezed into the same rush-hour tram car. Little by little, she grew accustomed to seeking out, in the tightly packed crowd, the back view that had moved her or the face that had disappointed her. If on a given day she hadn't run into him on the tram or in the student cafeteria or in a common lecture in the great hall, she got anxious and felt like a lost soul. She started worrying about what she wore and how her hair looked. That autumn evening, when the light blue color of the window curtain set off the beauty of that body—for many years, it had lain on her like a bitter iceberg, crushing and paralyzing her little-girl self-respect. When she compared herself to Sumi, her face and figure, even her hair and her nails, everything in herself seemed to her vulgar and tasteless, and she never dared to hope that she could ever move a man's heart. She invested all her energy in her studies, and she rejoiced in the fact that her parents had given her a smart brain, and her outstanding performance in school compensated somewhat for the feeling of inferiority produced by her plain appearance. Every time she got involved in endless conversations with male classmates about Heidegger or Freud, philosophy or psychology, her face flushed with excitement. Gesticulating and dancing about with joy, she would have a bout of self-confidence, and would fancy that if Sumi could witness a few such episodes, she might envy her a little. These moments of satisfaction, however, were short-lived; if one of her attractive fellow students was assiduously courted and asked to go for a walk in the suburbs, or, at a student-organized dance, if she was asked to dance out of pure compassion for a token couple of tunes, her self-contempt once more overwhelmed her. It frequently occurred to her that if only she had Sumi's beauty and her own intelligence—well, what luck that would have been. She had never expected him to notice her in the way that one notices a woman; but again, she hotly hoped for just that kind of attention.

Then, one day, at last, it happened: the unthinkable, yet completely predictable thing.

She was sitting next to him. It was much the same as usual, sitting in a row in the streetcar like many times before; but all those times they had never been thrown so close. As a rule, he seemed quite intent on maintaining a suitable distance between them. That day, maybe the streetcar had been particularly crowded. Or maybe it hadn't.

Suddenly she felt his arm on her shoulder, neither light nor heavy, but resting there in a way that was both deliberate and natural. It looked as if they had simply taken the seats of two people who had got off, and when they sat down, his arm had just happened to land in that position. She caught sight of the reflection of his face in the glass, so peaceful as to seem almost indifferent. That was a man's trick. She simply understood this, by herself, without needing to be taught. It was a long way, and the tram car wiggled slowly on the tracks, so slowly that it seemed it might stop anywhere. He and she sat stiffly, without moving; there was no further advance, nor was there any rejection. But she had no doubt that the position of his arm was a kind of sign. She just couldn't imagine that he could carelessly put his arm on a woman's shoulder and not notice. They didn't speak a word; there was no need to say anything.

The next day, when school let out in the afternoon, it was still light; she stood at the streetcar stop and let three cars go by, until he ran up in a great rush, his head covered with sweat. Again they sat in the same seat, and again his arm fell on her shoulder. She rested her head on his arm, and that shoulder felt to her as it had felt that day long ago, so broad and strong. When it was time to get off, neither of them moved. His jaw was resting on her forehead, and the stubble of his beard tickled and scraped. Finally she couldn't resist making the suggestion: let's not get off, all right? Let's go all the way to the terminus. He replied very tenderly, and at the same time he kissed the spot on her forehead where his beard had scraped her. All right. She felt a kind of pang in her heart, not a mental pain, but a real hurt in her physical heart. Even today, when she was another man's wife and a mother, when she thought about that scene in the streetcar, her heart contracted with pain.

The day Sumi married, she rushed to bring her best wishes. Her present was a pair of male ivory dolls. Afterwards, Sumi gave birth to twin boys. Sumi said: it's the will of heaven. The gods had realized what she had wished for her. These words of Sumi's moved her deeply. Once more, as before, Sumi held a special place for her, even though she now had a husband and had become a mother. Sumi treasured those two dolls, and kept them in a prominent place in the bookcase. She didn't know whether Sumi meant this to express some sort of apology. She knew perfectly clearly that Sumi had no reason at all to apologize to her, but she had an intuition that deep in her heart, Sumi simply had to feel she owed her an apology. After Sumi was executed, she once wrote a letter to Sumi's husband, asking to be given those two dolls as a keepsake, but the answer she got was that the two dolls had disappeared, he didn't known when. Could it be that she had dismembered them at the same time?

At the wedding, she met Sumi's husband for the first time. She saw a handsome man, thin and tall. You couldn't accuse Sumi of having made a bad choice. Judging by his bearing and conversation, you had to say he seemed quite worthy of Sumi. Still, she was altogether unwilling to engage him in conversation. She thought there was something hypocritical about his tone and his smile, as he invited people to eat sweets or to sit down, or chatted idly about good and bad weather. When they were courting, Sumi had never expressed any intention of getting her to meet him—no doubt she was being far-sighted. Sumi knew that her meeting him was bound to have bad consequences. She would no doubt behave as she had in the past, sabotaging all Sumi's relationships with any man whatever, putting forward a thousand, ten thousand considerations calculated thoroughly to destroy their relationship. She thought Sumi's attempts to avoid her meddling were altogether a waste of effort. She felt nothing worse than a certain distaste for this man, nothing you could really call loathing. Sumi's marriage actually hadn't proved as unbearable as she had imagined it would be. Nevertheless, when she visited their new house, she felt a twinge of distress when she saw the huge mirror that adorned the wall next to their large Simmons bed. She thought about how Sumi's lovely body would be wantonly ravaged by a man in this very spot, and how this mirror would keep a scrupulous record of their lovemaking sessions, and she found it hard to regain her good humor.

All day long, she refrained from looking in Sumi's direction. She knew that Sumi's beauty was surely nothing less than terrifying. Every time she heard the happy, spring-like breeziness in Sumi's voice, she could barely stop herself from leaving the noisy cursed place, and running off to take refuge in the strong and warm embrace which was hers for the asking. She was obscurely conscious that everything that happened between him and her had much to do with Sumi.

It occurred to her that if he had been a fine figure of a man, perhaps she would have told Sumi all about what passed between them. As it was, she just couldn't open her mouth. She was convinced that Sumi would think his ugliness would make their love completely worthless. She understood Sumi all too well. If this was indeed the case, she might waver. She felt unworthy of him. And so, every time he embraced her, she harbored an inexpressible feeling of guilt, and in her heart a sentence kept recurring: Oh, forgive me, I am a girl quite given over to vanity.

I walked past that low hedge of oleanders. It was an amazingly fine day. The warm rays of the setting sun were shining, and the oleander leaves were bathed in the warm light, and had acquired the brilliant splendor of gold. Once there had been a thirteen-year-old girl who could tell no one her secret, wandering to and fro by the oleander hedge. That day, every leaf on the oleanders was covered in melancholy drops of rain, like numberless staring eyes all brimful with feeling. The mysteries of human feeling, human nature, human life: they all seemed to be held in the speechless gaze of those eyes, and before her was the limitless and unfathomable space she was about to enter, her future as a woman. Now the space had vanished, the doors of her destiny had suddenly closed, and the ice cold pool of golden light remained immobile for a long time, without thought or feeling.

A red dragonfly flew by, and went off who knows where. Perhaps it would never return.

The fetus had begun to move inside my belly, restlessly, day and night. It swelled up savagely, stretched the skin of my abdomen until it was as taut and shiny as a drum. I had edema in my insteps and calves, which periodically felt like they were being jabbed with a needle. I'd stopped looking in the mirror for quite a while already. I knew that what I'd find there would be just grotesque. Again I thought of Sumi. Amazingly, her pregnancy and delivery hadn't diminished her beauty by a hair. Until the moment she set down her burden, and returned from maternity leave, her figure and her face were as attractive as before; indeed, in her eye there was now added a new kind of mature womanly charm. Whenever I saw her, it was as if some hope was withering away. I had made a kind of opportunity out of Sumi's pregnancy, an opportunity for myself. For it was she who taught me to be a woman, but again I felt oppressed by the thought that I could never really become a pure woman. It was hard to say whether she was my friend or my enemy. When I witnessed the miraculous recovery of her beauty after she had given birth, my heart was filled with a confusion of incoherent feelings, of deep loss and of guilt. I drowned in boundless bitterness. Sumi was like an iceberg that would never melt, pressing down on my head. In the ocean of bitterness where Sumi had left me adrift, I never glimpsed the other shore, the one that belonged to real women.

That evening, in my twentieth year, when the weather was so amazingly fine—when I walked by the low oleander hedge: was it because I was looking for that red dragonfly?

I don't know how he was able to leap out of that distant sea of strangers in a far away southern land, and walk straight into my life. The first time he told me I was beautiful, I wasn't sure whether I had imagined hearing it, or whether he was just talking nonsense. I had never in my life dared set my hopes on hearing a single syllable in praise of my looks. Your beauty doesn't show up when you are just sitting there. It's in your expression, when you are alive with talk and laughter: at those times, you can really touch a man's heart. I scrutinized his eyes, looking for the marks of insincerity. But his two thin, wide eyes were pure and clear, and I couldn't sense the slightest trace of hypocrisy. That's when I really became stuck on him, that's when I started to feel I wanted to melt my being into his. Only in his tight embrace could I experience the quivering breathlessness of a real woman. Heidegger, Sartre, Freud—all that I had studied for my degree exams, the familiar world in which I had struggled so hard to excel—it had all lost its meaning. I just wanted to become weak, to become the sort of person that anyone could dupe. He would protect me; he would know how to protect me. He was my only guardian angel. Ah, how wonderful: I was a woman.

The station at the end of the tram line was called Lichee Bay. Actually she thought that name was a sort of ironic joke. In this northern capital, lichees could only be found at banquets, and as soon as they heard this word, people couldn't help associating them with the legend of the courtesan Yang for whom countless post horses raced to death to satisfy her craving for lichees. If you have a chance, come and visit my house, we have plenty of lichees there, he said to her.

They walked forward along a desolate stony path, and didn't notice the darkness falling. Then they reached the gate of a thousand-year-old temple. The ticket sellers had already gone home, and there was no one to stop them going in. It was as if the two of them simply fell down on the long green bench, and all words were stopped in their throat by a passionate kiss. After a long silence, she asked him what he was thinking. Mischievous, he refused to answer. I won't tell you. She insisted, wouldn't give up. He put his lips close to her ear, and in a low voice said: I was thinking we need a bed. She felt his face suddenly turning crimson. Nothing can transport the heart of a woman more than the bashfulness of a mature man in the heat of passion. At that moment, her heart was bursting with the desire to cry out: I am willing, I want to give myself to you.

The crowds of people were far away; the world seemed as alien as a wilderness. They caught the very last streetcar back to town. The deserted countryside was silent, waiting for the melodious far-away sound of the evening bell in the old temple.

Are you willing, will you give yourself to me? On her wedding night, these turned out to be the very words used by the man who was now her legitimate husband. Unfortunately, these words genteelly spoken from his mouth just made her feel that he had got them from a book or was imitating a role played by some second-rate actor on TV. Perhaps it was merely a routine formality, much as he might have asked a patient: So what seems to be the problem, after leafing through the medical history. It had no effect beyond awakening in her the memory of that night in the ancient temple of Lichee Bay, to make her remember the power of his embrace and the cry that had burst from her soul. She nodded, said nothing. Her husband, quite satisfied and in a mood of exaltation, had made love to her with an expression of pure tenderness on his face. To be married to such a man had to be her good fortune. The youngest physician in charge of the surgical ward in the University Hospital, obliging towards all, cultivated, elegant; his hair was perfectly combed every day, the pleat of his pants sharp as a penciled line, his shoes polished to a shine. His career was successful, and his character excellent. Before her mother arranged a formal introduction, she hadn't in fact been willing to trumpet his virtues, though nothing could have been easier. She decided that any woman faced with this knight on a white horse would naturally love him with every limb in her body. She told her mother that she would have to think about it, but in fact at the moment she said this, she had already decided that she would never give the matter a second thought for the rest of her life.

When Sumi came looking for me, her whole body was still redolent of disinfectant. She told me that today during her shift they'd had seven women delivering in a row. She was so exhausted she thought her bones would come apart. Having said that, she dropped like a lump into the sofa, as if lacking the strength even to change position. I poured her a glass of fruit syrup, not quite understanding why today, exhausted as she was, she still had run to my house. In the past, she had always insisted that the secret of middle-aged women keeping their looks was to get proper nourishment, that getting too tired from overexertion was a sure way to accelerate the vanishing of youth, which no amount of makeup could restore. I guessed that she had something important to say to me. But it hadn't occurred to me that the reason she was beating about the bush was that she wanted to hear what I might have to say about my impressions of that young doctor. What about you? I asked her. Naturally, one has to reckon he's not a bad choice. But as for the question to marry or not to marry him, you'd better form your own opinion. As she answered the question, her gaze drifted off, but I caught in her eye, for just an instant, a look of frustration and envy. I've made up my mind, I plan to marry him as soon as possible. As soon as these words had slipped out, I myself thought them absurd. I hadn't even managed to meet this prince yet. Who knew whether he'd even be willing. However that might be, I couldn't help giving that answer. For the rest, we'd have to see later. Not unexpectedly, my words evidently left Sumi extremely depressed. When she said good-bye, I noticed that her step had lost its usual brisk bounce, which had never happened since I had known her. A malicious pleasure surged through my heart, almost entirely wiping out the thought of the single life to which, a moment ago, I had been firmly committed. All I could say was that it was all the hand of fate.

At her first trial, the prisoner Sumi was condemned to death and permanent loss of political rights for the murder of her children. Because of this news, the evening editions of newspapers must have printed a hundred thousand extra copies. The last line of the report stated that if the criminal refused to accept this judgment she had three days to appeal to the superior court. Why was there no photograph? I asked my husband, throwing the newspaper on the floor. This evening on the local television news, they'll have a shot of the opening of the court session, if you really must watch it... My husband, watching me carefully, was trying to probe my state of mind. I won't watch, I don't think any of you should watch either, I coolly answered, throwing their expectations off track. You're getting near the time of your delivery, the fetus is already mature, if you restrain your emotions a bit it won't do any harm. My mother talked to me in her special tone of voice for giving obstetric advice, seemingly all empathy and understanding. No, I don't want to see it, and you two can't watch it either. I gave a shout, as I started to get another cramp in my calf. Any moment, it seemed I might erupt into a hysterical fit. In unison, they threw down the dishes and carried me to bed.

I closed my eyes and imagined Sumi as the judgment was being passed on her. I wished she could always arrange her hair in the same refined way as before, and throw back her beautiful head, in the unchanging way that she always would in my memory.

As the prison van sped by, the dust it raised in the city square concealed it from the crowd's line of sight. Inside the prison van, could Sumi remember the light blue curtains, and the little girl with the dry, brownish hair in the boat in the middle of the lake?

The rainwater dripped wordlessly, and the long thin leaves of the oleander were like numberless eyes flowing with tears. A red dragonfly flew by. A gigantic dragonfly, humming and whooshing as it flapped its thick heavy wings, let out a metallic sound and dropped down on the oleander hedge. Branches and leaves fell one by one, draping the ground in a disorderly tangle. The red dragonfly's body was cut in two, its blood spurted out, and left stains all over the little girl's white skirt.

I woke up from my bad dream, my whole body drenched in sweat. The musical chime of the clock made a pleasant sound, telling me midnight was near. The fetus started violently moving and banging about; at one go, I felt something warm gushing out of my body, and became aware that my time of delivery was imminent.

Right until the day he took his degree, he never told her about his wife. When he did, she was exerting all her talents to make him dinner. They were celebrating his degree, and it was a farewell dinner, too. That afternoon, she had told him that her mother was out of town. He seemed very happy and said how good that was, let's get home early, spend the rest of the day together. They bought a bag full of fresh vegetables, apples, roasting chicken, ham sausage, and also a stuffed pastry. They seemed like a young married couple, as they made their leisurely way home. At that time, she still had no idea that a few thousand miles away from this city, there existed another woman, a woman who like her belonged to him.

It was all as natural and harmonious as she had hoped it would be. As she heated the soup and fried the vegetables, she was making a dinner combining sophisticated and simple flavors and smells and colors, while he sat in the living room smoking and watching television—just like a husband waiting for a model wife to serve him attentively. She was happy to be toiling and busying herself so. She was almost afraid that he would come and keep her company in the kitchen while she cooked, or from time to time ingratiatingly ask, do you want some help? Had it been so, this would have thrown into disarray their brief but genuine and peaceful moment of domestic life. What she really longed for was to be able to act like a wife to him, to serve him and work for him, to look after every little detail, and then, like a wife, without any bashfulness, to give herself to him.

Yet he did come into the kitchen, and silently watched as she bustled to and fro. At last, he finally spoke: Won't you hold it against me that I'm not helping? At home, she's always spoiled me. She? Who's she? she asked, the knife held motionless in her hand. Wife. My wife. His answer came out in two sentences. The knife edge resumed its motion over the cutting board, and suddenly the white shredded radish was smudged with red. You've cut your finger. He came up and placed her wounded index finger to his lips and sucked it dry of the oozing blood. Neither of them spoke another word.

It was a silent dinner. Looking at each other was all they craved. You mustn't think I tricked you, he said. No. This isn't so important to me, she replied. So why did you cut your hand? he asked. Just a pure coincidence, she said. Are you saying I can have an easy conscience? he asked. Of course. I, too, can have an easy conscience, she said. And it was while looking at him then that she finally realized: she had never had any intention of marrying him.

There was no need for preconditions. Neither had any need to convince the other of anything. They were linked by a tacit understanding at some high level. The conventional patterns of suspicion and jealousy in any couple of lovers were miraculously dispensed with, their hearts plunged into a space of limitless transparency. Ah, that really was a precious moment on Earth.

They heard the sound of a distant piano. The glow of the lamp was warm and peaceful. Outside, the wind might blow, the rain might fall, the whole Earth might have sunk to nothingness, poured into the ocean. They wouldn't have known.

I put too much trust in premonitions. It's because when I was thirteen I had intuitions about the future. On the strength of these intuitions, I knew that the most beautiful girl in the class, Wan Xiaoyan, would end up falling in love with the physical education teacher. Some ten years later, I got an invitation to their wedding. The rumor was that because of her marriage, Wang Xiaoyan's family, whose circumstances were highly privileged, cut off all relations with her. A primary school physical education teacher has a hard time showing the right qualifications for a powerful father- and mother-in-law. This news filled me with regret for the hatred I used to feel and my behavior toward her, especially when I threw into the garbage pail behind the schoolroom the eraser she had borrowed from me. I rummaged through my mother's room quite a while, and picked a pair of light green flower vases as a present. After this my mother gave me a lengthy scolding, saying this was a Qing Dynasty antique that had been part of her mother's dowry. I could hardly take back the present I had already given away; what's more, I didn't think the present extravagant, for they had confirmed my predictions, so I still felt I owed them repeated thanks.

A young girl, just thirteen that year, just beginning to understand life. The dragonfly on the oleander hedge told her that life was as fragile as her wings.

All along, there had been a kind of presentiment churning around inside me: this baby couldn't possibly drop uneventfully into life. My life would be torn apart by it, like a banner on the far-flung frontier, rent to pieces by a gale, floating above a desperate struggle between life and death. After I had been harboring the fetus for eight and a half months, I was often awakened by a nightmare. In my nightmare, I was walking ahead strenuously in a barren and desolate plain, unable to stop. The road wound on, unending, and I was like an exiled prisoner in forced labor, driven forward by a shapeless force, toward an unknown destination in the dark. Sometimes it seemed to me that I stood at a crossroads with no signposts, and that my mother, my husband, Sumi, and him—they each stood there, alone in one of the four roads, and silently watched as I struggled. I was dragging fetters, and the backs of my feet were dripping with blood where they rubbed, with my deathly white ankle joints bursting right through. As always, they stood unmoved. I looked frantically at the four roads around me, and in a rush of panic chose the direction where he stood. The three others then turned into raging fiends, and pursued me, beating me with whips and cudgels. I turned to him and begged him to save me, but he just stood there, far off, without moving, his eyes cold and expressionless like a lifeless statue. I completely lost all hope. No one on Earth could help me. Every time I woke up from the nightmare, I once again reached the same conclusion. After that I couldn't help thinking about him. Undoubtedly he would be fast asleep, with his arms clutched around his wife's shoulders.

Everywhere there was just the stillness of night. Occasionally, a car would speed out of the darkness and speed back into the darkness again.

When I was taken to the delivery room, the pains in my belly had already evolved into regular contractions. Every spell of pain was more violent than the last. In a daze, I saw the fetus in my belly as some sort of green-faced, long-fanged monster. It was using its sharp fingernails and toenails to claw into the walls of my belly, doing its utmost to tear my flesh, chew it to bits with its sharp teeth, mix in my warm blood and swallow up the whole hash. It seemed like a ravenous and efficient beast, tirelessly consuming everything in my entrails, sparing not a single organ. I let out a desperate scream, as I felt myself losing all my insides; my body had turned into a cavern teeming with a confusion of blood and flesh. It was gradually growing cold, and dry, and it began to float lightly round and round in a rising vortex of icy wind. Gradually the pain faded, and in its place was a feeling of comfort like nothing I had ever experienced. The black clouds of smoke seemed to be dispelled, and before my eyes was a gentle glow, while I heard what sounded like an organ playing solemn hymns, and to the music of the hymns I peacefully went to sleep.

The one night that belonged to them, a little before midnight, they rested on the pillow in the languor of love. He smoked a cigarette, exhaling his happiness with the smoke and, with an expression of love in his eyes, he caressed her soothingly. Talking had become burdensome, and neither spoke a word.

If I died, would you weep? she suddenly asked. I don't know. But I'd be very sad, he answered, with a long and meaningful kiss. She embraced him with renewed tenderness, and her heart was filled with the feeling that they were parting forever. Unawares, tears flowed down and dribbled from her temples onto his arm. What is it? What are you sad about? he asked, a little surprised. Suddenly a violent grief seized her heart; she made an effort to control her tears, but this only made her sob out loud. He caressed her forehead with his chin, and gently said: Perhaps, many years from now, when I have forgotten everything, I will remember only your tears. Every gentle and subtle feeling ever felt since the beginning of humanity seemed to gather and fuse together and flow to her now, and she felt its weight engulfing her. She really didn't know whether it had been good luck or bad for their lives to have crossed in this world.

Slowly the feeling ebbed and went, and she was quiet again.

Are you going to sleep? he gave her a tap. Let's not sleep tonight, all right? This suggestion lifted her spirits. She understood what he meant: our time is too short. Good, I'll go and make some coffee. She put on his broad cotton shirt, and went into the kitchen, her footstep lithe and graceful. She felt like Cinderella in the fairy tale, young, pure and kind, felt that in the selfless service of others her soul was being purified to the highest degree.

The coffee was too strong, a little acrid and bitter. Lifting their cups together, they slowly drank it, as if this acrid, bitter taste was that of happiness itself. This day must be fixed in our memory, it has to become a feast day that neither of us can ever forget, he said. In wordless answer, she tapped his cup with hers.

The white poplar trees swayed in the whistling wind, making a whooshing sound. Slowly, the day dawned.

In twos and threes, black shadows hovered before me. The metal instruments made a clear melodious clanging sound. A halo gradually spread, and the shadowless lamp shone brightly in my eyes. They brought salt water to rinse off the infant. I was just able to pick out my mother's voice, but her tone had lost its customary dignity. Quick, get hold of it, it's a boy. Then another voice spoke. Why isn't he crying? It was my husband, in anxious tones. Slap, slap—it was what I'd heard my mother talking about before: the head nurse was slapping the baby's bottom. Whah! a cry sprang up, though only a feeble one. When it's washed take it to the warm room. What about her blood pressure? My mother again. Her blood pressure and pulse are back to normal, the nurse answered. She should wake up now. My mother moved right up close, called my name. I shut my eyes tight and didn't move. I regarded myself as a creature who had just been humiliated and injured by all of the people present, including this newborn baby; these were the people who had terrified me and treated me to all kinds of deadly indignities, after which they had dug out what they wanted from me. Say something, I know you can hear me. My mother, as if bent on laying me bare, indifferent to my privacy, just revealed my little stratagem. I still didn't move a hair. Don't pay any attention to her, she's having a tantrum. Once again my mother was beginning to abuse her dignity. The patient wants to hoodwink her doctor, and the daughter wants to hoodwink her mother. It's all just wishful thinking.

I didn't hear my husband's voice any more. I knew he had followed that half-dead child to the infant care room. Simply an iron certainty, that outcome: it had long been clear to me that for him in there my own importance couldn't measure up to a finger of that baby. If he had married me, looked after me, it was all motivated by nothing more than conventions, reason and the proliferation of his posterity. I should be grateful to him, it was thanks to him that once, just once, I had felt proud and elated in front of Sumi. Come to think of it, this was quite funny. Now I had put my own life at stake to produce another life, to pay him back for his affection, so I could rest easy. Really, I was just too tired.

On that wet afternoon so many years ago, when that thirteen-year-old girl trembled in awe of the red dragonfly on the oleander branch, and came to the realization of the whole meaning of human life, no one knew, then, whether it occurred to her that one day she would live the life of a woman, and endure so much suffering. That is a secret locked away forever. No one can know.

All the while, she'd been waiting for him to say: I love you. But he didn't. He just said, as was his habit: I like you, I really like you. Just once, when she pushed him and wouldn't let go, he said it in English: *I love you.* I always feel awkward saying it in Chinese, he explained to her. This incident made her think he wasn't as obliging as she'd imagined, after all. Reminiscing happily about all this, she waited for him. She wanted to take him to the railway station. She was determined that the leave-taking would not be filled with anguish. She was confident that the distance between them could increase and deepen their longing for one another, and engrave their love even more deeply into the core of their being. The feeling that from now on, there would be someone, somewhere several thousand miles away, who would miss her from time to time, filled her to bursting with boundless joy. The big city where she had long lived, everything she had gone through in the past, next to that now seemed paltry, confined, and dull beyond endurance. She was willing to suffer the sleepless nights that would follow their parting: in the dead stillness of the dark, she would be able to think about him, to pray for him and wish for his happiness. Nevertheless, the fact was that he did have to leave her, to return to a world dominated by another woman. Perhaps he would soon get bogged down again in the reality of his role as a husband and father, in the life which he was doomed to want to go back to, and the memory of her would gradually fade away. To imagine that made her shudder, and it was as if the lovely brilliance of the sun were suddenly eclipsed to spread darkness in her heart. Let me just split myself squarely in two, one half for you, one half for her: he had said that to her one time, while caressing the hair on her temples. But when she had been seized by that feeling of bitter solitude, of having no one to lean on, and he had looked at her so mercilessly—then she had wanted to throw herself in his arms and cry out: I want my half! I'll trade all of me for it!

He was late. There was just enough time left to rush all the way to the railway station. Some good friends insisted on giving me a farewell dinner, I really couldn't get out of it. Faced with her resentful expression, he looked like a child who had been naughty. But you should have let me know. You knew I was waiting for you. She felt aggrieved, she had to let it out. She had been busy the whole morning preparing things for him to eat and drink, getting ready things he would need, including a traveling shoe brush, paper towels to wipe his hands with, and books to distract him on his journey. She'd put everything in order, carefully setting out alternating meat and vegetarian snacks in the container so as to make it most convenient for him, so he could eat first one and then the other, with coffee for the morning and tea for the afternoon. She felt like an idiot, taking care of this mountain of things, waiting for him anxiously, while at that very moment he was raising toast after toast with people with whom he hadn't the least thing in common. Please don't be angry with me. I can't bear to part with you like this. He hurriedly kissed her hair. If you forgive me, hoist the book bag with your left hand; if you don't forgive me you can still use your right hand, he said. He knew all along she'd change the book bag to her left hand, she wouldn't and couldn't deny him anything he asked. She raised the book bag into the train window with her left hand, just as the train started to pull out; he didn't have time to say anything more, and only could throw her a last look, empty and bewildered.

The train drew away into the distance, leaving the rails trembling slightly behind them, with an inauspicious sound. She ached with the pain of parting in every inch of her guts. The speeding train, just like the red dragonfly, had flown away never to return.

While I was struggling to emerge from the cavern of death, Sumi was stepping on the path to death. She hadn't appealed the decision of the first court, and so her remaining time of life had contracted still more. Both of us were brushing against the boundaries of life and death, but we were headed in opposite directions. I felt in this an intimation of the secret tie that bound us. There never had been any clear explanation of the impulse that had led her to kill her own sons: there was only the fact that, as a result of the examination conducted by the hospital, the court had rejected the claim that she was schizophrenic, and had decided that for her to evade execution would fail to satisfy public outrage. There would be the sound of a gun shot, and Sumi would turn into an unfathomable mystery, and no one would ever draw any connection with me, and even I would be unable to get clear exactly what part I really played in this riddle. I merely celebrated the fact that she left with her beauty intact. Since heaven and Earth had forged such beauty in her, it wouldn't have done for her to live on if that beauty were spoiled. They said that before her execution she scribbled a note to her husband, saying that she was about to be reunited with her children. In life, one could only be together a brief spell, while parting was forever, but after death, it was parting that was brief, and one could be united forever. She had chosen to be with them forever. By the time the note was conveyed to her husband, Sumi had already wafted away like a puff of incense. It was all ranting, she really was mad. Her husband, in the extremity of grief, wept without tears. Everyone who knew her was filled with pity, said that right till her last moments she displayed all the signs of insanity, but it was too late. They would never in all of time understand Sumi. By the same token, they would never in all of time understand me. Sumi had died, her secret held close within her; I was living, my own secret held close inside me. We were two completely similar women; we were two completely different women. Or perhaps it wasn't just us, it wasn't just women: every human being on this Earth is born and dies with a riddle that is never unlocked. Enigmas we come, enigmas we go.

A long, long time passed; it seemed like a hundred years. The rainy afternoon roused countless memories, as I walked with my son past the oleander hedge. The oleanders hadn't flowered yet, and rain dripped on their leaves in pearl-like tears. I saw the thirteen-year-old girl, walking to and fro under the wall of trees, her heart filled with the longing to confide the secrets of her life. A boy, who knows where he sprang from, ran up and squeezed the life out of the rain-drenched red dragonfly on the tree branch. The boy's round head was covered in shiny black hair; it looked like the glistening black fur of the cat that the girl had once so painstakingly raised. I straddled to avoid the dragonfly on the ground, and continued to walk. And suddenly fathomed how brief indeed is every human's path from birth to death.

It was because of Sumi that she hurried her wedding. It was because she had seen in Sumi's gaze, just the time of an eyeblink, the shadow of disappointment and envy: this was what determined her to tell her mother that she intended to marry the young doctor. A few thousand miles away, somewhere in a large southern city, lay a scarcely imagined piece of ground that floated in her dreams, and there, an image forever conjured in her dreams, was the man who had already left her.

Altogether, he had written her just two letters. They were short, and had neither salutation nor signature. Just before leaving, he had told her he might not be able to write her even a few words, but that he would think of her longingly. She took the implicit message in these words to be that he didn't want to get into trouble on her account. She realized that as a husband and a father he had to act this way. The forbearance of a woman in love is as broad as the ocean: she just needs the man she loves to be willing to dive deep into that ocean. After a few years, she still could recite by heart every sentence in those letters, and the last sentence he had written was fixed especially clearly in her mind: I think of you, from far far away. The first letter she had written him had been a poem, a very clumsily written poem. He had written back that women always turn the past into poetry, even if it was just a quotation or a comedy routine. This remark had left her feeling wounded for a long time, but she couldn't help herself and wrote him more letters, and to the patter of rain in the night, or to the howl of icy wind, or in the chill of early morning, she poured out onto the cold white page the twisting hurt and anguish of her innermost heart—like an over-heated patient opening her veins to let the hot blood stream out to save her in the extremity of a fever close to death. At the end of every letter she repeated that there was no need to answer. As a result, sure enough, no more letters came.

The boy threw the red dragonfly on the ground, and scampered off. They told me he was my son, but I couldn't make sense any more of the meaning of this word *son*. I didn't need to know who he was, I felt no need to understand who he was, where he came from or where he was going. Would he resent me, this boy, now scampering off?

It looked like a bundle of light soft cotton flowers that had fallen on the floor; as in a trance, my hand opened and the infant dropped from my chest. I expected an ear-piercing cry, but it never came. There was a faint sound, then not a stir came from the swaddling clothes. Ah—I stopped my own mouth, but a scream escaped me as in my nightmare. My husband rushed in from outside the door, his hands covered in soap bubbles. What happened? he asked in an urgent voice. I just stuck my head in the pillow, didn't look at him and didn't answer. I guessed that he must already have picked up the child, and with his most practiced skill was administering first-aid. For sure, that child's lips were purple, he was choking. The child uttered not a sound. He was certainly dead, no doubt about it. In one second, I had emulated Sumi, and I didn't know if it had been an accident or the effect of some irresistible fate.

The prison van sped by on the road, sped to the place of execution. The cloud of dust it raised blocked the view, and people couldn't peer inside at the criminal on the way to meet her death.

Come now, you must take your sedative, your pulse is racing. My husband was passing me a glass of warm boiled water and a little white pill. How's the baby? I asked in a faint whisper. He couldn't breathe for a second, but everything's all right now, he said. But you do need to be careful, don't keep getting all upset. I looked at the child, sleeping peacefully on the pillow next to me, and obediently nodded and took the pill. Since you came home, things haven't been easy for you; there can be after-effects of a difficult delivery. My husband was forgiving me, magnanimously. He was a doctor, not a judge; he brought everything back to the medical angle, so he couldn't see the crime for the sickness. Take care of yourself and you'll soon be well. Now just go to sleep for a while. He made sure the quilt covered me snugly. I gathered the child up on my breast, closed my eyes and hummed a lullaby, exerting myself to the utmost to produce an atmosphere overflowing with mother love.

I've always been silent as a tomb about all that. If some mother should happen to mention to someone that her small child fills her with terror and hatred, I affect to treat it as a big joke. I cradled my newborn baby, and thought about how savagely he took over my entrails, and grew larger day by day, drawing support from the warmth and nourishment of my body; about how he used his sharp nails and teeth to tear the walls of my body, and swallowed up my blood and my flesh, how he suddenly used to terrorize me. He had now metamorphosed into a sweet looking, mild-eyed human, so that no one could know what he was really like. But he had only to open his mouth and get absorbed in sucking my breast's milk, and right away I could see his insatiable self again. From the first day of his existence, I was at his mercy. He concocted this intimacy of our flesh and bones, playing to perfection the conventional role expected of him as a member of the human world, and ceaselessly exploited me, sucking from me countless times a day the liquid substance he required, using his still toothless gums to grind away at my breasts until they dripped with blood. He was a machine, knowing neither fatigue nor compassion, who bit by bit dug away at my life to make it his own. My blood was being channeled in a steady stream through my mammary glands till it dried up without my even knowing it. I didn't really love him, but as before I conscientiously fulfilled my duty to feed him at the well of my own life so that he would grow big. About that nightmarish failed attempt at murdering him, I can only seal up the secret tight, silent as a tomb. Thanks to this pretense of conscientiously fulfilling my duty, people all imagine I'm capable of being a good mother. I well know that if a mother fails to love her son, she can't expect anyone in the world to love her.

She had pined for love.

She never thought their reunion would be like that. Under a lonely lamp, by the silent window, she had fantasized a thousand times about their reunion after long parting, but in truth nothing could have matched the reality of that reunion. You had to say it pleased him that she showed up. It pleased him: nothing more.

How did you get here? he smiled. Smiling was his habit, a habit that was second nature. How did I get here? Here's how I got here. In her room, among the jumbled piles of curtains, tablecloths, pillowcases and bedspreads, she had left a letter telling her mother and the man she was about to marry that she had to go on a trip, and had then gone to the ticket office of the People's Airline to wait for someone to return a ticket. You always were daring and rash, he said. Before deciding to go, she had been using the sewing machine to make her dowry linen, whistling a tune all the while—it was the tune that he had incessantly sung in her ear: "Goodby, my love." It was when they were together that she had learned to whistle. They used to whistle greetings to one another, or else messages that only they could understand. Suddenly, she felt like whistling that song for him, suddenly felt a violent desire to see him. For some reason, she didn't tell him all that. As soon as she saw him, she sensed an atmosphere of unease. She discovered that he wasn't the same as those few years ago, he no longer seemed as interested in listening to her, especially her expressions of feeling. He looked at her in a very friendly way, a little as an older brother might look at his little sister, kind, but not intimate. They sat in the flower garden in the median strip in the road; the flower bed was large, allowing them to sit at quite a distance from each other, as if to advertise the fact that their relationship was open and aboveboard. In spite of this, he still scrutinized the passers-by from time to time, just as he used to do, as if he were afraid that someone he knew might see them. She became stiff and formal, her hands and feet fidgeting, not knowing what she must say and what she mustn't say to him. In the past, she could tell him anything she wanted, there were no constraints, she never felt anxious about being indiscreet, never thought he might scorn or ridicule her. Now, for the first time, she felt oppressed at his side. Who would have thought that in the past he always made her feel so relaxed, so happy, so natural—so much in harmony with him. She was aware of having in the past lost all self-consciousness when she was in his presence. All in all, the result was that she had just lost all her glamor: to love a man beyond measure meant turning into a fool and having to endure being ignored as a fool, eroding away her last scrap of self-confidence.

She fixed him with eyes full of reproach, and he read the meaning of her gaze, and politely looked away. Did you think about me? To ask such a question at such a time amounted to nothing less than self-torture, and her pride should have stopped her, but it came out anyway. I thought about you when I had the time, but you know I've been very busy, he answered, without a trace of feeling. You've changed, she said. When the scenery changes, so does the heart, he answered. A man can't play the same tune all his life long. I'm willing to follow my natural inclinations, but I can't force myself. He said the same things in many words, using many different similes; but the one thing she heard was: that was then, this is now. She felt he was humiliating her. I've already begun to be afraid of you, she said in a pitiful tone. I like women to be afraid of me. He felt no pity: on the contrary, he rather seemed to be gloating, quite pleased with himself. She simply couldn't believe that this cold-hearted and commonplace man was once the one she remembered as so considerate and warm. She cast her mind back to the many evenings when the two of them had dined together, and the things he had said then. Look, we seem to be in our own home. It's as if the two of us were writing an abridged version of a novel. He was very light-hearted, she very serious. Abridged, because the rhythm of their every emotion was an accelerated one, rising to a climax right after the beginning, and after the climax winding down to an ending. The thought of that ending left her distraught; it seemed to her that this novel's ending was ill-fated. Despite being ill-fated, she would just let the process go on without limit; she would have wanted the novel just to have a beginning, just to have a climax, but to go on forever without an ending.

His comparison was borne out by reality; her own fancies vanished and turned into calamity. Her heart began to ache again, but this ache tasted quite different from that which sprang from being in love.

At that moment, I felt overcome by the feebleness of old age. The skin of my face became lined, as if it had dried up in a parching wind; my hair and my teeth fell out continually, and the old-age spots one sees on old people covered my neck and the back of my hands.

Don't be so downcast, when you're upset it ages you. Sure enough, he had noticed my old woman look. He walked over and made me conscious of it, giving me a fleeting kiss on the forehead, like a brother kissing his little sister. Do you still like me? I asked. It seemed I still wanted to drag some hope out of despair. I like you, he said. But I couldn't hear the same tone of voice if I looked in his eyes. No you don't, you don't like me any more. I wanted to cry, but I had no tears. If I say I like you, you still won't believe me, so what am I to do? He was being deliberately evasive. Really? Until I'm an old, old woman? I asked, my tears bursting out, but quickly suppressed. Cheer up a bit, when you're cheerful is when I like you. You're a cheerful person, deep down. He just didn't seem to understand why I was or wasn't cheerful. It seemed he had no inkling that my cheerfulness was fake, that by nature I was really rather gloomy. Now time had passed and it was a different place, and he no longer understood me, nor did he feel any need to understand me, for to him I had already turned into an indifferent stranger.

We have to go. There are too many mosquitoes. In truth, when he uttered this suggestion, it was altogether reasonable. Nevertheless, she couldn't have uttered it herself: if, like her, he hadn't brought it up, she would have been happy to continue sitting there for a few centuries, until they had become fossils, dug up by future generations and taken off to be exhibited in a museum of natural history. He stretched out his hand towards her, and hoisted her up from the stone seat, and the momentum of that gesture made them cleave together. He kissed her, in that way that used to intoxicate her. But she felt it was only an empty, arid and unemotional parting kiss. Perhaps it was a polite gesture made out of a sense of duty, perhaps a kind of condescending pity—who could tell? In any case, whether he loved or not, whether he was loved or not—it was all up to him. The barriers were there in plain view, the distance couldn't be denied, and she was in despair.

I had wanted to confess. But I knew that nobody would believe me. That boy quickly grew up to be a perfectly contented sort, as if to proclaim to the world that I was a good mother. To all appearances, we were very close, indeed inseparable, and if there was any strife between us, we both tacitly determined to seal it up and keep it secret, a private matter which wasn't anyone else's business. As always, he controlled my destiny; my life was regulated in accordance with the rules he laid down and approved of, and every day by my expressions of love I sought to prove that I was indeed a good mother. But actually I was befuddled by my fantasies about the deep bond between mother and son; I was often intoxicated with mother love and quite forgot the essential conflict between that boy and myself. The years passed, day by day he grew stronger and more vigorous, while day by day I withered. The day would soon dawn when I would want to vanish from this world, and let him live in my place.

The lake surface was shrouded with purple mist. On the shore, willow catkins were flying about, tossed here and there by the wind. All around the little boat, spawning fish were struggling and darting about, and then sinking away. We were just like those fish: bound to grow, to spawn, then decline into old age and die. Soon after drawing up the blueprint for our lives as women, Sumi had died, so she didn't even reach the decline of old age. Maybe this was a mark of her courage: she really felt no terror before death. Or maybe it was a mark of her cowardice: that she was terrified by the process of growing old. In comparison to her, maybe I was the coward, because I was terrified of death; but maybe it was I who was brave, because I was willing to face old age. She had evaded old age, and thrown herself into death as a refuge; I was willing to endure old age, but in the end death's summons would not be evaded. We two women were completely alike, and completely unlike. We led our lives in our own different ways. No one could judge us: each of us lived out her fate.

All alone in the world, I walked the streets, and all around me was the glow of the big city in the night. The confused noise of the city filled earth and sky, and strangers appeared by my side and vanished like ghosts. The headlights of cars flashed and twinkled uncertainly like will-o'-the-wisps in a field, now near, now far. I seemed to be in some place that was both heaven and hell; I had turned into something that was neither ghost nor human, going I knew not where.

He must be home by now, he would have finished dinner; his hair would be soaked from taking a shower and he'd be drying it with a towel; he'd be smoking a cigarette and watching television; or else he'd be playing with his wife and children in a carefree, leisurely way. He wouldn't remember or miss me, he wouldn't care where I was; he had his own unchangeable life. In his life, I was just a brief interlude, that was as certain as fate.

Again I returned to my room, strewn all over with its jumble of curtains, tablecloths, pillowcases and bedspreads, and resumed making my wedding dress. No one reproached me. Just so long as you've returned safe and sound, that sets our minds at rest: my mother and this man who was about to become my husband said this in unison, as if they had agreed on it beforehand. Their forbearance moved me: could it be that they were the people on this Earth who genuinely loved me? Actually, I really didn't deserve this love. In this life and world, I could only struggle to do my duty as a daughter and a wife; I couldn't possibly love them with the kind of love that would meet their expectations. I had loved enough already.

She phoned him to say goodby, and to announce that she was getting married immediately upon her return, but deep in her heart she was still hesitating. It seemed that she'd only now realized that this trip of a few thousand miles, her throwing herself at him, were all designed to ask his advice. It's your decision; you have to have some clear and definite and reasonable plan for your own future life, he advised her in measured, amiable tones. And suddenly she felt that talking to him about these things was a waste of time. She didn't understand why she had sought him out to ask his advice—after all, what did it all have to do with him? What about you? Her question was incoherent, and he misunderstood what she was saying. I won't destroy one beautiful thing just for the sake of another beautiful thing. His answer was ingenious, well phrased, and at the same time quite unemotional. She wanted to say to him: Don't think I'm that devoted to you. But the words wouldn't come out. What's the matter now? he asked. Nothing, she answered. Well, that's that then. And without waiting for her to respond again, he hung up the phone.
Well, that's it then. Truly a tragic ending.

The boy, whose round head was covered with shiny black hair, threw down the red dragonfly and scampered off, and in the twinkling of an eye he had disappeared without a trace. I felt no need to know where he had gone: it seemed, that one time, like parting forever.

The city streetcar rails are beginning to be dismantled. Except for the tourist area in Lichee Bay park, which have become part of a complex of tourist facilities, all the other rail tracks have been converted to asphalt roads. At the streetcar stop where he and I so often met that year, the sunshade canopy has already vanished who knows where, and all that is left are two dilapidated stone blocks, like two gravestones that no one has swept clean for ages. We had pledged to meet at this tram car stop, on the tenth anniversary of our special feast day, and stay there until we saw each other.
I didn't write to tell him about the dismantling of the tram tracks. There was no need. When he had slammed down the phone with a bang, I clearly saw that he wouldn't come to keep our appointment. Yet I still silently keep waiting for that day. I will wait for him stubbornly, as I did that evening ten years before, until the last bus had sped by. I will remind myself to put on more

clothes, because there won't be someone there to smile and protect me from the wind. Though the bus stop won't return, the two stone stumps will still be there, like two desolate tombstones. His and my names will have to be carved on them.

The red dragonfly, its wings pinched and broken, fell to the ground. The round-headed, black-haired boy scampered away. I stepped wide to avoid the dragonfly, and continued on my way.

Maybe a long way. Maybe not.

Translated by Ronald de Sousa

池　莉

Chi Li (b. 1957), a native of Wuhan, has been a
teacher, a doctor and an editor. She began to
write in the late 1970s. In 1987, she published
"Troublesome Life" (Fannao rensheng), which
brought her instant recognition. Critics consider
her a *xin xieshi* (new realist) but Chi Li is
reluctant to accept this label because she expects
to experiment with many different writing styles.
Nevertheless, her writing since "Troublesome
Life" has focused on the everyday lives of
ordinary people in urban China.

Hot or Cold, Life's Okay
❖
1991

It was about four o'clock that afternoon. A shirtless man riding a dilapidated bicycle screeched to a stop in the gutter in front of Xiaochukai Tang. He didn't get off the bicycle, but kept his balance by touching the ground with his toes. With both hands he crumpled a sweaty bill into a ball and flicked it right onto the counter top.

"Hey, Cat. Get me a thermometer."

"Sure thing," Cat answered cheerfully, and went to get the thermometer.

Hanzhen, the cashier, made change and asked, "Who's that?"

"I don't know him," Cat replied.

"You don't know that guy who just called you Cat?" Hanzhen exclaimed.

"Everybody on Jiangnan Road knows I'm called Cat," he protested.

"Oh. It's like you're some big shot," said Hanzhen.

"I'm just telling you the way it is," Cat said.

Hanzhen opened her mouth, but she couldn't think of anything appropriate to say, so she kept quiet. She adjusted the fan toward her face, and through her wind-blown eyelashes turned her blurry vision toward the street.

Cat went to the edge of the gutter to hand over the thermometer to the customer. In an instant both of them were slick with sweat. Something suddenly startled them, then, roaring with laughter, they both cried, "Son of a bitch!"

Cat fetched another thermometer and gave it to the customer. Hanzhen asked, "What happened?"

Cat just laughed heartily and tossed over the money for the other thermometer.

"Well? What happened?" insisted Hanzhen.

"Take a guess," Cat said.

"You're going to make me guess on such a hot day. You're too much!" Hanzhen said.

"Take a guess. It would be amusing. You'll never guess in a million years," Cat said.

"I really must persuade Yanhua not to marry you. Hell, you're not enough of a man at all," Hanzhen said.

"What do you mean 'Not enough of a man?' That's shallow. All right, I'll tell you. Pop! The thermometer exploded and the mercury spilled out!" Cat said.

Hanzhen opened her eyes wide and said, "I don't believe you!"

"You don't believe me? Like this. Pop!" Cat made an animated motion.

"The world really is intriguing," Hanzhen said.

Cat gave her a look of disdain and mimicked the speech of Jiang Kun, the host of the talent-search TV program *The World Really Is Intriguing.*

They laughed, clutching their stomachs. The remaining hours passed quickly that day. They didn't doze off as usual. Instead, they talked about many strange, interesting things.

Cat originally had intended to go home after he got off work, but now he changed his plans and decided to go to Yanhua's instead. The temperature was skyrocketing and, on such a hot day, he should help out Yanhua. Since they were dating, he should show her a little consideration.

He left the store and, after walking along the main street for three minutes, he reached Yanhua's home. It was an old-fashioned house left over from the old society. The front entrance was small, but inside it was huge, as complicated as a rabbit warren. It was impossible to tell how many families lived there. Just inside the front door there was a steep, narrow staircase. Yanhua and her father lived in a two-room unit on the second floor. Yanhua had one room and her father had the other one, fifteen square meters in all. In the Jiangnan Road area, this kind of housing was unspeakably good. That made Yanhua even more attractive. Cat considered it: if Yanhua wasn't attractive, then who was? She had looks, she had an apartment, she had skills, and as for money, she was an only daughter. Yes, if Yanhua wasn't attractive, then who was? Yes, you had to say that Yanhua was attractive. Cat had confidence in himself.

Old Mrs. Wang, who lived on the first floor, was sitting on a small stool at the foot of the staircase shelling beans. Old Mrs. Wang was as regular as clockwork. Every evening at six o'clock, she was always sitting there trimming vegetables.

"Mrs. Wang. Hot, eh!" Cat said.

"It sure is, Cat," she replied.

Cat gave old Mrs. Wang a box of Rendan pills and said, "Mrs. Wang, it isn't cooling down, so take a few Rendan pills."

"Oh, why should I take them?" she said. "I'm just a troublesome old woman getting on in years. I just hope that I stop breathing. It would be a nice relief."

"Nonsense," said Cat.

Old Mrs. Wang shook out a few of the glimmering silver pills, and keeping them on her tongue said ambiguously, "Cat, Yanhua was on the morning shift today, so be careful."

There was no need for old Mrs. Wang to remind him; he knew what to expect. Yanhua was a city bus driver and every week she switched shifts. On the morning shift she set out at four a.m. It was impossible to get a good night's sleep on this shift. Whenever Yanhua switched to the morning shift, she directed her wrath at Cat, which was why Cat originally had planned to go straight home today.

Yanhua was in the communal kitchen washing vegetables. She was wearing a mannish sleeveless shirt and cotton print pants. The back of her clothes, including the waist of her pants, was stuck to her with sweat. The kitchen was shared by several families. A few of the women were bustling about with their meals, just as sweaty as Yanhua. Cat thought it was just like a sauna in there.

"Hot, eh ladies," declared Cat.

"You're such a sweet talker, Cat," they replied.

"Yanhua," called Cat.

Yanhua, who was briskly washing the vegetables, did not reply.

"Let me help," said Cat.

Yanhua ignored him and continued to wash the vegetables.

Cat, who was facing the women, made a signal for help and so they said, "Yanhua is such a stubborn girl. She can't enjoy her own good fortune."

"Quite right," said Cat.

Yanhua held up a finger, wiped off the drops of sweat on her face with a splash and said, "Go away. Didn't you say that you couldn't come today? Didn't you say that your mother was sick? She sure recovered fast!"

"You don't know what happened today," Cat said. "I've come specially to tell you."

Yanhua shot him an angry glance.

"What happened? What happened?" the women all asked.

"I was selling a thermometer," said Cat. "I took it to the street to give to the customer. The sun only shone on it for a few seconds, then 'pop!' the mercury ran out, the thermometer exploded."

"Ha. You see, it's this damned Wuhan heat! It's so hot!" said the women.

"You're exaggerating," said Yanhua.

"I'm exaggerating? Am I the kind of guy who exaggerates?" asked Cat.

"You think that you don't exaggerate? Nine out of ten men exaggerate," said Yanhua.

"Then let these ladies decide," said Cat.

"Cat doesn't really exaggerate," said the women. "Don't be so unfair to him, Yanhua."

"What are you all up to? Ganging up on me!" Unable to stop smiling, she turned around and walked away.

Cat took off his t-shirt and began to wash the vegetables. Then he cut them up and fried them. *Clang, clang,* he worked enthusiastically, dripping with sweat.

"Eh, henpecked Cat," the women said.

"It's only fear," said Cat. "What's the scandal in fearing your wife. It's the big trend nowadays. In fact, I feel sorry for her. The morning shift is really tough."

"Cat really is a good man," they said. "He's considerate and hard-working. And he doesn't go gambling or whoring."

"You don't pick up johns, so how do you know that I don't go whoring?" asked Cat.

One of the women walked over and pinched his mouth. A few of the others said, "Fuck you."

Cat laughed.

The meal was ready now. Yanhua's father returned. The old master chef was completely gray. He looked like the God of Longevity. He was the retired bean-curd-skin chef from Laotongcheng Restaurant. On the first day of his retirement, he had been enticed back by the high salary. It was said that he had been one of the chefs who had prepared bean-curd skins for Chairman Mao. There was no one in the neighborhood who did not allude to this and admire him.

Everyone in the kitchen greeted him.

"Master Xu, you're back."

"Yes, yes. It's so hot today," Master Xu said.

"Yes, it's so hot," they all replied.

"Cat, you're sweltering. Run inside and cool off with the electric fan," Master Xu said.

"It doesn't matter," said Cat. "It just blows hot air."

Yanhua had taken a bath with cool water. She looked handsome and bold, her breasts and thighs clearly showing through her sleeveless black top and white skirt. Cat, facing her, snapped his fingers. She turned and was about to go.

"Yanhua! Help Cat put out the food," Master Xu said.

The sun was sinking now little by little behind the buildings on the west side of the street but the remaining sunshine was still blinding. The water truck passed back and forth; they could hear the sound of sprinkling water. On the street, white steam rose up: soon the street was dry again. Although dusk had not yet come, the daytime breeze already had died down. This cursed Wuhan summer!

Yanhua carried out two buckets of water. Then she poured the water all over the street in front of her building, turning it a wet black color. By the time she stood upright, several households had moved out their bamboo beds.

"Cat!" shouted Yanhua.

"Coming," Cat replied from upstairs.

After a few minutes Cat still had not come down.

Yanhua was not pleased. She called out loudly, "Cat!"

Cat came down with a bamboo bed.

"You took your time coming downstairs," Yanhua said. "All the good spots have been taken by the neighbors."

"Hey. Lower your voice a little, okay?" Cat said. "Look at you. Everybody has got the usual spot for his bed. Everybody has to get some sleep. If we have to squeeze in a little, that's just the way it is."

Yanhua lowered her voice a little, but she was not convinced and said, "You're so sensible, so upright, the neighbors find you so likable. Goodness!"

"I'm just being realistic about it," Cat said.

Cat and Yanhua talked in whispers as they worked. They set up a bamboo bed and two deck-chairs, with the fan at one end of the bamboo bed and the television at the other end. A couple of half-grown boys were darting about like fish, making the electrical cords swing back and forth. "Shoo," said Yanhua. She chased them away as if they were small animals. Cat, who thought this was quite amusing, said, "Boys will be boys."

Master Xu came downstairs waving a folding fan. He'd already had a bath and was wearing an old pair of blue silk underpants. Sitting down on a deck-chair facing Yanhua and Cat, he looked completely contented.

In the middle of the bed were four plates of food and one bowl of soup. You shouldn't assume these ordinary dishes didn't make it into cookbooks. This was the type of food perhaps most loved by the people of Wuhan: red chilies with cold snow-white lotus root slices; thinly cut lean pork fried with green bitter gourd; long fish pan-fried a golden yellow and cooked with scallions, ginger, soy sauce and vinegar; and a small dish of pig ear stewed and thinly sliced. As for the soup, it was a light broth with towel gourd and egg flower. A layer of sesame oil floated on the surface.

Yanhua poured her father a cup of wine and then a cup for Cat. The smell of the wine mixed with the aroma of the dishes to envelope the whole street. All the surrounding neighbors said, "Such good food, Master Xu."

Master Xu used his chopsticks to point at the dishes and said, "Come and have a drink!"

The neighbors replied, "Don't be so polite!"

"Someone is happy," Master Xu said.

"Disgusting," Yanhua sneered to herself.

"Old folks," Cat said.

Across the street, beds also were lined up. Some people who were chatting called out, "Master Xu, what good fortune!"

"Thanks," replied Master Xu.

Yanhua turned on the television just as the national anthem came on. On both sides of the street people were on their beds starting dinner. All around people looked busy eating. Master Xu was drinking with great relish. So was Cat. He was eating heartily, a damp towel on his shoulder. Almost immediately he had to wipe away a trickle of sweat. Yanhua filled a bowl with meng-bean porridge. Bored to death, she drank slowly, her chopsticks haphazardly poking out of a dish.

"Isn't my dish delicious, Yanhua?" Cat asked.

"You think so," Yanhua replied.

"What do you think, Uncle Xu?" asked Cat.

"It's delicious," said Master Xu. "You're incredible."

"I'm not hungry," said Yanhua. "How can anyone eat in this heat?"

"That's because you haven't been sleeping well," said Cat. "The morning shift is too hard. That's the reason why I didn't go home and came here to cook for you instead."

When Master Xu heard this he laughed. "He's so glib," said Yanhua. "Before, he said it was because of the accident with the thermometer."

Cat slapped his thigh forcefully. How could he have neglected to tell his future father-in-law that day's big news! "Master Xu," he said. "A strange thing happened today. A thermometer burst on the street and the mercury poured out!"

Master Xu tilted his head, thought for a while and then exclaimed, "This is truly one of the world's great marvels. How high does a thermometer go, Cat?"

"Forty-two degrees Celsius," Cat said.

"Damn it! It's so hot!" said Master Xu.

Yanhua put down her bowl and said, "It's sweltering. I can't eat any more."

"Don't pay any attention to the temperature; eat some more," Cat said.

"Stupid," said Yanhua.

"If you don't eat something now, you'll be hungry later," Cat said.

"Stupid," said Yanhua. "I am alive. Will I starve to death so easily? The street will be full of food stands later."

"Okay, okay," Cat said. "We'll go have something to eat at midnight."

"You're so pleased with yourself," said Yanhua. "Who wants to go out with you? Earlier today I made plans with some people."

"Who?" asked Cat. "With who?"

"Are you Public Security?" Yanhua asked. "You make everything your business."

"Don't pay any attention to her," said Master Xu. "She's like too much chili in your food. It burns your mouth. She should be more like a girl."

"What is a girl supposed to be like?" Yanhua asked.

"A girl should be gentle and quiet, dutiful and meek," Master Xu said.

"That's old-fashioned," Yanhua said.

"Master Xu, don't antagonize her," Cat said.

"Let's ignore her," Master Xu replied.

The two men, one older and one younger, went to watch television. Yanhua let out a snort, turned around and, looking into the street, went to sit down. Her feelings were reflected in her panicky eyes. Girls usually do not show this kind of expression in public, and out-of-towners who were walking along the sides of the street couldn't help but be alarmed when they saw her.

On the street, pedestrian traffic was a little lighter but not by much. In Wuhan, there are almost four thousand people per square kilometer on average. Jiangnan Road is the area's most bustling commercial district, so where were people to go? There always was heavy traffic. But when the sun set, all the bamboo beds came out and the traffic was squeezed into the middle of the street. Local people saw nothing unusual in this, and together with city buses and bicycles, they made their way in the middle of the road. People from out of town were simply astounded. Slowly, they walked sideways; all along the length of the street, arms and legs, men and women were indistinguishable, everywhere the glint of flesh. What a sight!

The television was broadcasting the international news.

"Hey, the international news is on," Cat announced loudly.

After Iraq had invaded Kuwait, Cat took on the task of reminding the neighbors to watch the international news. The men of a few households ran over carrying their rice bowls. Iraq had annexed Kuwait and now wanted to get hold of Saudi Arabia.

"This son of a bitch Iraq, it's already stuffed," Cat said.

"Son of a bitch," all the men sighed.

Someone said, "This son of a bitch will ruin the Asian Games. Can't they wait until the Games are over?"

Master Xu said, "Chairman Mao said, 'The invaders will not come to a good end.' Don't you think so?"

"I think so," said Cat. "The wealthy countries will all send troops. Sooner or later this will be settled."

"That's hard to say," said one of the men. "As a matter of fact, the Arab League doesn't like the Yankees. We should send troops. We'd get foreign exchange, decrease the population and uphold justice, too. Something positive could come out of this situation. I don't know if Secretary Jiang has thought about this or not."

"How can you think like that?" asked Master Xu. "Is this how young people are today?"

"What are our ideas compared to you, armed with Mao Zedong Thought," declared the crowd.

Master Xu knew this was a joke but he smiled politely.

"Stinking Iraq, and now this foul unceasing heat wave."

Commercials came on next, stinking commercials. While the stinking commercials were on, people gradually dispersed.

As soon as Cat put down his bowl, Master Xu said, "Yanhua, take in the dishes."

"I want to wait for Hanzhen," she said.

"Ah, Hanzhen," said Cat. "You two are so tight-lipped, neither of you told me anything."

"You're such a big shot that we have to tell you everything," Yanhua said.

"Yanhua, take in the dishes," said Master Xu.

"I'll do it," said Cat.

"No, Cat," said Master Xu. "All the neighbors are watching. In this household there is still some parental authority. Yanhua, take in the dishes."

Unwillingly Yanhua got up and cleared away the bowls and chopsticks. Cat gave her a hand.

Old Mrs. Wang and the women watched Yanhua and Cat go upstairs, then said to Master Xu, "You did the right thing. Yanhua is a little hot-tempered. Cat is a fine boy. Yanhua would be worse off with somebody else."

"You're right," said Master Xu. "Where would you find an honest and tolerant boy like Cat nowadays? It's popular for girls today to look for foreigners. Will a foreigner cook bitter gourd for his father-in-law? If Yanhua weren't going to marry Cat, I'd break her leg."

Yanhua thought that Cat was going to wash the dishes. Who knew that he would put down the rice cooker and leave.

"Cat," said Yanhua.

"What?" said Cat.

"Okay, okay," said Yanhua. "I've finally seen through you."

"You've been making such a mean face today," Cat said.

"What kind of expression is okay, then?" Yanhua asked, revealing a smile.

"That's right," said Cat. "Now we are dating and we should act as such."

Cat pulled Yanhua to him and embraced her tightly. "It's too hot," she said, but her arms stayed around Cat's waist. The two of them stumbled into the room. It was like an oven: the walls, the floor, the furniture, whatever they touched was hot. When they came out, they were both woozy from the heat.

Hanzhen arrived at eight-thirty. Yanhua changed again into a fashionable sun dress and they left. Gleefully, they called to Cat, "Bye-bye!"

All the houses were empty now. Men and women, young and old had moved their beds out on both sides of the street. The bamboo beds, densely crowded together, formed a row on the street stretching as far as the eye could see. Before long, groups of people relaxing and enjoying themselves sprang up.

Originally, Master Xu had wanted to play mahjongg. Chef Wang, whose acquaintance he had made recently, came by. Chef Wang was from Wuhan. For thirty years he had worked on an ocean steamer. He had retired not long ago and returned to his old home town. Captivated, he sought out Master Xu to discuss Wuhan's exquisite dishes. They had a faithful audience in old Mrs.

Wang. She had spent most of her life around the Wuhan snacks Master Xu talked about.

A woman neighbor invited Cat to play mahjongg.

"Cat, go have some fun," said Master Xu.

"I don't like mahjongg," Cat replied.

"What do you like?" asked the neighbor. "There must be something you like to do for fun?"

"I'm going to chat with somebody," Cat said.

"What on Earth do you have to talk about?" the neighbor asked. "Stupid! Didn't you hear: of one billion people, eight hundred million gamble and two hundred million go dancing. Everybody else is stupid."

"Then I'm stupid," Cat said. "People nowadays aren't afraid of criticism."

The small boy at the neighbor's knee tried to climb up onto the bamboo bed, tumbled and fell, and began to wail. From a distance the husband yelled, "You damned deaf-mute! The kid fell down!"

The neighbor pinched the boy and said, "You bastard, you're always causing trouble!"

"You fool," said Cat. "If he's a bastard, then what does that make you?"

Laughing, the neighbor gave Cat a slap and said, "Are you scolding me? I said nothing but a common phrase: don't pretend you aren't from Wuhan."

Cat took the boy in his arms and carried him over to his family's bamboo bed. The husband gave Cat a cigarette.

"Master Wang, I'll tell you a story that will give you a fright," Cat said.

"Damn," said the man.

"Today, at four o'clock today that is, at our shop a thermometer was in the sun for just two minutes when the mercury broke through the glass tube," Cat said.

The man raised his eyebrows, "Really?"

Cat was pleased and blew out a string of smoke rings.

"That is frightening. Too hot! How can we survive!" the man said.

Cat laughed heartily and said, "Damn it, let's stop living!"

Someone in front called out, "Cat, come sit over here."

Cat went over. A big crowd was talking and watching television. Cat turned off the television and gave a vivid account of the incident with the thermometer. The people listened excitedly. Some suggested writing an item for the Wuhan Evening News. Some suggested phoning the Mayor's special telephone line: on such a hot day how could you still make people work the whole day? This stirred up the crowd. Someone put forward the idea that the government was to blame, that it did not permit the radio station to report the weather forecast truthfully in order to avoid alarming the population. Immediately some people came forward to refute this and said that measuring the atmosphere was not like surveying streets. Science stressed science. Those engaged in science could not lie. Cat joined the debate. The small crowd he was arguing with said the incident with the thermometer possibly was not a question of temperature, but rather a question of the quality of the thermometer. Cat became extremely indignant because the thermometer was his stock in trade. It was a high-quality product.

Master Xu also became a central figure in the conversation. All those around him, except old Mrs. Wang, were old men having their heads shaved clean.

Master Xu obviously was reveling in his few minutes of glory. He was saying that when Chairman Mao had finished eating the bean-curd skins, he came into the kitchen and shook hands with the chefs one by one, last of all patting him on the shoulder and saying, "Your bean-curd skins are delicious!"

The old folks beamed like small children. Master Xu self-mockingly said, "Ah, it's a little like the advertisement for Nescafé."

Old Mrs. Wang said, "Tell us the story again about the Korean who ate at the Four Seasons Restaurant."

Master Xu repeated the story about Kim Il Sung, who in such and such a year, in such and such a month, and on such and such a day had come to Wuhan and had visited the Four Seasons Restaurant. When he finished eating the dumpling soup, he left and went to Beijing. A couple of weeks later Kim Il Sung set out to return home. Before boarding, he suddenly said to the senior government official who was seeing him off, "I still have a small problem that I haven't figured out." The official asked him to explain and Kim Il Sung said, "It's about the Wuhan Four Seasons dumpling soup. How do they get the soup into the dumplings?"

The old folks were overwhelmed with joy, gleefully drinking mouthfuls of tea.

"Hell," said Chef Wang. "I've traveled across the ocean. I don't know how many countries and cities I've been to, but damn it, everywhere I went the deep-fried oil sticks were all soggy. Only the oil sticks in Wuhan are crisp."

"Don't even mention it," said Master Xu. "Talk about Shanghai. People eat rice gruel for breakfast. They soak the leftover rice from the day before in boiling water and have it with salted vegetables. This is the old Shanghai! As for the capital Beijing, they eat baked wheat cakes and noodles, noodles and baked wheat cakes. In Guangzhou and Shenzhen, an open economic city, there are rats, snakes and insects. Whatever disgusts people, you name it, they eat it. Is there any other city that can compare with Wuhan? Let's count only the dishes for breakfast. Come on, we only have to list a few famous ones."

Old Mrs. Wang began to count on her fingers: Lao Tongcheng's bean-curd skins, Yi Pinxiang's savory steamed buns, Cai Linji's hot dried noodles, Tan Yanji's boiled dumplings, Tian Hengqi's rice-noodle soup, Hou Shengli's mixed bean-curd jelly, Lao Qianji's beef with fried bean-curd threads, the small stuffed dumplings in soup at the Minsheng Restaurant, Wu Fangzhai's sesame-lotus stuffed dumplings in soup, Tong Xingli's deep-fried dough sticks,

Shun Xiangju's steamed shaomai, Minzhong Dessert Shop's fermented glutinous rice, Fu Qinghe's beef with rice noodles. There was a gap in old Mrs. Wang's teeth. She exhaled and emitted a string of saliva. Ashamed, she used her hand to cover her mouth and said, "I'm so embarrassed. This old mouth is watering."

The old folks clapped their hands.

"You are a true Hankou native," said Chef Wang. "You know how to eat well! I like eating all kinds of street food. At dawn, noodle nest, glutinous rice cakes, butter cakes, walnut cakes, glutinous rice chicken. I have some of everything. Delicious!"

"No place in the world can surpass Wuhan at dawn. That's no exaggeration," said Master Xu.

The old folks felt really proud and said, "You're quite right."

In this manner, the evening wore on slowly.

The city bus no longer resembled the noisy and frenzied operation of the daytime. Gasping contemptuously, and carrying half a load of passengers, it went past only to come by again much later. The voices of those playing mahjongg became more distinct. Because it was too hot to sleep, those people lying on the bamboo beds tossed and turned endlessly. The gold jewelry on the ears, necks, wrists and fingers of the women sparkled under the light of the street lamps. It was hard to see that the bamboo beds had slowly turned red while soaking in people's sweat.

Yanhua was on the street to her home. She and Hanzhen had invited two former classmates from their middle school to go out. The four girls were wearing the latest fashion. Their bangs were moussed, towering on their foreheads and heavy makeup was colorfully applied to their faces. They looked like models on a runway. Walking down the street they looked spectacular. Although doing nothing in particular, they felt really happy.

They did not go dancing or to a movie. They just strolled along the main street. From Jiangnan Road they strolled to Liudu Bridge, from Liudu Bridge they strolled back along Jiangnan Road. They ate ice cream, then some jellied bean curd; one of them got out her money and paid one time, another got out her money and paid the next.

Hanzhen told them that day's news about the thermometer.

Yanhua recalled the incident on her bus that day of the ticket-seller Xiao Mie and the passengers swearing at each other. She explained that two men from the north had passed their stop. Xiao Mie wanted to fine them. The northerners were not willing to pull out their money, in addition to complaining about feeling wronged. So Xiao Mie said, "You're shameless. Even with that piece of meat in your pants."

The northerners, seeing that Xiao Mie was a young girl, did not believe their ears and asked in a loud voice, "What?"

Xiao Mie also in a loud voice replied, "Penis. Don't you understand?"

The northerners, red in the face, quickly fished out their money.

The four girls fell into fits of laughter. Yanhua quickly retorted, saying, "Damn it, at home an old man and a boyfriend, but I couldn't tell them any of this. I feel so oppressed."

"Then get married and become a wife," said Hanzhen. "I think Cat has been kept waiting long enough."

The other two classmates said, "Yanhua may be a wife already. Is Cat a well-behaved guy?"

Yanhua took a friendly swipe at her classmates' mouths. They held hands together and turned into a circle under the neon light.

They also talked about movie stars, the price and the styles of gold jewelry, their boyfriends, and "Juan Lan" and "Liang Lan," who had been murdered by thugs. All this talk made the four women heave a sigh.

"What would you do if you met with a thug?" Hanzhen asked.

"I'm not afraid," said Yanhua. "How could he get any money? Is it easy for our company to make a little money? We drive all day and all night just to make a profit. Evil cannot suppress what is upright. The more you are afraid of it, the more evil occurs."

"That's right," said the girls. "Being afraid of a thug is not going to stop him killing you."

Walking along and talking, they eventually parted company.

Yanhua bought a midnight snack to take home.

Master Xu sat resting in the deck-chair with his eyes closed.

"Papa, have some fermented glutinous rice," Yanhua said. "What's Cat up to?"

"He's out front amusing himself," said Master Xu.

Yanhua stood on her tiptoes and, looking ahead, saw row upon row of bamboo beds. But she did not see Cat.

In fact, Cat was within Yanhua's line of sight, but he was lying on Si's bed. Si's bed was different from everyone else's. The legs were short and so it was out of sight.

Si was a slightly older single man. In the neighborhood it was said that he was a writer, a belief he neither confirmed nor denied. Si was his childhood name. Many people disliked his phony and pedantic manner. Cat, however, liked him a little because he and Si could talk nonsense.

"Si, I'll give you a little material to write about, okay?" said Cat.

"All right," replied Si.

"A thermometer exploded in our shop today," said Cat. "Don't you think that is extraordinary?"

"Oh," said Si.

"What do you think of it?" said Cat. "Not sentimental enough?"

"Damn," said Si.

"Damn it, Si," said Cat. "What name do you use when you publish your work?"

"Don't ask me where I'm from," sang out Si. "My home town is far away. Why do I roam, roam to distant places, roam about?"

"Si, you really know how to enjoy yourself," Cat said.

Si, his big head swaying back, gazed enigmatically up at the starry sky and asked, "Is your name Cat?"

"My real name is Zheng Zhiheng," said Cat.

"No," Si said. "Your name is 'human being'!"

"Of course," said Cat.

Later on Si chatted to Cat about one of his plots; Si said it would make Cat cry. When Si was in the middle of his story, Cat fell asleep. Si lowered his voice, insisting on finishing his story.

Yanhua took a bath, put on a t-shirt and shorts, and went along the street calling out, "Cat! Cat!"

Si heard her but did not respond. Let men have a little freedom, he thought.

It was one o'clock in the morning. Returning to her own bed, Yanhua felt like sleeping for awhile. Old Mrs. Wang whispered in her ear, "Child, Cat is a good fellow."

"I know," said Yanhua.

Old Mrs. Wang heaved a deep sigh but did not utter a word.

Yanhua slept fitfully for awhile. Her whole body was sweaty and she woke up hot. It was three-thirty; she had to go to work.

Yanhua's first bus started its run at four o'clock sharp. As always, Xiao Mie was the ticket-seller. When the bus passed along Jiangnan Road they found Cat. He was sleeping on Si's bed, his arms and legs spread wide without the least modesty. Yanhua, who hated Si more than anyone, said, "That bastard, any place is good enough to sleep."

"Cat has a boner," said Xiao Mie.

"Bah, you pervert," said Yanhua.

"Shit, he has a boner right on the street," said Xiao Mie. "Should I gouge my eyes out if I'm lying?"

"The son of a bitch," said Yanhua.

"Marry him," said Xiao Mie. "Don't be humiliated."

Xiao Mie laughed uproariously.

"Lower your voice, partner," said Yanhua. "Wuhan is getting a little sleep now."

Xiao Mie covered her mouth, but she could not suppress a smile.

Driving the two-section bus, Yanhua slowly passed through the passage-way of bamboo beds. Trying her best not to accelerate quickly, she made the bus ramble along quietly like the people.

Translated by Michael Cody

王安憶

Wang Anyi (b. 1954) is one of the best-known
contemporary writers in China. She was born in
Nanjing and grew up in Shanghai. Wang began
to write in 1975, and her early publications
consisted mainly of children's literature. "Who
will be the Future Leader of Middle Troop?"
(Shei shi weilai de zhong duizhang?) won a prize
for excellence in children's literature in Shanghai
in 1980. Since then, she has published several
volumes of prose. Her best known works include
the "love trilogy": *Love in a Small Town* (Xiao
cheng zhi lian, 1986), *Love on a Barren
Mountain* (Huangshan zhi lian, 1986) and *Love
in a Brocade Valley* (Jinxiugu zhi lian, 1988).

Sisters

❖

1994

Our village was famous for its prosperity. People from remote villages would come to look with admiration at our "village of brick homes." From a historical perspective, you could say our village reflected the characteristics of a mature agricultural society. First of all, there was our land. It was known as the "Lake" and was located at the southern end of our village. We called it "South Lake" in full, and you could tell from the name that it was a vast lowland. To plant crops in lowlands you need the foundation of civilization—irrigation. If we are to speak of this subject, we'll have to expand our survey.

Within the county where our village was situated, there were countless embankments. To reach the town ten miles away, you had to climb an endless succession of embankments. Locals called the embankments *fanzi* or concave hills; to climb an embankment was to climb a *fanzi*. In this county, there also were many places called *yu*, which were lowlands with rings of embankments around them to prevent flooding. The *Ci-Hai* dictionary contains an allusion to *yu* in the *Records of the Grand Historian, Hereditary Household of Confucius*. It says that Confucius "was born with a *yu ding* (or concave) skull." The dictionary then follows with a quotation from *Sima Zhen's Index*: "Yu ding means a hollow in the top of the head. Confucius's head looks like the inverted roof of a house (*fanyu*), low in the middle but high at the edges." In this sentence both *fan* and *yu* are used in the same sense as they are used to describe our county's topography. From the use of these terms, we know that we can trace the language of our village back to ancient times.

South Lake was surrounded by one embankment after another in order to keep flood waters in check during the Huai River's high-water season. When it rained, did the lake become a large water basin? Not at all, for we had ditches! We had a big ditch at South Lake that transported water to the lower reaches of the Huai River. And if, as in the worst of times, the water rose and flooded the crops, we still had another way out. That was buckwheat.

South Lake had two crop seasons each year; one was wheat, the other was soybeans. During wheat season, the weather usually was favorable. It was the golden time of the year. Crops were sown in autumn; the seeds slept in the soil through the winter. When spring came and the fields were green, the heads of wheat were so thick that reaping it was like scratching fleas. Afterward, when the southwest wind started to blow, people sharpened their knives for cutting and prepared the land for sowing, planting, ploughing, harrowing and leveling. Although both the Huai River and the weather were calm during this period, what we feared was several days of unbroken rain. While our hearts fluttered, these days passed; then all was fine. Unfortunately, soybean season was the worst time of the year. Come July, flood season was upon us. It rained most of the time. If it rained for a day or two, so be it. But when it lasted a week or so, then the soybean crop had had it. It was at this point that buckwheat arrived on the scene.

Buckwheat has a short growing season; it can be planted both in spring and autumn. It is well suited to intercropping and interplanting. Buckwheat was the savior of the poor in those days. When the buckwheat bloomed, the fields were snow-white. The farmer's resentful heart was soothed, and he began to plan for sowing the wheat.

Our village's wheat was sown together with peas. The wheat ripened along with the peas. People taking care of the wheat and children picking greens for the pigs liked to grab the tender peas and eat them raw; others waited until they grew longer, then cooked them. Since the season for cutting wheat was approaching, those days did not last very long. Our village's wheat was always mixed with peas, so when the wheat was ground, the flour was green.

Now let's turn to work in the village. In this area, our village's oldest traditions were displayed. We converted labor, the basic means of survival, into a form of artistic expression. At the same time, it became a spiritual activity. Ever heard of the older men's *haozi*, the work songs they sang while driving cattle? Full-throated, the songs poured forth. And though they seemed free and unrestrained, they had their own rules of composition. Otherwise how could one explain a sudden turn followed by a sudden finish when the song strayed far from the subject, or moved from a high pitch to a low one. Moreover, when you listened carefully, you could tell it was just like the four steps in the composition of an essay. The first line made people long for the next line, their hearts full of expectation, excitement and worry. This was the driving force of the melody. And the next line fit in exactly with your wishes. This showed it still had its own logic, and suited the subject. Ploughing the fields, raking the soil, threshing the crops, driving the cart, whenever they used cattle in physical work, the men sang these songs. And the cattle were as enchanted by the songs as were the people in the fields.

Those were the work songs. There was also the harvesting of the wheat. In our village, instead of using a sickle to cut wheat, we used a scythe, similar to the scythe Levin used to cut wheat in *Anna Karenina*. Even the handling of the scythe was about the same. We would stretch out both hands evenly, press the handle against our ribs, and walk forward one step at a time. Maintaining the harmony of waist, back, and arm was extremely important. What does this coincidence suggest? The history of livestock farming in the Huai River valley? Or that our village had contact with nomadic tribes from the North? It always has been the men's job to cut wheat. Apart from the scythe, they also possessed cloaks. The cloaks were made of bleached cotton gauze a meter wide and a meter-and-a-half long. The cloaks were tied about bare shoulders and backs. They looked more like costumes in the fields than protection from the scorching sun. Just imagine the scene: the blazing sun above a field of rippling wheat, among the wheat a row of strongly built men brandishing their scythes, their white cloaks fluttering in the wind.

During the harvests, another image stood out: the burning of wheat and soybeans. During their breaks, people would rub wheat heads, mix them with stubble, and light a match. Instantly, sparks flew off in all directions and you would be greeted by the sweet smell of the wheat. The outer layer of the wheat was hard but the inside was thick and chewy. It was easy to burn soybeans. You just gathered the soybean shoots and lit a match. The pods and straws would burn together. The soybeans buried in the ash also burned on the outside, but their insides were still hard. It took a lot of strength to chew them. From an aesthetic point of view, burning soybeans was more picturesque, especially during the second break in the afternoon. While the sun was setting in the West, the light was turmeric yellow, mellow and quiet. The autumn sky was high and clear, the air almost transparent, a few strands of thin cloud changed color in the evening glow. The dark soybean stalks lay scattered on the harvested fields. Suddenly, a stream of smoke would rise, and since there was no wind, the smoke floated straight up. It stood out sharply in the clear air; small pieces of ash dancing about the smoke were to be seen clearly. Just like an oil-painting.

Our village, which had a long history, suffered numerous droughts and floods. I have no idea how many times it had been destroyed and rebuilt before it became its present impregnable self. From a distance of two to three kilometers, the village could be seen, its brick houses scattered helter-skelter on the highly built terraces, their roofs visible to the naked eye.

The village faced south and rows of terraces were arranged from west to east. Below the terraces were the "streets" of the village, "lanes" which ran from south to north, and the wide road that went down to South Lake. In the southern-most part of the village, facing South Lake, were the cowshed and grain field. They were our village's public place and political center. Meetings, the recording of workpoints and discussions of village matters took place there. Travelers and beggars also would stop there for the night. In the late months of the year, when it snowed and there was no work to be done in the fields, the women stayed at home, while the men met in the cowshed to chat. The odor of cow sweat and cow manure mixed with cigarette smoke to create a warm, unpleasant atmosphere. It was quite pungent. One traveler who squeezed into the cowhand's bed happened to play the *erhu*. He stayed without cost in our village for a few days. He didn't leave until the snow had stopped falling. Then he set off on his way. After the wheat harvest, people had already ploughed half of the field in front of the cowshed with sorghum. Big sorghum was corn; small sorghum was just sorghum. When corn and sorghum were harvested, laborers would prepare the soil and wait to cut the soybeans. Our village had many young men and it seemed that there was not enough land. We had to plan and budget everything carefully.

Why was it said that our village was impregnable? Well, because its platform was built solid and tall. When our streets were flooded and both sides of our homes had become rivers, that platform did not budge at all. Credit should be given to the texture of the soil, which contained very little sand and had a high viscosity. When it rained and the streets were extremely muddy, large clods of soil would stick to the bottoms of your feet when you went out. Built with this type of soil, the platform was extremely solid. Instead of crushing it, the flood made the platform even more solid. Our platform was grand, stable, massive, and orderly. Our village had a large population, and had many houses packed together. The platform created an image of great prosperity.

Even in the days of drought, we were not afraid, for there were three wells in the village, one in the east, one in the west, and another in the center. The well in the west was a sweet-water well. Using sweet water, rice is easy to cook, flour is quick to rise, clothes are easy to wash; drink it, it tastes good. The other two wells were ordinary. There were also a few ponds where people washed their rice and vegetables, fed their cattle, and washed their clothes. So, our village did not fear either flood or drought. We lived and worked in peace and contentment. In good weather, after finishing work, we saw smoke rising from every home's chimney back in the village. People carrying water from their shoulder poles walked leisurely on the village's path. The buckets went "clank clank" on the rope. And a middle school graduate played a bamboo flute. It really was the picture of prosperity.

Our village's civilization also was reflected in the way villagers saved every little scrap. The village's prosperity was an accumulation of grains of wheat and bits of straw. As soon as children could walk, they went to the fields to pick green feed for pigs; women carried rakes wherever they went. They would gather every single leaf and put it into the stove. Old people always went about with a basket on their backs. They would collect turds wherever they went. So, in our village, whether it was South Lake's main road or the village streets and byways, it was clean everywhere. Seldom would you see a straw of wheat or a dropping. The people deserved credit for keeping the pigs' green feed cut cleanly. And when it rained or snowed and we could do no work, we ate only two meals a day. We wouldn't get up until noon but would go to bed before it was dark.

Our village was masterful at storing up grain, fodder and all sorts of agricultural goods. Take sweet potatoes for example. In the autumn, when sweet potatoes had just come out, everyone dug pits in front of their homes. The sweet potatoes spent their winter there. Later, when they split, a thick juice flowed out, or, as the saying went, "They sweated through." That was when they were ready to eat. The big ones were cut into slices, dried and ground. The smaller ones were cooked in porridge. Sweet potatoes were the most difficult food to preserve. Others, like wheat, soybeans or sorghum are much easier. The key point is to dry the grain in the sun—what kind of sun, the direction of the wind, what type of temperature was suitable—we knew these things like we knew our own palms.

The key to storing straw is stacking. Wheat straw, soybean straw, sorghum straw, all have their own way of stacking. The basic principle is to make sure that the wind can't scatter the straw about, nor the rain drench it, nor water soak it. The straw pile should not only be durable but also ventilated; it must be convenient to pull out and must not collapse when you only want to take a little. The pile should stand firmly until the last bit of straw is taken.

In our village, there was a special way of making pickles. Beans, peas, garlic bolt, garlic clove, carrot, outer leaves and stems of vegetables could be pickled. And each had its own way of being pickled. Anyone tasting these pickles would be surprised, for no matter how long ago they were preserved, whether in winter or summer, they always tasted fresh and crisp.

All these things prove our village learned from the past. Even during years with a good harvest we didn't forget the hungry years. We made long-term plans. It was a sophisticated village.

Like other civilizations, we paid dearly for development by destroying our natural environment. This could be seen in the scarcity of trees in our village. While our high platform and magnificent homes were being put up, the once beautiful scenery disappeared. There was nothing worth seeing. Our fields and village were well laid out but they were far removed from the concept of nature. The biggest regret was that there were too few trees. Along the big ditch at South Lake, there were two rows of elms. Although they were green and lush in the summer, this one highlight failed to fulfil our needs. In all fairness, I have to say that while our village might seem prosperous, in fact it was boring and dull. And, since existence determines consciousness, the people in our village definitely were not romantic types. Their aesthetic ideas were strictly rational—not coming from nature, but cultivated and taught by society. The examples are too numerous to list.

A young married woman, Xiao Ma, was, as everyone acknowledged, the beauty of our village. And though I had been in the village for quite a while and had heard her name mentioned everywhere I went, I had not seen her. She said one thing about our village that really hurt: in our village there weren't any pretty Sisters. All the Sisters were deeply hurt—not because of the words themselves, but because if the beautiful Xiao Ma said it, it had to be true. Her beauty gave her the authority to judge things. Her husband was a technician in the commune's hydroelectric station; he had a stable monthly salary, which was enough to support her. She rarely worked in the fields and people rarely saw her.

Before I saw her, I thought Xiao Ma must be a sorghum type of beauty: healthy, strong, with thick eyebrows and big eyes, like those seen in oil paintings, the kind of girl perfect to be a laborer. I just thought our village must appreciate that kind of beauty. I realized later that I was using a typically urban, especially intellectual, view of the countryside when I imagined her. Their demand for beauty was not as simple as what we thought it was. "Simplicity" is the urbanite's basic misunderstanding of country people. It was Xiao Ma who taught me otherwise.

I eventually saw Xiao Ma. It was at a meeting that the commune held for women who didn't work in the fields. The Sisters pointed her out to me through the window. That was Xiao Ma.

Xiao Ma had bent her head forward while stitching the soles of a pair of cloth shoes. I saw her short, pitch-black hair cut at the ears, with the top braided into a small circle and held together by a clip. This wasn't anything, though. What really struck me was the pair of socks she wore. It had just rained and was still overcast. The mud on the village path was overwhelming. That day she wore a pair of long gray cotton socks slipped over her trousers, which reached below her knees, and a pair of very common cloth shoes. Her way of wearing stocks didn't become popular in the cities for another twenty years, but then and there, Xiao Ma had already invented it. On her it looked so natural, so appropriate, and so pleasing to the eye. There was nothing strange or ridiculous about it. I then saw her fine, exquisite face. It was oval in shape and its features were delicate and symmetrical. Later, when she stood up and walked out before the other Sisters, I noticed her shapely figure and nimble movements. She was not strong, but not frail either. Her manner suggested a lively, vivid intelligence. To tell the truth, she looked rather like a college student. Only when she walked deliberately and quickly down the muddy village path did you realize that she was a locally born-and-bred country girl. To this day, her steady, fearless eyes remain clearly in my memory.

In our village, people generally considered beauty to be based on balance. They didn't like either fat or thin. The concept of balance required that one look at things comprehensively, not simply at particular parts. Xiao Ma, for whom everyone had the greatest esteem, was a typical example. Everything about her fit together perfectly. There was nothing outstanding, and in some respects she was a little plain. But considering her beauty as a whole, it glowed with extraordinary brightness. Her beauty was restrained and modest, for there was more to her: She was not like the wild, rapid surface of a river; she had depths you always were learning new things about. While her beauty was dignified and restrained, it was impossible to ignore. Indeed, Xiao Ma was proof of our village's high standards of beauty.

If you suppose Xiao Ma's beauty was of a material nature, then I will give you a different example to show our village's understanding of a more spiritual form of beauty.

There was an Elder Brother in the village who also had things to say about the village. He said that there were two remarkable Sisters in our village, who dressed in the same materials as everyone else, yet when they wore them, the clothes were quite different. The two Sisters were Liu Pingzi and Xiao Yingzi. His comment was insightful. The two Sisters were average looking; one might even say that they had a few noticeable shortcomings. Their temperament, however, made them outstanding, or "sensitive." Liu Pingzi and Xiao Yingzi had the strongest characters among the Sisters in the village. They were high-spirited, independent-minded and creative. One time, Liu Pingzi made herself a gown with an oblique front and thin waist. When she wore this old-fashioned gown, carried a wooden basin, and went to the pond to wash clothes, the other Sisters' eyes became dull. Her attitude was solemn. She seemed to be saying: Look, even old-fashioned clothes look good on me. Xiao Yingzi spent a few years in school and, as a result, she was more conscious than Liu Pingzi of being an individual. Her family arranged dates with her future husband, and they would go to the foot of the county sluice gate. If a fellow from the village ran across them and asked her who the man was, she would answer, "This is my friend." Both girls were independent. They were more enthusiastic about life than the other Sisters. These characteristics gave them a special quality. People found it difficult to define them, so instead they said the two girls had a "foreign flavor." This had many connotations: modernity, fashion sense, refinement and so on.

Elder Brother also was a very important character in the village. He went to school in the county, and afterward spent a few years in a Sizhou opera troupe. He was our village's famous *houzi* singer. When the season for soil preparation arrived, he drove the stone roller ahead. Once he opened his throat, the ox and donkey behind him obediently moved with the beat. The stone roller went *gulu, gulu*, the soybean stalks and wheat stalks went *kaka, kaka*. All these sounds seemed made for him. His wife also was considered to possess "foreign flavor." She was average looking, but had something of the student about her. So Elder Brother was qualified to speak in these matters. At a certain level, he set our village's aesthetic standards; he intellectualized our village's understanding of beauty. Beautiful Xiao Ma was the incarnation of this understanding, as were Liu Pingzi and Xiao Yingzi.

It happened once that a Sister was going to be married. At the time, I was in Shanghai. When I heard the news I bought a bolt of dress material to give to her as a wedding gift when I returned. The cloth was poplin, a greyish-green checkered fabric. My mother strongly criticized my choice. She said I had to go back to the store and buy another one. She thought it was inappropriate to give somber-colored material as a wedding gift. According to her, what village girls liked was either bright red or bright green. In order to convince me, she even invited the old granny from the third floor, who was considered to be very knowledgeable about dress material and etiquette. She took my mother's side. The two of them made my ears ache. However, I insisted and would not give in. The material won that Sister's heart. She didn't say anything when I gave it to her but on the day she paid a return visit to her parents after the wedding, we got together. She had her head lowered and was sewing a new piece of clothing. Suddenly, she raised her head and said, "The material you gave to me, I'll use it to make a short-sleeved gown." "Short sleeves" referred to the frill in place of the shirt's cuff. Usually, our village's Sisters' shirts didn't have frills. This type of short-sleeved shirt was worn by people from the city and was considered to possess "foreign flavor." After I heard what she was going to do with the gift, I understood that I had done the right thing.

These stories—don't they explain our village's rational aesthetics? A big village like ours, with a very large population, flourished and prospered. The villagers' thinking had been cultivated for a very long time and they had gone far down the road of civilization. They had long since cast off boorish ways; poetry and books lay deep in their bones. In our village, you didn't hear primitive or wild chants or vulgar country slang. On the contrary, stories with a scholarly flavor were popular. Intellectuals like Elder Brother were responsible for spreading these stories.

Elder Brother told the following story.

Once, there was a scholar who was about to go to the capital to take the imperial examination. Being very nervous, he had a dream that night. The dream was extremely strange and he did not know whether it was an ill omen or a good one. He got up early the next morning to go to his mother-in-law's house because she was an expert interpreter of dreams. When he got there, his mother-in-law had already gone out. As he stood there feeling disappointed, his sister-in-law came out and said, "For many years, I have studied dream interpretation from my mother and I'm practically as good as she is. Here, let me try." So the scholar told her every detail of his dreams. In the first dream, he was riding a horse on the top of a wall; in the second dream he was holding an umbrella in the sun; in the third dream he was hanging a coffin on a tree; in the fourth dream, the scholar slept with his sister-in-law. The sister-in-law then explained his dreams. The first dream: Gone never to return. The second dream: Superfluous. The third dream: Death without a burial place. The fourth dream: Wishful thinking! After hearing this, the scholar felt hopeless. In despair he was about to go back home. Unexpectedly, the mother-in-law returned and asked him why he was so upset. He told her the reason. The mother-in-law said, "Your sister-in-law has only studied for a short time. She's no expert. Now let me tell you. The first dream: You will succeed on your first attempt. The second dream: Perfectly safe. The third dream: You will become the highest official. The fourth dream . . ." When Elder Brother's story came to this point, he noticed there were several Sisters among his listeners. So he stopped and said, "That's all." Then he got up and left.

In this abruptly ended story, the fourth dream is part of popular folklore. But since he left off at this point, the listeners were left in suspense.

Our village called these types of stories "ancient chats." Elder Brother was good at "ancient chats," which embodied traditional ideas and could be traced back to the ancient past, though not all of these stories were necessarily ancient. Another form of entertainment people were fond of was listening to the playing of stringed instruments. Usually, it was from Sizhou opera. The melody was quite simple; it had only four basic phrases, but they were sung in different sequences over and over. The verses were usually about the people and the court from ancient times or the three cardinal guides (ruler guides subject, father guides son, and husband guides wife) and the five constant virtues (benevolence, righteousness, propriety, wisdom and fidelity) as specified in the feudal code.

During the early seventies, when I was in the countryside, the old operas were forbidden. Over time, some of the older opera troupes were dispersed. In our county, the opera troupe became a song-and-dance ensemble. Once in a while, they would perform one or two newly edited modern versions. People in our village could enjoy the wonder of Sizhou opera only through their recollections of the past.

One time, when working for the winter propaganda team, I wrote the verses of a song based on the deeds of a model worker, Madam Dong. I invited Elder Brother to sing the song. At the time of the performance, the audience crowded about the stage. The string was plucked; Elder Brother clapped the board. His first sentence was a success. The audience was very excited. Their eyes lit up, staring keenly at Elder Brother. Elder Brother was good at maintaining an audience's interest. The opening line was extraordinary. For a while it stayed that way and excited the audience. After a few lines, however, people lost interest. These new verses, with no roots or meaning for them, were boring. Some people began to pick up their stools and prepared to leave. Elder Brother, a really sharp fellow, noticing the audience's disinterest and not caring whether the story was finished, came to the conclusion, struck the beat, and ended the song. Without the old stories, no matter how good a voice the singer had, the four-phrase melodies just would not grab the audience's attention.

As you can see, our village's entertainment was based upon traditional moral tales. Those new songs and new melodies, which lacked historical foundation and worldly wisdom, failed to sway the audience or gain their trust and appreciation. This made our village's atmosphere much too solemn, and unavoidably boring and dull. However, our village's charm was its wisdom and deep understanding of the manners and morals of the time. It was good at hiding inadequacy by keeping quiet. Our village was like a man of great wisdom who appears slow-witted.

By understanding our villagers' way of talking, one could learn the depth and range of their self-restraint. There are words which Sisters can never say, nor have said in their presence. For example, the word *gan*, which means "to do." Sisters definitely cannot say *gan huo*, which means "work." Instead they can only say *zuo huo*. Other taboo words were *zou*, meaning "hit," and *gao xing*, meaning "happy." Sisters would be greatly offended if men used these words in front of them. Indeed, a serious argument might break out. Why? Even now, though the idea is vague, there is a feeling that some words, especially *gan* and *zou*, are related to a sexual offense, similar to the commonly used *cao*, which means "fuck." But how the word "happy" violated this taboo we did not really understand. In our village, you would have found that the words in the Modern Chinese Dictionary were too limited; our village used many words and terms you could not find in the dictionary. The language situation was so complicated here. The word *sha*, which means "kill," was one of the most insulting terms around—even men would not say this to each other. It conveyed the most serious insult and humiliation. I once saw two men, one a demobilized soldier and Communist party member, get into fight because of this word.

In our village, complications occurred once people started using curse words. For example, we said "grandson of a bitch" instead of "son of a bitch"; and instead of "turtle's son" (bastard), we cursed "turtle's grandson." Removing the curse one generation made it seem milder. However, if someone wanted to make lewd comments to a Sister, they would do so indirectly with words like *guai guai*, which, though it meant "little darling," afforded quite a bit of pleasure. The words *guai guai* had the meaning of being improperly familiar with women, carrying these overtones from Ming and Qing ballads. So Sisters had to be on guard against this word. *Wu liao*, which means "senseless," also was a derogatory term, connected to male and female decency. You couldn't just say it, for if you did, it meant the person had no manners. It's difficult to understand how this adjective developed such a meaning. Our village's taboo of certain words reflected not only our moral norms but reflected how extensively our village's language had developed.

Our village not only liked listening to "ancient chats" and "string music," but also delighted in word games. Those who possessed quick tongues enjoyed a high reputation in our village; they received nicknames that both flattered and mocked them. One was called "Mister Right," another "Mister Ideas," and yet another "Iron Mouth." Wherever Mr. Right worked, work would always slow down. Once when he was hoeing the fields, Mr. Right put down his hoe and started talking. The rest of the workers dropped their hoes to listen to him.

They all forgot about work, and because of this, the production team deducted work points from Mr. Right. Iron Mouth was one of the Sisters, an unmarried girl who dared to talk back to the wildest and boldest of men. Not only could she defend herself, but she could also attack those men. Our village was quite repressed in terms of language—it was like living in a minefield of words. But Iron Mouth moved about freely and always established herself in unassailable positions. She understood the gist of the situation, and she also must have had exceptional talent. Many people wanted to debate her, in order to measure their own strength, as well as to learn from her. And even if it went wrong, they had no regrets. Elder Brother's "ancient chats" also were a kind of word game.

Language standards are like that. Likewise, social behavior also has its own set of unwritten rules. At first glance, these rules don't seem to make much sense. However, once you've thought it over, you find there is a profound insight involved. For example, our village never married daughters to men from the same village or the neighboring village. Once there was a girl named Ying Chun. She and Xiao Niu from the same village were in love. Ying Chun's parents were strongly against this marriage. And for only one reason: Xiao Niu was from the same village. As for Xiao Niu's family, they didn't much care. Ying Chun was irritated because her parents beat her about this matter, so she left home and went to Xiao Niu's house. Xiao Niu's mother rejoiced. With the entire village looking on, she went out and about, buying quilts, bowls and busily prepared for the wedding. Ying Chun's family, on the contrary, were too embarrassed to go out. Not long afterward, the marriage's drawbacks appeared. First, we heard that Xiao Niu beat up Ying Chun. Then, Ying Chun was chased out of the house and beaten up by Xiao Niu on the street. Finally, Ying Chun was driven back to her own family. Should Ying Chun's parents open the door to their daughter or not? Ying Chun's family lost face, but no harm was done to Xiao Niu's family. In fact, things like husbands dragging their wives by the hair and beating them, either inside or outside the house, happened every day. However, since the wives' parents were far, far away, no one could laugh at them. Also, Ying Chun's pregnancy embarrassed her family. In order to avoid the embarrassment, they did not go to the same pond to wash clothes. The daughter was humiliated in full view of her parents. Something about the marriage rule moved people. It protected the dignity and honor of a family. It was pitiful but it maintained a family's prestige.

Social etiquette also was strict and impartial.

When someone got married, only those invited could go to the wedding banquet. On the other hand, for a funeral, we went directly to the mourning family's home without waiting to be invited. This custom also was reasonable because it showed sensibility and sympathy. If you stole the ripe dates from a neighbor's courtyard, you would be cursed. However, if you met him selling dates in the market, he would press them on you. He would not give in, no matter how much you refused. Affection and reason are different and you must not confuse the two. It is not appropriate for neighbors not to visit each other, but it is not necessary for neighbors to be too close to each other. In our village, there was a young man named Xiao Ren, transferred from Bangfu. After he returned to the city, he continued writing letters to his landlord. The landlord wrote back twice, but in the third letter he wrote, "You are very busy in the city now. You have to take care of your parents, and you must work. We understand your feelings; please don't waste stamps by writing to us." This curbed Xiao Ren's enthusiasm.

Our village was so serious, old-fashioned and well-behaved that, without careful observation, its profound human nature would not be understandable. In order to survive, its human nature was constantly being altered, giving up freedom as the price. But it believed in what was good. Its human nature was not poetic, but it maintained a streak of the rational in its oppressiveness.

Nevertheless, it was our Sisters who really made us feel our village's human nature. They were its freest and most beautiful expression because of their youth and innocence. They added a charming, lively air to our dull, depressed village, no matter whether they were sad or happy, self-sacrificing or pursuing a happy life. Since they all had to leave our village and get married to some fellow from far away, they left us their brief, flower-like girlhood. This was our village's glory, which shone over the years of our dull, strict life. Through strictness and regulations, our village took the utmost care of them during that time. Their shyness, self-respect, restraint and friendliness were the best features of our village's human nature. When a little girl's hair suddenly turns black, her cheeks bloom red, she grows up to be a real Sister. Her eyes shine with dignity. It was the best time to open the heavy curtain.

With spring's arrival even our dreary village filled with tenderness and affection. The water in the ditches rose, the elms grew leaves, the wheat in South Lake became green, and the sun was bright and charming. The power of nature was everywhere. It was the master of the world.

In our village, we called the unmarried girls Sisters.

Sisters liked to add *Xia* to their childhood name, as in Gen Xiazi and Lan Xiazi. Sometimes *Xia* alone became a childhood name, so the Shun family's Sisters were named Shun Xiazi and the Liu family's Sisters were Liu Xiazi. *Xia* doesn't have the least connection with being female. I guess the word is *ya*;[1] it is pronounced *xia* in some areas of northern Jiangsu. Although I've already said a lot about our village's language, I need to add that many sounds lack a written form and origin. I prefer to think that the *Xia* used by the village is written as the character *Xia*, meaning "rosy clouds." However, all of the village Sisters who could read and write believed the *Xia* in their name was

---

1. *Yazi* means child or kid.

from the character meaning "chivalrous." Sisters were usually seventeen to twenty years old. Before seventeen, they were still children and couldn't be called Sisters; after 21, they were members of their mother-in-law's family. The days of being a Sister were short, so people were able to put up with their willfulness. Parents would let them buy an extra piece of clothing, make an additional pair of shoes, let them boil water to wash their hair, or take baths. The married women also had to tolerate their harsh words. Sometimes when they couldn't take it any more, they would curse, "Next year, when you're married, let your sister-in-law bully you." On hearing this, the Sisters would feel that their weak point was being exploited and that they had shrunk a few inches. Though they wanted to argue, they just couldn't do it. Some would return home crying. Since the days of being a Sister were so valuable, the Sisters did more or less whatever they wanted.

Sisters always went to work in throngs and came back home in crowds. On the way to South Lake you could hear their laughter from afar. People passing by held them in awe and veneration, yet kept a little distance from them, afraid of annoying them or being annoyed by them. In the fields, they always sat together, in a sacred manner. People talking near them needed to be careful not to say anything that might violate a taboo, especially before those Sisters who already had a marriage arranged. During the famine years, people left their homes to beg for food. However, parents who already had arranged a marriage for a daughter would not allow her to go begging. Although our village did not look down on begging, it was not regarded as honorable. At autumn harvest, the family would buy a new piece of clothing for the Sister, even though the rest of the family wore ragged clothes. With this kind of care, step by step, our Sisters approached the day they got married.

Our village never called the Sister "bride" on her wedding day, for this was considered demeaning to her and her family. This custom created a dreary atmosphere, expressing as it did the desire to maintain the Sister's innocence and chastity up to the last minute. There was something of "flowers will die, do what one may" to the whole business. On the contrary, when our men got married the whole village bustled with noise and excitement. Everywhere you could hear "bride," and everyone seemed immensely proud.

With this kind of tender care our village's Sisters were cultivated to have a gentle and kind nature. They always saw the good side of things and treated people accordingly. They never complained about their difficult environment. In this hard grinding life, they had the best fruit of human nature—sympathy. They were merciful and understanding. They respected other people. Of course, they could be a little narrow-minded and sometimes would lose their temper, but they always took the whole situation into account. Even petty matters reflected reality.

There was an old villager who heard that I was going back to Shanghai after the autumn harvest. He brought his daughter to see me and said the child had suffered for a year and asked if I would bring something back for her. He would give me the money later. Then he asked the girl to tell me what she wanted. The girl flushed, held back her excitement, and looked up at the sky. Then she lowered her eyes, and looked down at the ground. She was silent for a long time; gradually the flush on her face faded and she calmed down. Finally, she said she did not need anything. She knew the difficulties of her family. Four elder brothers were all married and living apart from the family, after taking their share of the family property. She and her sick old parents remained at home. Every year, the family was in debt. Her old father promised to pay me back, but who knew when? No matter how we tried to persuade her, she still didn't want anything. The old man sighed and took her home.

The production brigade's propaganda team held rehearsals on snowy days. At noon, Xiao Yingzi, the girl who lived on the east side of the village, always felt too lazy to walk back home for lunch. I brought her a steamed bun from Sun Xiazi's home where I ate. Sun Xiazi's mother said nothing the first two times. The third time, she was not happy, and said, "This is not a long-term solution. Every family is short of food, we have to hold out until the wheat harvest." After she said this, I did not know what to do, for Xiao Yingzi was still waiting for me to bring her a bun. After lunch when everyone left, Sun Xiazi secretly gave me a bun. Her eyes were full of pity when she looked at me. She knew that I was in a dilemma and passed a bun to me. I knew she disliked Xiao Yingzi. Xiao Yingzi was a middle-school graduate who thought highly of herself and looked down on the other Sisters. I also knew Sun Xiazi was unhappy and jealous that I was close to Xiao Yingzi. Regardless, she understood my situation and gave me a steamed bun for Xiao Yingzi.

During the winter, food was in short supply. Nothing could be grown in the fields from autumn to spring, a whole half year. When digging a ditch, Sun Xiazi would say, "To do this work, I'm content with a wheat bun and a bowl of sweet potato porridge." At that time, every family was eating the rationed sweet potato noodles and bean cakes. When people gathered together in those days, the only topic was eating, what to eat and how to eat. Da Zhizi's family had just arranged a marriage for her. The boy was short and thin, the oldest one in the family. He had a bunch of brothers and sisters, but his family was considered rich. Da Zhizi secretly told me that even then his family still had three bags of flour! Everyone was talking about leaving home to go out begging. However, the commune sent a document that said begging was not allowed. Everyone had to stay at home and provide for oneself by engaging in production. People secretly left home, leaving chains of footprints in the snow.

That was the most depressing time in our village; everyone felt devastated. Most of the days were cloudy and windy. People put their feet in fur shoes and walked slowly along the village's path. If they saw someone's house was open, they would go up and chat with them. Everyone got up very late—some slept in for a whole day and no smoke came out of their chimneys at all. Even in a situation like this, when people met, they still used the same greeting, "Have you eaten?"

That winter I waited for the recruiting workers' notice before I gave up all hope. The road had already been covered with snow. Sun Xiazi and Da Zhizi helped me carry my luggage to the port. They only wore thin unlined shoes, yet cleared the path along the way. When we walked on the two-mile road on the dam, they even held my hands to help me along. Eventually, we arrived on the outskirts of the city, in sight of the sluice gate. Our hands parted. At that moment, the snow was falling thick and heavy, and the sky was overcast with dark clouds. The two Sisters' shoulders were covered with snow, their shoes were wet, but there wasn't a trace of sadness on their faces. On the contrary, they were very happy and relieved to see me leave that place. I walked toward the sluice gate without looking back. I left the hungry, cold, lonely winter behind, left the Sisters behind, left them patiently waiting for spring to come.

Their calm outlook could endure either good or bad days. With enthusiasm and sincerity in their hearts, they walked past their youth one step at a time. Even though these were ordinary years, they didn't waste their time. Their youth brought life to our dull village.

Sun Xiazi's family promised to make her a short winter gown. She had been planning on a gown for a long time. She was a girl of personality and she did not want to conform to a conventional pattern. She wanted to choose a unique piece of patterned cloth. That was easier to say than to do because the colors and patterns at the fabric store in town were very limited. All the Sisters I knew were wearing almost the same clothes. It was almost impossible to fly your own colors. In the end, she chose a thin staple rayon with black flowers and white background, which was generally used to make summer shirts. Due to the softness of the material, the gown was somewhat shapeless and the sleeves looked uneven. Every once in a while one sleeve would get longer than the other and needed to be folded up. Obviously, this kind of material wasn't suitable for making a winter gown because it was not warm enough for the winter. But the gown really was unique. Its unadorned pattern of black and white gave the impression of stark coldness, catching one's eye easily. Its striking effect conveyed an unyielding spirit, nothing could stand in its way. Xiao Yingzi also had a unique coat made of coarse blue cotton. This was not successful either. The color was too bright, and it looked a bit countrified. The coat itself was not as well-pressed as khaki cloth. No matter how you looked at it, it appeared uncomfortable. Nonetheless, it achieved its purpose of being different. The Sister's clashing coats added color to our village, made it less serious, younger and more charming.

The Sisters wove rings from wheat straw. Liu Pingzi was the most talented at this. She could be described as vain. She behaved frivolously and was manipulative. Girls like that always invite gossip. Her thinking was more complicated than the other Sisters. She understood men very well, she seemed to possess this talent innately. She was contrary when it came to our village customs, but she possessed a feminine charm that was so lively and attractive. Her mouth was as sweet as a honey pot. You could say she was a hypocrite, but you could also say she was tactful. Listen to how she flattered me, "Please lend me your cute pigtails, your bright eyes, and high-bridged nose. I will take a photo at the photo shop and return them to you later!" She wove ten wheat straw rings for her ten fingers, two wheat straw bracelets for each wrist. The bracelets glittered when the sun shone over them, as if she were wearing genuine jewelry. When she carried her hoe, she tied her little handkerchief to the handle, making it look very pretty. When working in the field, she wore it about her neck, also making her pretty. Her clothes were always well cut to show off her waist, her pants tight down to her ankle, so you could see the shape of her calves. Her shoes were different too, more delicate than the others. People looked at her with indignation. Yet they were unable to resist looking at her. You needed courage to behave like her.

Zong Mingzi was a high-school graduate. Her father was the director of the people's commune. Her mother was our village's leader in charge of women's affairs. This put her in a completely different world from the other Sisters. Her temperament, her thinking, her lifestyle, even her fate in the future seemed more similar to an educated youth from the city. For example, when she was eighteen, and still not engaged, the villagers took it for granted. No one tried to make a match for her. Not long after, the commune recommended that she be sent to university. But despite the great difference in her background, she would sometimes unintentionally display the same nature as the other Sisters in the village. And this surprised you. Take, for example, the unfortunate accident with the piglet.

She was working with the commune's cooperative medical team at the time. One day a piglet in her home was sick, so she took penicillin home to give it an injection. That piglet was her favorite among all the piglets. It ate a lot and was very plump. When someone came to buy a piglet, she always drove it into her room and bolted the door. She didn't want anyone to pick it. She took care of the piglet very well. However, soon after she gave the piglet the injection, it died. Needless to say, the piglet was allergic to penicillin. When she understood what had happened, it was already too late to do anything, so Zong Mingzi ran into her room, grabbed a towel, covered her face, and began to cry. From this, I realized that no matter how privileged Zong Mingzi was, she was still one of our village's Sisters.

Because she was privileged and educated and had experienced the world, her character was more liberal and easy-going. She was not afraid of displaying her nature. You could say she took the Sisters' qualities and explored them fully, displaying them distinctively and vigorously. She bravely pushed out into the open everything that was oppressive. The most spectacular scene was her grandmother's funeral. Because of her father's position, many people attended the funeral. From early morning to late night, we saw official-looking people riding bicycles to our village. They brought either a wreath or a long sheet with an elegy. These sheets were, in fact, made of cloth. They hung in the newly built shed in great numbers. Their different colors, layer upon layer, transformed the funeral's gloomy atmosphere. To my great surprise, one day, I saw Zong Mingzi looking at the sheets in the shed with great interest. She was planning which ones she wanted and what kind of clothes she would make from them. This behavior was inappropriate, and yet it was somehow lovable. It was innocent, yet seemed to carry within it a philosophy. Our village's wisdom was summed up in this.

What the Sisters most wanted was for people to call them by their real names. They might be illiterate, but they all knew how to write their own names. Their real names seemed useless to them, because everyone called them by their childhood names. People might not even know their real names. After they got married, people would call them by their last name temporarily. For example, our village called one married woman Xiao Ma (*Xiao* means "little," *Ma* was her family name). After a year, a child was born, and she would become "someone's mother." What was the point of having a real name? According to city people, real names always conformed to convention, while childhood names were highly personal. For example, Xiao Mianzi (*Mian* means "diligence"), Xiao Zhuizi (*Zhui* means "pendant"), Xiao Bianzi (*Bian* means "pigtail"). These childhood names are full of local color. We would rather call them by their childhood names, which disappointed and angered them. They wanted us, the city people, to call them by their real names. For them, it was as important as changing history. In their eyes, the real name represented a broader and bigger society, which was different from the world they knew.

The most distant place the Sisters had ever visited was the county town, which had only two criss-crossed streets. But, for them, the town could almost be called "great." In their eyes, the women attendants in the department store were fairy-like figures. They clicked their tongues in admiration: How can they be so beautiful? They described the town as a bustling, busy shopping center. Beverage peddlers on the street had green and pink water in bottles; fruit sellers had baskets full of green melons and dark purple apricots. In a giant vat, golden fried dough twists and balls were floating in bubbling oil. There was snow-white bean jelly seasoned with vinegar, garlic, pepper and sesame oil. You could eat one bowl after another. There was lots of meat hanging over and under the counter in the butcher's shop. And in the department store, there were clothes, hats, socks, dress material, knitting wool, woks, bowls, gourds, ladles, spoons. . . . The most interesting item was the baby stroller—how did they invent such a thing! From the blacksmith's shop came the "ding, dang, ding, dang" of the anvil. From the giant chimney of the coal pit came the "puff puff" of smoke. Distillers' grains from the brewery were everywhere on the street. What a rich and populous place! And there were ships at the pier. They had never been on a ship. For them, a ship was one of the most remarkable things in the world. Across the street, they listened to the blowing whistle of the ship from Bangbu approaching the pier.

They had never even seen a train.

The outside world was too far away for them to reach. On the east side of the village, there lived a mute. It was said he was separated from his parents while escaping from Japanese soldiers. He wandered destitute into our village. The Sisters said the mute came from Shanghai; the world outside of the village was more mysterious now.

They admired their brothers who joined the army, who could go to very far-away places: Jinhua, Yunnan, Tianjin. One of them even went to Vietnam. The soldier came back and said most Vietnamese Sisters were prettier than Chinese Sisters. That was also very mysterious.

In fact, although most Sisters could move only from one village to another in their life, this did not stop them from yearning for the outside world. They were especially enthusiastic in learning about the places they would never have the chance to visit. When outsiders came to our village, the Sisters would run up to look at these strangers. Since they were very shy, they didn't talk; they didn't even raise their eyes. They just buried themselves in their needlework and listened. While they were listening, they pricked up their ears. They didn't want to miss a single word. They admired the strangers, but they also took pity on them because they were so far away from their homes. In their eyes, people far from home were pitiful, like us young people who were sent to the countryside and their soldier brothers. People from other places were always treated very well. That was the case with me. They understood that the world was big and confusing even though they couldn't go very far. So they looked upon the mail with devotion. Every time the postman came, he became their center of attention. If someone got a letter, immediately everyone knew its contents. They particularly liked listening to people read letters aloud. It didn't matter whose letter. The words and sentences in the letters had traveled a great distance. This alone made them feel the letters were unusual.

That year I was very busy looking for a job. I did so much running around that I almost died. The last day before the application deadline, I ran from the commune to the town, then from the town to the commune. But to no avail. It was closing time and the only one left in the commune's office was a clerk, who had nothing to do with recruiting workers, and the school graduates. I was feeling so desperate that I started to cry. The clerk stood up from his chair, walked to the window, looked at the harvested soybean fields outside of the window. He didn't try to comfort or educate me, he only said that there were many Sisters living and working in the village. Something in his words hurt me, but at the same time moved me. I wept even harder in sadness; I cried all the way back to our village. I sympathized deeply and was overcome with grief.

After I left this village, I never thought of coming back. I didn't like the village at all. It was remote from the city and it was far from being natural as well. Its shrewdness alienated me. A village like this had a long history; everything had to be considered carefully. Domestic things and foreign things were distinct, as were advantages and disadvantages. Certainly the village was not simple and unsophisticated. Even to a lonely outsider like me, sometimes the village would play a dirty trick. But I couldn't find any fault with the Sisters, I really couldn't. Whenever I was grinding my teeth, swearing I was going to leave this place, as soon as I thought of the Sisters, my heart filled with grief. Because of the Sisters, people did not want to complain in the least. Thinking of them made people's hearts ache.

They filtered plant ash to wash their hair because they did not have money to buy soap. They patiently rubbed their hair, making it black and smooth. They locked themselves in a room to sew their underclothing; they didn't want anyone to see. They peeled the skin off sorghum stalks, chewed the pulp, sucked the sweet water . . . . . .

Marriage was the most important thing in the life of a Sister but they were utterly helpless in deciding who they were going to marry. The story of Da Zhizi demonstrates this.

One day, her cousin, a married woman in our village, called Da Zhizi to her house and said, "In my parents' village, there's a very good young man whose family is well-off." Then she asked Da Zhizi whether she would agree to marry the fellow. Upon hearing this, Da Zhizi wasn't very happy. She said, "Cousin, what's wrong with you? You should have talked to my mother about this, why to me?" What she said reminded me of Xue Baochai, a heroine in *Dream of the Red Chamber.* When Xue Baochai's mother asked her opinion about her engagement to Bao Yu, she also said: "Ma, what you said is not right, a girl's marriage should be decided by her parents, or brother, why come to ask me?" What the two girls said seemed to be cut from the same cloth. Xue Baochai's principles came from the books she read, but Da Zhizi's? Hers were from our village's customs. Her temperament was very tender; she turned a deaf ear to her own marriage and let her mother and cousin arrange everything. It turned out to be a successful engagement. "When spring came, there were still three bags of grain in the house" was the talk about her fiancé's family.

You can see the position the Sisters took in the matter of their own marriage from Da Zhizi's words. They neither discussed it nor were they present when it was discussed. This was not because they were weak, but because they were respectable and guarded their chaste status. But who knows what they were thinking in their hearts?

Sun Xiazi's parents arranged her marriage a long time ago. Her parents were very good at planning and calculating. They were among the best in our village in this respect. Sometimes their porridge was thin, sometimes thick; sometimes their work was busy, sometimes not. They were asked to take care of my three meals and I did not feel that I had to put up with the food they provided. Sun Xiazi's father was the most skilled worker in the field. Because of his competence, he was on the village's policy-making team, our own think-tank, even though he was not a party member or from a big family. He handled many things: spring wheat, autumn soybeans and summer floods. When he walked to South Lake with his hands clasped behind his back, our village held its breath. Even though he stammered when he talked, that didn't matter. Sun Xiazi's mother was a good talker! Sun Xiazi's mother was that type of woman our village described as "magic." She spoke in a lively manner on extremely interesting subjects and was convincing in argument. One time, Sun Xiazi's little brother had trouble with a student from the primary school. The kid chased him home. His mother stepped out of the house and said to the big kid, "You're a student, he's a commune member, are you the same as him?" Rendered speechless, the kid ran away. Because she was such a good talker, she also participated in men's conversation. She smoked a tobacco pipe, too. Her lips were thin; her voice sounded like a duck's. When she laughed, her laughter sounded like a duck's as well.

Their life was the best in our village. Everything they did, they did in proper measure. Sun Xiazi's engagement was neither too late nor too early, it was exactly at the right time. I saw the young guy—really not a bad match: He was tall, pleasant-looking and had broad shoulders and a high-bridged nose. Also, he was very honest. One day, he suddenly showed up at Sun Xiazi's home. When Sun Xiazi returned from the fields at noon, he had already told the whole story. In the afternoon, everyone in the fields knew that Sun Xiazi's future in-laws wanted them to get married soon. His nine-year-old sister had died of typhoid, and since she was too young to be buried, they could only use a straw mat to roll her up. They left it on a hillock and let wild dogs eat her. His mother wept day and night for her daughter. Then she thought about her daughter-in-law, and wanted Sun Xiazi to marry her son right away.

Sun Xiazi later told me that at noon that day, when her father had gone out to the field, her mother was cooking in the kitchen and she was washing clothes in the living room, the boy started talking to her. "What were you talking about?" I asked. "All nonsense, not worth remembering." But for Sun Xiazi, this first conversation couldn't have been so simple. She didn't tell the other Sisters about this. She only told me, because I was from the big city and, in her eyes, I would understand.

As for the wedding, Sun Xiazi's mother did not promise anything, but insisted on postponing the marriage until Sun Xiazi's soldier brother came back. This was an excuse. Her purpose was to make the future mother-in-law do more work, so that she would treasure her hard-earned daughter-in-law. And on the wedding day Sisters to be married all would cry for the same reason. Others said, they were crying for their dowry. Dowry was the last thing the Sisters asked for from their parents. The last few pieces of clothing from their own home also were something the Sisters could not ask about, but were related to the honor or disgrace of their position in their husband's household. It would also decide her future family's economic situation. They had the right to cry, because once the dowry was on its way, everyone knew what the Sister's reputation was worth.

The dowry came in different-sized sets: small three-piece, small five-piece, large five-piece. . . . The three small pieces were the basic items: a bed, a cutting board and a suitcase. The five small pieces had two more items than the three small pieces: a stool and a desk with three drawers. The five big pieces included a desk that had a cupboard. There was also the large seven-piece set. But in those days you rarely saw a large five-piece set. The most common dowry was a small three-piece set. A small five-piece set was plenty for a bride's reputation. A small three-piece set included the basic necessities for a family: sleeping, eating and storage. The furniture was painted bright red. Red was bright and eye-catching when it was not quite dry, but once the color dried it became dull, looked old and coarse, not pure. When you saw it, you couldn't help feeling depressed, unable to cheer up. There usually were ten pieces of clothing in the suitcase. A cotton-padded jacket was considered as two pieces because it included both the outside layer and lining. A piece of corduroy clothing also was required, and about 250 grams of wool, which was enough for a sweater. That was a dowry in our village, which you might call quite a sum. But from then on, the Sisters had to depend on themselves. The Sisters would say, "Within ten years, don't think of asking your mother-in-law for one piece of clothing." Crying for your dowry actually was crying for your future.

It was frightening to think about life in the future. A strange village, strange people, a strange home, even you yourself became strange. You would spend the rest of your life in strangeness. The married women in our village all had the same experience, and who could look at them with admiration? But what about not marrying at all? A twenty-year-old Sister who hadn't found a husband wasn't easy to read—it was hard to say what she really thought. After all, her parents' home was not her own home. She could only rest easy once she'd found a husband. From this point of view, crying on the wedding day seemed phony. Our village once had a laughing bride, Xiao Yingzi's sister-in-law. Xiao Yingzi's brother was a teacher in a primary school run by the local people. He could play the flute. I've mentioned that Xiao Yingzi wore a unique blue coat. Her brother had one, too. On the wedding day, the rain had just stopped. It was muddy everywhere. The bridegroom carried the bride into the house in order not to dirty her new shoes. Lying on his back, she started laughing. Her laugh seemed to shake the earth and batter the heavens. The guests were dumbfounded. But the bride was a real beauty—different than Xiao Ma—with an oval face and rosy cheeks darkened by the sun, long eye lashes, and red lips. Everyone forgave her for misbehaving.

There was someone who really cried, who really didn't want to get married. That was our own Xue Baochai, Da Zhizi. On the day of the wedding, I was still in Shanghai, buying the dark green material for her. No matter how hard people tried to convince her, Da Zhizi didn't want to leave home. She cried and cried, and made all the Sisters and married women in our village shed tears. Everywhere you went, you could hear people crying. News later came from her husband's village that Da Zhizi was sick. What type of sickness? Mental illness. She would be doing needlework, then suddenly stretch out her arms, begin to laugh, and afterward she would continue with her needlework. Why did she get this way? Because she loathed her husband. She couldn't stand him. One look at him made her sick. When they were having dinner, she had to fill everyone's bowl with porridge. After she had finished filling the last bowl, the first bowl was empty again, and she had to start over. She did not have a chance for her own bowl. When Da Zhizi came back home to visit her parents, I watched her closely. I never saw her stretch her arms out and laugh. She looked very calm and she wore new clothes. Besides, she was a quiet person and didn't like talking much. If I have to say something about how she changed, it was that she did not look at people any more when she spoke. She only watched her needlework. Throughout our conversation, I had little opportunity to look at her eyes. I didn't know what she was thinking. She had been one of my closest Sisters when I was in the village. She treated me like a younger sister. I felt that she only spoke about a tiny portion of what she was thinking. She hid everything deep inside. Later, she didn't even show her feelings with her eyes. Although I never saw her stretch her arms and laugh, my heart ached when I thought about the way people described her. It seemed that I saw the same thing with my own eyes.

Iron Mouth was the only Sister who still didn't have an arranged marriage by the time I left the village.

Iron Mouth had a brother named Guang Pingzi. They were the most handsome people in our village, but neither of them was engaged. That was because they belonged to the Rich Peasant class. Their father had died when they were still very young. They lived together with their widowed mother. Their mother was very tall. She had an oval face and bright eyes. She curled the smooth hair at the back of her head. She didn't talk much, but she was knowledgeable and educated her children well. Through her cultivation Guang Pingzi graduated from junior middle school and Iron Mouth became a good worker. Whatever a man could do, Iron Mouth could do as well. I have mentioned the men cutting the wheat with scythes. In fields of several hundred acres, Iron Mouth was the only woman who could do this. Iron Mouth could be seen from a distance wearing her flowery gown in the middle of a row of white cloaks, moving in equal strides with the men. She held the scythe as steady as the men did. The wheat she cut, "swoosh, swoosh" fell to the ground at the same speed as the men's, leaving only low stubble. She was such a pretty, capable, talkative Sister, yet her marriage prospects were ruined by her class status. There were several similar stories in those days. One production team leader in our village married a rich peasant's daughter when class status was not so important. But later the Party would not accept him as a member and so he was never promoted. Every day he beat up his wife and desperately wanted to divorce her.

Previously, people didn't care much about class status. Guang Pingzi used to be as proud as a peacock. At the age of twelve, when he was in primary school, there was a girl student on the school's propaganda team who was very fond of him. This student was one of the best Sisters in our village, Xiao Yingzi. Guang Pingzi lent his cotton-padded jacket to Xiao Yingzi one rainy day. After the rain, the sun began to shine. Xiao Yingzi went to Guang Pingzi's home to return the jacket. She said to him, "When we grow up, let's spend our life together." Guang Pingzi was young and arrogant—he didn't care much for what she said. Time zipped along and, before you knew it, years had passed by. Both Xiao Yingzi and Guang Pingzi had grown up. But Guang Pingzi was still a bachelor and no one wanted to marry him. One winter, men were digging ditches in the northeastern part of the village. Guang Pingzi went to look for water to drink during the break. He went to Xiao Yingzi's home. Xiao Yingzi was there alone. For no particular reason, they started to talk about the past. Xiao Yingzi was already engaged, but she still felt sentimental about Guang Pingzi. She said, "At that time, your family was high class; I wasn't a good match for you." What could Guang Pingzi say? He could blame no one for missing that moment in time, so he left with many regrets.

That was Guang Pingzi's romance. Iron Mouth did not go to school. She spent her time in the fields—led a quiet and virtuous life while her twentieth year drew nearer and nearer. Some warm-hearted people in the village tried to find a husband for her, but all failed. Guang Pingzi's situation was the same as his sister's, but it wasn't as tough for boys. They usually were thick-skinned and at least could talk about girls, even if they were afraid of people's teasing. A Sister, on the other hand, had to experience the bitterness on her own, for she couldn't talk about it with others and others couldn't talk about it with her. She could not show any signs of impulsiveness, even after she became an old spinster.

Xiao Mianzi was the proudest Sister in our village. Her fiancé was not an average person—he was an officer in the army and had been promoted to battalion commander. Their engagement was considered the most desirable one in our village. He was from a neighboring village. He had joined the army after graduating from junior middle school. People swapped stories about him when news of his promotion was heard. People talked about how he picked pigweed; how he carried the water bucket; how he sold dates at the market. However, bad news came with the good news: he wanted to break off the engagement to Xiao Mianzi.

Xiao Mianzi was already in her twenties. She had been waiting for him for years, and now he wanted to break it off. Who could stand for that? One day, after finishing work, Xiao Mianzi, her mother and the matchmaker went to the neighboring village. The three of them walked on the high embankment, the afterglow of the setting sun shining upon them. Under the vault of heaven, their figures looked lost and melancholy.

Xiao Mianzi started to learn to read soon afterward. Her textbook was *Chairman Mao's Quotations*. Everybody had one in those days. In this way, Xiao Mianzi was different from the other Sisters. She was the most driven concerning her own fate. Furthermore, she dared to smash the bonds of traditional taboo. She did not get married when she was supposed to marry. And she deliberately went to her fiancé's home when he wanted to break off the engagement. Her bravery was different from Liu Pingzi and Xiao Yingzi. Their bravery was shown in minor things, wearing outrageous clothes and saying outrageous things. That's excessive. Xiao Mianzi's bravery was displayed in her definite views and resolution of the issue of her own fate.

Xiao Mianzi's family were outsiders in our ancient village. Their family name stood alone from the rest. Their home at the foot of the village's platform had only two adobe rooms. A bad life or a good life depended entirely on the family themselves. For this reason, there was a real drive in the family, even though they were poor and had nothing saved up. Their little rooms were extremely clean. The patches on their children's clothes were neat and even. The children seemed healthy and good-looking. The parents were industrious and frugal commune members, and the children were students of good character and scholarship. Gradually, the family gained an importance that the villagers couldn't ignore. For example, when the "Learn from Da Zhai" work team was stationed in our village, Xiao Mianzi's mother was appointed to cook for them. The commune's director, whose home was in our village, got a few dozen workers enrolled. He gave one quota to Xiao Mianzi's brother. Xiao Mianzi's good engagement can't be separated from her family's good reputation. Children who grew up in such a family knew how to control their own fate. They were willing to pay any price for their goals. They were the least prejudiced, most open-minded and smartest in the village.

Xiao Mianzi's intelligence was different than Xiao Yingzi's and Liu Pingzi's. She was deeper and more rational. She was no different than the other Sisters in appearance, nor did she act unconventionally or outlandishly. She was well-behaved, peaceful, steady and honest, but her expectations were much greater than that. This was partly because she was a few years older than the other Sisters, partly because she had an even temper but also because she grew up in a good environment. She never went to school, yet she saw the world more clearly than a student. She had her own judgment and her own ideas. She didn't panic when bad things occurred. She never said anything about her engagement to the army officer, but I felt that deep in her heart, she had a confidence. This confidence was not simple, because the relative strength and weakness of the two parties were obvious. She had to have a very strong character to deal with that. Later events confirmed that: you plant melons and you get melons, you sow beans and you get beans.

Liu Pingzi and Xiao Yingzi were more superficial and sentimental than Xiao Mianzi. But they were as enthusiastic and spared no effort in whatever they were doing. However, by the end, they just couldn't get out of the Sisters' set pattern of life. They were a world apart from Xiao Mianzi but in fact belonged to a group of extremely bold and active Sisters. Therefore, married life was perhaps more difficult for them. Their vitality, nonetheless, always made people feel a sense of beauty, made it hard for people to forget them.

That year, Xiao Bianzi also became engaged.

Xiao Bianzi's parents died when she was very young. She lived with her younger sisters, elder brother and sister-in-law. Life was very hard for them. Her elder brother worked very hard to support two sisters and two kids. In the freezing cold winter, the beds in their home were still covered with summer straw mats. Xiao Bianzi never wore new clothes—her clothes were full of patches. Her sister dressed even worse. She wore her elder brother's and sister-in-law's old clothes. The pants were so long that they covered her to the knees. The other Sisters all had needlework to do, but Xiao Bianzi did not. Every day she would carry a basket on her back to pick up straw. She was tiny and short. In this way, she looked even more like a little kid. But day after day, she grew up, with red cheeks, black hair. Sometimes she had a sharp tongue and could be narrow-minded. One day, Sun Xiazi's mother said that she wanted to find a good husband for Xiao Bianzi. Who was the young guy? He was her cousin's son. Sun Xiazi should call him cousin. He was a student, still at school. Sun Xiazi's mother did what she said she would. A few days later, the young boy and his other sister came to visit Sun Xiazi's mother.

When you saw the brother and sister, you knew both of them were gifted. The sister's words and deeds were out of the ordinary. She carried herself with ease and confidence, as if she were experienced and had seen the world. It turned out that she was a cadre in the women's association. She often went to the town or district meeting. The brother was much less experienced. His complexion was quite fair and he looked extremely gentle. When they were having dinner, Sun Xiazi's sister, Lan Xiazi, a girl of twelve or thirteen, suddenly stretched out her hand and touched the back of the boy's hand. She exclaimed in admiration: my cousin's hands are so soft!

Everyone said Xiao Bianzi's luck had changed. The kid who had suffered so much now had a good husband. Xiao Bianzi's brother invited the boy to dinner. First, he made sure he was comfortable in his home, then returned to Sun Xiazi's home to borrow money to buy cigarettes and wine. Sun Xiazi's mother said, "You don't need to treat him like a guest; he is still a little boy." Xiao Bianzi's brother insisted, no matter how much Sun Xiazi's mother tried to dissuade him. Xiao Bianzi's brother treated his sister's engagement very seriously. He was afraid of people gossiping that he treated his sister badly. Because of the dinner, Xiao Bianzi and her sister-in-law got into a fight over kneading dough. Xiao Bianzi ran to Sun Xiazi's home right away and complained, "She insisted on me making the dough, and made a pulpy dough. I couldn't even pull my hands out of it." They were making buckwheat dough, and buckwheat flour is extremely sticky. If you were not good at making dough, your hands would be stuck in the dough, even if the flour basin broke. If a mother-in-law wanted to be mean, she would have her daughter-in-law make buckwheat dough for the first dinner, to see if the daughter-in-law were clever. This was also done to subdue the daughter-in-law. Xiao Bianzi was angry for a few days because of that dinner, and complained that her sister-in-law deliberately undermined her situation. Afterward, she was also angry with Sun Xiazi on the matter of stitching the soles of cloth shoes. She wanted to make a pair of shoes for her future husband, as well as show off her needlework to her mother-in-law. Out of kindness, Sun Xiazi wanted to help her cut a shoe pattern. She felt sympathy for her, because her mother was dead and no one had taught her how to do needlework. Xiao Bianzi, however, would not let her do it. Sun Xiazi was straightforward and had a sharp tongue. She told Xiao Bianzi that her shoe pattern was no good and insisted on cutting it for her. A few more words were exchanged. They took a dislike to each other. Xiao Bianzi bore a grudge against Sun Xiazi's family. She was even suspicious that Sun Xiazi's mother gossiped about her to her future mother-in-law. That was Xiao Bianzi's narrow-mindedness. Warm-hearted matchmakers can easily cause trouble for themselves. They have to control all conflicts since they are between the two families. Both families are suspicious of the matchmaker, suspicious that the matchmaker might say something improper to the other family. Only people who are warm-hearted and like to poke their noses into other people's business tend to be matchmakers. Sun Xiazi's mother expected that, so she didn't blame Xiao Bianzi. This was because she had a very good temper and was easygoing. She sympathized with Xiao Bianzi for losing her parents when she was young and didn't blame Xiao Bianzi for her misbehavior.

Xiao Bianzi started to make the pair of shoes by herself. In order to demonstrate that she could do it alone, she did the very opposite of what Sun Xiazi suggested. If Sun Xiazi said to the left, Xiao Bianzi went to the right. It was impossible to praise that pair of shoes: The uneven needlework caused the soles to twist; the stitching was crooked. But she did it with her whole heart. Also, she was secretive. She covered the shoes with a piece of cloth and kept them hidden from other people. During break time in the field, she would run to a quiet secluded place, hide there, and sew the shoes one stitch after another. Another time, I saw her sitting in the wheat field. The wheat was waist-high, and she sat there, sewing the shoe one stitch at a time. The top of the wheat stroked her pitch black hair. The sole of the shoe seemed so big in her hands that she appeared to have difficulty grasping it. She looked like a child playing at being a mother, but her earnestness was so moving that you had to take her seriously.

Sun Xiazi's mother couldn't help asking about the shoes when they were nearly finished, for this not only concerned Xiao Bianzi but involved her own reputation. She insisted on stitching the shoes for Xiao Bianzi and refused to hear another word about it. Xiao Bianzi obediently gave her the sole and the upper. Then she stood aside and listened to Sun Xiazi's mother's instructions while watching her sew the shoes. Xiao Bianzi pouted from start to finish, but dared not say a thing. After all, it was very important, so she couldn't be too willful and flaunt her superiority. She showed a sensible attitude on this point, even though she was young and quick-tempered.

Later, Sun Xiazi took Xiao Bianzi to her cousin's home. They dressed up, carried some gifts, and took the new pair of shoes with them. They walked single-file and forgot about the grudge between them. They were very happy now that both of them were engaged. Though their future was unclear, they couldn't imagine anything bad happening. Hope is a beautiful thing. At that time, they were the happiest Sisters in the village, unlike those little girls whose futures were uncertain or the married women who already had their whole life set. They were in between those two situations. Their hearts were both calm and excited; they had not obtained what they hoped for, and yet had not lost it either. They were climbing the embankment as the sun was rising, under a blue sky with white clouds. People working in the fields used their hands to shield their eyes in order to look at the two Sisters, admiration clearly showing on their faces.

During this visit, her mother-in-law gave her a set of expensive gifts: a length of corduroy dress material, a length of cotton dress material, and 750 grams of knitting wool. Xiao Bianzi began not long after to knit, and she carried her needlework with her wherever she went.

In our village, everyone quickly found out about Xiao Bianzi's new harvest and went to take a look at her dress material and knitting wool. They were laid out on her bare summer sleeping mat in the house made of sun-dried mud. It really had become a palace instead of a pigsty. Xiao Bianzi was proud, but afterward she felt resentful toward Sun Xiazi, for Sun Xiazi went around bragging about the match. Obviously, she intended to claim credit for herself and brag that Sun Xiazi's family was Xiao Bianzi's savior. This, of course, might have been the truth, but there was no evil in it. An orphan like Xiao Bianzi, growing up in her brother's home, would be very sensitive and could behave unreasonably. You could tell she was nervous about her future. She was cautious and afraid of making a mistake that might cause her a lifetime of regret. She didn't have Xiao Mianzi's brains, but she was careful. Even though she was suspicious, she treated her friends sincerely. The year that I went back to Shanghai, she saved a chunk of pork from Spring Festival and every day went to the village crossroads to wait for me. But at that time my heart wasn't in our village. I was thinking of leaving all the time. I stayed home even when March rolled around. The meat rotted. That would be nothing for other families, but for Xiao Bianzi's family it was something. How many times she had to quarrel with her sister-in-law and coax her little nephew so that she could save the chunk of meat for me. When I came back to our village, wherever I went, people would tell me about the meat Xiao Bianzi had saved for me and how it went rotten.

When Sisters became engaged, their future seemed to possess something hopeful. What they hoped for was more or less the same thing that many generations already had experienced. Still, each individual cherishes her own hopes. Even if these hopes are nothing new, it is a once-in-a-lifetime experience, so fresh and exciting, that it feels as though this is the very first time it has ever occurred. When the married women were in the fields talking about insignificant things in their daily lives, the Sisters listened with their heads lowered. Sisters all said to themselves: our future must be different from theirs. But how? They didn't know. The only people they could consult were these "must-be-different" married women. Therefore, they were very interested in the married women's conversations. They listened carefully to their talk.

That's a different world. They couldn't step into that world as long as they were still Sisters. What was inside that world? What type of life was beneath the married women's calm appearance? What did that life mean? In the Sisters' eyes, the married women were mysterious and gave them the feeling of "being oh so close, and yet so far." That was especially true for extremely young married women, who couldn't use their own mother as a comparison. They were so familiar with their mother's life that it was too ordinary. Besides, mothers always belong to another category. But those young married girls in our village were different. Even though the Sisters and the young married women were about the same age, the married ones had already "climbed over the embankment" and knew what the other side was like!

She Huizi's wife was the youngest married woman. She Huizi was the same age as Xiao Bianzi, while his wife was two years younger than Xiao Bianzi.

She Huizi had lived with his widowed mother. Life was good and he didn't need to worry about anything. The daily life was work, eat, eat, work.

He got the same points as the women, and he didn't need to do hard work like harvesting that the other men did. His job was to take food and drink to the people working at South Lake. But that year, his mother died and She Huizi was all alone. On the day of the funeral procession, She Huizi carried a long white flag, broke a yellow basin, and carried the coffin to the cemetery behind his house. Everyone cried: what kind of life was the boy going to have? His two-room house made of sun-dried mud looked like it was going to fall down. She Huizi slept there by himself at night. Some old people suggested that a wife be found for him. Once he had a wife, he would have a home. Every day getting up early for work and returning home late, She Huizi was lonely. Xiao Mianzi's mother then introduced her niece to him, Xiao Mianzi's cousin.

The little wife was smaller than Xiao Bianzi, though she had similar chubby cheeks. She went into She Huizi's house with her head lowered, neither laughing nor crying. The next morning when people passed She Huizi's house, they saw the door was open and the bride was feeding pigs. She Huizi squatted in front of the door, eating porridge. Seeing someone pass by, he raised himself slightly, and using the tip of a chopstick, tapped the edge of the bowl. He greeted the guest, "Come in and eat with us?" She Huizi had grown up overnight. When the following year's wheat harvest season came, he had his wife cut a piece of white gauze. He tied it to his shoulders. He then took a large scythe and joined the men in cutting wheat.

Bai Suizi, who was brought up by his grandma, also got married. Bai Suizi was a handsome boy with red lips and white teeth. He was pretty enough to play the young female role in opera. He also had an amiable disposition. He got along well with both children and adults. After finishing work in the fields, you could see him fly down the road carrying water. He carried water from the good well in the West and poured it into everyone's water vat, as if he had a lot of energy but no use for it. His wife, Xiao Guo, had a fair and clear complexion. She was very delicate, her eyes were not very big but they were bright and black. She plaited her long, thick hair in two huge braids. This couple was truly a match of gold and jade. It was difficult to determine a newlywed woman's temper. They were always seen working with their heads lowered, either in the fields or at home. You couldn't tell whether they were happy or sad. Their new clothes showed off their happiness. They returned to their old clothes after a while. Life as a married woman passed day by day. Xiao Guo's face gradually turned yellow, and not long after that she became pregnant. It wasn't long before her swollen belly forced her clothes tight against her midriff. Brown speckles appeared on her cheeks. After the child was born, she became a shrewish woman. She dared to say what she wanted, dared to hold up her shirt and breast-feed her baby in the field, and to throw her man on the ground and untie his belt. She became a real married woman, her days of being a Sister were gone forever.

In truth, to be a married woman means to shoulder life's burdens formally. She has to serve parents-in-law and raise children from then on. Life isn't as easy as when she was single. How many things she has to worry about now! In the past, she only got sad or angry for not being able to make a new dress. But now? She can't even think of it. Her man's clothes and shoes, her children's clothes and shoes, are all arranged before hers; and oil for the lamp, soda for making dough, salt for pickling vegetables take priority over her things. Don't blame married women for their fussing about trifles and coveting petty things. Life makes them like that. If she didn't fuss about trifles, who would? No matter how, she can't make her man fuss about trifles. Men need respect and that, too, is a woman's duty.

I never got along well with the wife of the family I stayed with. At first, I had my bed in their central room. The sorghum that surrounded the bed left just enough room to walk by. Sometimes when I went to town for a few days, my blanket would be gone when I came back. The wife took my blanket away to warm up her kid's feet. Even though I never caught her, I'm sure she often came to my room to look over my things. Otherwise, her rules would not have been so obviously directed against me. My room was thrown open when the sorghum straw was removed to cook food. It was more convenient for her. This woman seemed honest but could be crafty. She frequently took little things like soap powder or clothes that I'd hung in the courtyard to dry. She never said anything, she just watched to see if I was going to look for my stuff. If I didn't, she took it for granted that I'd forgotten about it and she wouldn't mention it. I felt awkward while I was living in someone else's house. I also felt embarrassed to ask her about those things. I never made it public and suffered the losses silently. She understood my thinking pretty well and took the initiative.

Even under these circumstances, she wasn't happy with me. She badmouthed me to everyone. My major shortcoming, according to her, was pettiness, by which she meant stinginess. There were two reasons for that. First: One year I had come back from Shanghai and I gave each Sister a handkerchief as a gift. She got mad and said that I gave them out to so many people but didn't give one to her daughter even though I was living in her house. That year, her daughter was only four years old, so I had not counted her. Second, after the autumn, I went back home. They drew the cotton rations that belonged to me. When I came back, I asked her for the cotton. She returned it but she was very unhappy, saying that a Shanghai person shouldn't care for such a small amount of cotton! I heard about her comments from Xiao Bianzi. If you were a Sister, you always despised married women.

My growing dislike for her changed one day.

I had come back from the town in the morning where I had picked up money sent to me by my parents at the post office, a five-yuan note, and a one-yuan note. I put down my bag and went to visit a school graduate in the neighboring village. I came back at noon and found the one-yuan note was not there any more. I was panicky for a while. I thought I must have remembered incorrectly because, until then, my money had never been stolen. After all, money is different than other things and it has a different nature. It seems that money is much more important than other objects. I dared not think further. I went to the field to work in the afternoon as usual. After work, I carried my hoe, walking along the field, while the wife walked behind me. Suddenly, she stretched out her hand and used her strength to scratch my back. She said, "Xiao Wang lost a one-yuan note." I felt her words in my heart, I turned around and asked her what she said. She once again scratched my back and said, "Xiao Wang lost a one-yuan note." She stared at me, her expression was a little evasive and noncommittal, but bold. Later, I thought over what she had said. I realized that she was saying "hello" to me. She felt guilty doing things like that. She had no alternative, otherwise she would never have done that. Consider her situation. It was not easy being a wife in such a family. She had two children and an ailing husband. He was devoted to his parents and didn't want to leave them. Her mother-in-law was a shrewish woman, and there was a sister-in-law studying in the town's middle school. She not only had to support the family but also had to keep the peace between all the parties. How could she possibly question what she did?

When you see those sloppy, dirty married woman walking swiftly in the village, talking dirty words, please don't give them the cold shoulder. Life changed them. They had three or four kids and they were like a mother wolf, always fighting for food to feed baby wolves. Those little mouths were bottomless pits. They wished for seven or eight pairs of hands, one for work in the production team, one for watering the garden, one for cooking, one for feeding pigs, another for sewing patches on their children's clothing.

A woman from the west end of the village came to see me. She was not from our production team, so we usually didn't see each other. The only connection I had with her family was that I used to be in the same criticism team as her husband when the criticism team traveled around the commune. I was one member of the criticism team, her husband was the one being criticized. Her husband's case was a typical example of the commune's "grasp revolution, promote production" movement. It was a civil matter. His sister had an argument with her husband and committed suicide by hanging herself. He insisted it was the husband who had killed his sister, and he would not allow anyone to bury her. He put his sister's coffin in a room and sealed the room for one year. When the work team went there to open the room, they found Chairman Mao's portrait on the wall. Thus he became an anti-revolutionary. We had been together for more than half a month. At the start, I made a clean break with him and maintained a distance. But, as we were together from morning to night, I became close to him. I found out he really wasn't a bad person; he was just a little stubborn and backward. Nevertheless, he was honest and kind. Later, the criticism meeting became a routine for both of us. We became actors. We just played different roles. Maybe because of this, his wife came to see me.

She begged me to knit two sweaters for her kids. She had unraveled some gloves and dyed the yarn green and red. I do not know how many gloves she unraveled. I told her I did not know how to knit a sweater, but she said I knew. Then she put the yarn in my hands and ran away. She looked as if she were afraid that I might run after her and give her back the yarn. Having no choice, I started knitting the sweater. I had never seen her two kids, and the knitting needle was the wrong type and the yarn was quite poor. I had difficulty with the sweater. I wondered why she had asked me. The reason was very simple. In their eyes, I was a big idler in the village, and had nothing to do every day after I finished eating. If they didn't come to ask me to do things, who else could they ask?

Eventually, I knitted the pile of yarn into two sweaters, one red, one green. Since she did not dye the yarn long enough, the color was not pure and a bit yellowish. I went to her place and gave her the sweaters. She bought meat and invited me for dinner. Her husband was a Muslim, so he never ate pork. She borrowed a wok and cooked the meat just for me. Later, people saw her two kids wearing the sweaters I had knitted. The neckband and the shoulder were fastened together with a pin so that they wouldn't come undone. The two kids wore those sweaters while they carried their baskets collecting grass, spreading my name far and wide.

Besides the pressures of life, there also were the men ordering the women about, which made the women wild and lacking in self-respect. Men tore apart women's defenses, exposing them to boorish male society. When you heard a woman's boisterous laugh and unrestrained talk, who knows whether she was immensely proud or just giving herself up as hopeless. A married woman was half like a man; she completely forgot what she was like when she was a Sister. We could tell the educated ones from the uneducated ones. Elder Brother, who performed "ancient chats" and was good at *haozi*—his wife was out of the ordinary. So was Xiao Ma. The former was educated, the latter was born beautiful and knew her own value. As well, their husbands were unusual; they respected women. The two women were like cranes standing among a flock of poultry. People regarded them with special attention, and their parents-in-law were afraid of them.

In our village, almost everyone beat up his wife. Even the gentle, girl-like Bai Suizi used to beat his wife, Xiao Guo. It seemed that if you didn't beat your wife, you weren't a real man. Some guys even beat up their wives on the street, just to show off their awe-inspiring reputation. One stupid young guy used a cutting knife to split his wife's hands. Married women, when beaten by their men, became "thick faced" even if they were not "thick faced" before. Once they were humiliated in public, they didn't care about manners. Actually, they were pitiful. Beneath their rough appearances were very weak hearts. Who had not experienced being a Sister? How much respect they had when they were still Sisters. Men were so careful when they were talking to them and they dared not utter one improper word to offend them.

But there was one married woman who dared fight back. She even wanted to divorce her husband. She had been married for only half a year and people couldn't remember her face. I recalled only that she was a tall woman with two braids hanging from the back of her head. Whenever she wasn't working, she would stand in front of the house of the leader of the women's association. She didn't talk much, but insisted on divorcing her husband. He was such a moron that he didn't care at all. He still went about the village having a good time. She stood before the women's leader's house for more than a month. Things eventually fell in with her wishes. I thought she must have been to school and that was why she could make her own decision. The women leader said, "Educated? Didn't you see that she was holding the divorce certificate as if it were a heavenly book? And she held it upside-down." This married woman was really tough and not easy to handle. She was the first one in our village to divorce her husband. In order to jump out of a settled routine and live a different kind of life, it all depended on the individual.

But besides their special basic instinct, what else could the Sisters depend upon? Our village's landscape never changed; the crops never changed. They waited for the elms to grow leaves, then they plucked elm-seeds and exchanged them for money. They bought some ribbons for their hair, hair pins or shoe uppers. Then they waited for cicadas to slip out of their shells. They gathered shed cicada skins to sell, then they bought some buttons and edging. The never-changing scenery limited their view and imagination. Xiao Mianzi, Xiao Ma, and the divorced woman were unique; one in a thousand.

The day that I went back to the village to arrange my transfer, I ran across Liu Pingzi. She had already married. Her husband was the one she picked out from many choices. He was a demobilized soldier and a Communist Party member, too. Liu Pingzi had curled her hair. It looked like there was a hen's nest on top of her head. This made her face look yellow and her eyes triangular. I hadn't noticed her triangular eyes earlier, but I had thought her eyes were charming. She kept cursing people from our village, very angrily. She told me someone had gossiped about her, and her mother-in-law had heard. She wore layer upon layer of new clothes but her straight pants were conventional. She was no longer unique, as she had been when she was still a Sister. Not married for very long, she already had become a nagging, mean woman. Gone forever was the lively, charming Liu Pingzi.

Like wheat growing a blade at a time, the Sisters grew up a blade at a time. When the wheat ripened, it was time for the Sisters to marry, for another blade of wheat was green. And even though all the wheat was the same, every blade of wheat was new.

Sun Xiazi's sister Lan Xiazi had big lovely black eyes with thick long eye lashes and a wide mouth. One day, when they were having dinner, her mother suddenly said, "Just for that pair of braids, I'm going to find her a good husband." Lan Xiazi retorted, "Pah!" then turned her head and ran into her room. Everyone laughed and someone said even little girls can become embarrassed. Lan Xiazi was four years younger than Sun Xiazi, only fourteen years old. Because she had a grown-up sister, she scarcely had a chance to wear new clothes. She wore her elder sister's hand-me-downs. She was a small girl, so she could wear any ragged clothes. One day, Lan Xiazi thought it over, felt very sad, and began to cry. All through dinner she sobbed that her mother had promised two years earlier that after the soybean harvest she would make her a new quilted coat, but when the coat was made, gave it to her older sister instead. Then her mother promised her one for the following year, but she did not make it at all. She had been cheated for two years. She kept sobbing, but no one took her seriously. She wasn't a Sister yet. She was still a baby. Every day, she carried her basket to pick grass. She was not a real laborer, so she couldn't earn much money. But she cried so often that, in order to stop her, her mother said, "When the soybean season comes, you can gather soybeans and sell them. Then you can make yourself a new quilted coat."

So, then came the season to harvest soybeans.

There was a rule about gathering soybeans. You couldn't go to the field to pick soybeans until the production team had finished the harvest and the fields were about to be ploughed. That year, soybeans didn't grow very well. July's flood didn't destroy all the soybeans, but they looked like they were diseased. The soybeans were very sparse and their pods shriveled. So the production team harvested very carefully, leaving very few soybeans in the fields. Lan Xiazi looked for soybeans very carefully, her head lowered, and her back bent. In the huge brown wheat field, a little girl was picking soybeans, her black braids hanging. She wanted to earn herself a new quilted coat. She flicked through the stubble and dug in the soil. She was overjoyed whenever she saw a pod. When she was tired, she would sit in the field, peeling the pods one by one, gathering the soybeans. She wrapped them in her handkerchief and hid them under the pigweed in the manure basket. Her face looked content and happy, as if her new quilted coat was waving to her.

The little Sisters could never get people's attention. If they didn't have an elder sister, things were better. Otherwise, they felt constantly oppressed. They felt they would never grow up to be a real Sister. When Liu Pingzi was washing clothes by the river, her clothes-stick fell into the river—one word and her little sister jumped into the water and got the stick back. Xiao Bianzi cursed her little sister. Why? The girl needed to pee but couldn't find a secluded place near South Lake, so she wet her pants. Xiao Bianzi said, "Why are you so embarrassed, can't you just squat and take a piss? Who would laugh at you?" When Lan Xiazi was crying for her new quilted coat, Sun Xiazi's expression seemed to say: Look, even she wants to wear a new quilted coat. Anyway, in the home, the elder sister was the Miss, the younger sister was the servant girl. On stage, the elder sister would play the lead, while the younger sister would be relegated to the role of supporting actress. Wherever they went, the younger sister was just a decoration.

But, without knowing how, these little girls gradually caught people's eyes. Even though they were still little and short, their brows and eyes became distinct and there was a glow on their faces. People from other villages passing by would turn their heads and take a second look and wonder whose family that little girl was from. One day, Da Zhizi said, "Xue Mingzi is better than me now." Xue Mingzi was her younger sister and only wore her hand-me-down clothes. Da Zhizi sighed when she said that, for when Xue Mingzi grew up, Da Zhizi would be married.

At sunset, the burned soybean smoke rose up into the bright, yellow sky. In the harvested fields, the red ribbon on Lan Xiazi's big braids touched the ground now and then, as she picked up the soybean pods left in the field. Many Sisters began to count the new clothes they put in their trunk at this time. Da He's mother bought meat and wine, invited a carpenter and lacquerer to make furniture, and prepared a dowry for her. The wedding day was just before her eyes.

Have you ever watched anyone walk along the South Lake road? When they get close, you see a young married woman, carrying a small bag and wearing new clothes. She walks faster when she becomes aware that the workers in the fields are watching her. In the distance, a fellow trails behind her. He looks about, pretending he has nothing to do with the woman in front of him. That was how the daughter and son-in-law returned to visit her family after the wedding. The sun was already high, although they had traveled only half of their the journey. Their clothes were covered with dust. You could see them reach the embankment, climb up and over—and then you couldn't see them any more.

Translated by Ihor Pidhainy and Xiao-miao Lan

Translators

MICHAEL CODY has a B.A. in film studies from York University and an M.A. in Chinese Studies from the University of Toronto. He has a particular interest in the social history and material culture of pre-modern China.

RONALD DE SOUSA lives in Toronto with his wife Jingsong Ma and daughter Qingting, named after the dragonfly of Jiang Zidan's story. A professor of philosophy at the University of Toronto, he rashly undertook to learn Chinese at the outset of his sixth decade.

FRED EDWARDS has B.A. in history from Trent University and a second B.A. in Chinese Studies from the University of Toronto. He also studied Chinese at Harbin Normal University and has lived and worked in China. He currently is an editor in the Business department at *The Toronto Star*.

XIAO-MIAO LAN has a degree in English from Sichuan Foreign Languages University. Her interests include Western literature, contemporary Chinese fiction and traditional Chinese medicine.

IHOR PIDHAINY is a graduate student in the East Asian Studies department at the University of Toronto. His interests include contemporary poetry, Chinese fiction and the Chinese language.

HEATHER SCHMIDT graduated from the University of Calgary in 1995 with a B.A. in English literature and a minor in Chinese. She studied in China for two years after graduation and currently is a graduate student at the University of Toronto.

SHU-NING SCIBAN received her Ph.D. in Chinese literature from the University of Toronto and currently is teaching at the University of Calgary.

MARTIN SULEV taught English in China for three years. He graduated from the University of Toronto in 1998 with a degree in paleontology.

YU-KUN YANG graduated from National Taiwan Zhongyang University with a Master's degree in statistics. She has taught mathematics at colleges and universities for fourteen years and currently lives in Canada.

Acknowledgment of Copyright

"The Embroidered Cushions" (Xiu zhen) was first published in *Modern Criticism* (Xiandai pinglun), No. 15, in 1925. Copyright permission granted by Hsiao-ying Chen Chinnery (2001).

"My Neighbour (Wode linju) was written in the early 1940s and first appeared in *About Women* (Guanyu nüren) published by Tiandi chubanshe (Chengdu) in 1943. Copyright permission granted by Chen Shu (2000).

"Love in the Fallen City" (Qingcheng zhi lian) was first published in *Magazine* (Zazhi) in the September and October issues of 1943. Copyright permission granted by Huangguan chubanshe (2002).

"Women" (Nüren) was written in 1956 and anthologized in *On Women* (Nüren ji) in 1980. Copyright permission granted by Wei Junyi (2001).

"Such a Beautiful Sunday" (Zheyanghaode xingqitian)was anthologized in the short story collection of the same title published by Wenxing shudian (Taipei) in 1966. Copyright permission granted by Kang Yunwei (1999).

"Bowls" (Wan) and "Frying Pan" (Jian guo) were written in 1980. They were anthologized in *A Girl Like Me* (Xiang wo zheyangde nüzi) published by Hongfan shudian (Taipei) in 1984. Copyright permission granted by Xi Xi (Zhang Yun) (2000).

"Rapeseed" (Youma caizi) was first published in *China Times* (Zhongguo shibao) in 1981. Copyright permission granted by Liao Huiying (1999).

"Jade" (Ai yu) was first published in *United News* (Lianhe bao) in 1985. Copyright permission granted by Ping Lu (1999).

"Waiting for Dusk" (Dengdai huanghun) was first published in *Harvest* (Shouhou) in 1990. Copyright permission granted by Jiang Zidan (2001).

Hot or Cold, Life's Okay" (Leng ye hao, re ye hao, huozhe jiu hao) was first published in *Fiction Forest* (Xiaosuo lin), No. 1, 1991, and anthologized in *A Winter Without Snow* (Yi dong wu xue), published by Jiangsu Literary Publishing House, 1995. Copyright permission granted by Chi Li (2000).

"Sisters" (Jiemeimen) was first published in *Shanghai Literature* (Shanghai wenxue), No. 223 (April 1996). Copyright permission granted by Maitian chubanshe (Taibei) (1999).

CORNELL EAST ASIA SERIES

113 Thomas Conlan, *In Little Need of Divine Intervention: Scrolls of the Mongol Invasions of Japan*

114 Jane Kate Leonard & Robert Antony, eds., *Dragons, Tigers, and Dogs: Qing Crisis Management and the Boundaries of State Power in Late Imperial China*

115 Shu-ning Sciban & Fred Edwards, eds., *Dragonflies: Fiction by Chinese Women in the Twentieth Century*

116 David G. Goodman, ed., *The Return of the Gods: Japanese Drama and Culture in the 1960s*

117 Yang Hi Choe-Wall, *Vision of a Phoenix: The Poems of Hŏ Nansŏrhŏn*

118 Mae J. Smethurst, ed., *The Noh Ominameshi: A Flower Viewed from Many Directions*

FORTHCOMING

Joseph Murphy, *The Metaphorical Circuit: Negotiations Between Literature and Science in Twentieth-Century Japan*

S. Yumiko Hulvey, *Sacred Rites in Moonlight: Ben no Naishi Nikki*

Charlotte von Verschuer, *Across the Perilous Sea: Japanese Trade with China and Korea from the 7ʰ to the 16ʰ Century,* Kristen Lee Hunter, tr.

Pang Kie-chung & Michael D. Shin, eds., *Landlords, Peasants, and Intellectuals in Modern Korea*

Fan Pen Chen, *Visions for the Masses: Chinese Shadow Plays from Shaanxi & Shanxi*

Ann Lee, *Yi Kwang-su, the Novel* Mujŏng, *and Modern Korean Literature*

Joan R. Piggott, ed., *Capital and Countryside in Japan, 300-1180: Japanese Historians Interpreted in English*

Brett de Bary, ed., *Deconstructing Nationality*

Kyoko Selden & Jolisa Gracewood, eds., *Modern Japanese Literature Readers*

Vol. 1 Stories by Tawada Yōko, Nakagami Kenji, and Hayashi Kyōko

Vol. 2 Stories by Natsume Sōseki, Inoue Yasushi, and Tomioka Taeko

Richard Calichman, *Takeuchi Yoshimi: Displacing the West*

Judith Rabinovitch and Timothy Bradstock, *Dance of the Butterflies:* Kanshi *(Chinese Poetry) from the Japanese Court Tradition*

To order, please contact the Cornell University East Asia Program, 140 Uris Hall, Ithaca, NY 14853-7601, USA; phone 607-255-6222, fax 607-255-1388, ceas@cornell.edu, www.einaudi.cornell.edu/eastasia/CEASbooks

SB/6-03/.7M pb